D1021192

Praise for the Angela Matelli series
by Wendi Lee

HE WHO DIES
"Lee delivers another fast-paced thriller..."

—*Booklist*

"Lee's prose is tight and flows at whirlwind speed...one entertaining ride."

—*Publishers Weekly*

DEADBEAT
"...strong, simple prose that has great wit and great heart."

—*Mystery Scene*

"Lee effectively combines a fast-paced story, a well-realized Boston setting, and a cast of rich and sympathetic characters..."

—*Booklist*

Praise for the Sheriff Dan Rhodes series
by Bill Crider

WINNING CAN BE MURDER
"...a keeper."

—*Booklist*

"Series fans and others will appreciate this return to rural Texas and Crider's memorable characters."

—*Library Journal*

DEATH BY ACCIDENT
"...will leave fans crowing for more."

—*Library Journal*

"It's a pleasure to watch him solve this case through intelligence, wit, and just a little bit of luck. Fans will definitely be satisfied..."

—*Booklist*

MURDER, MAYHEM
—And—
MISTLETOE

Terence Faherty
Aileen Schumacher
Wendi Lee
Bill Crider

WORLDWIDE.

TORONTO • NEW YORK • LONDON
AMSTERDAM • PARIS • SYDNEY • HAMBURG
STOCKHOLM • ATHENS • TOKYO • MILAN
MADRID • WARSAW • BUDAPEST • AUCKLAND

MURDER, MAYHEM AND MISTLETOE

A Worldwide Mystery/November 2001

ISBN 0-373-26401-1

THE HEADLESS MAGI Copyright © 2001 by Terence Faherty.

CHRISTMAS CACHE Copyright © 2001 by Aileen Schumacher.

STOCKING STUFFER Copyright © 2001 by Wendi Lee.

THE EMPTY MANGER Copyright © 2001 by Bill Crider.

CONTENTS

CONTENTS

THE HEADLESS MAGI
by Terence Faherty

ONE

"IF MARJORIE should call back, tell her *The Bells of St. Mary's* is on Channel Nine at eleven. That always cheers her up. Though why a movie about a nun getting tuberculosis should cheer anyone up is beyond me. May be some Catholic school issues there."

The speaker was a nun herself, but not the least bit tubercular. Even a minor chest cold would have prevented her from bustling about the tiny office as she was doing, collecting hat and coat and mittens, while keeping up both ends of our conversation.

"That's the scariest part about being a religious—walking through a crowd of strangers, knowing that about half of them were taught by nuns and that some percentage of those have been harboring dreams of revenge ever since. No wonder I prefer sweat suits to habits."

Sister Agnes Kelly was a sparrowlike woman, which is to say, small and apparently frail, with a self-consuming energy, bright eyes, and a sharp nose so prominent that it seemed to be what her entire face had set itself to achieve. The room in which I sat and around which she ricocheted was the headquarters of just one of her many ministries: a crisis phone service she'd set up in an old rectory turned Catholic Life Center in a quiet corner of quiet Elizabeth, New Jersey. The service was called Adullam Line, after the cave in the Bible where David hid from a jealous King Saul and where all the "discontented gathered themselves unto him."

"I hate to leave you here alone, Owen, fresh out of training. Not that my training amounts to much. Honey over at Domestic Justice—that's another crisis line, you know—always says that my training consists of the laying on of hands, and she might be right. But a person has the knack for listening or he doesn't. That's what I say."

Anyone who spent much time in Sister Agnes's company would develop a knack for listening, like it or not, I thought. Aloud I said, "I'll be fine."

"Speaking of Honey, she got an interesting call the other night. What?" she interrupted herself as my three-word message got through. "You'll be fine? Of course, you will. But I usually have someone sit with novices on their first night. It's just that it's so close to Christmas, and my other volunteers have families. I mean, I'm sure you do, too, Owen. A nice family. Somewhere."

She sidled then, physically—toward the door—and conversationally. "Like my nieces who always want me to come to their Christmas pageant." She pushed back coat and sweatshirt sleeves and squinted at her watch. "For which I'm now late. Not that I'll miss more than three percent of the total running time. I can remember when a Christmas pageant was two kids in paper halos knocking on inn doors and one chorus of 'Silent Night.' Now it's *The Sound of Music* with shepherds.

"That reminds me. If an out-of-town guy should call looking for a room for his very pregnant wife, offer him the couch downstairs."

TWO

WHEN THE LAST echoes of the front door's slam had faded away, I went from enjoying the quiet in the second-floor-bedroom-turned-office to missing Sister Agnes in a heartbeat. I coped by centering the old black rotary telephone on the contact-paper mahogany of the desktop and drawing two binders closer to hand. One was what Sister Agnes called the *Code Red Book,* though its cover was black. It contained phone numbers for emergency agencies and social services in Elizabeth and the cheek-by-jowl communities in this damp edge of North Jersey's urban sprawl. The second binder was known as the *White Book,* and it actually was white. Within it, yellow tabs divided shorthand instructions for dealing with various types of calls.

I had a book of my own, a private-eye paperback by Ross Macdonald, but I was saving that for later, when I'd be fighting sleep. So I opened the white binder and began to page through its overview of human misery, wondering what I'd be dealing with before the end of my shift.

The *White Book* handled the big ones first: suicide, physical abuse, substance abuse. I flipped through those quickly, especially the last one, which might have set me thinking about a scotch on the rocks. The next categories, depression, loneliness, and anger, were also familiar to me. I'd experienced them all in the two years since I'd quit a steady and relatively respectable job in New York City and moved back across the river to my native Garden State.

Job Problems was the next tab in the binder, but I didn't

linger there, either, having had enough personal experience in that area to counsel an entire union. In part, my history of job failures stemmed from the type I chose: uninvolving, undemanding jobs that left me free mentally to explore my own interests. But it was those interests that accounted for the bulk of my career difficulties. I was an amateur detective, to state things in the most flattering way possible. Or a compulsive meddler in mysteries that were none of my business, to give the opposing view.

The next tab bore the legend Friendship, and I did pause there, friendship being a subject I'd been thinking about a lot this Christmas season. Why so few took and why the ones that did endured so much. Those issues weren't considered in Sister Agnes's notes, which were mostly suggestions on making friends that read like advice you'd give your five-year-old if he came home from school and announced that no one liked him. Take an interest in other people. Smile. Change your socks.

The next tab, Religion, likewise promised more than it delivered. Here Sister Agnes's emphasis seemed to be on not offending anyone's religious sensibilities, however bizarre. All the pussyfooting created the impression that belief in God was just another delusion that had to be humored, like the idea that President Reagan was reading one's mail. An odd attitude for a nun's notes to reflect, but then I was finding the early eighties to be an odd time in general.

The *White Book*'s final section was a catch-all of lacks relating to poverty: lack of food, lack of shelter, lack of clothing. All things I was too close to experiencing firsthand to want to read about. So I shut the book and turned to examining the room, the water stains on its papered ceiling and the collage on the wall opposite me. It was made up of dozens of human faces, cut from newspapers and magazines and taped up at random.

Then the phone rang. I reached first for the spiral note-

book that served as the office log and then for the handset.
"Adullam Line."

It was Marjorie, one of Sister Agnes's regulars, a woman
with too many kids and not enough of anything else, including friendly ears. She didn't seem to mind breaking in
a new pair of those, especially after I passed on the news
about *The Bells of St. Mary's.* She wanted to talk about her
oldest daughter, who was skipping school, so I listened,
saying "uh-huh" occasionally while outside my window a
car with a powerful stereo passed every ten minutes, as
regular as a police cruiser on patrol, which it might even
have been.

As I listened, I went back to examining the wall of pictures across from me, looking for a face that matched Marjorie's very tired, somewhat nasal voice. I found the right
one near the upper edge of the mosaic, a glossy color shot
of a stout woman with clear blue eyes and a square jaw. It
occurred to me that Sister Agnes had taped the pictures
there for that very purpose: so her volunteers could put
faces with the voices, making it easier to think of the callers
as human beings and not just disembodied woes.

When Marjorie signed off, it was so close to nine on the
dot, I deduced that some favorite television show or old
movie was about to start. Maybe *Going My Way.*

I was deep into the adventures of Lew Archer, private
eye, when the phone rang again. This time the caller was a
man, an angry man.

"This the crisis line?" he asked, sneering the crisis part.

"Right," I said.

"What'dya call it? Adullam?"

"Yes?"

"What's that supposed to mean?"

I told him the story of David, hiding in the cave from
the wrathful King Saul and being visited there by troubled
Israelites, who preferred David's judgment to the king's,
which had bummed out Saul in the first place.

"That's damn stupid," the man said.

"Is it?" Ask open-ended questions, the *White Book* advised. It was easy advice for me to follow, a man for whom all questions were open-ended. I noted the time in the log, expecting a hang-up. The man hadn't offered me a name, so I gave him one, writing "Saul" next to the time.

"You're taping this, right?"

"Nope," I said, "no tape." Sister Agnes thought taping would break Adullam Line's implicit promise of confidentiality. Not to mention breaking our budget.

"I'm supposed to believe that?" Saul demanded.

"Your call," I said, the laconic voice of Archer still fresh in my ear.

It turned out to be the right tone to take. Saul started talking, hesitantly at first, about his ex-wife. She'd talked him into a divorce, claiming an unhappiness that was pushing her toward suicide. He'd given her the divorce and most of their joint possessions in the settlement. Too late he'd learned that she hadn't been unhappy at all, largely due to the attentions of the young man she'd been seeing for a year and more. Now the boyfriend was living in Saul's house, sleeping in Saul's bed, watching Saul's television.

I found I was staring at the collage, at a black-and-white picture of a balding guy with intense eyes that stared back into mine. Sister Agnes had cut him from some medical ad, I decided. He was the doctor who recommended the latest wonder drug. The more I listened to Saul's clipped anger, the more I wondered which he missed more, his wife or his television. I sensed that he'd been happy to go along with the divorce at the onset. Now he was very unhappy. Because his wife had finished the game with more chips? Because she'd gotten them through trickery? Or was it because all the possibilities he'd seen in divorce hadn't panned out, starting with the chance to see himself as a man who had made a noble sacrifice?

I was trying to connect the dots, a tendency of mine that

Sister Agnes had warned me against during my training. I reached for the *Code Red Book* and found a phone number for a counseling service for divorced men and another for an anger management class. Not much to offer, but then Adullam Line's major service had already been delivered. Someone had listened to Saul's side of things, which had calmed him considerably.

When he ran out of gas completely, I had him copy the phone numbers down. We were encouraged to arrange for call-backs, so I suggested that he sleep on things and call again.

"Will you be there?"

"Someone will be," Archer said.

I got up to stretch and make a pot of coffee. Sister Agnes bought hers in five-pound cans from Thriftway. It was the last thing she should scrimp on, I thought. Then the phone rang again.

This time the voice was very young and very frightened. "Help me," it said.

THREE

"YOU GOTTA HELP ME."

I stifled an impulsive "I will," which would have violated Sister Agnes's second most sacred rule: "Never promise help until you've identified the problem. Then don't promise."

"Tell me about it."

My FM radio calm was wasted on the caller, who was nearing hysterics. "Ain't no time for talking. We gotta save him. Now."

"Who?"

"My brother. Benjy. He's gonna snatch him. He said he would and he's gonna do it. Tonight. I know."

"Benjy's going to snatch—"

"Benjy's gonna get snatched. Shit. Listen to me. I'm talking, and you ain't listening. Shouldn't have a guy on this phone that don't listen."

Oddly, my incompetence was having a calming effect on Benjy's brother. "You new at this?" he asked, concerned for me now, it seemed.

Something in his voice told me that he wasn't new to his end of it, new to dealing with problems too large for him or anyone else. I said, "Yes," quickly, anxious to keep us in the pocket of calm we'd blundered into. "I just started."

"Shit," the voice said. And then, "Sorry. But this ain't no call about boozing or paying electric bills. This is an emergency."

"I know," I said.

"If I wanted somebody who didn't know nothing, I'd call the cops. They'd really mess things up."

"Right," I said, taking my hand away from the *Code Red Book*. I reached for the log instead, wrote the time and asked, "What's your name?"

"John," he said, after the slightest hesitation. "But everybody calls me Jackie. What's yours?"

Sister Agnes had advised me to select an Adullam name, one that would protect my own anonymity. I'd egotistically considered David, after the biblical cave dweller and counselor, but now I impulsively gave my own.

"Owen? What kind of name's that?"

"South Jersey. Are you okay yourself?"

"Okay?"

"Somewhere safe?"

"I'm always safe. Don't worry about me. Russet don't bother me. He don't even think about me. I'm not his."

"Not his son?"

"Damn right not his son."

"But Benjy is?"

"Russet thinks he is. Momma told him he is. But Benjy don't look like any Russet to me. Russet's an alien. Benjy's human."

"An alien?"

"From space, like that one that comes out of your chest, rips you apart and kills you. That's Russet."

"He's not really from space though. Is he?"

"You nuts and new both?" Jackie piped. "No, he ain't from space. But he ain't from South Jersey, either. And he's big. Big and sweaty. Benjy's little and pretty. Russet can palm him, he's so little."

"Benjy's a baby?"

"Yeah, a baby. Momma told Russet that Benjy's his to keep him from beating her. But nothing keeps Russet out of a beating mood for long. The Nets winning a game's about the best thing. But the Nets don't win that many."

By then I'd relaxed sufficiently to scan Sister Agnes's photo lineup for a likely Jackie. The closest I could find was a preteen with large eyes and a seventies afro. But the photo kid was smiling, and there was more wrong with the picture than that. It had been cut from a glossy ad, cut generously enough to include a hint of bright green background around the kid's head. A sunlit field, maybe, in soft focus. A Kodak moment. There was nothing bright or soft about the moment Jackie was calling from.

"You there, Owen?"

"I'm here. Why does Russet want to take Benjy?"

"To hit Momma. To hit her without hitting her, worse than really hitting her."

"To punish her?"

"That's right, to punish her. Cause she likes Benjy more than him. Like who wouldn't? So he's gonna take Benjy away."

"And do what with him?"

"Lose him. Take him across the Hudson and leave him on the subway. Or just use the bay. This is the best place in the world for losing stuff. The Mafia knows that. That's why they hang around here. You got Mafia in South Jersey, Owen?"

"Some."

"Yeah? Well, I bet when they want to lose a guy they bring him up here. Then he stays lost. We got a smelter near here that does guys all the time. They go in, but they don't come out."

"What's a smelter?" I asked.

"You don't know or you don't think I know?" Jackie shot back. "Smelter's a big black place with smokestacks. It's where Benjy's going if you don't do something."

"And you don't want me to call the police?"

"No. Momma won't say a word to them against Russet. Then, when they leave, he'll beat her again. No social workers, either. Russet beats on them first and Momma second.''

''But not on you?''

''I'm too fast for him,'' Jackie said, but without his earlier, easy conviction. ''Benjy's no faster than a brick. He just lays in his crib smiling at you. This time tomorrow, Momma's gonna be kneeling next to that crib crying, cause it's gonna be empty.''

An odd thing happened then. A siren started to wail—not in itself an odd thing in Elizabeth. But I heard two sirens, one through the thin walls of the old rectory and one over the phone, their risings and fallings perfectly matched. Jackie was very close.

''I can be there in a few minutes,'' I said, breaking Adullam Line's most sacred rule: ''Keep your body out of it.''

''You?'' Jackie said. ''You'd come here?''

''Yes.''

''You are a rookie. Nobody's ever said that before. You'd come here right now, and Russet showing up any time?''

''Just tell me where.''

''Wait a minute. How do I know you won't screw things up worse? Or get scared and run?''

''You'll have to trust me.''

''Trust you? I don't know you. Listen. I ain't got much time. Tell me something about yourself. Something bad.''

''Something bad? Why would that make you trust me?''

''You trust me first, with something you don't want anybody to know. You trust me, and I'll trust you. So tell me something bad. Tell me about some time when you got scared and ran.''

I didn't have to rack my brain for examples. ''I was going to be a priest. I was in school for it, a school out west. I got scared that I wouldn't measure up, so I ran away.''

''Ran here?''

Via a series of stops, I thought, some of which were further examples of my cutting and running. I said, "Yes."

"Shit, Owen, this ain't no place to run to. You run *from* here. You get the hell away from here."

"Let me help you then. And your mother and Benjy."

"I gotta think. I'll call you back."

"Wait. Don't hang up." I scrambled for some way to keep him talking. "I told you something about me. Tell me something about you."

"Something bad?"

"If you like."

The silence lasted so long I thought I'd somehow missed the click of the connection being broken. Then Jackie said, "Sometimes I'm Russet," and the line went dead.

FOUR

THE POLICEMAN, one Sergeant Grabowski, was unhelpful. "Kidnapper name of Russet?" he asked in a voice only slightly louder than the static on the line. "Sure we aren't talking about a spud napper? Is that a first name or a last name? Wait, I remember. You don't know. Address? Also unknown. Ditto time and place of the crime."

I liked the ditto. I hadn't seen it coming, unlike the rest of Grabowski's spiel. In honor of the ditto, I tried to be patient with him. "The guy's been in trouble before for beating his girlfriend. Or maybe his wife. Somebody down there should recognize his name or the names of the two kids. Jackie and Benjy."

Grabowski was also patient, to give him his due. "It's going on eleven, Mister, ah, Keane. I'm a lot of all the somebody down here who's down here. And I never heard of any wife or girlfriend beater named Russet, first name or last. To speak the truth, we've so many of those creeps around this town that it would be hard to know half of them. But I'll ask around. Can I reach you at Adullam Line?"

"Or at home," I said, giving him the number of the phone in my tiny apartment.

"Got it," Grabowski said. "And give Sister Agnes my regards. Tell her Merry Christmas for me. Not Seasons Greetings. Merry Christmas."

"Got it," I said, but I never did pass on the message. The nun returned shortly afterward, aglow from the pageant

or the cold night air. Before she'd gotten her scarf of many
colors unwound, she'd started to tell me about her evening.

"You would have liked this play, Owen. Really. It was
a mystery, like you're always reading. The hero is a detective who's trying to find the true spirit of Christmas. He
visits all the shops in a mall, which gave all the grades in
the school a chance to sing a number. That padded things,
let me tell you. In the end it turns out that the detective is
really an angel. He takes off his trench coat and a long
white robe drops down. This is after he's found one person
out of all the ones at the shopping center who still remembers what Christmas means, which is exactly the ratio you'd
expect at a Jersey mall."

Then she caught my eye and stopped. "Owen. Something
happened while I was gone. Tell me, tell me, tell me."

I did, getting through all of Jackie's story and as far as
Sergeant Grabowski's name before the nun interrupted me.

"Owen, Owen, Owen. You never called the poor police
over that, did you? You did. What will they think of us
now, of our credibility, when we need them in a real emergency?"

"This wasn't a real emergency?"

"No. It was a prank, like that call Honey got over at
Domestic Justice the other night. I told you about that."
She stopped and held a mitten to her open mouth. "No, I
didn't, did I? I started to tell you and got distracted. So I
guess this whole thing was my fault, after all. My mind will
wander."

"What about the other call?"

"Oh. Some child called Honey and wove her a tale about
his mother being attacked by her boyfriend for stealing
some of his drug money so she could buy food for her
babies. That part rang true, God help us, so Honey tried to
get some details. The child told her his mother's name was
Angela and that her boyfriend had cut her hands as a pun-

shment and that they were red with blood and her dress was red with it, too.

"Honey was still taken in at that point, so I guess I can't be too hard on you, Owen, you being a rookie and Honey an old pro. She started to get suspicious when the boy wouldn't give her his name and address. He just kept piling up lurid details.

"Then he overstepped himself. He said he didn't know Honey well enough to trust her. He asked her to tell him something bad about herself. Something she didn't want anyone else to know."

Sister Agnes didn't have to catch my eye this time. She'd been studying both my eyes, watching for my reaction. 'Aha. I thought so. He asked you the same thing. What did you tell him, Owen? Was it about your time in the seminary? Never mind, I don't want to know. Forgive my curiosity.

"Anyway, that was the tip-off for Honey. She knew then she was being strung along. The callers who ask you to say something nasty or to repeat some fetish word that turns them on are the classic time wasters. Like the ones who ask our female volunteers what they're wearing. I always disappoint those guys," she added, tugging down the sleeves of her sweatshirt.

"This boy seemed very young to Honey to be into that kind of thing, but when she confronted him—gently—by suggesting that he was making up the bloody hands stuff out of whole cloth, he didn't argue with her. Didn't say another word. He just hung up. He would have given up with you, too, Owen. If you'd been more…"

"Rational?" I suggested, so embarrassed that the under-heated room suddenly felt oppressively warm.

"Forceful," Sister Agnes said. "And don't be hard on yourself. We all make mistakes when we're starting out. When we've been at this for years, we make new mistakes. Go on home now. I've some paperwork to do and I can

listen for the phone until the midnight relief comes on. It'
Rhoda tonight, I think. She'll bring cookies and I'll cadg
some from her. All those dancing sugar canes at the pagear
gave me the munchies.

"Be careful on the front walk, it's icy. Don't slip an
land on your keester."

Yet again, I thought.

FIVE

TWO NIGHTS LATER I had a social engagement, a rare event for me. It was a dinner at the home of friends who lived in Morristown, not a long drive from Elizabeth in a normal car, but quite the haul in a barely heated Volkswagen Karmann Ghia. The friends were the Ohlmans, Harry and Mary, two people I'd known since my first year in college, which is to say, for almost fifteen years. A decade and a half. It was this amazing span of time that had gotten me thinking about friendship, the resiliency thereof, this Christmas season, or rather the Ohlmans' invitation—pressed on me in the face of many subtle hints and outright refusals—had.

I would have been thinking of friendship as I drove—northwest on 82 and then 24 past Millburn and through Chatham and Madison and Convent Station, the towns getting nicer if not noticeably farther apart—if I'd been able to put Jackie out of my mind. I'd waited all day for a call from Sergeant Grabowski and had even casually dropped by the Adullam office on the off chance that Jackie had called back. But there had been nothing there for me, not even leftover cookies.

I'd been quick to accept Sister Agnes's pronouncement that Jackie's call was a hoax and I still doubted the story he'd told me, Russet the alien's imminent kidnapping of innocent Benjy, but I'd gone back to believing the call itself. By that I mean that I now believed again that it had been a genuine call for help. I had just failed to determine what the real problem was. That failure and the nature of Jackie's unstated problem haunted me as I drove through frozen marshland, patches of ice in the weedy darkness beyond the road reflecting an elusive moon.

Suburban Morristown's zoning seemed to restrict builders to colonial homes, the bigger the better. Harry and Mary's was a nice brick example in a subdivision too new to have many trees. That was just as well, as those trees present were strung with enough electric lights to distract the airliners swarming Newark. An unfamiliar car was parked on the Ohlmans' sloping drive, a sleek Audi, but that didn't surprise me, Harry being as sentimental about cars as George Steinbrenner was about managers.

So I rang the front bell, worrying only about whether I'd be able to make two hours of small talk with my old friends, the woman I had once loved and the man who had won her away from me. But as soon as the door opened, I knew I was in far worse trouble. I could hear Harry's deep voice a room or two away, speaking to someone who was not the couple's two-year-old daughter. And there was the look on Mary's face, the how's-Owen-going-to-take-this? look. I knew then I was being set up, not the way paperback detectives were set up, to take the fall for someone, but the way unmarried friends were. To fall for someone. Some stranger.

"It's not too late to run," Mary said. "I thought you might when you saw Beth's car in the drive."

"I'm not that fast mentally."

She didn't disagree with me. "Tenacity," she said as she hugged me. "That's your strong suit. Owen, you're frozen. That car of yours. Come inside."

I'd already noted that she was very warm. And soft, in a mauve cashmere sweater with a floppy turtleneck collar. As we did the little dance required for her to take my coat, I further noted her brown, calf-length skirt and matching boots. Her short, honey-colored hair was arranged more formally than usual, which had the effect of making her look older. All grown-up. Or maybe it was the setting, the formal entryway, all warm wood and antique brass, with fresh greenery draped over its doorways and wound around the banister of the staircase that led to the shadowy second floor.

Somehow I'd held on to the present I'd brought for Amanda, the two-year-old. "Wrapped it yourself, I see," Mary, who was something of a detective in her own right, observed. "That's so sweet."

I was still holding the package as we entered the softly lit living room, where a fire crackled aggressively and smoked slightly.

"Damn fireplace isn't drawing right," Harry said as we shook hands. His large hand switched to smoothing his dark, thinning hair self-consciously the second I released it. He also directed my attention to the extra pound or two he'd put on by sucking in his stomach. "Should have pre-heated the flue. That column of cold air acts like a cork."

"I'm fine, Harry," I said. "How are you?"

Then Mary was introducing me to our fourth, who was seated on one of the twin love seats that faced each other at right angles to the hearth. "Beth, I'd like you to meet Owen Keane. Owen, this is Beth Wolfe."

Beth was a slender woman in a rust-colored knit dress that was doing what clinging it could with what was available. Her facial features were also slender, in a very regular, very classic way: her lips thin but not wide, her nose straight but not sharp, her cheekbones visible but not hollow. The elegance of the whole was offset by a dusting of old freckles on her very pale skin and by her eye makeup, which was a bit on the heavy side. All the eye shadow and mascara made her dark-brown eyes look very dark indeed, as did the up-from-under look she gave me from beneath chestnut bangs. Her thin hand felt cold even to my frozen one, and her legs were not so much crossed as clamped, one atop the other. This icy reserve relaxed me as thoroughly as the double scotch Harry handed me. Beth wanted no more to do with Mary's ambush than I did.

Though my secret ally looked like a model, she was actually a teacher whom Mary had met while working as a volunteer for the local school board. Mary mentioned this in her introduction, also that Beth was a Jersey girl, a native of Metuchen, and a graduate of Drew, the school I'd driven past that evening about the time I'd been losing the feeling in my feet.

I was anxious to hear how Mary would summarize me to Beth, but that tale had evidently been spun before I'd arrived. So we passed immediately to small talk.

Harry, poker in hand, led off by demanding, "What are you doing to run down that crèche vandal, Owen?"

I begged his pardon.

"Over in Elizabeth. Somebody's been screwing with Nativity scenes. It was in today's paper. Probably a hit squad from the ACLU. I thought you'd be right on top of that. It sounds like your kind of case."

"Case?" Beth repeated, the question barely escaping the depths of the love seat.

"Sure. Owen dabbles in crime detection," Harry said. "Or palmistry. His technique is somewhat idiosyncratic."

He was close to undoing all the careful obfuscation Mary must have done on my behalf. Or so I guessed from her serrated expression, which Harry was taking pains not to notice. He was saved by the entrance of his daughter in footed pajamas, one tiny balled fist working one half-closed eye, her blond hair informal in the extreme.

"Amanda, honey, you're supposed to be asleep," Mary said, crossing to her. "Now that you're here, you can say hello to Beth. Can you say hello?"

Amanda could and did.

"And you know who this is, don't you? He brought you a present. Can you say who this is?"

"Uncle Owen," Amanda said.

The uncle part was news to me, and to Harry, too. Mary must have been coaching her all day long in secret. Harry liked my new title about as much as Mary had liked his palmistry crack, which evened their score.

I liked my promotion in general, and Amanda seemed comfortable with it, as well. She led me by the hand to the Christmas tree, the fire's rival as the room's principal source of light. She showed me where to put her unopened present—a snow globe containing an angel—and then identified various ornaments for me—balls and birds and bells and drums—letting me pick her up so she could point to the higher branches. We'd reached the star at the top when Mary arrived beside us.

"Your reprieve is over," she said, addressing Amanda or me or both of us. "Dinner is served."

SIX

THE OHLMANS' dining room was dark blue and large. The table it contained was proportionally large most nights, but tonight it had lost more leaves than the front yard maples and was no bigger than a generous card table. An intimate setting for a somewhat restrained dinner.

Or maybe I should say constrained, conversationally at least. The food couldn't have been better, a brothy soup supporting chopped green onions followed by a tossed salad garnished with nuts and cranberries followed by beef tips on rice, the beef the most red, unground meat I'd had in months. Harry kept a series of wine bottles circulating, for his own benefit chiefly, but they didn't do much to help the talk.

The problem was suitable subject matter. The Ohlmans and I couldn't lose ourselves in old times without excluding Beth or, worse, accidentally mentioning one or more of my earlier "cases," which would have blown my cover as an average, eligible joe. Mary and Beth couldn't discuss their mutual interest, the school board, without leaving Harry and me to our own devices, which would have given us more leash than Mary intended us to have.

The solution, of course, was for Beth and me to question one another politely, with Harry and Mary filling in any dead air that occurred. But Beth was uninterested and I was uncooperative, at least initially. My second glass of wine softened me. I waited for a break in the chewing and then asked Beth what she taught.

"Men to be bastards, lately," she said in a voice that while soft was not without its edge.

No one dropped a fork during the ensuing silence, but it would have been a nice touch. Beth looked as shocked as Harry and Mary. As shocked as I did, for all I knew.

"Beth's recently divorced," Harry confided, his tone more sober than his eyes as he chalked up a point against Mary the matchmaker.

"She teaches high school English," Mary said. "Owen was an English major, like me, Beth."

The hostess and I discussed a class we'd once had until Beth regrouped and rejoined us. "What do you do for a living, Owen?" she eventually asked.

I'd more or less invited the question, but I found I had no desire to answer it, not while I was seated in the Ohlmans' plush, candlelit dining room, not within earshot of the tiny golden cherubs that hung from golden ribbons from the golden chandelier. For one thing, I was afraid the revelation would inspire Harry to award himself another point at Mary's expense.

Luckily I had a fallback. "I'm doing some volunteer work for a crisis phone center in Elizabeth. Adullam Line."

I told them a little about the place, keeping it general, not mentioning any real callers, least of all Jackie. Even so, I could see that Mary was concerned, as much as if she'd heard an alcoholic friend was a volunteer tour guide at a brewery.

Beth wasn't interested in Adullam Line, but she was still struggling to be polite. "How do you like Elizabeth?" she asked.

"And what about those manger scenes getting splattered with paint over there?" Harry cut in. He hadn't forgotten Mary's opinion of that topic, but she'd slipped into the kitchen to start the coffee.

"I hadn't heard about it," I admitted. "I'm not taking a

paper just now. Somebody's spray painting Nativity scenes?''

"Throwing paint," Beth said. "Red paint. It was in the paper. But only one of the incidents involved paint."

"You're right," Harry said from deep inside his wine glass. "The other church had something stolen. One of the statues stolen."

"Baby Jesus," Beth said. "I remember thinking, 'What's Jesus doing in the manger already, anyway? It's not Christmas Day yet.'"

"Maybe that's a clue to who stole the statue," Harry said. "A frustrated traditionalist." Then he heard himself, on some drinker's internal tape delay, and blushed, though it was hard to be sure, the wine having rosied him generally. "I didn't mean you, of course," he stammered to Beth.

"If the shoe fits," she said as Mary reentered, carrying slices of chocolate cake dolloped with whipped cream that had been drizzled with something red.

Harry made short work of his, sensing perhaps that he was close to being sent to bed without any. He held up his last forkful of the reddened topping in a salute to Beth "Like the statue's hands," he said.

"Hands?" Mary and I asked together.

Beth answered us. "In the manger scene desecration. The red paint was thrown on the Virgin Mary's hands—"

"Back on that, are we?" Mary asked her husband pointedly.

"—and across her dress," Beth finished. "Some woman hater probably," she added, looking somewhat pointedly at Harry herself.

"Don't forget the stolen statue at the other church was Baby Jesus, a male," Harry said.

"No better way to express your hatred for a woman than to steal her baby," Beth replied.

And that did it. That echo of Jackie's story, of Russet's motive for kidnapping the beautiful Benjy, finally brought into focus the feeling I'd been having that this was all some-how familiar. The idea had sprung to life when Beth men-tioned the Virgin's red hands and splattered dress, the very way the prank caller to Domestic Justice had described his wounded mother. Now I suddenly realized that both hoax calls, the kidnapping and the knifing, were perfect parallels to the desecrations.

"What's the matter, Owen?" Mary asked. "Did this hus-band of mine spoil your appetite? I can get you a piece of cake with plain whipped cream or no whipped cream."

I did want something, but I placed my order with Harry. "Do you still have the newspaper article about the vandal-ism?"

"Sure. It was in this morning's *Star Ledger*. No, wait. I used it to start the fire."

"Best move you've made all night," Mary said.

I stuck it out through coffee and then started looking around for my coat. Beth let me bear the brunt of Mary's disappointment at the early evening, then announced that she was going also. The Ohlmans saw us to the front door but not beyond it, the night having become positively frosty.

So much so that when Beth spoke to me as we neared her car her breath was as white in the glow of the garage light as her very pale face. "If you really want a copy of that newspaper article," she said, "you can have mine. It's at my apartment, which should be on your way home."

I did want the article, but it wouldn't be any job to find a copy. I'd made a mental list of likely sources while sip-ping the Ohlmans' arabica supreme.

"Look," Beth said before I could word an excuse, "I'm sorry I wasn't better company tonight. I should have told Mary it was too soon for me. Let me make amends a little."

I said sure and followed the Audi twenty minutes east to Beth's apartment complex, where I said sure again to her suggestion that I come in and warm up a minute.

I waited in her living room, coat unbuttoned and gloves in hand, while she looked for the paper. Though bigger and nicer, the apartment reminded me of my rooms. Its decor had the same just-passing-through motif.

Beth reentered minus her coat and her shoes. She carried the *Star Ledger,* but she was flipping it toward the sofa almost before she'd said, "Here it is."

Then she was inside my coat with me, kissing me with incredible hunger and squeezing me harder than two people with bony chests should ever squeeze one another. I say "one another" because I was squeezing her back by then and kissing her back, though it had been the farthest thing from my mind a second earlier. A second later we were in the bedroom, where we made amends, twice.

SEVEN

I AWOKE around three from a dream of splattered blood. For a moment I couldn't remember where I was. Then the smell of wood smoke in the hair of the woman sleeping beside me brought back Harry's cranky fireplace and then the whole evening. I thought of the newspaper waiting in the living room, tried to stop thinking of it, and found I couldn't.

I got up quietly, collected my pants, and slipped out into the front room. It was quite cold out there. Luckily I'd left major units of my wardrobe scattered about, including a sweater. I crawled into it and switched on a lamp next to a sofa that was as firm and spare as its owner.

Beth had left me the entire paper, and it took me some time to find Harry's article. The story was a brief bottom dweller on page twenty-one. Nevertheless, it contained some important additional information, notably the dates of the vandalism. The paint incident had occurred first, on the previous Tuesday. The Infant Jesus had been stolen two nights later, on Thursday. The day after my maiden shift at Adullam Line. Though I'd have to check the date the Domestic Justice message was received, it seemed the hoax calls were warnings of the desecrations, not after-the-fact gloating.

More significant still were the names of the target churches, because they confirmed that this wasn't all a wild coincidence. The statue had been taken from a manger outside a church called St. John Leonardi. Jackie had given his

formal first name as John. The church that owned the
bloody Virgin was Holy Angels, the second word of which
was very like Angela, the name of the caller's wounded
mother.

I looked up from the paper to find Beth standing in the
bedroom doorway. She was naked and leaning against the
jamb with her hips cocked outward, all of which I took to
be good signs. But she was holding my shoes, which I took
to be a bad sign, perhaps even a criticism of my leaving
her alone.

"You know where the light's better?" she asked.

"No," I said.

"Your place," she said, dropping my shoes. Then she
returned to the bedroom, shutting the door behind her and
locking it.

EARLY THAT SAME MORNING, after a quick stop at Adullam
Line, I visited the scenes of the crime. Bright and early, as
I'd been unable to get much sleep after leaving Beth's in
the wee small hours. I'd tried talking with her through her
bedroom door, but hadn't gotten an answer. Hadn't heard
a thing, not a snicker or a sniffle or a snore.

Elizabeth was an old city, founded in the seventeenth
century no less, that had been victimized by twentieth-
century modes of transportation. Newark Airport pressed
down on it from the north and from above, too, if you
counted the racket produced by an endless stream of airliners. Next to the airport, on Newark Bay, was the giant Elizabeth Port Authority Marine Terminal, no great enhancer
of the local quality of life. But the worst offender was the
New Jersey Turnpike, a shaft of bad air and noise that had
been driven right through the city, dividing the old waterfront from the hilly, disheartened downtown.

I found St. John Leonardi first, it being closer to the
center of town and my apartment. It was a small brownstone
church with a stone steeple still stained by the pollution
from long-dead smokestacks.

Father Ross, the pastor, was a balding man with a full beard and glasses so thick they had to be mentioned prominently on his driver's license. He also had a manner as energetic as Sister Agnes's. I used the nun's name in my introduction, without her permission, implying that I was somehow representing her and Adullam Line. That was more lying than I needed to do, Father Ross not being one of the church's great listeners. He mistook me for a concerned parishioner and led me outside, talking away while I wondered if he'd be a terrible confessor or the one of choice.

"We put the manger scene in its usual place, you see, right next to the front steps. Thirty years, same place. Keeps it out of the wind."

That wind was blowing off the bay this morning, and the priest had come outside in only the cardigan sweater he wore over his clericals. I pulled my overcoat tighter in sympathy as we examined the straw-covered patch of frozen ground and the manger scene, a fairly small one, the kneeling Mary and Joseph no more than three feet high. The stable was just a suggestion of one, a black wooden frame heavy enough to hold a plaster angel aloft. The crib or manger was also little more than a frame and it contained only additional straw, some of which blew away as we watched, despite the protection of the steps. Mary, hands spread wide, gazed down at the emptiness. I thought of Jackie's words: "Momma's gonna be kneeling next to that crib crying, cause it's gonna be empty."

Father Ross could add little to the newspaper account. The Jesus figure had disappeared sometime during the night. There'd been no witnesses and no clues, not even footprints on the iron ground. None of the other figures had been tipped or even touched.

I asked the priest why he'd had the Christ Child out so early.

"You're thinking of the old days when the Babe appeared on Christmas morning and the Wise Men on the

Feast of the Epiphany. Let me tell you, that Twelve Days of Christmas stuff is history. Christmas is Advent and out these days. It starts the day after Thanksgiving at the latest and by noon Christmas Day it's gone with a puff of smoke. After that it's all Super Bowl. So we have to get the word out early if we're going to do it at all."

His red, streaming face suddenly lit with a smile. "Get it? We have to get the word out early. Jesus, the Word Made Flesh. We have to get Him into the manger early. That's actually a pretty good play on words."

And the start of next Sunday's sermon, ten to one. "Very good," I said.

"I hope whoever took our Jesus needed Him, that he just didn't throw Him into the bay. Either way," he added, giving me a hopeful look, "I guess we'll have to start collecting for a new one."

"Just send me the envelope," I said.

HOLY ANGELS WAS a few blocks south, on the other side of the river, beyond the green space called Williams Field. It was newer than St. John Leonardi, but not new, its 1960s angled slab of a roof and stylized I-beam bell tower more dated-seeming than the older church's gothic touches.

Holy Angels's manger scene sat on a concrete plaza between the church and the street. It was larger and more three-dimensional than Father Ross's display, but that was all I could tell about it, as the whole thing was covered by gray tarps. But I knew I'd come to the right place. Just below one of the tarps, the cement showed a string of bright-red spots.

No priest was available to waste his time with me in the church's classroom-size office. I had to make do with a modern substitute, a "permanent deacon," a man empowered to handle some of a priest's workload, such as funerals and baptisms and dealing with amateur sleuths. This particular deacon's name was Walt Majeski, which fit him, as he was very large, with a fifties rocker's wave of greasy black hair that went not at all with his lumberman's shirt.

I tried the same cover story on him that I'd used on Father Ross, but Majeski actually listened to it. "What's Sister Agnes's interest in this? She gonna start some new project now? Maybe a branch of the Inquisition?"

Majeski wasn't moving, and he was a man who could do not moving as well as any small building. I decided I'd have to give him more.

"We got a call the other night at Adullam Line we think might be connected to the vandalism. We wanted to get some details from you so we could test the guy if he calls back."

"What details?" Majeski asked.

"Anything the real vandal would know. Like the time of night it happened."

"I can give you a range on that. I locked up after a late wedding rehearsal. A little after eleven. At twelve-thirty, I was back to pick up the Blessed Sacrament. I'd gotten a panic call. One of our sick parishioners was failing. Wanted to receive. I found the Blessed Virgin statue with red paint all over it. The stuff was too dry to wipe off, so it must have been thrown just after I left the first time, just after eleven."

"Any witnesses or suspects?" I asked.

"No and no," Majeski said. "I was so mad at first I couldn't think. Then I thought it might be some liberal who can't stand Christmas being about religion. Then I thought no, it can't be that. A hater like that would have trashed the whole display, not one statue. So then I thought it might be someone with something against the Virgin Mary. Maybe some fanatical Protestant obsessed with Mariolatry. But who on earth would care enough about that in this day and age to commit a crime? No one.

"Anyway, I've since heard about what happened over at Leonardi. If it's the same guy, his grudge is against the

Holy Family. Look for somebody's St. Joseph to be hit next.''

I asked if I could see the statue.

"Too late to see the paint. It's cleaned off by now. We didn't touch it for a day or two so the police could have a look, not that they were very interested. But we can't keep the crèche closed forever, vandals or no vandals. So the paint's gone.''

There followed a loud sniff, originating from the church secretary, who had been moving back and forth behind Majeski during the whole interview.

"Got something to say, Belinda?''

"Just that if you're counting on Ray to be getting that paint off you shouldn't. He was out back smoking a cigarette when I came in this morning, and he was still out there fooling around a minute ago.''

That news set Majeski in motion, and I followed. Luckily for me, he went first to the basement workshop where Ray was supposed to be, giving him the benefit of the doubt. The handyman wasn't there, and the deacon pounded off in search of him.

I stayed behind to examine the statue, which lay on its back on a workbench under lights that barely had space to hang beneath the low ceiling of ducts and pipes. The piece was much larger than its counterpart at St. John Leonardi, but otherwise very like it, a kneeling figure whose heavy base hung over one end of the bench. As the *Ledger* article had said, both the hands and the front of the dress had been splattered. I confirmed now that it had been done in multiple passes and that the white plaster dress had received its own treatment and had not just caught the excess from the outstretched palms. The vandal had gone to some trouble to recreate the details given to Honey at Domestic Justice.

When I heard Majeski coming back through the rear of the building with an alibiing Ray in tow, I slipped out the front.

EIGHT

I HAD TO GO to work then myself, to the job I'd been reluctant to tell Harry and Mary about: stocking shelves at an Acme not far from the county courthouse. It wasn't the kind of work that keeps your mind anchored. That day mine was especially prone to wander, though I was careful not to glance toward the large clock on the wall above the deli counter, both because it would have made the clock run more slowly and because it might have tipped my supervisor that I was planning an escape.

When my lunch break finally came at one, I dashed out to my car, which I'd parked in the full sun in the hope of some passive solar heating. I drove to the offices of Domestic Justice. They were in a nondescript block of a building, on a side street that plunged from the main road, Elizabeth Avenue, like a luge run. The first floor of the brick cube housed a beauty college whose sign featured menacing golden scissors three feet high. The crisis line's signage was far more discreet. So much so that the words *Domestic Justice* didn't even appear on the little pink square next to the stairs leading down to the basement entrance. In their place was an alias, Telephone Contact, Inc.

When I'd stopped briefly at dawn at Adullam Line to glance at the log book and to get Domestic Justice's address, Rhoda, the volunteer on duty, had explained the situation to me. "The location is strictly confidential, Owen. Don't give this address to anyone. They do a lot of domestic abuse counseling and they get a lot of threats. It would be hard to get people to work there if the security wasn't so good.''

That security, in the form of a receptionist seated behind tollbooth-grade bulletproof glass, gave me a very hard look when I showed up asking to see Honey, but I was eventually buzzed in. Rhoda had assured me that Honey would be there if I waited until afternoon, that she only went home to sleep the morning away, that she was more of a nun than Sister Agnes, her cloister being Domestic Justice.

I found Honey in a small, damp-smelling office whose door bore no name or title, only a bumper sticker: Hatred Is Its Own Excuse. Beyond that grim assertion was a large woman seated behind a small woman's desk. She was wearing a Seton Hall sweatshirt, and her blond hair was held back from her broad, shiny face by brightly colored plastic clips placed at random or in a design that was too avant-garde for me. Contrasting with this playfulness was her expression—flat-eyed wariness—and the cigarette that clung to her lower lip as though pasted on.

"You've come from Sister Agnes?" Honey asked, repeating the information the receptionist had passed her along with my name.

"I work for her," I said.

"Shame about that eye patch they've got her wearing," she said, testing me unsubtly.

"Goes well with the peg leg and the parrot," I replied. That failed to get a hand, so I described the nun in general, flattering terms, though the simple reference to her sweat suits on which I ended would probably have sufficed.

"A shared weakness," Honey said, tugging on the *S* in *Seton*. "What do you want, Mr. Keane? Have a seat, by the way."

I did, noticing belatedly that the entire block wall behind her was papered in bumper stickers. The subjects covered included domestic violence, racism, air and water pollution, gun ownership, and medical testing on animals. Sitting there was like being stuck in traffic behind a gigantic Volvo.

"I'd like to ask you about a call you received the other night."

"You surely know I can't discuss our calls with you. They're confidential."

"You discussed this one with Sister Agnes. It was a prank call from a kid who told you his mother's hands had been slashed."

"Sister Agnes is a confidant of mine. Someone in the same line of business. We consult with each other often. When she gets a caller yanking her chain, she lets me know. And vice versa. As a professional courtesy."

"I'm in the same profession," I said.

Honey finally acknowledged the cigarette stuck to her lip by peeling it free and stubbing it out. "You may have passed Sister Agnes's screening. I doubt you'd pass mine."

So did I. Afraid that the crushed cigarette was a cue for me, I dug out my hole card, the *Star Ledger* article, and slid it across the little desk.

Honey had scanned it through dismissively and was in the process of sliding it back when the contents registered. She pulled the clipping toward her again and bent over it. "The call I discussed with Sister Agnes," she said looking up.

"Exactly," I said. "It was a prediction or a warning of what was going to happen at Holy Angels. At least I think it was a warning. Sister Agnes was a little vague about when your call came in."

"Monday evening, about ten. I can get you the exact time from the log."

"The statue was vandalized a little after eleven on Tuesday night."

Honey shook her hair clips and pursed her big lips down to nothing. "He didn't seem like that at all. I mean, yes, he was wasting my time. But when I called him on it, he didn't laugh or gloat. He didn't seem malicious. He seemed..."

"Lost," I said.

She gave me a rapid reexamination and shook a fresh cigarette free of her pack. "You've spoken to him, too?"

I pointed to the clipping, but she had it memorized. "The stolen statue. What did he tell you? That he was going to be taken from his mother by someone? Some social workers?"

I shook my head, mentally declining the cigarette she hadn't offered me. "That wouldn't have fit the pattern." I recounted Jackie's story while Honey lit up and inhaled deeply.

"I see what you mean. Threatening boyfriend in each scenario. Made up or real?"

"I don't know."

"You couldn't know, could you? But you know why you're here, what you're after. What is it?"

"I want to know if he's called again. I checked Adullam Line's log this morning. He didn't call there last night."

"You're thinking he'll do it again? Why?"

"Because no one's caught him."

Honey liked that. "And being caught is the point of the exercise. Otherwise, why would he call twenty-four hours before he strikes? And he has to figure it will take some time for someone to figure it all out, so he has to keep at it. You're seeing all this as a cry for help."

"Yes," I said.

"These days, a kid's cry for help can be pretty damn dangerous," Honey observed. "For innocent bystanders especially."

"Is that your feeling about this kid?" I asked.

"No."

"So did he call here last night?"

"No."

"Who else might he have called?"

"Let's get something straight. Is this about protecting some statues nobody looks at twice anymore? Or is it about helping the kid?"

"Helping the kid."

"Okay. I'll do some digging. Where can I reach you?"

"I'd better reach you," I said. The Acme frowned on incoming calls.

"Give me an hour."

NINE

I ENDED UP giving Honey several hours. A truckload of frozen turkeys had arrived for a special sale, which was an all-hands-on-deck situation at the Acme. It was going on five when I used stiff and swollen fingers to dial the direct-line number she'd given me.

"You'll be lucky to catch him this late," Honey said right off in a voice so much warmer and softer than her office persona that it checked me up. So did the statement itself, which I interpreted as meaning it was too late to catch Jackie before he struck again, though it was barely dusk.

"Catch who?" I managed to ask.

"Edward Hennix. President and CEO of a corporate counseling service called Hand to Hand."

"Never heard of it."

"Must not be in your benefits package. It's a fringe some of the fatter corporations are starting to offer, confidential psychological counseling for employees and their families. Supposed to cut down on trouble—drinking, drugs, depression—in the workplace, keep the worker bees buzzing."

At the Acme, they used free coffee. "How does our caller fit in? His mother work for AT&T?"

"Probably not," Honey said. "But this Edward Hennix is an interesting character. I could tell you so much about him you'd miss him for sure. Slum kid from Newark who worked his way through Rutgers studying psychology. Was going to be the Albert Schweitzer of North Jersey, but got switched onto the John D. Rockefeller track by mistake.

Been piling up money ever since. Conflicted as hell about it, too, which is where our mystery caller comes in. Hennix has this big fancy call center with more capacity than his business needs right now, so he donates some time to the county, taking welfare agency calls during their off hours.''

"And his center got one of the hoax calls?"

"I think so. He wouldn't say much about it, except that it was really off-the-wall."

Bingo. "Can you give me his number?"

"He asked me to give you his address. He wants to meet you. It's a trust thing. Hennix has some problems with trust."

Honey had had them herself, earlier in the day. As she read off the address, I decided I'd passed her screening after all. So had Hennix, evidently.

"Don't let his hard nose fool you. Eddie is a good man. I'll let him know you're on your way."

THE GOOD MAN'S OFFICES were in a very sleek building in an office park so close to Newark Airport the blue lights of the taxiways seemed to run right up to its back fence. Unlike Domestic Justice, Hennix's company didn't go in for pseudonyms on its outdoor advertising. Hand to Hand appeared in large backlit white letters on a low sign beside the front walk. The chrome door at the end of the walk opened itself for me when it detected my approach, just like the ones at the Acme, only faster. The door had to be fast to open for me, since I was very nearly trotting, afraid I'd miss Hennix and the vital clue.

A receptionist, working without the benefit of armored glass, called my name when I was two steps inside the door and then waved me down a hallway like a third-base coach waving a runner home. Or maybe just like a woman who was anxious to head home herself. Hennix's office was at the far end of the hallway, and I spotted him through its open door.

He was speaking on the phone and gesturing away like he had his listener across the desk, every movement of his free hand accentuated by the office lights hitting a heavy golden ring. He was more trim than thin and very dark complexioned with short hair worn like a Marine recruit's. His nose was set high and high arched, and his eyes kept track of my approach while smiling away with his wide, mobile mouth. He wore a white shirt and a blue silk tie, the shirt looking as if he'd just gotten it out of the cellophane.

He wasn't nearly my age, but he'd made much better use of his postcollege years. I suddenly wished I had Harry Ohlman along. He and Hennix could have compared club memberships and mutual fund balances and exchanged secret handshakes in general while I looked on from the sidelines.

"Got to go," Hennix said when I reached his doorway. "Right. Got to go. Right. See you."

He was up out of his seat, extending his hand, before he'd hung up the phone, and he stayed up, using our handshake to pull me back in the direction I'd come. "You almost missed me. I'm pitching to a company in Linden. Express package shipper, employees all tensed up and overtimed out, all screwed down tighter than a skydiver's toupee, ready to take off like that toupee, ready to be generally unproductive and obnoxious—"

"Like the toupee again," I said, more to arrest him than top him. To stop the practice pitch certainly, but also his escape. After leading me back to the doorway of his office, Hennix had extracted a suit coat and topcoat from behind the office door and slipped them on, almost simultaneously. Another snappy line of dialogue or two and he'd be out the door and gone. I planted myself in the doorway.

"Honey said you were an interesting study," Hennix observed, standing chest to chest with me, not moving me yet, but sizing up the job.

"She likes you, too," I said.

"I can guess what she told you about me. Child of the ghetto, so guilt ridden he can barely look at his bank statement. That bullshit's one of the occupational hazards of being a psychologist. All your peers analyze you, even the well-meaning amateur peers like Honey. I could give you a few theories about her, Keane, including why she hangs on to a first name she hates, one that reflects an image of women that she hates, one that fits her about as well as—"

"A bad toupee?" I asked. "We're wasting your pitching time."

"Right. Come back tomorrow."

"Tomorrow will be too late."

"Why? Sister Agnes going to find out what you're up to and clip your wings? I guarantee I would if you worked for me and I found out you were running around playing Joe Private Eye."

A plane passed so low overhead I almost ducked. "Tomorrow will be too late because that call you got will be old news by then. I'll be able to read about the results in tomorrow's paper. The chance to help this kid will be gone."

"Help him how, Keane?" Hennix demanded, backing me into the hallway. "Do you have the slightest idea what he's up to? You ever even met a kid like him, head full of brains and no chance to use them? Have you ever been inside a housing project? Do you have any idea what that kid's up against, day in and day out, what you'd be up against if you found him?"

His tone was giving me déjà vu, and I remembered Jackie's exasperated condescension. "How do you know so much about this kid?" I asked. "You must have taken the call yourself."

"Wrong," Hennix said, drawing out the word like a game show buzzer. "I listened to the tape. We tape every call that comes in here, even wild fairy tales."

"What was this fairy tale about?"

"I'd be wasting your time telling you, because it's not going to do you any good."

"Waste my time. I'm not selling to any corporations tonight."

That reminder of the meeting he was late for tipped Hennix my way, though he headed for the front door as he spoke. "It was about a mob hit. Kid called in to say his momma's badass boyfriend was going to whack a Mafia guy over some drug deal. Plus the Mafia guy's two bodyguards.

"Honey told me about the manger scene stuff, so it was no big job deciphering this call. Three Mafiosi or wise guys equals the Three Wise Men. The Magi. No problem, except that, according to Honey, the clue to where the vandalism's going to happen is in a name, and the kid didn't give any names, not for himself or his momma or her man. Not even for the Mafia kingpin. He was just 'Mr. X.' Like out of some spy movie, which is probably where the kid got it."

We'd reached the main entrance. Once outside, Hennix paused for a moment to punch a number into a keypad next to the automatic door, disabling it, I guessed, to protect the night shift from prowlers and return visits by me. Then he marched to the nearest parking space, which held a silver Audi, as sleek as Beth Wolfe's, though larger.

"Feel free to drive around Elizabeth all night trying to catch this kid in the act, Keane," he said in parting. "You won't, not in a month of trying, which means you'll be safe from him. And he'll be safe from you."

TEN

IF HENNIX HADN'T secured the front door of his building, I might have snuck back in. Not to bother the help, but to borrow a phone book. I wasn't as discouraged by Hennix's brief recounting of the third call as he'd intended me to be, because I knew a little more about the Catholic Church than he did. Specifically, I knew a saint's name that began with an X, as in Mr. X, St. Francis Xavier, missionary hero of the Jesuits who had taught Harry and Mary and me. If I was right, Jackie had passed on the name of tonight's target church in his subtlest way yet.

I wasn't familiar with a St. Francis Xavier Church in greater Elizabeth, but finding it only required a phone book. I stopped to ask for one at a diner just south of the airport and so proud of the association that it was referenced twice in its name, Skyways Jet Service, though, from the look of the parking lot, they were serving more truck drivers than jet jockeys.

I ordered coffee, resisting the urge the place inspired to call it java, and the yellow pages. It turned out to be supporting the toothpick dispenser and the after-dinner mint dish next to the cash register. I sat on a very low stool at the very low counter and looked up Churches, Roman Catholic. The book contained a decent-size list, this very industrialized corner of America having attracted waves of European immigrants. But there was no church in Elizabeth named for St. Francis Xavier. I tried under the *F*s and then under the *X*s, of which there were none at all. While I was moving my finger back up the list to check again for Francis, I spotted the correct answer to Jackie's riddle, a church called St. Pius X. Mr. X himself, for anyone unfamiliar with Roman numerals, and an Italian big shot to boot.

I celebrated the discovery by ordering dinner, a big one, hamburger steak, mashed potatoes with gravy, and green beans. The waitress, concerned for my cholesterol perhaps, tried to steer me toward the turkey, but I'd played catch with too many of those that afternoon. I justified this break in the action by telling myself that it wasn't yet eight and I couldn't expect Jackie to appear much before eleven, that a place that promised jet service was sure to be fast, and that a greasy meal would help me stay warm on a long stakeout in an unheated car.

As a further precaution against the cold, I ordered a large coffee to go, but it was tepid by the time I parked in the shadow of St. Pius X. The church was another old one, sited on a hill overlooking the bay and built of brick that had once been painted white and was now going back to natural. There must have been some money in the parish at one time, because its Nativity scene was a near life-size beauty, Holy Family, shepherds, angels, and even farm animals, arranged against a flat wall painted to represent a stable and lit by a single floodlight. A little to one side were the Three Magi, weeks early for their traditional appearance and arranged in ascending order according to height: kneeling king, bowing king, standing king.

All three were untouched, as far as I could tell. I didn't go in for a close inspection, afraid that Jackie was somewhere nearby on a stakeout of his own. I was expecting him to be especially wary tonight. I still felt that Honey and I were right, that Jackie's calls were cries for help, that he wanted to be noticed and caught. But I understood that he was ambivalent about the process. Hence his elaborate game and the hesitancy in his voice when I'd offered to come to him. So I was determined not to scare him off.

And not to freeze to death. By eleven, that seemed like a real possibility. I was getting regular exercise, scraping my frozen breath from the inside of the windshield, but that wasn't enough to keep my blood circulating. I decided I had to do some pacing, and climbed out of the car as quietly as I could. I paced away from the church, down a barely lit side street and back again. I made no noise myself in my rubber-soled, stock-boy shoes, and I heard very little, there being almost no traffic on the nearby streets or on the bay. The occasional jet that passed low overhead sounded like a freight train in the general hush.

I hadn't been on my feet very long before all the coffee I'd drunk began demanding to part company. I was taking care of that in a little alley that ran behind the church when I heard the faint sound of a blow being struck and the fainter thud of something heavy falling.

I circled the church at a run, aware as soon as I'd reached the street that something had changed. It was the lighting. The single flood that had lit the Nativity scene was off. I'd neglected to take the Ghia's flashlight with me, and I didn't stop for it now, making do with the residue from the nearest streetlight, which reduced the colors of the scene to shades of blue and gray. Still, I was able to spot a second change. The standing king was missing his head. So was the stooping king, who now looked like he'd been bowing for a headsman's ax. The sight of that damage dropped me from a run to a very deliberate walk. I stopped altogether when I saw that the kneeling king had yet to be beheaded. Jackie hadn't finished the hit, which meant I'd either frightened him off or he was hiding somewhere in the shadows.

"Jackie, it's me," I said as conversationally as I could when I'd caught my breath a little. "Owen. We talked the other night. I came by to see whether you wanted to talk again."

Nothing. I stood there like the latest addition to the statuary, but couldn't hear the sound of movement or any breathing but my own, which gradually slowed with disappointment.

I started forward into the grouping itself, speaking a little louder now. Jackie might still be somewhere nearby, listening. "If you don't want to talk tonight, maybe you'll call—"

I caught a flash of movement to my right, from behind the tallest king. I turned my head toward it and saw him, saw a single wide eye peering at me from behind a raised bat. Then I saw the Star of Bethlehem itself, but only very briefly.

ELEVEN

I WOKE UP in a bed in Elizabeth General Hospital, though all I knew at the moment of waking was that it was a hospital somewhere. Before I could puzzle out where I was exactly and how I'd gotten there, I was presented with a far more interesting mystery. I heard a chair scrape against the floor and Mary Ohlman was standing over me, her sky-blue eyes youthful without all the dinner-party makeup but dark, too, with concern.

"Owen, thank God," she said.

"How?" I asked, which was short for "How did they know to call you?" I was afraid someone had found some old college love letter I'd tucked into the lining of my wallet and forgotten or, worse, that I'd absentmindedly listed Mary on a next-of-kin line of an Acme insurance form. Name: Mary Ohlman. Relationship: One True Love.

Mary understood the question and probably the concern. "The map I sent you so you could find our house for the party. It was still in the pocket of your coat. It had our phone number on it. Your wallet didn't have much in it, much they could use to contact someone, I mean. So they called me. I left Amanda with a neighbor and drove straight over here." She was still wearing the stadium coat she'd thrown on for the drive, wearing it tightly buttoned, like someone who couldn't stay.

"Thanks," I said. "Where's here?"

She gave me the name of the place, also the date and the hour. I hadn't been out all that long, not if you factored in a normal night's sleep. It was only midmorning of the day after my stakeout.

Mary had her own take on the timing. "You're lucky they found you so quickly. It got down below freezing last night."

A young doctor joined us then. He was blond and excessively tall, and his nose hair needed professional attention. He brought with him yet a third point of view regarding the time scheme.

"You had us worried. You were out for a long time for no harder than you were hit. I mean, judging by the lump and the bruising, you were hit more of a stunning, glancing blow, but it put you right under."

While he spoke, he examined my left temple. "I gave your X ray a closer look. There appears to be an indication of a prior injury to that area. An old one. Were you struck there before?"

"Yes," Mary said. "With a rifle butt."

"A rifle butt?" the doctor repeated with interest. "You were a soldier?"

"No," I said. "Just a poor judge of character."

The doctor, whose name was Steir, was a good judge of character, or else his X-ray machine had revealed other interesting information regarding my head. Perhaps a table of contents. He smiled stoically. "My advice would be to get hit somewhere else in the future. In the meantime, I'd like to run some further tests."

I shook my head and immediately regretted it. "I don't think my health insurance covers anything beyond the ice pack. Besides, I have to get out of here as soon as possible. Holiday business."

Mary reacted to that with a visible jerk, as though a current had been run through her by some unseen cardiologist. In another second, she would have been authorizing every test in the catalog. Luckily, Sister Agnes Kelly burst in just then, which meant that the Pope himself, had he been visiting, would have been demoted to looker-on.

"Owen, what have you been up to? Never mind, don't tax your imagination. Honey's already told me all about it. Traipsing around looking for some boy you think is in trouble. Who turns out to be trouble. This is why I have my rule about keeping out of the line of fire. This is what can happen. You end up in the hospital or worse. If Father Andrus hadn't found you when he did, worse it would have been. All for some old pieces of plaster that will be glued back together before you are."

And on and on. Dr. Steir decided after a paragraph or two that his time could be better spent elsewhere. Mary remained, patience being her long suit, especially where I was concerned. I decided that it was in my best interests to keep the nun talking.

"How did Father Andrus happen to find me?" I asked when she appeared to be flagging.

"What? Oh, that. Somebody rang the rectory bell. Some hooligan. I say hooligan because when Father Andrus opened the door there was no one there, just a blast of arctic air. He was looking around for whoever did it when he noticed the light was out in front of the Nativity scene. The rectory's right across the street from the church, you know. The bulb, he thought. Nowadays priests change lightbulbs themselves, God help us, so he bundled up and went out to do it.

"When he got out there, he found that the old bulb was halfway unscrewed. He tightened it, it worked, and he saw you, lying next to the manger. Like an uncle who'd dropped in unexpectedly and decided to stay the night was how he put it. Except he said something about your having too much to drink, too. An uncle who'd drank too much and decided to stay the night. That was it. Because he thought you were drunk at first. Then he tried to rouse you, it being too cold out even for drunks, and saw the bruise on your head.

"So it seems that hooligan accidentally saved your life. Or do you think it was some passerby who only wanted someone to see that the light was out?"

Mary said, "I'm guessing that Owen thinks it was the boy who hit him. He thinks the boy rang the rectory bell so someone would come out and find him."

"He beans him, then he rescues him? Why?"

Mary delegated that one. "He didn't mean to hurt me," I said. "I scared him, showing up in the middle of things and accidentally cornering him in the scene itself. I thought he was off somewhere by then in the shadows listening to me. I didn't realize that I had him trapped. He only hit me, not hard, to get away."

"He hit you hard enough," Sister Agnes said, leaning across the bed so that her very pointed face was pointed at me, first at my lump and then at a spot between my eyes. In her own way, she was as insightful as Mary. "You're still soft on this kid, aren't you? You're still going to try to help him."

"Yes," Mary said.

"If you do, you can forget about representing Adullam Line." The nun had gone over to the other side, gone from running interference for me to double-teaming me with Mrs. Ohlman. I needed another timely entrance to save me, and I got one. A uniformed patrolman entered stage right, unzipping a well-filled nylon jacket and extracting a notebook. Not the interruption I would have picked, since the last thing I wanted to do was give a statement in front of Mary and Sister Agnes. Those two would give me no room to maneuver with respect to the truth.

But luck was with me that morning. I'd just begun to describe the crèche vandalism in general terms when the cop lowered his pencil and said, "You Catholics and your frigging statues. Why can't you just worship the frigging trees like the frigging Indians?''

The next thing he knew he was being pushed into the hallway by a tiny woman in a track suit, who was demanding to know the number of his badge and precinct and the names of his lieutenant and captain and mother. Forgetting her own recent dismissal of "old pieces of plaster," she then launched into a lecture on the Catholic Church and its use of iconography that promised to last a while, starting as it did way back with the Byzantine Empire.

Mary was smiling as she listened, but the smile faded when she turned to me. "Owen, what am I going to do with you?''

In the interlude that followed, she considered her question and I indulged the fantasy of a future time when doing something about me might actually be Mary's business.

Then I shook it off. "Tell Amanda her Uncle Owen sends his love."

TWELVE

LATER, as I sat in the chair Mary had used, awaiting my promised release, Edward Hennix walked in. Unlike me, he was not wearing his outfit from the prior evening, but today's had come from the same haberdashery. The mouse-colored topcoat was slung over one shoulder and was therefore undistinguished, a foil only for the white shirt with the fine silver stripe that perfectly matched the silk tie, the black blazer, and the charcoal slacks. Hennix's expression was also a new one within our brief acquaintance: sheepish contrition.

"Damn, Keane," he said, "I feel like this is my fault. I underestimated you and I overestimated you at the same time, if that's possible. I mean, I never thought you'd actually track down that kid, and I humbly ask your pardon for that. But I never would have guessed you'd let him slip up behind you with a bat, either. You're an honest-to-God investigator, but you're not like the ones I read about growing up."

I'd often had the same thought, but I didn't dwell on it now. I was feeling bad enough already. The dull ache in my temple had spread to my left eye, making the afternoon's cheerful sunlight a penance. To move the discussion away from my uniqueness, I said, "How did you find out?"

Hennix waved his golden ring dismissively. "The news ran through our grapevine like lightning. We're a close-knit little group, the help-line people, the telephonic tongue waggers. Honey and Sister A and me and a few of the others working this edge of the garbage dump of humanity, we stay in touch. You lit up the board this morning, let me tell you." He'd dropped his coat on my unmade bed before settling comfortably on the spare one. "So give. How did you find him?"

It was my chance to use a dismissive gesture, but I lacked a golden ring to set if off. I described the correct reading of the Mr. X clue, wishing it were something more elaborate even before Hennix began shaking his head.

"It's always some little thing like that in detective books," he said. "They have all those words to work with, you'd think they'd have the solution hinge on some complex human interaction, instead of a bit of trivia."

"The better ones do," I said. I was pondering some complex human interaction in the here and now. Specifically, I was wondering why Hennix had come to see me. With Mary's recent example as my guide, I decided to be patient and not ask him directly. So I asked instead how his sales pitch had gone.

Hennix waved the nugget at me again. "It went okay. Bunch of people whose only real problem is incipient gout. No emotional hang-ups a good night's sleep wouldn't cure. But I don't want to be offering my services to people who really need them. That would be like selling health insurance to smokers. Too much overhead. Too much work.

"So I should have been at the top of my game with that crowd, but I never really found my rhythm. My mind kept slipping back to you and your little problem. When I should have been making empty promises to my prospective clients, I was trying to remember what you'd told me about that kid. But I couldn't remember much. Couldn't even remember what your guess was about why he's doing this."

"You didn't give me a chance to guess," I said. "You had those gouty people waiting." He had other people waiting somewhere right now, I was certain. And yet here he was in an overheated hospital room in Elizabeth, drawing admiring stares from passing nurses, several of whom seemed to be passing very regularly.

"I know I stiff-armed you, Keane, and I'm sorry. I was sorry all night. Not about being rude to you—you don't make that good a first impression—over the kid. Over not offering to help with the kid.

"I don't know how much that boss of yours or Honey told you about me, but I grew up pretty much like this kid you're hunting is growing up. Wild and scared. That may be reason one why I should have helped you. Why I feel like helping you now.

"Reason two is that I got a hand up when I needed one. A teacher here and there who told me I had brains and a mother who wouldn't let me quit. More than this kid has maybe.

"Reason three is the one you maybe heard from Honey. How I was going to be a Moses to my people once upon a time. I was going to help the neediest, instead of which I've ended up squeezing the wealthiest. So I've got this whole thing going about falling away from a call to grace. I don't know if you can identify with that."

In fact, he knew I could. He told me so with an uncharacteristically furtive glance out the window. A member of his grapevine, Sister Agnes probably, had filled him in on my own past and my own failures, supplementing my poor first impression. Once I would have been offended by that breach of confidence. Now I'd come to accept that it was how some people defined me. A failed seminarian now and forever.

"Hell," Hennix said turning back to me. "It may just be that it's Christmastime, with all the shit that goes with that. I'm speaking of the secular stuff now. The idea of being Scrooge and having a change of heart. Maybe saving a Tiny Tim.

"Which brings me back to the question of what this kid is up to. What you think he's up to, I mean. I know you believe this is all a cry for help or attention, and I think you're right about that. But why is he doing what he's doing? Why has he picked this specific pattern of vandalism?''

It was the moment for him to pause so I could make my guess, but Hennix didn't pause. He went back to his pacing, this time with a surer step.

"If you're thinking the kid might be hitting out at religion in general, at the idea of religion or the idea of God, I'd have to say I don't think so. There are statues all over town all year long he could be defacing, not to mention the buildings, the churches and temples and mosques. Same objection applies to the idea that he could have some grudge against Catholics. Why strike now? And why not hit the churches themselves?

"The targets were Nativity scenes, not churches. Not the religious beliefs the Nativity scenes stand for either, or else the churches would have been more logical targets. So what else do the scenes stand for?''

He stopped pacing and directed the question at his audience, so I answered it. "Christmas.''

"Exactly. Christmas. The day every kid loves except for the kids that don't get any Christmas. The ones who watch all the lights and decorations go up and listen to all the corny songs and know that at the end of it all there's going to be squat for them, that they're being screwed over again. Christmas could come to represent the entire world a kid like that, a kid from the projects, is cut off from. The world of a normal childhood.

"So the specific act a kid like that might choose as his cry for help might be a blow against Christmas itself.''

Tiny Tim as urban terrorist. It was certainly a new twist.

Hennix was moving on. "Not that that gets us much of anywhere. You're still looking for a needle in a haystack. A potentially dangerous haystack for you, a white guy straight off the bus, to be wandering around in. What I'm saying is, think twice about following this kid's trail any farther. I sold you short last night. I know now you have the kid's best interests at heart, that your intentions are good. But good intentions aren't much of a shield in this world.

"If you want, I can do some poking around. In fact, that might be best. Pass the buck to me and give that cracked head of yours a rest." He retrieved his topcoat. "I'll let you know how things work out."

My cracked head was throbbing with new urgency. I was straining it, still trying to figure out why Hennix had come. Had it really been to take the Jackie problem off my hands? No. That offer seemed like an afterthought. To warn me off the case, perhaps at Sister Agnes's request? Then all his speculating about motives and targets had just been filler. That wasn't easy to believe; he'd worked so hard at putting it across.

While I was still grinding away, Hennix gave me yet another possible reason for his drop-in. He reached into the pocket of his topcoat and extracted a cassette tape.

"This message came for you late last night. Should have gone to Adullam Line, but it came to us, I guess because the Mr. X call had come to us."

He tossed the tape spinning to me. It passed through my outstretched fingers and landed in my lap.

"Don't let that get you fired up again," Hennix said from the doorway. "Think of it as a good-bye."

THIRTEEN

ADULLAM LINE didn't tape its calls, but the ministry did own a tape recorder. I knew that because part of Sister Agnes's cursory training consisted of listening to tapes of sample crisis-line calls that had been compiled and published by the University of Georgia.

So when I was reluctantly sprung by Elizabeth General, I retrieved my car from the shadow of St. Pius X, stopped by the Acme to trade glimpses of my damaged head for a sick day, and then drove to the old rectory where it had all begun. The phone was being staffed by a college-age volunteer who barely looked up from her fashion magazine when I introduced myself and asked after the tape player. I found the little plastic portable in a corner filing cabinet and carried it into Sister Agnes's private office, which I'd already determined to be empty. I even sat at the nun's desk. There was no point in observing the proprieties when my pink slip was already in the works.

The cassette Hennix had given me was a pristine one in an unscratched case, but it sounded old and crackly on Sister Agnes's machine. I leaned forward as the hissing began, thinking that Jackie had gotten a bad connection for his call. The static lasted so long, I began to wonder whether Hennix had forgotten to rewind the tape. Then Jackie came on.

"Tell Owen I'm sorry."

That was it. I listened to the four words again and again, but I never detected a secret meaning or anything in Jackie's voice but sincere regret. Around the fifth replay, I stopped listening and went over to asking myself the question Hennix had asked: Why had the apology call come to him and not Adullam Line? Hennix's guess had been that he'd gotten the follow-up call because he'd received the earlier Magi warning. Since I'd shown up at St. Pius X, Jackie could rightfully assume some ongoing communication between Hand to Hand and me.

It was an answer, but it didn't satisfy me. I fell into thinking of Hennix's breezy description of the loose federation of local crisis-line operators, or "telephonic tongue waggers," as he had put it. He'd also referred to the grapevine that had spread the news of my bonk on the head, and I wondered if Jackie had somehow known of this grapevine or taken it for granted. Maybe that was why each of his three calls had gone to a different line. To Jackie, they might simply be different extensions of some interconnected, invisible world of the knowing and the powerful.

As I popped the cassette out of the machine, I thought of a third explanation for Jackie's misdirected call, one that was less philosophically tangled than mine and more plausible than Hennix's. It was that Jackie had tried to reach me through Adullam Line, been told I wasn't there, and had then tried Hand to Hand.

The theory had the advantage of being easy to check, as all calls to Adullam Line were logged. I rejoined the coed who was cramming for her *Mademoiselle* final. She didn't look up as I returned the tape recorder and barely did when I reached for the log. Someone named Wilson had been on duty around the time they were X-raying my head. He'd gotten several calls in a row involving holiday stresses and strains, which he'd written up at novella length. I flipped ahead and found a very brief entry logged at midnight. "Personal message for O. Keane." But no word of the message itself.

The fashion major looked up when I cleared my throat.

"It says a message came in for me last night. Any sign of it?"

She didn't answer right away. She might have been considering the makeup challenge presented by the bump on my head. Finally she mumbled, "Personal messages aren't allowed," but began searching the desktop. Beneath her magazine was a textbook in a related field, marketing, and beneath that a yellow slip. She handed it over without asking for ID.

It was the message for me all right, but it wasn't from Jackie. My midnight caller had been Beth Wolfe, the divorcée who'd given me the interesting evening and the free copy of the *Star Ledger*. The complete text of the message was her phone number. I filed it in my shirt pocket.

THE RECEPTIONIST AT Domestic Justice remembered me but pretended not to. She called Honey or pretended to. Then she told me with a straight face that was all pretense that Honey—the secular nun who never left her bumperstickered office—wasn't in.

I'd driven there in the first place because going back over Hennix's hospital-room lecture, during which the psychologist had worked his way down the motive list from hatred of religion to hatred of Catholics to hatred of Christmas, had gotten me thinking in terms of layers. And that had led me in turn to observe that Jackie's own work was multilayered. On the surface his calls were cries for help from a kid facing some immediate threat from an abusive male. Peel that layer back, and they were prank calls. Beneath that layer they were clever warnings of impending vandalism. And one layer further down they were cries for help again, this time from a kid facing an undefined threat. Or so I still believed.

Which meant that the calls themselves were still the vital clues. That is to say, if I was right about Jackie, if he really was as clever and complicated as I judged him to be, the original calls would have, buried deep inside them, all the information I needed to track him down.

Following that bolt from the blue, I'd sat freezing in my Volkswagen, writing down every stray detail I could remember from the call I'd received, using the back of the envelope full of paperwork the hospital had given me as my official notebook. Then I'd hurried over to Domestic Justice to interview Honey and add her memories of call number one to my list.

And been lied to for my trouble. I stood there on the wrong side of the receptionist's greenish Plexiglas trying to think of a password that would get me in. The young woman, whose head was very nearly shaved, still had one hand on the phone as though she expected me to try again.

"It's about the prank call we discussed yesterday," I said.

"She's not in," the woman repeated.

I caught sight of my reflection in the glass, of my haggard, greenish face and the discolored bump on my head, and realized how much I looked like an abusive husband who'd been taken out by a well-thrown pot and was now looking for round two. And I suddenly knew that the woman held on to the phone with a twitching hand because she was a second away from calling the police.

I retreated to the Ghia, where I considered using the direct-dial phone number Honey had given me. I decided she would have anticipated that move. The line would be busy today or unanswered. So I started out for my next stop, Hand to Hand. Started slowly, as the late-afternoon traffic was thickening like old gravy. It gave me plenty of time to consider Honey's rejection. The receptionist might have been reacting to my appearance, but what was scaring Honey? Some threat from Sister Agnes? Guilt over my narrow escape?

I decided Hennix could tell me, which was an example of my intuition failing me. I moved right on to calculating the odds of finding Jackie with just two pieces of the puzzle, mine and Hennix's, without pausing to wonder whether the psychologist had been gotten to by whoever had gotten to Honey.

The sun was sinking behind one of the airport terminals as I pulled into the Hand to Hand lot. I shivered my way up Hennix's front walk, shivered violently, as though my body were having a flashback to my nap in St. Pius's stable. I grabbed at the front door's chrome handle eagerly. It was ice-cold, and the door it was attached to was locked.

The reception area lighting had been turned low, but I could see that the central desk was empty. The woman I'd kept late last night must have claimed her comp time this evening. The keypad Hennix had used to secure the door had a button marked Assistance. I pressed it and then went back to yanking on the door, expecting someone to buzz me in. Instead, a man who sounded as if he were speaking through a cardboard tube inquired, "Can I help you?"

I gave my name, asked for the head man, and added that it was damn cold outside.

The voice said, "Mr. Hennix has left for the day."

I looked over my shoulder to the spot where Hennix's Audi had been parked the night before. It was parked there now, reflecting the last of a very pale sunset. I pointed this out to the man on the other end of the tube.

"Mr. Hennix has left for the day," he repeated.

I could have threatened to stay there until Hennix came out, but I was flirting with frostbite as it was. I thanked the disembodied voice for its courtesy and left.

FOURTEEN

THE ROOMS I rented were always overheated because the old woman who owned the house had a susceptibility to drafts or, to borrow her own diagnosis, "hollow bones, bones the wind whistles right through." That night the place felt just right to me, which caused me to reflect that my own bones might be near to whistling. Certainly the collection of bones I called my skull felt hollow as I sat at my table-for-one in the little bay window alcove in my front room, poring over the list I'd scribbled on the hospital envelope, the list of stray details from Jackie's call, trying to spot some useful information.

I'd noted the names Russet and Benjy, Jackie's interest in the Mafia and smelters and science fiction films, his familiarity with two of a crisis line's more routine functions: advising on alcohol problems and unpaid bills, and his contempt for the New Jersey Nets. Not much to work with. If only I had a similar list from Honey and another from Hennix, the facts from each list might have linked themselves together in some pattern. If only.

I considered the possibilities offered by Jackie's reference to a smelter. A big black place with smokestacks near where he lived, he'd said, daring me to challenge his expertise. I could ask around the next day, see if any functioning or defunct smelter in Elizabeth matched that description. And then what? Canvas the immediate neighborhood for Knicks fans?

To save all my energy for thinking, I put my head down

on my folded arms. It worked so well, I promptly fell asleep.

The phone woke me. I scrambled to reach it, so intent on the idea that it was Jackie calling back that I almost said "Adullam Line" instead of "Hello."

"Owen?" a woman's voice said. "Owen Keane? It's Beth Wolfe."

We'd slept together, and we were still using last names. Guilty thoughts of that made me miss my cue. Beth said, "Are you there?" but meant, "Have you forgotten me already?"

"I'm here, Beth, sorry. I had a little accident, and it's left me groggy."

"A traffic accident?"

"No."

"Something to do with your case?"

She managed to say *case* very naturally, without the rhetorical quotes Harry and even Mary put around the word when they were discussing one of my mysteries.

"Yes," I said, "but it's only a bump on the head. I got a message that you'd called. I'm sorry—"

"I want to talk with you about the other night. Have you eaten anything? I made some lasagna."

Just the thought of getting back in my car started me shivering again. The vibrations must have traveled down the phone line, because Beth said, "I'll bring everything over there. You're in downtown Elizabeth, right? Just give me directions."

My instinct was to dodge it, but something in Beth's voice, a little tremor of vulnerability, made me think it over. She was facing down the risk that I'd turn out to be another bastard, lowering her guard in a way she hadn't even done when we'd been naked together in her bed. Her courage, and a growling in my stomach that had started at the mention of lasagna, changed my mind.

I gave her the route I'd used on the night of Mary's party

and then fell into cleaning the place, prioritizing as follows: kitchenette first, then bathroom, then main room. My tiny bedroom I left for last. I didn't think I'd be entertaining there in my condition, but then I wouldn't have guessed, only an hour earlier, that I'd be so interested in Italian food.

I would have spent some time fixing myself up next, but I heard my landlady greeting Beth at the front door as I was tucking in my emergency sheets. Then my blind date was at my doorstep, pink from the cold and struggling with a large cardboard box.

The box got us past the awkwardness of the first few minutes, since it had to be taken into the kitchen and unloaded, the lasagna going into the oven and the salad into the refrigerator, the interior of which seemed brilliantly lit to me now that it had been emptied of old milk cartons. The perfect guest, Beth had even brought a bottle of Chianti, which we opened while the main course was warming.

We sat on my fourth-hand sofa, a vinyl number with bare metal legs and no arms that belonged in the waiting room of a rental car agency. For all its faults, it was softer than Beth's own sofa, as she observed herself. She looked softer tonight, too, and less emaciated in woolen slacks and a cable-knit sweater. Casual, but not relaxed. She drank half of her first glass of wine in a gulp, her Gothic eyes giving me their trademark peekaboo through her overcoated lashes.

Here it comes, I thought, the apology. But it didn't come. "Tell me how you got that egg," she said instead.

I told her at some length, recounting my whole investigation to date, the telling taking us right through the first helpings of dinner and relaxing us both.

"What about the targets?" Beth asked as she poured out the last of the wine. "Why aren't they on your list?"

We were seated by then at the little table in the little alcove, Beth in my spare folding chair, the window nearest her open at her request to give her a break from the heat. The cold draft felt good to me as well, the meal and the wine having restored me amazingly. I wrote the names of the three churches on my trusty envelope, but that didn't satisfy her.

"Have you given them any thought?"

"The targets?" I asked.

"Yes. You're looking for some secret message in the calls, but maybe the message is in the targets."

"Well, yeah," I said, "the attack on Christmas thing."

"I'm not talking about the symbolism of the Nativity scenes themselves. I mean the churches. Why pick those churches in particular when there's a church with a Nativity scene in every neighborhood around here? This kid has such a complex mind, the way you tell it, it's like he's playing chess with you. And you're right to think of him that way. I've got some fourth graders in my class who should be designing crossword puzzles. So maybe there's some pattern to the churches. Maybe if you put pins in a map, you'd come up with something."

"There's only three of them," I said. "They could only form a straight line or a triangle."

Beth laughed at herself, and for a second, her pale skin seemed to reflect a light from her eyes. Then the second passed. "I guess I've watched too many detective shows on television," she said.

"Nothing wrong with that, I hope."

She pushed her plate away, running it into mine. "I'm stalling anyway. I mean, this case of yours is interesting—it's interesting that you're still trying to help this kid, bump and all—but it isn't what I came over to talk about. To apologize for."

"You've nothing to apologize to me for," I said. "I shouldn't have left you to read that paper."

"I wasn't going to apologize for asking you to go home," she said.

She hesitated, so I fired off another guess. "If it's about

the dinner party, I was uncomfortable myself. Mary should have warned us."

"Owen, shut up and listen for a minute. If you keep coming up with things that I should be apologizing for, that I hadn't even thought about apologizing for, you're going to make me cry."

"What is it then?"

"Having sex with you."

"I'm usually the one who apologizes after that."

"Don't make jokes, either. I'm serious. I used you and I'm sorry. I don't want you to think that I'm that way. That I go around sleeping with strange—with men I barely know. I haven't been myself lately. It's my divorce. It has me scared all the time."

"Scared of what?"

"Of being alone," she said, her eyes glistening in spite of her best efforts.

It was like working Adullam Line without the protection of a telephone. "You're too young to be worried about that."

"Not alone for the rest of my life, Owen. Alone for Christmas. Doesn't that bother you?"

"Some," I said.

"I don't mind it so much the rest of the year. But at Christmas, when family is such a big deal, when Norman Rockwell images of family are everywhere you look, it bothers me. I had a family like that once, but they're all gone. All I had left was Gary, my husband. Now, right before Christmas, I don't have him."

She was crying now but good. I led her back to the sofa. There, despite the collective angularity, Beth's and mine and the sofa's, I tried to comfort her.

"Let's make a pact to be together at Christmas," I said, addressing the top of Beth's head, her face being pressed into my shirt, wet mascara and all. "Here or at your place. Or we could drop in on the Ohlmans. Unannounced."

"Would serve them right," she said.

FIFTEEN

BETH DIDN'T STAY the night. Perhaps she didn't feel up to another apology. It was just as well, both from the point of view of my throbbing head and because I would have ended up leaving her alone in bed for the second time. Around two I awoke from an uneasy sleep with visions of our dinner dancing through my head. And I remembered something Beth had said, something that got me out of bed and pacing the hardwood.

It was the idea that she dreaded Christmas because she didn't have a family. At the time she'd said it, I could focus only on her tears and pain. But when her words came back to me in the still of the night, they made me think of Jackie, made me see the whole mystery from a new angle.

Beth hadn't been interested in Nativity scene symbolism, but I still was. Edward Hennix had left me with the idea that the crèches were symbols of Christmas and targets for that reason. I hadn't questioned his conclusion at the time, but now I did. I thought of the many other symbols of Christmas dotting the landscape, and I asked myself why, if there wasn't some religious issue at work, Jackie had picked on manger scenes. Why not plastic Santas or neon reindeer or aluminum trees?

Beth's fears gave me a possible answer. Nativity scenes could also be seen as symbols of the family. An intact ideal family: father, mother, and baby. It was an image that could bring pain to a lonely soul like Beth Wolfe. And perhaps cause someone else, a boy who, like Beth, was without a

family at a time of year when families are so important, to
hit out at the world.

The more I paced, the more certain I was that someone
had come close to telling me this earlier in the investigation.
I searched backward and remembered Walt Majeski, permanent deacon at Holy Angels, and his guess that the target
of the attacks was the Holy Family. He'd been right about
that, but wrong when he'd predicted that the next victim,
after Mary and Jesus, would be Joseph. It had been the
Magi. Why had Joseph escaped?

And how had Hennix, a trained psychologist, missed all
this? How had he failed to see that Christmas was only
important as the general context of the attacks, as the time
of year when a person, a child, without an intact family
would most resent it? Had he in fact missed it or had he
been intentionally misleading me? I remembered Hennix's
own nervous pacing, back and forth in my hospital room,
and decided that the misdirection had been intentional. He'd
wanted to send me down the wrong path. That was why
his offer to take over the case had been so offhand. It hadn't
been what he'd been building to. It had been a postscript,
something he'd thrown in after he'd achieved his real purpose: planting a false idea in my cracked head.

But why? Because his old friend Sister Agnes had gotten
to him, asked him not to encourage me? Easy enough to
believe, but then why tell me anything? Why even come to
the hospital? Why not drop the tape of Jackie's apology in
the mail or, better, in the trash and forget the whole thing?

A siren started wailing somewhere in the night. I went
to the alcove and opened the window. The sound came in
as crisp and clear as the night air. And it grew louder with
every cold breath I took. I remembered the moment during
Jackie's call when I'd heard a siren in stereo, through the
old rectory's window and through the phone. Jackie had
been very close that night, and he was close now. The answer to his mystery was close. I could almost touch it.

The sound of the ambulance began to recede. I shut the window, anxious to avoid the suggestion that my answers were also slipping away, and sat down at the table. My list of clues was still there, right where I'd left it after amending it at Beth's insistence. My pen lay beside it. I picked it up and, by the glow of my landlady's security light, added a name to my list of clues. Edward Hennix.

Then I waited for the alchemy to occur, for the addition of Hennix's name to magically transform the scribbled list into something valuable. And it happened. My eye strayed upward from the psychologist's name to the churches Beth had had me add to the list. And I noticed that Hennix's name ended in the same unusual letter as St. Pius X.

I grabbed up the pen again and crossed out part of each church name, leaving the H and the E of Holy Angels, the two Ns of St. John Leonardi, and the I and X of St. Pius X. Hennix.

A coincidence? Or did I owe Beth Wolfe a very nice dinner out? She'd suggested that the target churches were themselves the message. If I was right, it was a very private message, one that only Hennix himself could be expected to decipher. More of a taunt than a message. But why even that?

Suddenly I felt so chilled I looked up to be sure I'd closed the window. But it was doubt and not physical cold affecting me. Doubt, my old traveling companion, telling me that I was overreaching, overanalyzing. I was attributing my own baroque patterns of thought to Jackie. The churches no more spelled out Hennix's name than the secret name of God. I was imagining things.

I still held the pen. I used it to scribble out letters of the church names, this time leaving only the O, N, and E of Holy Angels, the L and O of Leonardi, and the S and T and the P and I of St. Pius. Together the letters spelled "One Lost P.I."

I tossed the pen away and went back to crawl between my now cold sheets.

SIXTEEN

I WENT TO BED ALONE, but I woke up with Edward Hennix. By that I mean that my first thoughts upon waking were of Hennix. And though I'd been quick to dismiss my predawn hunch that he was somehow at the bottom of this—had been able to sleep because I'd consciously dismissed that hunch—it came back to me in the first few moments of the new day with the force of a conviction.

If Hennix was the key to the mystery, the key to Hennix was Sister Agnes. By Hennix's own account, he and the nun "went way back." And way back was what I wanted. Honey might also have served as a source of serious gossip, but Honey was cocooned in bulletproof glass. Sister Agnes's protection consisted solely of her moral superiority. And I thought I'd detected a crack in that, one big enough for me to slip through.

At nine sharp I was at the Catholic Life Center, checking the parking spaces along its narrow street for the nun's Plymouth station wagon. It was there and in a prime spot, only half a block from the old rectory's front door. Better still, there was an open stretch of granite curbing right in front of the wagon for me to park in. I took that as a sign that the karma of the universe, or at least of Elizabeth, New Jersey, was turning my way.

I had reason to doubt that augury only a minute later when I was all but knocked down on the center's icy front walk by Sister Agnes herself. She was exiting the building with her usual head-down determination and only checked herself when I called out a desperate "Good morning."

"Owen! I can't talk now, which is a lucky thing for you. What were you doing in *my* office yesterday with *my* tape recorder? And what did you mean by going back over to Domestic Justice to bother Honey? I'd sack Rhoda for giving you directions to the place, but I'm going to be short-handed as it is. Now that..."

"Now that I've been sacked?" I asked.

The nun's sigh froze in the air between us. "You don't have the right temperament for this work, Owen. You have to be able to leave the problem alone once you've hung up the phone. Otherwise you're not there for the next caller. Mentally or, in your case, physically. Do you have any idea how many different souls have called while you've been running around looking for that one boy?"

"The phone's been covered," I said. "It's about more than me being gone."

"Yes. It's also about you being obsessed. It's about you running around, getting yourself hurt, trying to accomplish something that will mystically undo a past failure."

Hennix had been right. Amateur psychoanalysis was an occupational hazard for crisis-line workers.

"I'm sorry, Owen, for being so blunt, but there it is. Now good-bye. It's cold out here, and I'm late. I've some donated soup to deliver to one of our kitchens."

"Canned soup?" I asked.

The nun's eyebrows rose toward her knitted beret. "Yes."

"Then it will keep. I have some questions I'd like to ask you about Edward Hennix. We can go inside if you're cold."

I was hoping she would go back inside, afraid my tough-guy act would be undercut by another shivering spell. But she held her ground. "What makes you think I know anything about Edward Hennix and that golden goose company of his?''

"He told me himself that you did. And I'm not interested in his company. I want his personal history."

"His what?" She backed me up a step as Hennix had done in his office, her technique being an unexpected leap forward. "Do you think I'd discuss Mr. Hennix's personal business with you or anyone else? Do you think I gossip about people?''

There it was. The moral superiority and the flaw, all in one sentence. "I know you do," I said. "You told Hennix that I'm a seminary dropout."

I'd no sooner made the accusation than I panicked, remembering another possible source for Hennix's information. I was positing some secret connection between Hennix and Jackie, and I'd told Jackie of my onetime plan to become a priest. Suppose he was the one who had told the psychologist. But the panic passed so quickly it never had time to show on my face. Sister Agnes herself saved me by breaking her iron eye contact and placing a mittened hand on her breast.

"He didn't know the first time I spoke with him," I said, "so Honey hadn't briefed him when she'd called to tell him I was coming. She didn't know me that well then, though she probably does now. But Hennix knew when he came to the hospital yesterday. You'd told him by then."

"Come inside, Owen. Please."

I'd forgotten the cold for the first time since leaving my rooms, but I followed her, anxious not to give her time to recover. She retreated no farther than the old house's glassed front porch. It was barely above freezing in there, but it felt like a greenhouse.

"I did tell Edward, Owen. And I'm sorry. He was curious about you, about what might be motivating you. And I wanted a second opinion about whether I might have made a mistake taking you on, given what I knew of your background. My only reservation when you first came to me was that you'd find call taking hard and leave. I was afraid, based on your history, that you were a quitter." She laughed mirthlessly. "A quitter you're not."

"What did Hennix say?"

"He called you an unacceptable risk. Not because you might run away but because you might still be driven by the needs and feelings that sent you to the seminary in the first place. If so, you'd have a hard time maintaining an emotional distance."

So the psychoanalysis the nun had hit me with earlier hadn't been amateur work after all.

"I apologize most sincerely for violating your confidence, Owen."

"Apology accepted. Now tell me about Hennix."

"Owen, Owen. Two wrongs can never make a right. I can't undo an injury to you by injuring Edward."

"I'm not worried about my injuries. I'm worried about the boy who's at the center of this. Edward Hennix has done something to him, and I think you know what it is."

"If Edward confessed anything to me—"

"You're not obligated to keep his secrets," I said. "You're not a priest."

"Neither are you," she shot back. "You can't repeat some ancient words and wave your hand in the air and make everything right."

"We can't refer this problem, Sister. It's been referred to us. To me. Let me try to help. I promise not to use anyone's words but my own."

"And as many of those as it takes," the nun said with resignation. "You'll need to talk with a woman named Louise Cooper. She lives here in Elizabeth—I'm not sure where. But she shouldn't be hard to find."

SEVENTEEN

LOUISE COOPER wasn't hard to find. In fact, I located her before I left the Catholic Life Center for the last time. After Sister Agnes hurried off to deliver her soup, I slipped into the ground-floor offices of an outreach ministry for divorced Catholics and borrowed their phone book. No Louise Cooper was listed, but there were no fewer than four L. Coopers. One of those lived on Russet Street.

I'd never even thought of looking up the name of Jackie's alien tormentor on the index of an Elizabeth street map. I did it now, using a map I'd purchased when I'd first moved to the area. I found the map under the passenger seat of the Ghia and Russet Street on its western edge, near the old industrial part of town, only a few blocks from where I was parked.

When I arrived on Russet Street itself, I was greeted by another clue I'd made scant use of, a defunct smelter, Amax Plant Number Four, according to its weathered sign. In the morning light, the place didn't look as black as Jackie had described it, but it was still menacing, razor wire gleaming atop its rusting fence.

In comparison, Russet Street was narrow and ordinary, its most interesting feature a stretch of the original cobblestones showing through a modern covering of asphalt. Opposite the smelter was a row of homes so alike in shape and size I deduced that they'd been a by-product of the plant, company houses for lucky foremen. They'd probably been identical in every detail then, but, like their street, they'd been recovered, some in aluminum siding, some in a kind of shingle stamped to look like brick, some in stucco.

The one I was after, 15 Russet Street, had acquired a thin veneer of limestone on its narrow front. Its sides were still wooden but recently painted. The very brief front walk—a square of concrete only—was bordered by the remains of mums, blasted brown by the cold.

I rang the bell before I'd begun to plan my approach to Louise Cooper, counting, as I so often did, on the inspiration of the moment. In the event, it wasn't Cooper who answered the door. It was a kid with a choirboy face and a mouth open wide for a high note. Jackie.

Our eyes met for a long moment through the glass of the storm door. Then he was gone, leaving the front door open behind him. Seconds later he was leaving the back door behind him, closed. The sound of that reached me before I'd had a chance to move. I didn't feel up to a foot race through the backyards and alleyways of Elizabeth, so I rang the bell again.

I heard someone call "Benjy" several times. Then she appeared beyond the glass, a petite woman with closely cropped hair and Jackie's oversize eyes. She was dressed in brown insulated coveralls, or rather dressing in the coveralls. She buttoned the last button as she examined me through the glass. My forehead didn't draw any special attention, but then it wasn't the spectacle it had been the day before.

"Yes?" she said.

"My name is Owen Keane," I said. And then, forgetting Hennix in the excitement of having found the boy, I added, "I'm a friend of your son's."

"A friend of Benjy's?" Copper repeated disbelievingly.

So Benjy, the name of Jackie's darling brother, had been another clue. "He and I have never met. Not formally. But we've spoken on the phone. He called a crisis line I worked for to ask for help."

"Help with what?" Cooper demanded, now both disbelieving and displeased.

I gambled then. "I think he wants help contacting his father."

That was the way it had all come together for me, the only way it made sense. It explained why, in each of the prank calls, the bad guy had been an abusive male and why the St. Joseph statues had escaped the vandalism. The father was the source of the evil, and everyone around him its victims. If Benjy really was directing these messages, these accusations, toward Hennix, it could only be because he believed Hennix to be the evil father. But the cryptic nature of the accusations suggested that their purpose wasn't to expose Hennix as a monster. They were more like repeated tugs on the psychologist's sleeve.

Explaining all that to Cooper through a locked storm door would have been a tough job. Luckily, I didn't have to try. She snapped the catch back and said, "You'd better come in and tell me about it."

We sat in a cozy front room that was more or less a Benjy Cooper art gallery. All around me were examples of a child's artwork in dime-store frames, the early ones in crayon, the later ones in watercolor. Many of the pictures were pastoral landscapes very unlike Russet Street.

Cooper, following my gaze, said, "Those are old drawings. I can't display his newer ones. They're all of monsters trying to tear each other's arms off."

She gestured vaguely to her coveralls. "As you can see, I'm late for work. So if you could make this quick..."

I put aside the questions about her job with which I normally would have stalled, and retold the story I'd so recently told Beth Wolfe, cutting it down by minimizing my investigation and completely eliminating my stay in the hospital. I also omitted names, especially Hennix's, not wanting to lose my welcome prematurely. In the back of my mind, I was wondering how I'd convince Cooper that any part of my fantastic tale was true. But that was another challenge she took off my shoulders.

"Oh, Benjamin," she said, addressing the nearest painting. And then to me, "You must think I'm one hell of a mother."

I thought it was interesting—and suggestive—that that would be her first reaction. "Your son's a complicated kid."

"Tell me about it. I never knew how complicated until this last year or so. I thought what we had here, what Benjy and I had, simple as it was, was also somehow complete. Sufficient. As sufficient for Benjy as it was for me. It isn't anymore. Maybe it never really was."

"He misses his father," I said, as something between a statement and a question.

"He misses his father," Cooper repeated wearily. "Tell me how that could happen, how Benjy could miss something he never really had, something half the kids in his school don't have, something even the television shows don't push these days. Tell me how he could miss a man he's never met, whose name he doesn't know."

"Your son doesn't know his father's name?"

"No. I've never told him. I've guarded that secret like I've guarded him. I thought I was guarding him by not telling him. I was protecting him from a man who didn't want him, from having to know that his own father didn't want him. But lately, when Benjy's been asking and asking about his father, I've wondered whether I haven't kept the secret all these years to protect myself."

"Protect you from the idea that Benjy's father didn't want to be with you?"

Another wrong guess. Beth Wolfe could have quietly kicked me for it if she'd been handy. Cooper only shook her head.

"No. When I decided to keep Benjamin, I rebuilt my life around the idea that I could raise him alone. That's what I've been protecting by denying him even his father's name—the idea I built my life on. My personal faith. Do you know how hard it's been for me to give that up?"

I thought I did, but revealing that would have gotten us

too close to my own secrets. "Ms. Cooper, I think Benjamin knows who his father is."

"What makes you say that?"

"He told me his father's name, in a very roundabout way."

Cooper wasn't going to be tricked out of the secret she'd protected so long. She waited for me to say the name.

I took a deep breath. "Edward Hennix."

I knew that, for once, I'd guessed right. Cooper slumped within her quilted outerwear. "His wildness, his slyness, his sneaking out at all hours. I've watched it all coming on these last few months and never guessed that Eddie was behind it. Never guessed he'd try to force his way into Benjy's life."

"Wait a minute," I said. "I don't think Hennix contacted Benjy. I think all this has been Benjy's way of getting Hennix's attention."

"Then who—" She thought of a name before she'd finished the question, but didn't share it with me. She sat up abruptly. "I want to pay for any damage Benjamin's done, but it may take a while. If you could give me some kind of figure…"

"We're not interested in any money," I said on the archdiocese's behalf. "We're interested in Benjamin's welfare. Would you let Benjamin's father come here and meet him?"

"I'm not the problem there, Mr. Keane. I've had my idea that I could go this alone seriously knocked around these last few months. If you're right that Eddie didn't contact his son, that Eddie hasn't changed his mind about wanting a son, then he's your problem. You'll never get him to even acknowledge Benjy, never mind come here."

I could only repeat the request I'd made of Sister Agnes. "Let me try."

EIGHTEEN

I DIDN'T ATTEMPT to contact Hennix right away. Cooper told me as I left her that she'd be gone until six and ordered me not to approach Benjy in her absence, with or without Hennix. So I passed the day at the Acme, slipping away just before five to return home and call the psychologist.

Locating him at five on a Saturday would have seemed like a hopeless task to me only a day earlier. Now I was so unconcerned I discarded my initial idea of making up some clever message based on Nativity scene imagery that only Hennix would understand. When I reached Hand to Hand and was told that the boss wasn't in, I simply said, "I have an important message regarding Mr. Hennix's son. Please have him call Owen Keane as soon as possible." Then I read off my home number.

Three Christmas cards had come in the mail that day. I decided to pass the time by opening them. While I was ripping the second envelope, the phone rang.

I got the better part of hello out before Hennix demanded, "What do you want, Keane?"

"Thirty minutes of your time."

"You've got from now until I get mad enough to hang up this phone."

"Not over the phone. I want face-to-face. Then if you get mad enough, you can hit me."

"I'm that mad right now," he said. He gave me an address and broke the connection.

He hadn't given me directions, and it was well past full dark when I found his place, a gentrified warehouse right on Newark Bay, just north of the Port Newark Terminal. Hennix's apartment was a large, largely open space overlooking the moving lights of the river traffic. It had old hardwood floors that creaked eloquently as he marched away from me and the open front door.

I shut the door behind me and followed him, not getting much noise at all from the floor. A series of iron posts supported a ceiling that was almost beyond the range of the muted lighting. When I drew abreast of the third post, Hennix said, "Help yourself to some Christmas cheer."

By then he was standing at the wall of riverfront windows, his back to me, a trim figure in dark slacks and a white dress shirt with rolled up sleeves. He gestured with his own glass to a little bar that stood against one of the iron poles, looking like a kiosk in a bus terminal. I crossed to it and poured some scotch into a glass. It was better scotch than Harry Ohlman had served me, and I made a mental note to mention that if I survived to recount the evening for Harry and Mary.

Hennix didn't seem very threatening at the moment. Still, from the several little groupings of furniture scattered around the vast room, I selected a pair of leather easy chairs well away from the windows.

He must have been following my progress in the windows' dark glass. When I was settled in nicely, he said without turning, "The clock's running, Keane. What do you want from me?"

Small mysteries first, I thought. "How did Benjy find out about you?"

"I'm only guessing, but I think it was Louie's—Louise's—mother. She called me a few months back. Gave me a talking-to she'd been holding in for years. Mrs. Cooper must be a big woman. She can hold a lot. Most of it was variations on the same basic resentment—I was doing great and her daughter was struggling to raise my son all by herself. Ruining her life doing it, too, giving up on school, doing road construction in all kinds of weather, breathing in filthy fumes from smudge pots. Tell me something,

Keane. When's the last time you saw a smudge pot at a construction site in New Jersey? EPA would have a fit. Woman's still living in the fifties.''

"You think she told Benjy about you?''

"Yes. And at about the same time. The old lady's mouth dam must have burst. Just after I got rid of her, we started to get calls down at the center from the kid. At first it was just, 'Tell Mr. Hennix his son called.' Then he started adding little teasers. 'Tell Mr. Hennix his son's been hit by a car. Tell Mr. Hennix his son's mother's had a heart attack.' Little love notes.''

"Did you answer any of them?''

Hennix finally turned to face me. "No.''

We sipped our drinks. I said, "What did you say to get rid of Mrs. Cooper?''

"I told her I didn't love her daughter and her daughter didn't love me. She was just an underclassman I happened to know when I was in graduate school. We had a few drinks one night and then we had sex. Blame it on disco.

"When Louie told me she was pregnant, I said, 'None for me, thank you very much.' Actually, I don't think I said that much. I just made myself scarce. I never thought she'd keep the kid. I sure didn't know she had. But it was her decision, not mine. The man doesn't get to decide these days.''

"Lucky thing for Benjy,'' I said.

While he bristled like a kicked cat, I wondered whether Hennix's desertion of Cooper and their child had been part of what had turned him from idealistic humanitarian to successful businessman. But I suppressed my curiosity in the interests of the task at hand.

"So Benjy was calling your crisis line. When the call came in about the Mafia hit, you knew who it was.''

"Not right away. Not when Honey called to ask if we'd gotten anything really offbeat. The fact that she and Sister A had both gotten calls first fooled me for a little bit. Benjy'd never called anyone else, so far as I knew. I'm still not sure why those first two calls didn't come to me. I'm not sure how the kid knew I'd hear about them."

I reminded him of his description of the interconnectedness of the crisis lines, adding my own guess that someone on the outside looking in would be likely to see them just that way.

"Are things so tight for Louie that her son's a specialist on help lines?" Hennix asked.

"She's getting by. Financially. Emotionally, she's pretty beaten up. When did you realize the Mafia call was Benjy's work?"

"Between the time I talked with Honey and the time you showed up. I had this bad feeling. So I pulled the tape of the call and recognized the kid's voice from listening to his earlier efforts."

"But you still gave me the gist of the message."

"To get rid of you. Look, I've already apologized for that. I didn't think you'd be able to figure out where he was going to strike next."

"I remember your apology. It was a cover for more of that stuff about Benjy being a child of the projects. Somebody I'd never be able to track down."

"So I tried to scare you off. Why shouldn't I try to protect the kid?"

I badly wanted a swallow of scotch just then, but I didn't dare look away from Hennix's eyes. He drank. And he looked away.

"Okay. So I was protecting myself. So what? So I didn't want to have this little scene we're having now. Who would?"

He pounded over to the kiosk bar and picked up a bottle. He didn't pour another drink, however. He doesn't want to go over there drunk, I thought, allowing myself to believe, for the first time, that he might actually go. Not that his next words were encouraging.

"You still haven't told me, Keane. Just what do you expect from me? How do you see this all playing out? Do you think it's going to be like some old Christmas movie?

Do you think I'm going to walk into their lives and we're going to magically be a family? That some relationship's going to suddenly spring up between me and that kid?''

"The relationship's already there," I said, getting to my feet. "It's always been there. Denying it is screwing up that kid. Your kid. I expect you to do whatever it takes to make that right. You were going to fix the world, once upon a time. Start with him."

It was the moment to deck me, if he was still in the mood. He might even have been thinking about it, but instead he began to roll down his sleeves.

"Come over there with me," he said.

NINETEEN

AMAX PLANT Number Four's resemblance to a prison camp had increased markedly with the coming of night, thanks to an impressive array of security lights. They kept Russet Street in perpetual dusk and all but drowned out its houses' meager Christmas decorations.

Louise Cooper's house had a single string of white lights framing the front door, a detail I hadn't noticed in daylight. I might not have noticed it now, in the glare of the plant, if Hennix hadn't kept us standing so long in the cobblestoned street, studying the place.

He was still mad at me. "Hope that little elf heart of yours isn't hoping for some Christmas miracle to happen."

"Hasn't for years," I said.

"Not a bad little place," he said, but that was as far as the architectural review got.

The front door opened. Silhouetted in the frame of lights were Cooper and Benjy, the woman much smaller than she'd appeared in her work clothes, the boy positioned behind her slightly. I wondered if he was frightened now that his big moment had arrived. I was. So was Hennix.

"Damn," he said softly and walked inside.

No one invited me in. I stayed in the street until the front door shut and a little while afterward. The door opened again just as I was starting for my car. Benjy came out, bent over sideways by a burden he carried in his right hand.

"Wait!" he called to me.

The load weighing him down so was a little pink figure with upraised hands, one of which Benjy was using as a handle. It was the Christ Child statue he'd taken from St. John Leonardi. So it hadn't been thrown in a trash can or the bay after all.

He used both hands to raise the statue up for me to take. Then we stood smiling at one another for a moment. I wanted to ask him if he'd really been trying to spell out Hennix with his church names, but I didn't. He might have said no, and then I would have spent long nights wondering who else might have been doing the spelling.

There was no time to ask questions in any case. Before I'd settled the surprising weight of the statue in my arms, Benjy was running back to the house.

I drove straight to St. John Leonardi, intending to hand over the figure to Father Ross. I found the old church lit up like the smelter. Singing was coming out to me faintly, through the heavy doors and the multicolored windows. A late Advent service or maybe a choir practice. The song was "O Come O Come Emanuel," appropriately enough.

I paused to listen near the church steps. The parish's little Nativity scene still huddled in its protected spot next to those steps, Mary, Joseph, and the angel, all staring down at an empty manger.

It occurred to me then that the best way to find a Christmas miracle was to go out and make your own, as Benjy had done. So I changed my mind about ringing the rectory bell. Instead, I tucked the Infant back into His bed of straw for the departing parishioners to find. Then I went home to call Beth Wolfe.

CHRISTMAS CACHE
by Aileen Schumacher

Acknowledgments

I am grateful to the following individuals for their invaluable help: Jeanette Toohey and Larry Perkins of The Harn Museum of Art, Tim Merrill of the Alachua County Sheriff's Office, Manny Terrazas of the New Mexico State University Campus Police Department, Drs. Kenneth White and James E. Botsford of New Mexico State University (Civil Engineering and Biology Department respectively), and Katharine Forbes, art student extraordinaire at Florida State University. As wonderful as all these people are, they may not, en masse, have prevented me from wandering off and making mistakes on my own. Thanks to Ann Henley for proofing and mailing. For getting this tale into print, thanks to Jake Elwell and Feroze Mohammed, the latter of whom gave some research assistance himself. Thanks to Janne Skipper, JoAnne Bowers, and Bobbye Straight, as always, and thanks to Tommy Chrestman for bringing me an amazing photograph. My husband, Richard Blum, is responsible for so much about which I knew so little being packed into so few words. I'm not sure I'm thankful for that, but I am immensely grateful for his blind faith that I will always somehow manage to write the ending sentence. Thanks to Kevin and Nicky for being who you are. *Balkan Ghosts*, by Robert D. Kaplan, was an invaluable resource for my particular needs.

PROLOGUE

HE LOOKED at his watch, at the illuminated digits indicating that it was two in the morning. A moonless night didn't make for ideal digging conditions, but life was full of trade-offs. Secrets were better kept in darkness. When one was counted among the hunted, darkness could mean the difference between life and death. Besides, long ago, he had learned how to work in the absence of light.

He took a last drag on his cigarette, dropped it, and crushed it out under his boot. Once, he could not have allowed himself this luxury while waiting to start a task. Those were times best left forgotten, times when a simple cigarette could mark the target for a sniper, or divulge the last hiding place of a desperate refugee.

Snipers and armed men in uniform were no longer part of his waking life, but that was a mixed blessing. Relegated to the land of dreams, such killers ranged unfettered by laws of physics or limits of logic, and fed his fears that the stuff of dreams might become the nightmare of reality yet again.

Adjacent rooftops might be deserted and there might be no one outside the door, poised to force entry to his house, but that didn't mean that he was safe. No matter what he was told, no matter how many reassurances he was given in this new place that he had come to, he would never let down his guard. If the enemy was not visible out in the open, the enemy might well be waiting just next door.

Someone could be watching him even now, but he didn't think so, and besides, he had taken the usual precautions.

Dressed in black, he was skilled at using his tools quietly—never in his hands would metal strike metal on a night like this.

Yes, he was skilled at this task of working silently in the dark to hide things, hide them where they would never be found, never uncovered, until he decided to retrieve them for his own purposes, in his own time. Because of the lives these things represented, and because of their potential future use, he handled them reverentially. This darkness, his black clothes, the careful digging, they were all part of a ritual every bit as holy as any other. Every bit as holy as any ritual performed in the light of day.

What was it that these people called this hard layer under the topsoil, that strange-sounding word? *Caliche*, yes, that was it. He remembered because it was like that other foreign word, *cache*, a word for things hidden.

Tonight he might have to dig through some *caliche*. If so, he had a pickax handy. He would get the job done, just as he had every time before. Silently shouldering his shovel, Hafiz Bamia walked out from under the eaves of his back porch and began to dig.

ONE

The Set-Up

TORY TRAVERS KNEW a set-up the minute one reared its ugly head. Her fork, bearing a load of turkey dressing, stopped midway between plate and mouth. She found herself automatically glancing at David Alvarez where he sat across the table from her. In this uneasy effort of theirs to form a new relationship, she found herself constantly checking for his reactions, as though they might affect her own. She didn't mean to be doing it, but she couldn't seem to stop.

David raised one eyebrow in response. Challenges, discussions, arguments, even some amazing good times, all had been known to materialize when he raised one eyebrow like that. Then again, the raised eyebrow could simply be a response to the fact that her mouth, not quite caught up with her mind, was still hanging open. Tory remedied the situation, let gravity pull her forkload of dressing back to rest on her plate, and turned her attention to where it belonged, on her sixteen-year-old son, Cody.

"What did you say?" she asked. Every other adult sitting at the table suddenly seemed focused on the food in front of them.

Even David was now studying the turkey on his plate as though it might reveal some major clue in an investigation. Well, it was Thanksgiving and he was off duty, and Tory hadn't prepared this meal; Sylvia Maestes had done the cooking. So even if he was a homicide detective, there was no reason for him to view the bird with suspicion.

Cody concluded a long, unhurried drink of water, carefully set the fancy fake-crystal water goblet back down on the table, looked his mother straight in the eye and repeated what he had just said. "There's something I'd like to discuss with you."

Yes, it was a set-up. No teenager ever broached a subject at dinner with his mother and four other adults, not unless those adults had been previously briefed and recruited to some cause. Cody was a cool one, this dark-haired lanky son of hers, this child who looked more like a man with every passing day. Losing her husband while Cody was still so young, Tory worried about the lack of a father figure in their family of two. But it appeared that Cody had managed just fine, using the men sitting at this very table as role models.

Cody's slow, easy way of talking surely came from Lonnie Harper. Lonnie's family first set foot in New Mexico more than four generations ago, and he owned more acres of ranch land than anyone Tory knew. He had been Tory's friend since she'd first come to New Mexico as a young college student. Lonnie lost his wife in an automobile accident shortly after Tory's husband died, and there had been a time when everyone, including Lonnie, assumed that he would become more than a friend.

But that was before Tory developed a penchant for finding dead bodies. Before David Alvarez came along to help her avoid becoming one of them.

Since Tory refused to consider stubbornness as part of Cody's genetic heritage from his mother, she was certain that he learned it from Jesus Alfonso Rodriguez, better known as Jazz, senior foreman and inspector at Travers Testing and Engineering Company. Jazz had never been known to lose an argument. He just changed his mind.

And lately, Tory had begun to notice Cody imitating

some of David Alvarez's ways—a detective's wary analysis that took nothing for granted, his gnawing at pieces of information that didn't seem to fit together. At least, not until they were assembled in a manner so obvious that you wondered why no one had seen the connections all along.

If Cody chose not to be a structural engineer like his mother, what if he decided to become a homicide detective like David? The thought of a teenaged son developing his very own "cop voice" was enough to make her shudder. But for such fears to materialize, first, Cody must survive his teenaged years. Tory firmly pulled herself back into the present.

So, there they were, the four men in her life, sitting together at Thanksgiving dinner. Cody. Lonnie. Jazz. David Alvarez. There was enough testosterone at this very table to stuff several turkeys.

There was one other woman sitting at the table. Tory glanced in Sylvia's direction, blinked in spite of herself. Sylvia was wearing a skintight sweater, a snakeskin print in lime green. Would Sylvia have the nerve to wear this sweater in the spring, when rattlesnakes started coming out of hibernation? It didn't matter, in this particular discussion, Tory's secretary would be of no help whatsoever. If Cody suddenly announced that he wanted to take flying lessons, he could look pleadingly in Sylvia's direction, and she would argue his case in a flamboyant verbal style every bit as aggressive as her sweater.

Tory looked at Cody, took a deep breath, and readied herself for whatever was to come. "Just what is it you want to discuss?" Tory asked her son.

"I've been offered a job," said Cody.

Tory was not so easily suckered. Entire battles had been lost by betting on the face value of a statement seemingly as innocent as this one. "You have a job already," she said.

"But only on weekends," Cody argued. "Lonnie got the university to offer me a job. They want me to house-sit, for

CHRISTMAS CACHE

102

a month or so. It's the best, Mom. I'd get paid just for living
somewhere else.'' Tory noticed that Lonnie seemed to have
the decency to wince at Cody's last statement.

''You're only sixteen,'' she said automatically.

''I'm old enough to drive,'' Cody pointed out.

''He's old enough to work,'' Lonnie added, sounding a
little defensive.

''Sixteen, that's old enough to drop out of school,'' Jazz
said around a mouthful of turkey. Jazz lived alone and felt
it was unnatural for a man of his age and heritage to learn
how to cook. Cody might be primed for discussion and
Lonnie might be feeling guilty, but Jazz wasn't letting any
conversation get between him and a home-cooked meal.
''Hey, kid, don't kick me under the table,'' he growled at
Cody. ''Your mother does enough of that for both of you.''

''Sixteen is old enough to get married,'' said Sylvia. Tory
shot her a withering look. ''In some states,'' Sylvia
amended.

That led Tory to her next pronouncement. ''You have a
girlfriend,'' she declared.

''Whether the kid has a girlfriend or not doesn't depend
on a house-sitting job,'' David said. He looked at Tory as
though she were now infinitely more interesting than the
turkey on his plate.

''Do you know anything about this?'' she asked him.

''I claim the right to be silent,'' David replied.

''It's a simple business proposition,'' said Lonnie. ''Henderson brought it up at lunch a few days ago.''

''Henderson?'' asked Tory. Charles Henderson was Facilities Director for New Mexico State University, a position of immense importance to anyone employed in con-
struction-related activities. Lonnie lunching with Henderson
was no surprise, since the Harper family seemed involved
with virtually every philanthropic activity in the county. But
Henderson needing a house sitter?

''He needs someone to live in a unit of experimental

housing for a month or so, and when he mentioned it to me, I thought of Cody.''

"Experimental housing?" asked David. Tory could have sworn he blinked now. "No one told me that part. I mean, sixteen isn't *that* old."

"It's *solar energy* experimental housing, those dual residences that the university built about ten years ago." Lonnie seemed to be talking faster than usual.

"So," said Jazz, "it's for the sake of science then."

"That makes it okay for my son to go live somewhere else for a month?" asked Tory. Was this the man whose professional judgment she relied on?

Jazz reached across the table, grabbed the remaining drumstick, waved it at Tory. "At sixteen, a boy is a man," he stated.

"He's a child," said Tory. "And don't forget who signs your paychecks. Besides, Henderson is head of facilities for the university. We work for him. It would be a conflict of interest."

"We're talking about me," interjected Cody. "Mr. Henderson is talking about hiring *me* to house-sit, Mom. Not your engineering firm. Not you."

"Well, that's a relief," said David. "At least I got that part straight."

"The university owns two houses on property up by Telshor," said Lonnie. "Two identical, one-bedroom houses with identical fenced yards, next door to each other. One is solar-powered, the other uses conventional energy. To compare energy use, each house needs to be continuously occupied by one individual. A permanent caretaker lives in the solar-powered house, a single graduate student or post doc has always lived in the other."

"Then why prey on innocent, unsuspecting high school students?" asked Tory. Cody broke off a small piece of the roll on his bread plate and threw it at his mother. She dodged it easily, frowning sufficiently to discourage subsequent attacks.

"The guy in Con House is moving out right before Christmas," said Lonnie.

"Con House?" asked David. "No one told me about this part, either. Henderson's *asking* for someone to stay someplace called Con House? Where I work, we don't give people choices about things like that."

Jazz looked positively gleeful. "Man, this is sounding worse and worse," he told Lonnie. "How long since you stopped smoking? Pretty soon, you're gonna need to go outside, have a cigarette with me."

"Con House—conventional electricity," Lonnie said. "Get it?" Easy going Lonnie was beginning to sound testy.

"They call the other one Reformed House, then?" asked Jazz.

Lonnie glared at Jazz. "Sol House," he said.

"Sol House—that sounds spiritual," Sylvia offered. Lonnie glared at her, too. "I was only trying to help," she protested.

Lonnie ignored her. "With the guy moving out the middle of December, Henderson doesn't have anyone to move in over the holidays. He needs someone with flexibility in schedule, flexibility in living arrangements."

"I'd like to discuss flexibility in the next structural design Henderson needs," said Tory.

"Henderson is a client," Jazz reminded Tory, waving the drumstick at her again, half-eaten at this point. "It's for the sake of science, *es verdad?* Lighten up and give the boy a break."

"The man living in the other house has been there for years," said Lonnie. "He's very reliable."

"Cody could earn some extra Christmas money," said Sylvia, but Tory refused to look in her direction. She hadn't forgiven Sylvia for the remark about marriage, a delicious Thanksgiving dinner notwithstanding.

"And the guy living in the other house is from Bosnia," Cody continued, taking up where Lonnie left off. "There aren't too many people from Bosnia here in Las Cruces, and I have that research paper to do over the break. I could earn money, help conduct research, and get extra insight into my school assignment, all at the same time."

"You're not taking world history, modern politics or even comparative religion," Tory told her son. "You told me you have to do a paper for your psychology class. You've over-reached yourself on this one."

David looked at Cody, shrugged. "That's a common problem," he told the boy. "No one is ever really listening until you make a mistake."

Cody flashed David one of his killer smiles. Not a good sign. "I'm writing a paper on Rebecca West."

"Who is Rebecca West?" asked Tory. She had a feeling of impending doom.

"She traveled through the Balkans in the thirties and wrote a famous book about it," Cody replied. "Our psychology teacher says she's one of the women of that time period who transcended her gender."

Tory recognized the bait, refused to go for it. "What does that have to do with psychology?" she asked instead.

"She also wrote a famous book about motives for committing treason," said Cody.

There was silence around the table. "In my line of work, that's where we say, 'gotcha,'" said David finally, and there was another silence.

Tory believed in being gracious, especially in front of an audience. "I suppose we could go together to talk to Charles Henderson and find out more about this," she said slowly. "Before I absolutely say no," she added.

"I'd like to go along," said David, "sit in on that conversation. Maybe ask some questions myself." Now the silence around the table was deafening.

Tory thought of five different responses, took a deep breath, thought of five more, picked one. "Okay," she said.

"I'm going to step outside," Lonnie announced, standing up and stretching as if he'd been confined in a small space for hours.

"Yeah, I'd like a cigarette, too," said Jazz.

"What's for dessert?" asked Cody.

TWO

A New Lease on Life

So, TUESDAY afternoon following Thanksgiving, Tory, David and Cody trooped into Henderson's office to talk about the potential house-sitting job. Almost immediately, Henderson told Tory that there was nothing to worry about.

"Some of my worst experiences start with those very words," Tory said.

Henderson negotiated contracts on a regular basis; it was no problem for him to continue on as if she hadn't spoken. "I never wanted any part of this, but all university-owned property falls under the purview of my office. Both of these houses must be continuously occupied by one individual. This stepchild of a study is finally coming to an end, thank God, but recent data is raising some questions, so things have to be finished out by the book. I don't want Mechanical Engineering complaining that we didn't discharge our duties properly."

"Someone needs to live in Con House, where the guy is moving out, just until the next guy moves in," said Cody. Did he really think his mother hadn't grasped these basic facts? "And it needs to be a guy," Cody added. "It can't be a woman."

This was news to Tory. "Why?" she asked.

"The resident of the other house is male," Henderson said. "We're supposed to make the two living situations as equivalent as possible."

"You know how girls wash their hair all the time, use more hot water than guys," Cody said, grinning. Tory shook her head at him. "Lonnie told me—for real—only guys can live in these two houses," Cody added.

"It's part of the grant conditions," Henderson explained, speaking fast. "And I don't want to discuss it, it's not my doing. Keep in mind that this damn study was started almost ten years ago."

Was that Charles Henderson, swearing? David laughed outright. "You try to shut out reality," he said, "and it still comes in through the windows sometimes. Maybe even if the windows are well insulated, *¿que no?*"

"The house Cody would occupy is the one that's hooked up to commercial electricity," Henderson continued, going for a smooth transition into discussing energy sources, like *that* was an important consideration in Tory's decision making. "The other place, Sol House, has conventional power, too, for backup as needed. That's what's got the ME Department all concerned—Sol House has needed more backup power for heating and cooling than in previous years."

"Forget energy efficiency," said Tory. "Why can't the current occupant in Con House stay until the next one comes?" It felt stupid, actually speaking the words "Con House," but saying "conventional" and "solar-powered" was getting to be tedious.

"Because he's Croat," said Henderson.

"I beg your pardon?"

Henderson sighed. "Josef Kunz, the young man moving out of Con House. He's Croatian."

"From Sarajevo," said Cody, "just like Mr. Bamia, who lives in Sol House. Mr. Bamia is Bosnian—*Muslim* Bosnian." Tory felt in over her head; it was obvious that Cody had prepared for this discussion.

"Josef Kunz is Croat, he's Catholic," continued Henderson. "I'm Methodist, myself, but you're Episcopalian,

Tory, so you should understand—it's about the same thing."

"It's not." Tory and David said it in unison.

"Besides," Tory added, reaching for some distant knowledge, "I thought the Bosnians and Croats were fighting the Serbs when the trouble started in Sarajevo, something like that."

"According to Rebecca West, the trouble didn't start then, it's always been there," Cody offered.

It took Tory a moment to remember just who the hell this West woman was. "I don't care what Rebecca West thinks," Tory told her son.

"Thought," said Cody. "She's dead."

"Whatever," Tory muttered, and could have kicked herself for using that inane response.

"Putting Rebecca West aside for the moment," said David, "what about Kunz and Bamia?"

Henderson sighed again. "Separately, they're fine. But next door to each other, they seem like mortal enemies. It probably started as political discussions, but discussions led to arguments, arguments to shouting matches, shouting matches to—" Henderson stopped himself. "It's not important. The point is, I can't referee any more—I won't have to, thank God. Kunz came in here a week ago, told me he'd talked it over with the Biology Department, and that he was moving out December 15, agreement or no agreement, Health Institute or no Health Institute."

"There's health department problems with these houses?" asked David. Henderson began to turn an unbecoming shade of red.

"He can't help it—he's a cop—that's how he thinks," said Tory. If David was such a hot-shot detective, couldn't he see that Henderson considered any university property to be hallowed?

"National. Institute. Of. Health," stated Henderson, giving equal weight to each word.

"NIH—they do research," explained Cody, ever helpful.

"I knew that," David said. "NIH. Doesn't come up often in my line of work.

Henderson shot David a serious frown before continuing with his explanation. "The irony of the whole sorry situation is that Kunz hasn't lived in Sarajevo since he was a child. He studied microbiology in Hungary—he's here on NIH grant-funded research. Living in Con House rent-free for a year was just something to sweeten the deal. Moving out won't affect the NIH funding for Kunz, but now I've got the ME's on my case."

"Mechanical Engineers," said Tory automatically.

"I've got that one down," David assured her. "But I still don't understand why these two guys can't live next door to each other for a few more months."

"That's a good question," said Henderson. "I've learned more about Eastern European politics than I ever wanted to know, just trying to keep peace between those two for one more semester. When fighting started in Sarajevo in the early nineties, Bosnian Muslims and Croatian Catholics fought the Serbians. The Serbs are Eastern Orthodox Christians." Henderson sounded as if he were reciting some creed from memory.

"I think I've got that," said Tory after a moment. This made Con House and Sol House seem simple.

"Then alliances fell apart, the Croats and Bosnians started fighting each other."

"The Catholics started fighting the Muslims?" asked Tory, trying to make sure she was keeping the players straight.

"Sounds about right to me," agreed David. "When I was in school, the nuns said Muslims and Protestants were all going to hell. They never talked much about anything called Orthodox, except Jews. Always seemed the nuns liked Jews better than the Protestants, especially the Methodists."

"So this Bamia person came here as a refugee?" asked Tory, trying to get back on topic.

"Not exactly," said Henderson. "Hafiz Bamia was supposed to teach, once he recovered from whatever happened to him over there. He taught Humanities in Sarajevo. I was told he came from an affluent and highly educated family."

"Was this one of those politically correct job offers?" asked David.

Henderson frowned some more. "We get state and federal funding, so we're part of a political system, whether we want to be or not. We have diversity goals, and yes, when certain people ask, we make staff positions available on a case-by-case basis."

"What does this Hafiz Bamia teach?" asked Tory.

Henderson looked off into the distance. "He doesn't. Teach, that is. For one thing, his English isn't too good."

"You made him a full-time caretaker?" Tory tried not to sound incredulous, didn't totally succeed.

"We didn't intend to," Henderson replied. "Hafiz Bamia arrived here by himself at the beginning of a summer term, so it was convenient to put him into one of those two houses. We thought it would help him get his bearings, get used to things. But when the fall semester rolled around, Hafiz just wanted to go on doing what he was doing." Henderson shrugged, looking uncomfortable. "Hafiz has never talked about why he left Sarajevo, or what happened to him, and no one wanted to ask. When he offered to take care of both houses, the ME Department said it worked for them." Henderson shrugged again. "It's hard to find someone to live there for a long period of time, someone who doesn't want to take vacations, go off for a long weekend."

"So," said David, "you inherited a political refugee, supposedly a professor of Humanities. But when it turned out that he didn't want to practice his profession, you couldn't exactly turn him out, leave him homeless, and without a job.''

"Well, yes," Henderson answered.

"Kind of like a refugee with tenure," David ventured.

"You do have a way with words," said Henderson, and he didn't make it sound like a compliment. "It worked out well from a facilities standpoint. At least, until we put Kunz next door. The very name seems to set off something in Hafiz, and Hafiz sets off something in Kunz."

"Wait," said Tory. "This Hafiz Bamia had to leave his country. Maybe he thinks Croatians are responsible. But what's Kunz's problem?"

"Kunz believes that Bosnian Muslims started the fighting in Sarajevo."

"But weren't the first victims mostly Muslims?" asked Tory, wondering if she was following this correctly.

Henderson nodded. "But some people believe that Muslim leaders killed some of their own people to start a fight for an independent Muslim nation. Unfortunately, Josef Kunz is one of those people."

Tory was still trying to figure out who was who when David spoke up. "That's quite a tale. But I guess none of it has to do with a sixteen-year-old Episcopalian."

"So there wouldn't be a problem with me house-sitting for a month." Cody sounded like a true believer. Tory would have been better off meeting with Henderson by herself.

After more discussion for another twenty minutes, Tory decided to cut her losses. "Two conditions," she said.

"I brush my teeth every night, and I come home for Christmas?" asked Cody.

Tory gave her son a look that would turn a less durable child to stone. "You and I are going to go meet this Mr. Bamia, see what he's like, take a look at the house."

"You always save the worst condition for last," Cody said.

"If you're going to be in a house by yourself for a month, you're taking Tango with you."

Henderson blinked this time. "He has to take a breakfast drink along with him?"

David shook his head. "Tango is a Transylvanian Hound," he told Henderson. "And before you ask, no, I'm not kidding."

"Pets aren't allowed in campus housing," said Henderson.

"Well, that's that," said Tory. It felt good to stand up and put an end to things.

"Until now," Henderson concluded.

THE HOUSE CHECKED OUT okay, such as it was. Both residences were sturdy-looking, with a mustard-colored stucco on the outside, standard gray shingles on the roof. New Mexico State didn't have a school of architecture, and it was obvious that the two buildings had been constructed with function in mind. Considering some architectural wonders Tory had seen, that wasn't necessarily a bad thing.

The houses were on lots that sloped slightly downward from back to front. Both had yards enclosed by a rock wall; in the front it was for appearances only, three feet high, separating small identical front yards covered with white gravel. The backyards were enclosed by a higher, more serious-looking wall, and displayed a sparse sprinkling of grass, a few shabby-looking trees. Maybe the vegetation looked better in the summer, but then again, maybe not.

Hafiz Bamia was a dark-haired, thickset man with an intense but polite manner, eager to show them his house. Bamia explained that it was part of his job to make routine inspections of both buildings. He had a budget for general maintenance, and he was responsible for keeping everything as identical as possible, including household furnishings and appliances. But since *someone* was living in the other house and it wasn't time for one of those scheduled inspections, could he please show Mrs. Travers and her son Sol House, since it looked exactly like the house next door? Mrs. Travers and her son said yes please and thank you very much.

The front door opened into a living room with a couch, television and two chairs. The living room transitioned straight into a dining area with a table seating four. A breakfast counter defined the start of a small kitchen with a sliding glass door opening into the backyard. Off to the side, a hallway gave access to a utility room with laundry facilities and a bathroom that opened both into the hall and into the single bedroom at the very back of the house.

The furniture was nothing remarkable, but there was a great deal of framed art on the walls in every room, even the bathroom. Some of these framed items were quite large, seeming unusual in such a small house. But Henderson had said Bamia taught courses in Humanities, so maybe he had an avid interest in art. Besides, Tory hadn't come to see the interior decorating.

She came to see that Hafiz Bamia lived in a secure little house with only two places of entry. A secure little house with two cordless phones, one in the kitchen and one in the bedroom. A secure little house with a nice, responsible adult man living there. And according to Henderson, a nice adult man who spent most of his time right there, next door to the house where Tory's son would be staying.

Cody said "Please mom can I," about ten times in ten different ways. Tory bargained for everything she could think of, including behaviors applying to college attendance and beyond.

And then she said yes.

ALVAREZ DROPPED BY Henderson's office the next day, walked in, closed the door, asked if the man could spare a minute. This was always so much more effective than calling ahead.

"This Bamia-Kunz thing," he said to Henderson. "You said discussions led to arguments, and arguments led to shouting matches. What I want to know is, did the shouting matches lead to threats?"

"Not really."

"Is that an answer to my question?"

"You think I'd let Cody Travers stay somewhere that wasn't safe?" Henderson asked.

"Just answer the question."

"There weren't threats, not exactly. Kunz and Bamia each ranted and raved about how insufferable the other one was, but there were never out-and-out threats. It got unbearable when Bamia started using art to go to war against Kunz."

Alvarez ran through his mental catalogue of acts of aggression. *Por cierto,* art as a weapon was not in there. "What do you mean, using art to go to war?"

Henderson's frown turned into a smile—a small smile, but a smile, nonetheless. "Be there when Cody moves in," he said. "Then you'll know what I mean."

None of Alvarez's other interrogation efforts bore fruit. He decided to stop making cracks about Methodists.

THREE

Warming House

ALVAREZ KNEW from the beginning that nothing about this house-sitting gig was going to be simple. Tory's reluctance to accept her son's approaching adulthood was one thing; adding Sylvia Maestes into the mix was another.

Tory insisted that Henderson be present when Cody moved in, punctually after school on December 15. She held Henderson responsible for the whole arrangement, and there was a certain irony in the Facilities Director showing up to see a sixteen-year-old boy move into a rather drab-looking single-bedroom house.

And never mind that Cody was only taking up residence for a month; Sylvia insisted on a housewarming party scheduled for 6:00 p.m., complete with pizza. If Henderson stuck around for the festivities, would he be adequately prepared for whatever outfit Sylvia deemed appropriate for the occasion? Tory's secretary was a striking young Hispanic woman with a knockout figure and a penchant for clothes that made people sit up and notice. Only Jazz seemed immune to either shock or titillation—Alvarez had once heard him tell Sylvia flat-out, "Whatever look you were trying for, you missed."

Regardless of any plans for later on, it turned out that Tory wasn't just being overprotective, making sure that she and Alvarez were there to help Cody move in. There was

an immediate, unexpected situation staring them all in the
face from the moment that their little convoy of three ve-
hicles pulled up to Con House.

Kunz might have vacated the premises that morning, but
it appeared that he had left behind an extensive array of
Christmas lights, a display that in spite of space limitation,
seemed to include most all of the holiday conventions.
There were lights outlining a manger scene, a star, a Santa
Claus and a snowman, in addition to even more lights
strung virtually everywhere in the small fenced front yard.

"Wow," exclaimed Cody, standing frozen on the sidewalk, holding a box of his belongings. "This wasn't here
when we were here."

Henderson had the decency to look guilty. "I found out
about this yesterday," he said.

Tory walked over to get a closer look at the life-size,
cutout manger scene. "I thought you couldn't put religious
displays on state property."

"You can't," Henderson confirmed. "But Kunz put a
formal petition on my desk yesterday. He wants this to remain in place as a display of Croatian customs, under the
auspices of diversity, international goodwill and all that."
Henderson looked miserable. "Bamia will protest, of
course, but any petition process takes forever, and it being
the holidays and all—"

Alvarez was going to ask if this was part of the art war
when Tory said, "Take it all down. The electricity needed
for these lights will blow any comparison study out of the
water."

Henderson stared at Tory for a moment, then nodded.
"That's inspired," he said.

"It's gonna be a truckload of stuff," observed Cody, son
of an engineer. "What do we do with it?"

"If Kunz didn't take it with him, I guess it belongs to

the university now,'' said Henderson. He looked worried again.

"Take it to Sylvia's house," Tory said without a moment's hesitation, and that was that.

But it still wasn't simple.

There was a list of grant-imposed rules longer than the list of rules that Tory had prepared, and that was a scary idea. Tory, Henderson and Cody sat at the dining room table to go over the user manual for Con House. Alvarez could hear bits and pieces as he carried boxes in.

The furnace had to be set to certain temperatures during the different time periods defining day and night. It being December, Alvarez hoped that Cody could skip the rules about air-conditioning. Laundry would consist of three loads a week, whether you needed it or not, and clothes were never, ever to be put outside to dry. The occupant of Con House should cook meals for one, never for guests. That must put the damper on any sit-down dinner parties Cody might have planned. Problems with any energy-consuming appliances should be reported to Bamia immediately, the same with anything needing repair.

Tory had told Alvarez about the abundance of framed art in Bamia's house; for his part, Alvarez had decided there was no reason to discuss his private conversation with Henderson. Still, even forewarned, Alvarez was surprised by the artwork displayed in the little house. There were a few standard motel-like pictures. But seven of the walls—Alvarez had counted—boasted huge paintings on black velvet, the type sometimes displayed by roadside vendors. Cody probably wouldn't care if the walls were painted with zebra stripes, but Tory might find this unsettling. On the ride over, she'd assured Alvarez numerous times that she wasn't tense, so he'd diplomatically decided that she was simply very, very alert.

While Tory was occupied with Cody and the Bible of

House Rules, Alvarez took a closer look at the place, like
a cop would look at it. Bamia was responsible for furnishing
and maintaining the two houses, so that must apply to the
artwork, too. Maybe Bamia had a warped sense of humor.
Maybe Kunz's Christmas display was a response to
Bamia's interior decorating. Maybe this was what Henderson had hinted at—it was certainly a better theory than
thinking that Cody's new next-door neighbor was totally
deranged.

Two huge paintings in the living room were garish ex-
panses of clashing colors that seemed to depict flowers.
They were unlike any flowers Alvarez had ever seen, but
he didn't know a lot about flowers, or paintings, either. He
also didn't know what prompted people to purchase large
velvet paintings displayed on the side of the road.

Two more velvet paintings hung in the kitchen. Perhaps
each could be called a still life. One seemed to feature ba-
nana peels as the primary object in the arrangement; in the
other, an onion and a potato competed for front billing.

The bedroom boasted two pictures of Elvis, larger than
life, so there must be a method to this madness, a pairing
by theme. Marilyn Monroe would have been a nice touch
in the bedroom, but Bamia must have been unwilling to
risk hanging something Kunz might enjoy.

It was in the bathroom that Alvarez found the crowning
touch, and started to truly comprehend the concept of wag-
ing war with art. In the bathroom, on the wall behind the
mirror, hung a life-size Jesus. Living in this house, a man
would shave every day with Jesus Christ literally looking
over his shoulder.

Alvarez felt certain that the Jesus painting exactly
matched the size of some framed artwork in Bamia's bathroom, so it could be argued that Jesus must stay where he
was. Alvarez felt a grudging respect for the man who lived
in the house next door.

As if Alvarez conjured him up, someone who looked to be Hafiz Bamia himself appeared in the hallway outside the bathroom, holding a large framed black-and-white print. "I put other things back on the walls now, things the boy can like to look at," he said without preamble. "I put these others to bother that Croat. The Croat, he said bad things to me, things no one should hear. He believed evil things. That Croat should live with these pictures. Not the boy, no."

Alvarez introduced himself. Bamia seemed to think that Alvarez was Cody's father; Alvarez let it go. If the situation was too complicated for Alvarez to figure out, how could he explain it to someone else?

Bamia went on apologizing. He pointed to the Jesus picture. "I mean nothing bad for others. But the Croat, he said bad things about me, about my people. So I put this thing in here."

"I'm surprised you hang any paintings, even prints, on the walls at all," Alvarez said. "You're Muslim, right?"

Bamia stiffened. "Muslim, yes. Bosnian. I thought you already know that, you, the woman, the boy. Is a problem now?"

"No problem," said Alvarez. He turned and took Jesus off the bathroom wall to exchange for the print in Bamia's hands. The ambiance improved immediately. "It's no problem at all," Alvarez repeated. "I'm just interested. I thought Muslims didn't collect art, not art like paintings." Alvarez pointed at the framed Jesus that Bamia was now holding. "That one there, it looks like a weapon."

Bamia went perfectly still. Alvarez leaned back against the bathroom sink, made sure he didn't use what Tory called his "cop voice." He gestured again at the painting Bamia was gripping. "It must have driven Josef Kunz over the edge. He'd see Jesus behind him every time he shaved. But the clincher is that every time he sat on the can," Alvarez said pointing to the toilet, just in case that didn't translate well, "he'd have to face Jesus straight on."

Then it happened—Bamia relaxed his stance and began to laugh, a good hearty laugh that seemed to come from deep inside. It was lucky no one else was standing there, because the two of them acted like a couple of teenage girls. Every time one stopped laughing, the other would start. Finally Tory stuck her head around the hall and said, "Can't you find something useful to do?"

"You, you come with me," Bamia told Alvarez. "We take these bad things down and put up nice things, things for the boy. He is a nice boy. He should have nice things to look at."

Alvarez and Bamia changed the seven velvet paintings for items Bamia already had on hand. They were mostly black-and-white prints like the one that went in the bathroom. One was an interesting close-up of a meditative-looking praying mantis in the midst of dense foliage that Alvarez wouldn't have minded having for himself.

Bamia told Alvarez that Islamic art, and a Muslim's approach to other art, depended, as did so many things, on the individual. Historically, Islam basically prohibited artistic representations of living things, since this might challenge or insult an all-powerful creator. These prohibitions had resulted in highly stylized depictions of animate objects, intricate geometric designs and the development of calligraphy. However, these same prohibitions were now considered irrelevant by many, and did not prevent numerous modern Muslims from collecting European-style art.

"If you could see my father's home, the paintings, the rugs, the porcelain," said Bamia, as he and Alvarez hung the last replacement painting. Then the man shook his head. "All gone now," he said. "All of it, gone."

"Do you still have family in Sarajevo?" asked Alvarez.

Forget Henderson's tactful restraint. A cop was used to asking the questions that no one wanted to ask.

"I do not talk of that," replied Bamia. It might have been an awkward moment, but just then the pizza arrived, along with the other guests, and the official housewarming began. Then it became apparent that while Bamia might be closemouthed on some subjects, he had discussed at least a few things with Sylvia Maestes beforehand.

When everyone finished eating, Sylvia pulled the curtains shut, then handed out index cards and flashlights to Jazz, Henderson, Bamia and Cody's girlfriend, Kohli.

"What's going on?" Tory asked when Sylvia doused the lights.

"Is it dessert?" Alvarez asked. If there was to be a performance of some kind, he rather hoped that Sylvia would jump out of a cake. She wore shiny white leather pants and a white fringed shirt, cinched in at the waist with a wide leather belt. The buckle was not ashamed to prominently display the initials *S* and *M*. It looked like a cross between Davy Crockett and a Ku Klux Klan costume, but maybe Sylvia was wearing something more interesting underneath.

"No," she answered. "This doesn't have anything to do with dessert. We're going to have a ceremony to give Cody some advice before we leave him here alone."

"*Alone* being the operative word," said Tory, looking at Cody, where he sat on the floor next to Kohli.

"Everybody ready?" asked Sylvia. No one answered, but she counted to three anyhow. Then Jazz, Henderson, Bamia, Kohli and Sylvia all switched on flashlights held under their chins, giving each of them an ominous threatening look, sitting grouped around Cody in the dark.

"I can't believe we're doing this," growled Jazz. There was one pure crystalline giggle from Kohli's direction.

"We five are gathered here to give you important commands," said Sylvia in a fake deep voice, "so listen closely. Your life may hang in the balance." There was a period of silence. "You're first," Sylvia hissed at Jazz.

"If you think you've killed the monster, never check to see if it's really dead," Jazz read in a disgusted monotone.

Henderson was next. "If you find that your house is built upon or near a cemetery, was once a church used for black masses, had previous inhabitants who went mad or committed suicide or died in some horrible fashion, move away immediately."

"I hope you had an environmental audit done on this property," Tory told Henderson.

"Shh," hissed Sylvia.

Bamia looked intently at his index card while he held his flashlight in the other hand. "Never read a book of demon summoning aloud, even as a joke," he said carefully.

"When you have the benefit of numbers, never pair off or go alone," said Kohli. "Stay together."

Cody put his arm around her. "I like that one," he said.

"Do not search the basement, especially when the power has just gone out," pronounced Sylvia.

"There's no basement here, so I can't be held responsible for that one," said Henderson.

"If *anything* goes wrong, I'm holding you responsible," Tory told him.

"Shh," Sylvia hissed again.

"If appliances start operating by themselves, move out," read Jazz. "There, I'm done." He turned off his flashlight. Sylvia gave him a look that appeared downright scary, especially since she was still maintaining the proper lighting effects.

"If your companions suddenly begin to exhibit uncharacteristic behavior such as hissing, fascination for blood, glowing eyes or increasing hairiness, get away from them as fast as possible," read Henderson. He seemed to have been assigned all the really long, formal statements.

"What if someone wears white clothes that look like they glow in the dark?" asked Jazz pointedly.

"Do not take, or borrow, anything from the dead," read Bamia, refusing to deviate from the scripted dialogue.

"As a general rule, don't solve puzzles that open portals to Hell," said Kohli.

"And here is the most important advice of all," said Sylvia, "so listen carefully. Beware of strangers bearing tools such as chain saws, staple guns, hedge trimmers, electric carving knives, combines, lawn mowers, butane torches, soldering irons, band saws, weed whackers or any device made from deceased companions. That's it. One, two, three." She hadn't finished counting before the flashlights began to go out.

Kohli turned the lights back on, and Cody duly applauded Sylvia's theatrical efforts. Alvarez would still have preferred to see Sylvia jump out of a cake.

He wondered how she had recruited her eclectic cast, with the exception of Kohli. "How'd she talk you into doing that?" Alvarez asked Bamia while everyone was cleaning up the remains of the pizza dinner.

Bamia shrugged, as if there were nothing to explain. "I like the boy," he said. "And I like Sylvia. It was nice to meet you," he added formally, and then went to tell the others goodbye.

"How'd Sylvia get you in on that deal?" Alvarez asked when Henderson passed by him in the kitchen.

Henderson looked around, lowered his voice. "She threatened to tell Bamia that Cody was a Born Again Christian with a quota of converts for the Christmas season," he said.

"How about you?" Alvarez asked Jazz.

"She promised to wear clothes of one color only, for a whole week, man."

Tory had decided that Tango shouldn't be in such a small

house with so many people and so much pizza, so she and Alvarez were driving back to her house to fetch the official watchdog.

"I wonder why Sylvia went to all that effort," Tory said as they walked to her car. "Cody's stayed by himself before, and he's not the nervous type."

Alvarez knew the answer to this particular question. *"Querida,"* he said, "the performance wasn't to reassure Cody. It was all for you."

FOUR

Good Fences Make Good Neighbors

CODY HADN'T SPENT all *that* many nights by himself. Although he had displayed the appropriate aplomb during Sylvia's theatrics, he was glad that Mr. Bamia was right next door. Cody was also grateful for Tango asleep on the floor next to his bed, even though he'd put a lot of effort into arguing with his Mom about the dog custody agreement.

Cody didn't want his friends to think he needed a dog for protection. He'd contended that it was stupid for an eighty-pound dog to hang out all day in a tiny house with a tiny yard. So this was the deal—each morning Cody would get in his bright-red, almost new, half-paid-for-with-his-own-savings truck, and drive down University Street to Mesilla. He would drop Tango off at home, then hope like hell that he got to school on time, or his Mom would be all over him. Each day, at some point after school, afternoon or evening, he'd reverse the procedure—pick up Tango to spend the night with him at Con House.

Cody reached down, picked up one of Tango's long, limp ears, rubbed it absently between his thumb and fingers. The dog continued to snore. If Hannibal Lecter fondled Tango's ear, the dog would probably sleep through it. This agreement about Tango was like hauling a kid back and forth to day care—it was ridiculous. Cody stopped rubbing Tango's ear. Hadn't his Mom always told him that there were some negotiations you *want* to lose? She'd gotten him to agree to an arrangement that insured he'd be returning home at least twice a day.

Cody turned onto his back and stared at the ceiling. Damn. He hadn't seen this one coming. Thinking about how hard he had argued for keeping Tango only at night, Cody had to laugh. It was either that or hit something.

Sometimes his mom made him really angry. Sometimes she did things that really scared him, but lots of times she cracked him up, just being herself. Mostly, he was really proud of his mom and he really loved her. But she needed to concentrate on building relationships with people who would still be there when Cody moved out, moved on. That's why this house-sitting job was so great, coming along when his mom needed to focus on sorting out other things.

As long as he didn't watch any scary movies late at night, Cody figured he would be okay. Staying in a house by himself was going to be a piece of cake.

He turned onto his stomach. When he finally fell asleep, he still had one hand hanging off the bed, resting on Tango's head.

MR. BAMIA WALKED UP TO Cody's truck as soon as he pulled up to the curb. "How was school today?" he asked. "I want to know how are you doing, Cody. Make sure everything is how you say it—okay."

"Everything is okay, Mr. Bamia. How was your day?"

Mr. Bamia seemed to think this over. "My day was okay, too," he said.

Because Cody had been taught to be polite, and because he was proud of having a place of his own, he took a first stab at entertaining. "Would you like to come in and have a soda, Mr. Bamia?"

There was another pause, then the man nodded. "I would like that, Cody. I would like that very much. But you are a man now, right? Now you stay by yourself in this house, you are a man.''

Cody had a momentary fear there might be some bizarre Bosnian rite of manhood having to do with staying in a house by yourself. "Well, yeah, I guess so." God, he sounded just like some goofy teenage kid.

"Then you must call me Hafiz," Bamia said, extending one hand, and they shook on it. Cody led the way into Con House and dropped his backpack onto the dining room table. "Please, sit," he told his guest, and handed him a soda from the fridge. When Cody sat down with a soda of his own, Hafiz pointed at the backpack on the table between them.

"You read that book?" he asked. Cody took a look. The only title fully visible in the half-open backpack was *Rebecca West: A Life.*

"Yeah," replied Cody. He wondered what Hafiz knew about Rebecca West. Henderson said Bamia didn't talk about his past. Well, if Rebecca West was a touchy subject, they could always talk about some other book in his backpack. *Precalculus: Tools for The Future,* for example.

"Why that book?" Hafiz asked.

"It's for my psychology class," said Cody. "I'm writing a paper about Rebecca West. She studied people who betray their countries.''

"I know about this woman," said Hafiz. "This woman, this Rebecca West, she went to Balkans, then write book about people, about countries. Sometimes not same thing."

Cody nodded. "*Black Lamb and Grey Falcon,*" he said, "a famous book about her travels in the Balkans, published in 1941." He wished his psych teacher was there to hear him rattle that off. He could also bring up the fact that Rebecca West had been the mistress of H. G. Wells, but maybe he should wait and see if Hafiz mentioned it.

"She wrote for people like you," stated Hafiz. "People like you read her book, go see just a little, write more books. Books about other books. Your president read these books about other books when there was fighting in my country. The newspapers in Sarajevo told about it.''

"Isn't it good to read books to try to understand things?'' asked Cody, trying to keep up his end of the conversation.

"No. To understand Balkans, you must live in Balkans.'' Hafiz made it a flat statement. Cody didn't argue—he was just writing a paper for a high school psychology class. "You fear people come to your door, maybe tonight?'' Hafiz asked Cody suddenly. "People who beat you with whips? As punishment—no, maybe not punishment. Maybe try get answers. Maybe answers you not know.''

"That doesn't happen here,'' Cody told him. He knew firsthand that David Alvarez was a homicide detective and he didn't beat people with whips.

Hafiz shrugged. "My people, we have a history of fear, hate, revenge. It is in our blood. We learn it like you learn history at school.''

"Why?'' asked Cody. "Because you're Muslim?''

Hafiz leaned across the table toward Cody. "I look Muslim to you?''

Cody shook his head. "But Hafiz, I don't know any Muslims,'' he said. "At least, I don't think I do.''

"You think Muslim, you think Arabian, sheik maybe. Dark, turban, horse, saber, you think this Muslim.''

"Well, maybe not all that,'' said Cody. But then again, maybe so. "But you're right, you don't look like a Muslim to me.''

Cody was afraid that he might have insulted the man, but Hafiz banged his soda can on the table to indicate agreement. "I am Slav,'' he said. "I am Bosnian Muslim. I am Bosnian Muslim from Sarajevo. But I am Slav, always Slav.''

"How is that different from guys in turbans?'' That came out as a pretty lame question, but it didn't faze Hafiz.

"When Turks come long ago, my people found way of

Islam, others did not. Turks not like these others, so my people, the ones who are Slav *and* Muslim, get land, power. Many years come, go. Invaders come, go. Evil wars, evil leaders, fascism, communism. Still, we hold land, power, not others. Not Croats, Serbs. You understand now, why those others come to hate us.''

Cody thought this over. "How do you tell the difference between Muslims and the others?"

"Is hard, but not hard," replied Hafiz. "Old ways change. Muslims watch MTV. Some even eat pork, drink alcohol, watch MTV. In Sarajevo, I was teacher—students in blue jeans, miniskirts—like here, no turbans. But names, other differences, always there. In Sarajevo, you know who is Muslim, who is not."

"Well, that explains things," said Cody. How could something that sounded okay in your head sound so dumb when it came out of your mouth?

"No," said Hafiz. "That explains nothing. I had family in Sarajevo. Now, no family. I do not talk of it. Now I live different life, much different. But we talk of other things. I like you, so we talk again, you and me." Hafiz downed the last of his soda and carefully set the can on the table in front of him. "Thank you for drink."

"Well, okay," said Cody. Hafiz stood, formally shook hands again, and left without saying another word.

Cody didn't think that his first effort at solo entertaining had been a complete success. But it was time to go pick up his dog, and Tango didn't require a lot of conversation.

THE NEXT AFTERNOON, Cody swung by his house after school to pick up a few things. No one was home, which wasn't a big surprise, considering the time of day. Cody loaded up Tango with the rest of his stuff, so he wouldn't have to make a separate night-time trip. Tango sat in the passenger seat, his head almost on a level with Cody's.

Riding in a vehicle always filled Tango with an enthusiastic anticipation about his destination. After any car trip, the dog was energized for a bit, running around, sniffing and poking, whether he'd ever seen the place before or not. It worked the same in reverse; returning home, Tango went running around for a little while as if he were in an entirely new place. Then the interest would wear off, and he would revert to the practice of sleeping most of his life away.

Cody pulled up at Con House. He leashed Tango and transferred the dog from truck to house, then from house to backyard, where Tango could explore to his heart's content. Then Cody turned around and went back to his truck to get his backpack and the rest of his things. Hafiz was standing by the truck.

"Was your day okay today, Cody?" he asked.

"Yeah," said Cody. Was this becoming a ritual? Would either of them ever admit to a rotten, horrible day? "How was your day, Mr. Bamia? I mean, Hafiz."

"My day was okay," Hafiz answered as Cody locked the door to his truck. "Okay until now. I did not know that you have dog."

Because of the idiotic custody arrangement regarding Tango, this might well be the very first time that Hafiz had laid eyes on the dog. "He's really my mom's dog," said Cody. This seemed so much like the sort of treason he was researching that he amended his statement. "He's a family dog."

"If he is family dog, why is he here?"

"He only stays here at night. Mr. Henderson knows all about it—he gave special permission." Cody felt like a real idiot. It would have been ten times better to have agreed to keep the dog with him the whole time. But it was too late for that.

"He is a very big dog," Hafiz observed.

"Yeah, he is. But he's a nice dog, really friendly."

"I do not like dogs," said Hafiz.

"I'm sorry to hear that." Why did everything that Cody said to this man come out sounding so lame?

Cody and Hafiz stood on the sidewalk looking at each other for a time that seemed to last forever. Finally Hafiz spoke again. "Do not let dog come near me, Cody. I like you, but not dog. So." Hafiz nodded a couple of times; maybe he thought Cody was slow on the uptake. "No more talk today," he said. Then, without another word, Hafiz turned and walked away. He went into his house and closed the door behind him.

Cody stood staring after him for a moment, wondering if he might have imagined this strange conversation. He wanted to be considerate of Mr. Bamia's feelings. But he still thought it was damned unfair to lump canines with Croatians.

THE FOLLOWING DAY, Cody drove straight to Con House after school—no picking up Tango during daylight hours from now on, not if he could help it. It was a good strategy, because sure enough, as soon as Cody pulled up to the curb, Hafiz came out of his house and waited for Cody to get out of the truck. Geez. Hafiz was getting to be worse than Cody's mom.

"Your day okay, Cody?" he asked.

"Yeah, my day went okay, Hafiz. How was your day?"

"My day was okay," said Hafiz. "I go to your house, drink soda with you, remember? You come to my house now, have beer, we talk."

Wow, what a switch. Dump the dog, and Hafiz and him were buds again. A beer. The guy was actually standing out here on the sidewalk, offering him a beer. Unbidden, an image of his mom flashed through his mind—major bummer. "I don't know," Cody hedged. "Maybe I better not."

"Why? You man now. Come to my house, have one beer. We talk, no problem."

Cody balanced on the knife edge of temptation. "Well,

I feel kind of bad about doing that. My girlfriend doesn't like for me to drink." Where had that come from? Talk about making up whopper lies on the spot.

Hafiz made a show of looking around. "Girlfriend here now?" he asked. Maybe the guy had a sense of humor after all.

"No," Cody admitted, "she's not."

"Then no problem."

Cody looked around for himself, and sure enough, Kohli was nowhere to be seen. Neither was anyone else that he knew. "I guess you're right, there's no problem," he said.

Cody shrugged his backpack onto one shoulder and followed Hafiz into Sol House. Cody sat down at a table exactly like the one in his house, and Hafiz reached into a refrigerator that was just like the one in Cody's kitchen. But instead of a soda, Hafiz handed Cody a beer, took one for himself and sat across from Cody. They drank in silence for a while.

This felt kind of strange to Cody. He tried to think of something to say to break the silence. He knew one thing—he sure as hell wouldn't bring up dogs as a topic.

"What you know of Sarajevo?" asked Hafiz suddenly.

So they didn't need to fish around in Cody's backpack to find something to talk about. "I don't know much," said Cody. "I know the Olympics were held there once, back when everyone got along, before the fighting started."

Hafiz made a snorting sound. "So much talk about those games, about when everybody in Sarajevo got along. Is lie. I know joke, from time right after Olympics. Fighting in Croatia but no fighting in Bosnia. Everybody ask, why no fighting in Bosnia? You know answer?" Cody shook his head. "This is answer," Hafiz said. "Because no 'warm-up' needed. Bosnia go directly to finals."

That didn't sound like much of a joke to Cody. He didn't know a lot about Eastern European politics, but he knew about Sarajevo, the Olympic Games and the fighting that came afterward. Everyone knew about that. "What about Sarajevo during the Olympics?" he asked Hafiz. "No one was fighting then. Different people lived together in the same city, and there was no fighting, there was peace."

"Peace on surface, on TV only," said Hafiz. "Always fear, hate, underneath, always. Where Muslims live together with other people, we must remember differences, never forget we are Muslims. Croats and Serbs the same, never forget. Hate Muslims, hate each other. Serbs—hate, torture, killing. Croats—hate torture, killing. No matter each called Christian." Hafiz made another sound of disgust. "You know why we drink beer together, not plum brandy?" Hafiz didn't wait for an answer. "Because Chetniks, they drink plum brandy."

"Who are Chetniks?" Cody thought he'd gotten a fundamental grasp on the Bosnians, Serbs and Croats, but who the hell were Chetniks? How did plum brandy figure into this? Wouldn't it be safer to go back to talking about Rebecca West?

"Chetniks—Serbs who want country with only Serbs, no others. Chetniks need plum brandy to do their work."

Cody couldn't help himself. He had to ask the next question. "What is their work?"

Hafiz leaned across the table, his beer forgotten. He was focused only on Cody. "Killing. Chetniks kill, kill, kill. Chetniks throw child up in air to land on knife. Chetniks tie man to burning log. Chetniks rape and kill daughters in front of mother. Chetniks cut off eyelids, make sure mother watches. Then Chetniks kill mother. That is work of Chetniks. After they do work, they go to church. They do these things and go to their church." Hafiz closed his eyes as if what he'd said was too much for him. It was certainly enough for Cody.

"I'm sorry to hear about that," Cody said. Why were his words so painfully inadequate whenever he talked to this man? Hafiz opened his eyes, and they sat in silence together again. "Thanks for the beer," Cody said after a while. "I better get going, I have a lot of homework."

Hafiz reached across the table and closed one hand around Cody's wrist. "What about you Cody? You are Christian, no? What kind Christian?"

"I don't know," replied Cody. "I'm still trying to decide." He really wished Hafiz would let go of his wrist.

"I had family," Hafiz said. "No family now." He tightened his grip on Cody for a few seconds, and then, just as suddenly, he let go. He leaned back in his chair, away from Cody. "Now I have different life, different work," he told Cody. "Much, much different. But I never forget, I must be always ready."

Hafiz gestured toward the kitchen counter, and for a moment, Cody actually thought that the man was going to offer him another beer. "I keep gun with me, always," Hafiz told Cody. "Before the Croat, I keep it in drawer. But others like him, out there, always somewhere." Hafiz gestured toward the front door. "Always others like that Croat. Serb, Jew, Nazi, fascist, communist, all same. Hate, torture, kill. Now gun stays with me. Never forget again, always ready."

Sure enough, there was a gun sitting right there on the kitchen counter. For a moment it seemed so huge that it occupied the whole room. How had Cody missed seeing it? Were guns even allowed on university property? Did that matter? Would he be allowed to continue house-sitting one more single minute if his mother knew about this?

"You're not scared of me, are you, Hafiz?" Cody asked his drinking companion. "I got confirmed as an Episcopalian, but I only did it to please my mother. Really."

Hafiz seemed to have withdrawn into himself, seemed to have lost interest in Cody's religious status. "No, not afraid of you, Cody. You nice boy, I like talking with you. But I think you should go home now."

"Well, okay," said Cody. It was the best exit line he could think of.

CODY DIDN'T SAY ANYTHING to anyone about his conversation with Hafiz, not even when he went home to pick up Tango right before curfew. Adults always told teenagers to put things in perspective, so that's what he was going to do.

After all, Cody had been raised around guns, knew how to shoot them, how to handle them. Ratting Hafiz out to Henderson might have terrible results for the man, and frankly, it might have terrible results for Cody, too, grant-funded study or no grant-funded study. Here he was in a house of his own, and he'd been so busy studying for semester finals that he hadn't had a chance to have his friends over yet, not even Kohli. Putting things in perspective meant considering that the weekend was in sight.

If Cody had been forced to leave friends and family to start over in a new country, if he'd seen the things Hafiz had seen, maybe he'd be a little jumpy, too. Hafiz had lived in the house next door for years without causing any trouble, and he seemed to have taken a liking to Cody, however fleeting and strange. And hadn't Hafiz said straight out that he wasn't afraid of Cody?

If Hafiz threatened him, or started acting dangerous, then Cody would tell someone about the gun—hopefully after at least one weekend in this house by himself.

By the time Cody got ready to lock up for the night, he was convinced he'd made the right decision. He'd stay put, wait and watch.

But.

Wasn't this waiting and watching the very same stuff Hafiz said he had to do? Cody decided to think about it tomorrow.

FIVE

The Windfall

LAST THING before going to bed, Cody made Tango wake up and go outside, the theory being that the dog should relieve himself before packing it in for the night. This "putting the dog out" endeavor was no small feat. Cody had to make sure that Tango was sufficiently awake to have at least a passing interest in his surroundings, otherwise the hound had been known to simply walk out a door, plop down next to it, and go back to sleep.

Cody leaned against the kitchen wall by the sliding glass door and watched Tango's dark shape. The dog sniffed around the backyard as if he knew he was being watched, and was therefore just going through the motions. This was going to take a while. Cody turned away, walked over to the sink and got himself a glass of water, then walked back to keep an eye on Tango.

Maybe Hafiz had good reasons not to like dogs. Cody was grateful for the solid rock wall between the two houses. A nice, sturdy, substantial rock wall—not one of those flimsy wooden fences that were easy to dig under. Cody wanted to avoid any more spontaneous interactions between his next-door neighbor and his dog.

There was no way around it, thinking about Hafiz and Tango made Cody think about Hafiz and his gun. Cody wasn't real comfortable about keeping something like this from his mom, all previous rationalizations aside. His mom could always come up with some question that finally tripped him up, no matter how cool he tried to play it.

Someday Cody should talk to David Alvarez about the idea of using regular everyday moms as civilian instructors for law enforcement classes. He could see it as one of those wacky ideas that catches on and results in a one-page story in *People* magazine. And besides, then, if his mom ever got tired of being an engineer, she would have a guaranteed job opening.

Cody knew he was just trying to distract himself. In the end, it came down to a matter of timing. Cody had moved into Con House on Monday evening. Tuesday, Wednesday and Thursday had already elapsed. That meant that Friday was right around the corner, and to every student in the world, Friday heralded the beginning of The Hallowed Weekend. Cody had plans for Friday night. He had plans for the weekend. Otherwise, what was the use of having a girlfriend, buddies, cash in your pocket and a house to yourself?

It wasn't like he felt great about his decision, but maybe it all came down to a don't-ask-don't-tell policy. Now Cody would just have to hope like hell that his mom didn't do any critical asking any time soon.

He opened the sliding glass door and whistled for Tango, his breath puffing cloudy in the clear night air. The temperature had already dropped significantly from a few hours ago. Tango ran up, his body wriggling like that of an over-size puppy. He had a stick in his mouth. It was sandy and slightly moist, as if the dog had just dug it up. Surprised by his dog's animation, Cody gave in to the canine hint.

Cody threw the stick for the dog a few times, then firmly commanded him to come in and leave his newfound toy outside. Cody locked the sliding glass door and drew the curtains, then bent down to give Tango a perfunctory scratch behind the ears before they both went to bed.

The dog had brought something inside besides a stick.

Cody hooked a finger into Tango's mouth and withdrew something green that was only slightly soggy from being masticated. It was a piece of paper. Wait, it was more than a piece of green paper—it was money.

Cody stood and looked at the bill in astonishment. He held the money in one hand and used the other hand to push Tango back down. Tango seemed to think that Cody was starting a new indoor version of throw-the-stick game; he was panting and wagging his tail as if he expected Cody to start throwing green paper around. But this wasn't the kind of money Cody would ever throw around. He had extracted a one-hundred-dollar bill from the depths of Tango's cavernous and drooling mouth.

Cody looked at the money once, twice, three times more, and it looked the same each time he examined it. He was holding a one-hundred-dollar bill in his hand, one hundred dollars that had materialized from thin air. Well, from thin air via Tango's tonsils.

Cody reached under the sink and got out a flashlight. He was conveniently outfitted with a flashlight, candles, matches, all kinds of survival gear, even a small can of pepper spray. He had Sylvia to thank for that, as his mother tended to think along bigger lines than pepper spray.

Cody left Tango looking sadly out through the sliding glass door, as if wondering why Cody would go outside to play alone. Cody made a quick flashlight inspection of the small yard.

He was somewhat amazed at the size and number of holes the dog had dug in the relatively little time he'd been at Con House, but it was something that could easily be remedied with a little effort and a shovel. He'd have to be sure and mention this to his mother, as a shovel was just about the only emergency tool Sylvia hadn't provided.

Try as he might, Cody couldn't locate the source of Tango's windfall. He went and peered over the back wall, but there was nothing but dark, undeveloped desert land.

One more circle of the yard, and Cody gave it up. He'd heard about things like this before, the sort of things that also rated one page write-ups in *People* magazine. But since he could find no purse or wallet, Cody couldn't see that there would be much point in reporting his discovery. Hell, how could anyone prove ownership of a one-hundred-dollar bill that just seemed to have found its way into someone's backyard?

Cody might as well hang on to the money. He felt fewer twinges of conscience about this decision. Maybe this windfall was an omen. It sure beat any previous omens in his life hands down. Maybe it was an omen that his other decision wasn't so far off a moral compass, after all.

Cody fell asleep immediately, contrary to the popular notion that people toss and turn over difficult decisions. But he didn't escape totally unscathed. He had a dream about some masked man chasing him and Tango across a desert. The masked man had a gun, and he was gaining on them. Cody came suddenly and completely awake, sitting up in bed so rapidly that his head spun and it took him a moment to remember why he was in unfamiliar surroundings.

Tango was snoring, a familiar sound, lying so close to the side of the bed that Cody could reach out and put his hand on the dog's head. Tango was real and tangible, not part of any dream.

The alarm said that there was a good hour to go until it was time to get up. In less than five minutes, Cody was asleep again.

SIX

The Price

THE FIRST THING Cody noticed when he woke up was the sound of the wind. Whistling around the outside walls and brushing scratchy fingers over the roof shingles, wind sounds filled the small house.

The really bad windstorms came with a vengeance in the spring. They turned the sky brown and left a fine dust of silt on everything inside a house, no matter how well-sealed the doors and windows might be. Still, even in the relative calm of winter, a sudden desert windstorm could come at any time.

Wind meant you had to make allowances. People would be edgy about a windstorm that had unexpectedly materialized in the early morning, like an unwanted salesperson who appeared uninvited at the front door. They would wonder if the wind would blow out by noon, or if it would feed on its own fickleness and become more of a nuisance by sundown. People would be churlish about the wind, whether they were on the road, inside a building or out in the weather.

When the wind was blowing, it was harder to get things from place to place—you had to make sure you were holding on to everything properly, or the wind would snatch it away from you. With Tango weighing in at over eighty pounds, at least Cody didn't have to worry about pitting the dog against the wind.

Cody rousted the hound, shook some dog chow into a bowl, opened the back sliding glass door and pushed the still groggy dog out into the morning gusts. "Hurry up," muttered Cody. "I don't want to be late for school." Tango didn't have a reply, so Cody left him to eat a solitary breakfast.

Then Cody took one of the fastest showers on record, gathered up his things, grabbed Tango's leash and went to call the dog back inside. Tango was right by the door waiting for him. There was some green stuff scattered around the dog, dancing in the wind, and more green stuff blowing around out in the little backyard. Not grass, not likely, not out on the desert in the middle of the winter. The green stuff blowing around was all just like the green stuff Cody had taken out of Tango's mouth last night.

All thoughts of schedules forgotten, Cody stepped out the door and dropped to his knees next to the dog. He reached out with both hands and grabbed some of the green stuff. Cody looked at what he held in his hands, and it added up to six hundred dollars.

Tango sat next to Cody, his tail swishing a steady beat back and forth on the concrete porch. Cody knew that Tango had some distant memory of obedience classes in his puppyhood, and the dog was already sitting. "Stay," Cody told Tango. Cody stood and stepped off the back porch and into the yard.

It didn't look much different than it had the previous night; there was still evidence of an amazing amount of excavation on Tango's part. Cody looked up at the sky. Maybe he was looking for some kind of hijacker, someone who pulled a heist in midair, didn't have the ability to land the plane, and was dumping currency in an effort to conserve fuel. Or maybe he was looking for a fat bearded man in a red suit and a sleigh, dropping hundred-dollar bills into the very yard where Cody had been hired to house-sit. But he knew he hadn't been *that* good all year—just yesterday, he'd had a beer with Hafiz.

The thought of Hafiz turned Cody's attention toward his neighbor's yard. The rock wall separating the two yards was a good, solid wall, just as he'd reflected last night. It was five feet in height for most of its length, but it had been constructed to appear level at the top, while the yards themselves followed the natural incline of the foothills. Because of the way the backyard sloped upward away from the house, the wall at the back of the yard was closer to four feet in height.

Cody turned to look back at Tango. The dog was staying in place as he had been told to do, but he wasn't sitting anymore, he was lying down. It was this very behavior that led one to underestimate the physical capabilities of an eighty-pound hound.

With a sinking heart, Cody went to look over the fence into the backyard of Sol House. Sure enough, it appeared that Tango had become bored with working merely at Con House, and had expanded his activities into excavating five significant holes in the yard next door. Even more green stuff was blowing around there.

Cody was up and over the fence in no time, and thankfully, Tango showed no interest in following him. Cody took a quick look into each of the excavations.

One contained a partially buried plastic bag, badly torn, leaking hundred-dollar bills into the wind. Three others looked like normal dog holes, if there was such a thing. But in the last, Cody thought he could see a flash of clear plastic. Sure enough, with very little effort, he was able to liberate another plastic bag with green stuff in it. The bag was covered with dirt but intact. Cody picked it and the leaking bag up as quickly as he could, also gathering the ten or so loose bills in immediate proximity.

Later, Cody would be told many times, and at great

length, that his subsequent actions were reckless. He would also be told that what he did saved a life. But neither mattered—in a time of crisis, one acted according to one's gut instincts. Cody's gut instincts told him that he was a teenager who had withheld information from his mother, and as a result, he was in deep shit trouble. Having that gut instinct made a kid want to put things right as soon as possible, optimally without any mother's involvement.

Cody was back over the fence in a matter of seconds, holding the plastic bags of money in one hand and pulling Tango into the house with the other. Cody closed a startled Tango in the bathroom, then used the phone in the kitchen to call home.

Alvarez answered. At another time that might warrant some consideration, but certainly not now. "Tell my mom that I'm going to be late bringing Tango over. There's something here that I need to take care of."

"Are you okay?" asked Alvarez.

Cody was really sick of that question. "I'm fine. Just tell my mom that I'm gonna be late, okay?"

There was a silence, and then Alvarez said, "Okay." No questions, just that one word. Based on that one word, at that one moment, Cody would have been willing to hug the man and call him dad. But there were more immediate matters at hand. Cody hung up the phone, grabbed the two plastic bags of money and went to face Hafiz, wanting to return his property to him, wanting to make things right.

Cody didn't think to grab up the bills on the floor in the kitchen, bills that totaled seven hundred dollars. And he didn't think about the fact that Tango wouldn't be able to answer the phone five minutes later, when his mother called, demanding an explanation. Cody was a man on a mission.

He tried the front door of Sol House first, of course, but no one answered. Hafiz's car was parked in its usual place, so it followed that Hafiz was at home. Cody walked around the side of the house, banging on any window in sight, but to no avail. All the curtains were closed, there was no chance to look inside. That left the sliding glass door in the backyard.

Cody strengthened his resolve and returned to the backyard at Sol House. He knocked on the sliding glass door with his knuckles, calling his neighbor's name. Then he cupped his hands around his face to peer into the darkened interior of the house. He immediately forgot about Tango, the excavated holes, the money. Hafiz was motionless on the floor beside the dining room table. He appeared to be lying in a pool of dark liquid, and Cody didn't see any overturned paint cans around.

There was a shovel leaning against the wall next to the sliding glass door. Cody dropped the bags of money, picked up the shovel, and put all his energy into breaking down the door. It didn't work. It simply didn't work. Cody must have spent a good two minutes whaling away at the glass door with no results.

Then he saw the pickax against the wall where the shovel had been. Two good strokes and there were spiderwebs of fractures. But it was still harder than it looked in the movies, and messier, too. The safety glass seemed to simply sag inward instead of shatter. It was going to take some effort to tear a hole big enough for him to climb through. Then Cody realized how stupid he was, and he concentrated on breaking out the glass around the handle to the sliding glass door. Even then, when he had a hole big enough that he could put his hand inside, it took some time to lift the latch and open the door. It seemed to take eons.

Once in the house, Cody dropped to his knees beside the prone figure of his next-door neighbor. He knelt in sticky, wet stuff. He was in a pool of blood forming under Hafiz, a pool of blood that was pumping weakly from his neighbor's blood-soaked shirt over his stomach. Cody stood, slid on some the blood, grabbed the phone in the kitchen, called

911. "Send an ambulance," Cody said. It sounded like someone else's voice. "There's a man here, and he's bleeding from his stomach."

"What's your name, and where are you?" said the sexless voice on the other end.

"I'm Cody Travers, and I'm at Con House, no, I'm not. I'm at the solar house. I don't know the address. I'm just the house sitter." Never had he felt so helpless. Here he was with a dying man on his hands, and he couldn't even give the emergency dispatcher the fucking address.

"It's okay, we've got a location on you. Tell me about the man, tell me how he looks. Is he breathing?"

"Yes, he's breathing. I mean I think he's still breathing. He's still bleeding, so that means he has to be still breathing, doesn't it?"

"He's bleeding from the stomach?"

"Yes."

"And he's lying down?"

"He's on his back on the floor. In a pool of blood. Didn't I already tell you that?"

"Cody, it is Cody, right?"

"Just tell me what to do. What the hell do I do?"

"See if you can find a towel, a blanket, a piece of clothing," the voice said with no expression whatsoever. You can use your own shirt—"

"I've got a towel," Cody yelled into the phone. Standing in the kitchen, it was easy to grab a dish towel. Why the hell was the fucking dispatcher one step behind him?

"Apply force where you see the bleeding," said the voice. "Try to stop the bleeding, but try to keep out of the blood. Do you have blood on you, Cody?"

With a cordless phone one could keep on talking while one did other things. "Of course I have blood on me," Cody replied. Could morons get hired as emergency dispatchers? The next time Cody had an emergency, he'd like to call somewhere else. "I was standing in a pool of blood, now I'm kneeling in it."

"Stay calm, Cody."

"What else can I do?"

"Can you tell me more about the man? Was there an accident? Has he been stabbed? Has he been shot?"

Cody took his first really good look at Hafiz, and saw that there were other objects lying in the pool of blood. "I don't know what happened to him," Cody said. "There's a framed picture next to him. It's facedown in the blood."

"A picture?" The voice on the other end slipped from expressionless to sounding puzzled. "What kind of a picture?"

"What kind of a picture? How would I know? Didn't I just tell you that it's facedown in the blood?"

"Calm down," the voice said.

"I am calm," Cody yelled. "What the hell is taking you so long? When will you get here?"

"Soon," said the voice. "Really soon. Help is on the way."

Cody recognized a hedge when he heard one. "What the hell does *soon* mean? I'll bet you tell every fucking person who calls you that help will be there *soon.*"

"What else can you see?" the voice asked him.

"There's a spool of wire, the kind you hang pictures with. And there's a hammer next to him."

"Is it bloody?"

"Of course, it's bloody." Cody was back to yelling again. "How many times do I have to tell you that there's a pool of blood here?"

"What else do you see?"

"Well, there's a gun. It's kind of hard to see from where I'm kneeling, but it's over there on the floor with the rest of this stuff."

"A gun? There's a gun? Do you have a gun, Cody? Are you armed?"

"Are you some kind of idiot? Of course I'm not armed, unless you mean a fucking shovel, a pickax and a Transylvanian hound, but the dog's in the bathroom next door, so that doesn't really count, does it?"

"Tell me about the gun," said the voice. The voice wasn't interested in tools or hounds.

"I don't know about the gun. It belongs to Hafiz. How would I know about it?"

"Who is Hafiz?"

"He's the man lying here bleeding to death. Didn't I tell you that?"

"Tell me what you know about Hafiz. How old is he?"

And so it went, for a period that seemed endless until Cody heard sirens so loud that he couldn't hear the voice on the other end of the phone any more. He dropped the phone on the floor and went to open the front door. His mother and Alvarez stood there, and Cody could see two medics sitting in an emergency vehicle parked streetside. In some insane order of things, it became obvious that Alvarez and his mother were coming inside the house, but the medics were not.

"Are you okay?" Alvarez asked as he pushed past the boy, a gun in hand.

"What are you doing?" asked Cody's mom.

"I'm clearing the house," said Alvarez. Whatever clearing was, it was a small house, so it didn't take long. Cody didn't care about any of that, or about his mother asking Alvarez why he happened to have a gun on him. Cody was busy yelling, trying to get the medics to come inside. His mother, to her credit, shut up and went to take care of Hafiz.

"Sorry, kid, it's policy," a grizzled black man called through a partially cracked window. A young woman sat next to him, and that's exactly what they were doing, just sitting there. "We can't go inside any building until it's cleared. We go inside before the cops get here, we lose our jobs."

Then Alvarez was suddenly by Cody's side, gun gone, but badge in hand as he walked up to the vehicle. "The house is clear," he told the medics. "There's a man in there bleeding to death."

"You're from Texas," said the female medic.

"Yeah," Alvarez replied. "I'm from Texas. And you know what, lady? There's still a man in there bleeding to death."

"Oh, fuck it," said the black medic. "I'm gonna retire this year anyhow." He climbed out of the vehicle and went in the house. The other medic hesitated, then followed her partner inside.

Cody slumped down onto the floor, his back against the wall next to the front door.

Another ambulance pulled up. Then the cops finally came.

SEVEN

Straightening Up

TORY HAD NOT been pleased to discover that Alvarez didn't quiz Cody about the nature of his delay, and that was putting it mildly. After her third phone call went unanswered, she told Alvarez that she was heading out to see for herself what was going on. Alvarez thought that she was overreacting, but offered to drive anyway.

He figured it was the luck of the draw that they had arrived before the police. Alvarez always tried to give law enforcement officers the benefit of the doubt; the systems were always overloaded, and besides, what with location, there might have been some confusion over who had jurisdiction, campus cops or Las Cruces PD. Hell, if Cody had tried to explain that he was calling from some place called Con House, the dispatcher might have thought the call was related to a prison break. Stranger things had happened.

The important thing was that Cody was all right. While the medics were doing their thing, in that short interval before the police arrived, Alvarez took a good look around. This left Tory to her own devices, which meant that she had Cody washing up in the kitchen sink, while she called Henderson and yelled at him to get over here fast, she didn't care what else he had planned. He'd gotten her son into this mess and he damned well better get over here to help her son get out of it. Charles Henderson arrived at Sol House barely five minutes after the two cops.

By that time, Cody was sitting on the couch and Henderson sat down next to him, a blank look on his face. Someone had draped a blanket around Cody's shoulders, and Tory was kneeling in front of her son, embracing him, blanket and all. The second set of medics had left with the injured man, sirens blasting, while the first two stayed behind. Alvarez knew that they wanted to talk to the cops, and Alvarez knew that he wanted to be as unobtrusive as possible.

He went to stand behind the couch, putting a hand on Cody's shoulder. The boy was pretty pale, but otherwise he seemed to be doing just fine. He didn't seem to be on the verge of throwing up, something cops dreaded. Someone could always be disarmed, but there was simply no way to prevent someone from barfing.

"Mrs. Travers," said the cop who seemed to be in charge, not making it a question. Sergeant Bobby Snow apparently recognized Tory right away. Alvarez just hoped that was a good thing. "Remember me? I'm the one who took the report when your employee Rodriguez was attacked, and then after—"

"Right," said Tory. It was understandable that she had no interest in rehashing old history, discussing a madman operating a rogue crane. Tory stood up. "This is my son, Cody Travers. You know Charles Henderson. He's responsible for anything having to do with this property." Even standing behind the man, Alvarez thought he could sense a wince. Tory nodded in Alvarez's direction. "He's David Alvarez. He's the El Paso detective that was involved in that other case." Since Alvarez had arrived on the scene in time to cuff a homicidal madman after Tory was done with him, Snow should know who Alvarez was, even if the two of them had never met. The two men exchanged nods.

The female medic stood quietly at attention, obviously waiting for her partner to decide what to say. The old guy cut right to the chase. "This Alvarez guy there, he showed up with the kid's mother, cleared the house. Got a problem with that?'' Snow shook his head, and the female medic let out an audible little puff of breath.

"Guy was gut-shot," the medic continued. "Unconscious, couldn't tell us anything. He'd been bleeding for a while—gonna be touch and go, whether he makes it. Concussed, too.''

"Before or after?" asked Snow.

"Can't tell," said the medic. "You think we carry a crystal ball or something?'' A gun, a bunch of blood, a dying man, everyone gets touchy.

"What can you tell me?" asked Snow.

"It's a strange one," said the medic. "Gut-shot, the guns we see these days, you woulda thought the guy'd be missing a lot more down there. Whatever shot him musta not had much firepower, or musta been something real small caliber.''

"Could he be trying to cap himself?" asked the second cop. "Maybe chicken out, lower the gun at the last moment?''

"Strange way to kill yourself," said the medic. "Wouldn't choose it myself. Didn't see no note, but then we just try to put 'em back together, we don't try to figure out who did what. You need us around any more? We're shorthanded today, two guys called in sick.''

"Same with us," said Snow. Alvarez had heard him call for backup, virtually first thing. "Go ahead, take off. We know where to find you if we need you.''

"What's the kid's part in all this?" asked the second cop, turning his attention to the little group gathered at the couch. This second cop was even younger than Snow, and now Alvarez could read Brett Reeves on his nametag.

"We know as much as you know," said Alvarez. The more he could keep Tory from interacting with the cops, the better off they'd all be. She didn't exactly have a good history with law enforcement, and stress seemed to bring out old behaviors. "Why don't we let Cody tell us what happened?"

So that was what they did. Cody did okay telling them, but just like everyone else, he didn't get in all the details the first time, and no one understood everything he was telling them the first time. Or the second. It was admittedly quite a story. There wasn't any more money blowing around outside, but at least one of the cops had brought the two money bags inside.

They were on their third go-round, and Snow was still asking questions. "So, in the time you got to know this guy, Hamiz—"

"Hafiz," said Cody.

"Hafiz," echoed Snow. "In the time you got to know Hafiz, did he tell you about anyone who might want to hurt him? Anyone he was afraid of?"

Henderson cleared his throat. "He had some problems with the man who lived next door. Before Cody." And then the cops had a second person telling a story, a story about a bizarre feud between two men, a feud having to do with paintings of Elvis and Christmas lights. It was admittedly quite a story, too—Alvarez was glad he wasn't the one telling it.

"We need to find this Josef Kunz," said Snow.

"He works for Skipper Botsford in the Biology Department," offered Henderson. "He should be there now. He works in Botsford's lab."

Snow nodded and spoke into a crackling microphone on his shoulder.

"Can we go now?" asked Tory.

Snow shook his head. "Not yet. Let me see what we find out from this Kunz and call the hospital to check on Hafiz, see if maybe he's come around and can tell us what happened. We need to hang on to your son a little longer."

"We'll take him down to the station, you're welcome to come along, ma'am," said the other cop.

"You are *not* taking my son to any station," Tory said.

"The kid's been house-sitting right next door," said Alvarez, nice and easy. "Why don't we go over there? There's a phone, we can all sit down and talk without having to worry about contaminating the scene." He'd carefully edited the word *crime* out of his last statement.

"I don't know about that," said Reeves. Shit, now the guy was pissed. "Kid could have a part in this, what with the money and all."

This time it was Snow who spoke up. "Let's slow down, Brett. Whole story has to do with the kid house-sitting. Soon as we get someone here to secure this place until it can be processed, let's go look at the kid's house."

"It isn't his house," said Tory. Damned if that wasn't a sticky issue, all the legalities that could be involved. In rental, the permission of the property owner wasn't always enough for a search warrant. And what was Cody's status? He wasn't renting the property, he was being paid to stay there. Alvarez couldn't recall ever executing a warrant with a house sitter involved, and Cody was a minor, to boot. Next thing they knew, there'd be six attorneys in the room, and five of them would be looking out to make sure the university didn't get sued.

"Henderson is Facilities Director, right?" said Alvarez, pointing out something that everyone already knew, trying not to be obvious about it. "So, if he gives you permission, and if the kid says it's okay, it should be all right to set up shop next door, at least for the moment."

Snow looked at Henderson, who nodded. "All right with you, kid?" Snow asked.

"His name is Cody," said Tory.

At sixteen, the kid had a better grasp on how to deal with cops than his mother did. "Mom," Cody said, "don't make things worse than they are already. Try being nicer."

"I'll start being nicer if this guy starts being smarter," Tory replied.

Alvarez bent down to speak softly into Tory's ear. "Sweetheart," he murmured. That always got Tory's attention. "You have the right to remain silent, so shut up."

"It's okay with me to go next door," Cody said. "I don't have anything to hide."

Now it was Alvarez who tried not to wince. He couldn't count the times that exact statement had gotten people into trouble. Maybe he was developing a split personality. He wanted to get Cody out of this situation as quickly as he could, while the detective in him wanted to suck as much information from the boy as possible. Before Alvarez had time to decide which personality to favor, Tory spoke up.

"Before we go next door, I want to look around," she said.

"What for?" asked Reeves, still pissed. "Think we're gonna plant evidence here?" Cody must want to pull the blanket over his head and melt into the couch. Alvarez didn't think that Reeves and Tory were going to develop much of a friendship.

"With all due respect, ma'am, it's a crime scene," said Snow.

"With all due respect, it's my son sitting here, and there's bags of money over there, and your partner thinks my son may be involved."

"Now that was a little hasty," admitted Snow, backpedaling fast. Reeves ready to cuff Tory at any moment, and Alvarez wasn't sure he wanted to use hardware to do it.

"I want to look around," said Tory doggedly. "You can watch me every moment. I won't touch anything. I want to see what was here when my son came in through the sliding glass door."

"Might not be a bad idea," said Alvarez, trying to sound helpful, maybe play on the fact that Snow knew that there were actually three cops in the room, not two.

"I don't see the harm in it," chimed in Henderson, surprising Alvarez that the man would weigh in on the side of anything that wasn't normal procedure. Well, if Alvarez was in Henderson's shoes, he'd want to suck up to Tory, too.

"Okay," said Snow. "Take a look around while we're waiting for backup, but don't touch anything and don't get out of my sight." Alvarez had already looked around, so he tracked Tory's gaze, tried to see what she saw as she walked over to the kitchen area.

The overwhelming image was blood on the tiled floor, so much of it, most already dried to a color verging on black. The reddish parts were mainly smear marks where the medics had done their work, some intruding into the clean spot where the unconscious man had lain. The next thing drawing attention was the gun, pushed to the side of the pool of blood. It was a big gun, that was for sure, a semiautomatic pistol of some kind. It seemed cheap, just from the look of it, one of the generic-type weapons that had proliferated everywhere.

There were all sorts of other items on the floor by the gun, things that had either been pushed aside by the medics, or were lying where they'd originally been—it would be up to someone else to figure that out. There was a hammer, a framed picture propped up against the wall, its back facing out into the room, a spool of wire, a small saw, a toolbox, a yardstick, what looked to be wire clippers, a box of nails, partially spilled. All of these things were strewn around randomly, but more or less contained in a relatively small area. There was a pencil, too, but it didn't really register with Alvarez as an item of interest.

"It looks like he was hanging a picture," observed Snow, breaking the silence.

"He was doing more than that," said Tory. "There's a rectangle marked on the wall." Trust Tory to be the one looking up when everyone else was looking down—damn, he should have paid more attention to that pencil.

"So he was making marks where he wanted to hang the picture," muttered Reeves. "So what?"

"No one draws a rectangle to hang a picture," Tory said. She made it sound as if Reeves were really stupid. "There's some plywood on the kitchen counter," she added. Sure enough, there were a few small pieces of plywood on the kitchen table. Alvarez had seen them when he'd first surveyed the kitchen area, but they hadn't been of interest to him then. Alvarez was trained to look for things that seemed out of place. The picture, the box of nails, the wire, all those seemed to fit in with a toolbox sitting on the floor. Until now.

"Hafiz waged a war with paintings," Alvarez said, thinking it out as he went along.

Tory turned back to look at Henderson. "You told us that there were problems with the energy study," Tory said. Snow looked really lost now. "Differences you couldn't explain. You said that this house was becoming less energy efficient, that it's taking more backup power to heat and cool."

"So what," said Reeves.

Tory ignored him. "That rectangle on the wall, it's smaller than the picture sitting there. A lot smaller."

"So what?" At least this time, Reeves made it a question.

"HVAC energy consumption depends on insulation effectiveness."

"She wants you to look behind the stuff hanging on the walls," said Cody. They were quite a team; the kid got it before Alvarez.

Reeves looked at Snow and Snow nodded. "Go ahead," said Snow. "I don't see where it could hurt."

Reeves turned to face one of the larger framed pictures, while pulling on a pair of latex gloves. Using one hand, he slowly nudged the frame to one side, as though he thought a venomous serpent might emerge from the wall behind the picture. What he found was a lot more innocuous—there was plywood behind the painting. Seeing this, Reeves lifted the picture off the wall, set it down at his feet. A neat rectangular surface of plywood faced out, flush with the wallboard it replaced, screws in all four corners holding it in place.

"Take the plywood off," ordered Tory. When would she get it through her head that this wasn't some construction site? She wasn't the one in charge.

"I've got a pocket knife with a screwdriver," Henderson offered, surprising Alvarez again.

"Do it," said Snow.

Reeves wasn't quick about removing the screws, maybe all of them watching made him nervous. Or maybe he was worried about what he might find, which turned out to be a rectangular plastic-wrapped package. Without looking for direction this time, Reeves lifted it out from where it sat, exposing the neatly constructed plywood niche in which it had been concealed. It was as if someone built a plywood medicine cabinet into the wall and hung a picture over it.

The package wasn't ticking, and it looked as if there were another painting inside the plastic. "Unwrap it over on that table," said Snow, before Tory could tell Reeves what to do. Everyone gathered around Reeves and his plastic-wrapped package. Anticipation seemed to run like a current through the room. Snow might have had to remove people at gunpoint if he hadn't told his partner to unwrap the thing.

Under the plastic was more plastic and a backing of plywood. But Reeves kept carefully cutting away at each layer, and eventually, a small painting was revealed, showing a group of women in ballet dresses.

It didn't do a lot for Alvarez, but Tory seemed stunned. "That's a Degas," she said.

"What's a day-gah?" asked Reeves, saving Alvarez from having to pose the question.

"Degas," said Henderson. "He's a famous artist, his work is pretty distinctive."

"Would you build a box into the wall to hide a copy?" Tory asked. She should know, since she'd grown up round the real thing.

Snow started to look behind more of the framed pictures hanging on the walls. Most hid a smaller piece of plywood, neatly inserted into the wallboard, and the Facilities Director seemed faced with facilities that had become too much for him. "Call the university Art Department," Henderson told Snow. "Get them to send Tommy Chrestman over here."

"Who's Chrestman?" asked Reeves.

"Head of the Art Department," answered Henderson.

Snow started talking into his mobile again. He asked for Chrestman and he asked for special help in processing the evidence—special help to make certain everything was identified and vouchered correctly.

"What's the deal?" asked Reeves.

"That painting that you took out of the wall looks like a Degas," explained Henderson. "It could be extremely valuable. If there's more like this, you'll need someone to tell you what comes out of the walls from behind all that plywood."

Snow cocked his head, listening to another conversation that only he could hear. "They can't find Kunz," he said. He looked at Henderson. "Your Dr. Botsford is coming over here."

"Why do we need a microbiologist over here?" asked Henderson.

"Because," replied Snow, "Botsford says Kunz hasn't shown up for work lately. After the first day, he started calling Kunz's home phone number—the new one, he says."

"Sounds like Botsford," said Henderson. "So where is Kunz?"

"Botsford says he's been calling for three days now, and no one answers." There was silence while everyone seemed to think that over, then two more campus cops showed up.

"I think it's time we moved everyone out of here." Reeves made it a statement, and Alvarez certainly agreed.

EIGHT

Arrival of the Wise Men

AND SO THE GROUP decamped to Con House, leaving the two new cops on guard next door. Snow kept talking into his mobile about processing. Alvarez wondered what crime scene capabilities the campus department had, what agencies they used for special expertise, and decided it would not be diplomatic to ask. It was telling enough that Snow told the two uniforms not to touch anything—he was obviously requesting cavalry of some kind.

Everyone seemed to mill around at Con House, uneasy with the situation, mixed alliances floating around everywhere. The campus cops didn't know whether Alvarez was really for them or against them. Snow wasn't totally comfortable setting up shop next door to the crime scene. Cody didn't know if he wanted to stick close to his mom or not, and Henderson looked wary of every single person in their motley group.

Tory dropped straight down onto the couch in the living room, the couch that was identical to the one Cody had been sitting on previously. Cody seemed to think it over, then sat on the couch next to her.

The cops took a cursory look through the small house, checking behind the pictures hanging on the walls, finding no plywood inserted into the wallboard anywhere. Then they gravitated toward the kitchen, as cops usually did.

If it wasn't a kid living in the house, there might have

been a decent chance for coffee all round. Alvarez followed
the two cops into the kitchen, opened the fridge. There were
a few food items and a six-pack of Mountain Dew. Alvarez
closed the refrigerator door.

Henderson couldn't decide where to place himself, with
the three cops in the kitchen, or with the two civilians in
the living room. "I'm going to the john," he said. He
headed down the hall. Then four things happened in quick
succession.

There was a knock on the front door. Snow walked out
of the kitchen area, past the dining room table, past Tory
and Cody. He opened the door. Henderson yelled, and
Reeves drew his gun. Snow swiveled his head back and
forth between the new arrival at the doorstep and his partner, who was swiveling his gun back and forth in the hall.
Alvarez was only a few feet from Reeves. Trying not to
move a muscle, he hinted to Reeves, "Gun control—use
two hands."

Henderson was frozen halfway inside the bathroom.
"What the hell are you doing?" he yelled at Reeves. Mean-
while, a man stood motionless at the front door, next to
Snow, who had his hand on his own gun now.

"What the hell were you yelling about?" Reeves shouted
at Henderson. Snow didn't draw his gun, but he still had
his hand there, and he was still looking back and forth between the new arrival and the action in hallway. Henderson
looked ready to bolt back into the bathroom for cover;
Reeves still hadn't lowered his gun.

Cody spoke up from where he sat on the couch. "I told
you that I put Tango in the bathroom."

"Don't shoot my dog," Tory told Reeves. At least she
didn't stand up to present a target. "Cody told you he was
in that bathroom."

"Why didn't you check the bathroom?" Snow demanded
of his partner, who was finally lowering his gun.

"Because the kid told us he'd put the dog in the bathroom, that's why I didn't check it," Reeves yelled back, obviously still on an adrenaline high, not willing to take the fall for the dog-in-the-bathroom encounter. "And we weren't clearing the damn house, that's why." In an interesting reversal of the usual sequence of events whenever someone drew a gun, Henderson now threw up his hands.

"I'm sorry," he told Reeves. "I didn't remember about the dog. He's really big, I stepped on him, then he started moving—"

"He goes to sleep whenever he's shut up in a room," said Cody, sounding defensive. "Sometimes it takes him a while to wake up."

"Why didn't you remind me he was in the bathroom?" asked Henderson.

"I forgot," Cody said.

"He'd already told you once," Tory added.

Tango came out of the bathroom. He squeezed past Henderson and headed for the kitchen area, appearing a little sluggish, but still wagging his tail at the unexpected company.

"That's one big dog," said Snow.

"What did I tell you?" asked Henderson.

"I'm Skipper Botsford," said the man at the front door. "I'm supposed to talk to the campus police—the ones who want to know about Josef Kunz."

"What the hell do we do with the dog?" asked Reeves. Tango was busy sniffing at Snow. Snow didn't seem like a man who liked dogs.

"Put him back in the bathroom," ordered Snow. It wasn't clear who he was speaking to.

"I'm Skipper Botsford," the man at the door announced again.

"But I need to use the bathroom," said Henderson.

"I'll put him out in the backyard," said Reeves.

"But that's how the whole thing started," Cody said. "If

you put him out in the backyard, he'll start digging more holes."

"For God's sake," snapped Tory. "I'll shut the dog in the bedroom. Is anyone going to need the bedroom any time soon?" No one said anything. Tory got up from the couch, took the affable hound by his collar, pulled him away from Snow, down the hall and shut him in the bedroom.

"I'm Skipper Botsford," said the man at the front door for the third time. Tory sat back down on the couch.

Snow seemed to be recovering from his hound encounter. "Come inside," he said.

"Could someone tell me what's going on?" asked Botsford. Alvarez thought that sounded like a fair question.

"Have a seat," offered Snow. He gestured to the dining room table, introduced himself and Reeves. Snow filled Botsford in on the recent events at Sol House. While Snow was still talking, Henderson returned and sat down at the table with Botsford. Maybe he'd finally found a group to join.

"Do you have any idea where Kunz might be?" Snow asked Botsford. The microbiologist shook his head. "Anything ever happen like this before?" Botsford shook his head again. "Kunz a good worker up till now?" Botsford nodded. Perhaps he'd used up his store of words by standing at the front door and introducing himself three times. "Kunz ever say anything about living here, about problems with the guy next door?" asked Snow.

Botsford glanced at Snow, glanced away. "Yeah," he said.

"What does that mean?"

"Josef had problems when he lived here. He told me about his next-door neighbor, said he started out asking him about his family, where he came from, who he was related to. Then the guy started arguing with him, insulting him. Finally started threatening him."

It was as if once the floodgates were opened, the professor had a lot of words stored up. "Josef talked to me about it, talked to other people who work in my lab. It got in the way of his work. I'm the one who told him he needed to move away from here." Botsford paused, looked around. "Funny, I always knew where this place was, but I've never been inside. It's kind of nice."

"So you told this Josef Kunz that he should get out, he should move somewhere else?" Snow tried to bring Botsford back on topic.

"Yeah." Botsford glanced at Snow, glanced away again. Maybe he'd be more at ease if Snow put questions under a slide in front of a microscope and let him focus his gaze there. "I told him he needed to do something about the problem, do something so he wouldn't be distracted. My work, it's really important. Not worth letting something get in the way, not something like a next-door neighbor, or living in a certain house." Botsford sent another quick glance in Snow's direction. "It's hanta, you know."

The silence in the room was deafening. Nobody wanted to ask the next question; it made Alvarez glad to be a bystander. It was a dirty job, but someone had to do it.

Snow leaned in close to Botsford. "You're faculty, right?" Botsford was back to nodding. "Got a doctorate, work in the biology department?" Botsford kept nodding. "But you're sitting here telling me that the house was haunted." Snow made it an accusation.

Botsford looked at Snow, blinked. "This house? It's haunted? Who said it was haunted?"

Reeves dropped into a chair at the dining room table, put his face a few inches from the puzzled professor. "You said it was haunted, buddy. I heard it. You just told my partner here."

"I'm called Skipper, not Buddy—Skipper," Botsford said, glaring at Reeves. "But it's Dr. Botsford to you. I don't like how you're talking to me. I came over here, interrupted my day, just to help out."

"There's no need to insult Dr. Botsford," Henderson told Reeves.

Alvarez decided there were too many people gathered around the table. He walked into the living room area and sat down in one of the two chairs across from the couch. "Too many cooks in the kitchen for you?" Tory asked him. At least she spoke quietly.

"Macho Law prevents me from answering," he told her sotto voce.

"I was talking about my work," Botsford told Reeves. "How important it is. HVS can be lethal. Just wait until there's another dry season and mice start coming into your home." That was certainly a threat that was new to Alvarez.

"He's talking about hanta, about hantavirus," Cody explained. "The thing that killed some people in the Four Corners area a few years ago. It's carried by mice. We studied it in biology for current affairs, and again in biochemistry."

"That right?" Snow asked Botsford. "You're researching something called hantavirus?"

"That's what I've been telling you," affirmed Botsford. "That's what we're working on—me, Josef, everyone in my lab—hantavirus."

Snow decided to abandon this line of questioning, looked at Henderson. "This Josef Kunz, he threatened the guy who got shot? The guy told you that?" Snow was getting ready to take an action; he wanted to be sure.

"Yes," said Henderson, back to looking uncomfortable. "But there were mitigating circumstances. They're both from Bosnia, different cultures, different—"

"I don't care if they were Hatfields and McCoys," growled Snow. "Did the guy who got shot, this Bamia guy, tell you that Kunz threatened him?"

"Yes," answered Henderson. He looked unhappy at his own answer.

"Let's put out an APB, pick him up," Snow said to

Reeves. He turned back to Botsford. "Think Kunz could be dangerous?"

"I don't know," said Botsford. "I suppose anyone could be dangerous. When I got here, your partner had his gun drawn, pointed at the Facilities Director and a dog."

Before someone could respond to that, there was another knock on the door. "Want me to get it?" Alvarez asked, and Snow shrugged. Alvarez crossed the room and opened the door. A short, dapper-looking portly man, with long gray hair tied back in a ponytail, stood where Botsford had stood before. He wore a dark-maroon jacket, black turtle-neck sweater, and black slacks. His shiny black shoes looked as expensive to Alvarez as the gun next door had looked cheap.

"I'm Tommy Chrestman," the man said. "Dr. Chrest-man, from the Art Department. Charles Henderson asked for me to come over here, take a look at some things—" His words faltered as he peered into the house. It seemed no one had filled him in.

"Come on in," said Alvarez. It was lucky he hadn't broken out the Mountain Dew. There wouldn't be nearly enough to go around.

Snow made introductions again. "We'd like you to look at a painting we found next door. Officer Reeves will go with you. We want to know if you think it's the real thing."

Reeves balked. "Shouldn't we wait for processing?" he asked Snow.

"I don't want to wait for anything." That was Tory is-suing orders again. "If it hadn't been for me, you wouldn't even know about the painting. Cody's had a horrible shock—I want to take him home."

Snow squatted, got on eye-level with Cody. "I'd like you to stay," he told the boy. Snow pointed in the general area of the dining room table. "You're the one told me that the guy over there was talking about hantavirus. You might be able to give us some more help. You okay with hanging around a little while longer? You're not feeling faint, are you, like you need to go home and lie down?'' Even for a cop, that was low.

''The kid needs to stay.'' Reeves was talking to Tory. ''You help us, we help you. Otherwise, we might have to impound the dog.'' Now that was really low. ''Material witness,'' Reeves added for emphasis.

''Evidence,'' Snow corrected.

''I'm okay,'' said Cody. ''I don't mind sticking around— I'd like to help.'' Tory gave her son a look capable of turning someone into granite.

Snow stood up again. ''Take Dr. Chrestman next door, show him what we found,'' he told Reeves. ''Maybe look behind one of the other pieces of plywood.''

''There goes the energy study,'' said Tory.

Snow ignored her. ''Last thing we need, cops getting sued over something valuable getting handled wrong.''

''Let's go,'' Reeves told Chrestman.

''Would someone please tell me what's going on?'' Chrestman asked.

''Tommy,'' said Henderson, ''just go next door, look at some things the officer wants to show you, come back and tell us what you think.''

For a small man in the hands of a determined cop, Chrestman didn't move an inch. ''I want to know what's going on,'' he persisted.

''Tommy,'' said Henderson again, ''go next door with the officer. We think there may be a Degas next door.''

''Oh,'' breathed Chrestman in a tone of awe. He turned and went without another word.

''Okay,'' said Snow, turning his attention back to the two men sitting at the dining room table. ''You both know this Kunz. You think he could be dangerous?''

Tory wasn't giving up so easily. ''So after you process the scene, then can we go? You have no idea what you're looking at over there—processing could take forever.''

"We'll discuss it when we start the processing," replied Snow.

"But you don't even know when that will be, do you?" asked Tory.

"Mrs. Travers," said Snow, "you'll know as soon as I do. Right now, I need to concentrate on getting information to put out an APB for this Josef Kunz." Someone else knocked on the door.

"Want me to get it?" asked Alvarez.

"Why not." Snow didn't make it a question.

Alvarez opened the door again. Con House was certainly getting to be a popular destination. This time there were two people on the doorstep, a young man and woman, both good-looking. The young man was tall and thin, with dark hair and serious eyebrows over an intense gaze. The woman was short but trim, with a mass of curly black hair and a friendly smile. "Hi," she said. "We're looking for Dr. Botsford. His secretary told us he was over here." She managed to make it a casual request accompanied by a smile, and it took a real optimist to ignore a pair of police cars parked at the curb.

Alvarez was a detective—he was trained to investigate. "Who are you?" he asked.

"I'm Josef Kunz," the young man answered. Alvarez stepped aside so the two men sitting at the dining room table, Henderson and Botsford, could get a good look at the couple on the doorstep and vice versa. "I want to know why there are policemen here." The young man seemed on a par with Tory at issuing commands.

"That's Josef Kunz," said Henderson.

"It certainly is," Botsford echoed. "It's Josef and Bridget."

Snow was a trained detective, too. "Who's Bridget?" he asked.

"She's a graduate student," said Botsford. "She works

with Josef in my lab. She hasn't been coming to work, either.''

Snow stared at Botsford. "Someone else went missing from your lab, and you didn't tell me?" His voice was as cold as his name.

"You didn't ask."

Alvarez closed his eyes for a moment. It was good that there were strict rules governing the use of weapons. Otherwise, a lot of civilians like Botsford would get shot during investigations.

Bridget didn't wait for an invitation. She came inside, taking Kunz by the hand and bringing him inside with her. "I'm Bridget Charson," she said. "Josef and I both work for Dr. Botsford, and he's right. We just up and disappeared for the last few days. That's why we wanted to find Dr. Botsford—we want to apologize, tell him what happened.'' Bridget gave Botsford a smile that would melt any employer's heart.

"What happened?" asked Snow, right on the ball.

Bridget's smile got even brighter. "It's one of those things, if we didn't do it on the spur of the moment, maybe we wouldn't have the nerve to do it at all." Bridget looked straight at Botsford. "We want to make it right—we're sorry we didn't let you know."

"Know what?" asked Botsford. Maybe he was detective material, too.

"We got married," Bridget said. "We did it on impulse. We just got in the car, drove to Las Vegas and got married.''

"But that's impossible," Botsford said, then turned an interesting shade of red.

"What do you mean, it's impossible?" Snow asked. Maybe Snow would shoot the microbiologist yet.

"Because—because—" stammered Botsford. "Because Bridget's Jewish," he blurted out.

"You're Jewish?" Tory asked blankly. "Your name is

Bridget, and you're Jewish?'' And she was usually so politically correct.

"Yes,'' Bridget told Tory. "I'm Jewish. You think we
all have names like Shoshanna Finkelstein? My mother
liked the name. I'm Jewish, and I'm named Bridget.'' Henderson put his elbows on the table, put his forehead in his
hands so he was no longer looking at the rest of them.
"Josef is Catholic, so what? We love each other, we got
married.''

"I'd say that definitely qualifies as an alibi,'' Alvarez
told Snow. He couldn't help himself.

"It doesn't matter if we got married or not,'' said Kunz.
His face looked stony; he certainly didn't seem to have his
new wife's sunny disposition. "If we miss work, we need
to talk to Dr. Botsford, not the police. Why are the police
here? Why is Dr. Botsford here?''

"Come in and sit down.'' Snow pointed to the two empty
chairs at the table. He asked Kunz a few questions and
explained the bare basics of what had happened. To their
credit, the newlyweds were doing a good job of looking
horrified when Reeves and Chrestman returned from next
door.

They didn't knock, so at least Alvarez didn't have to play
doorman again. Chrestman was about five steps ahead of
Reeves, talking excitedly from the moment he walked in
the door.

"It's a Degas, you were right,'' he told Henderson. "We
found some drawings, early Picasso, I'm almost certain.''
Chrestman rattled off a few other names Alvarez didn't recognize. "And—there's a Kadensky,'' he ended reverentially.

"How'd he come up with all that?'' Snow asked Reeves.

"Where'd they come from?'' Reeves asked in response,
looking at the two newcomers.

"What's a Kadensky?'' asked Tory.

"It's a blue rider," said Chrestman. "Not only a Kaden-sky, but a blue rider."

"I couldn't see it," stated Reeves. "Not the painting, I mean, the blue rider."

Snow didn't seem to care about any blue rider. "How does Dr. Chrestman know about all this stuff?" he persisted.

"You said to look behind one more piece of plywood," answered Reeves. "Once we got started, Dr. Chrestman here, he didn't want to stop."

"Can I be there when you open up the rest?" asked Chrestman.

"That's a good question," said Tory. "When will you get someone here to start processing the scene? I want to take Cody home."

"Who are those two?" Reeves could be persistent himself.

There was yet another knock on the door. This time Alvarez answered without asking.

A UPS deliveryman in a heavy jacket stood outside. Alvarez could see that his van was parked a ways up the street. Admittedly, street parking in front of the two small houses had become scarce.

"UPS," the guy said, and no one challenged his statement. "Has something happened to Mr. Bamia?" he asked. "I'm looking for Hafiz Bamia."

NINE

Holiday Deliveries

TORY FELT LIKE calling out a warning to this newest arrival standing at the doorstep to the crowded House from Hell—run, run, before they make you come inside. But Snow jumped right in with his finely honed interrogation techniques. "Why are you looking for Hafiz Bamia?" he asked, and it was too late for the man to save himself.

"Because I'm UPS," said the hapless man.

Snow walked over to the front door where David was still standing. "You better come in," he said. "I need to talk to you."

"I'm on a schedule—"

"I don't care," Maybe Snow was starting to snap, try saying that three times real fast and see where it got you. "I'm telling you to come inside and talk to me. It'll just take a few minutes, but I'm not going to talk to you standing there."

"Well—" The UPS man wavered, and again, the moment for escape was lost. Snow ushered him into the living room, into the midst of all the people gathered inside. "Take a seat," Snow told the UPS man, something that was easier said than done. "No one is going anywhere until I get some answers."

"You have no right to tell me what to do—" Kunz said immediately. Tory personally thought Kunz had the right idea, but his new bride cut him off midsentence.

"Don't be ridiculous, Jay," she told him. Jay? "It will just make things more difficult if we don't cooperate now. Besides, I want to find out more about what's going on. I especially want to know about the Kadensky."

"What's a Kadensky?" asked Botsford.

"Never mind," Henderson told the biologist, but his words didn't matter.

"Kadensky's a Russian painter, the father of abstract art as we know it today," said Chrestman. He looked like a man who had seen the Holy Grail.

"I thought that was Picasso," said Botsford.

"Dr. Botsford," began Snow. "Unless I ask you a direct question, please be quiet." Botsford opened his mouth, closed it. "Like I said, take a seat," Snow said to the UPS guy.

Chrestman dropped into one of the two vacant room chairs, the UPS man sat in the other. It wasn't like they had a lot of choices by this time. Snow remained standing in the living room while his partner hovered over the group at the dining room table. David leaned on the wall by the front door. Maybe he assumed he was part of the group that didn't have to take a seat, then again, maybe he was positioned to open the door for the next caller.

"So, you're looking for Mr. Bamia," Snow said to the UPS guy. The man was still staring at everyone; maybe he hadn't had time to count them all yet. "Do you have something to deliver to him?"

"No."

"Are you picking something up, then, something he's sending somewhere?"

"No."

"Then why are you looking for Mr. Bamia?" Snow sounded downright peevish. "And don't tell me you're the UPS man—that's not an answer to my question. You could be the milkman, and you wouldn't have any business looking for Mr. Bamia unless you were delivering milk or picking up the empties, would you?'' asked Snow. Had anyone in this room ever even seen a milkman before? It probably wasn't a good time to pose the question.

"I stop at Mr. Bamia's house every day," said the UPS man. "Every weekday, that is," he amended carefully, looking up at Snow. If someone didn't do something, they would all go on sitting in this house together forever, all eleven of them in this little one-bedroom house, and at some point, there were certain practicalities to consider. Tango hadn't been outside in quite a while, and Tory didn't want her dog accused of any more wrongdoings, especially not in Henderson's presence.

"You stop at Bamia's house every day?" asked Tory.

"Yes, yes, he did," said Kunz suddenly. "When I lived here, next door to Bamia, I see this man and his truck, many times. Every day I see them."

Snow shot a warning look in Tory's direction, but she ignored him, focused on the UPS guy. Up close, he was kind of good-looking, "That's unusual, isn't it, daily UPS pickup at a private residence?"

The UPS man seemed to consider whether this might be a trick question. Tory needed to ask him his name, stop thinking of him as the UPS man. "Yeah, it's unusual, but there's nothing wrong with daily pickup at a residence."

"I know," said Tory. "We have daily UPS pickup at my office."

"Good," said the UPS man. "UPS appreciates all our customers. I hope you get good service."

Maybe Tory didn't want to know this man's name after all. "But we have to pay extra for it," she said. "We pay for UPS to come every day to the office, whether we have something to send out or not."

"You could do it the other way," the UPS man suggested. "You could call every time you have a pickup, but then you'd have to pay for each pickup." He seemed apologetic about having to give Tory the downside of this alternative.

"So if Mr. Bamia paid for daily pickup, he must be sending out a lot of items, using UPS a lot," said Tory.

"You could say that," the UPS man ventured. "It depends on what you call a lot."

Quantifying "a lot" could wait for later. Maybe never. "Have you been on this particular route a long time?"

"What do you call a long time?"

Tory should have seen that one coming. "How long have you been on this route?"

"Three years. That's considered pretty long, although—"

"So you must know something about where Mr. Bamia sends things, where his deliveries come from."

"Of course," the UPS man answered. "But is it okay to tell?"

This was Snow's cue. "Of course it's okay to tell. Mr. Bamia was hurt sometime early this morning."

"That's terrible," said the UPS man. "I knew something was wrong the minute I saw policemen at his house. They wouldn't answer any of my questions. That's why I came over here to ask about Mr. Bamia."

"We're trying to find out what happened," said Snow.

"And me telling you about where Mr. Bamia ships things, where his deliveries come from, that might help you figure out how he got hurt?"

"Yes," said Tory. Why give an explanation when a simple answer would do?

"Do you want to know about now, or before?" The guy was on a roll.

"Both," said Tory, jumping in again before Snow could speak.

"When I first got the route, Mr. Bamia, he shipped big things to New York City, and little things to Bosnia. I noticed that early on, Bosnia being kind of unusual, and he gets stuff regular from Bosnia, too. Then, eight, nine months ago, poof, no more big stuff for New York. Now everything is Bosnia, just Bosnia, back and forth.''

"Do you know where he sent the big things to, back when he was sending things to New York City?" asked Tory.

"That's easy, because he always shipped to the same person, and after you see a name over and over, you remember. Bamia used to send stuff to a guy named Ernie Lerner.''

"Ernie Lerner?" asked Chrestman. His newfound glow seemed to fade a little.

"That name mean something to you?" Snow asked Chrestman.

"I'm familiar with it,'' said Chrestman.

"Why?" Snow asked.

"Ernie was a graduate student of mine, he went to work for a gallery in New York after he finished here, a gallery called Nuance." Chrestman paused. "He still works there.''

"Ernest Lerner?'' Now it was Henderson joining the conversation. "An Ernest Lerner used to live here, right here in this house. This Lerner works at a gallery in New York now? And his old next-door neighbor had a *Kadensky* hidden in his house, behind some framed print?''

"*In* the wall,'' stressed Tory. "That's important. Remember the problems with the energy study? Bamia was removing insulation and replacing it with artwork.''

"Mom, no one cares about the energy study,'' Cody interjected.

"Mrs. Travers—'' Snow began.

"What? If I talk too much, are you going to tell me to leave? That's fine, as long as Cody comes with me.''

"There's always the dog—'' said Reeves.

"Don't even start with me,'' Tory told him. "You will not win. I'll make one call, get an attorney over here, and we'll see who gets to keep the dog.''

"Okay, Okay," said Snow. "Calm down, you two. Exactly where are you going with this, Mrs. Travers?"

Tory didn't really know, so it was fortunate that Chrestman spoke up. "There's something maybe you should know about Ernie," said Chrestman.

"Yes, something you maybe need to know." Henderson sounded like an echo.

"What, the guy has a record?" asked Reeves.

"No," said Chrestman. "Not anything like that."

"What then?" Snow demanded.

There was another pause. "This is awkward," said Chrestman.

"Yes, awkward," echoed Henderson.

It looked as if David was losing patience with his role of objective observer. "What's more awkward," he said, "is for somebody to get shot, and someone else is too embarrassed to say whatever might help the cops figure out what happened. I know we've got a Jew, a Catholic and a Latino in this room. If someone in this room is gay, I don't give a damn. What do the two of you know about this guy who used to live here, this Earnest Lerner?"

"He's from the U.K.," said Chrestman.

"He's black," added Henderson. Tory felt as if they were playing guessing games with Henderson and Chrestman on one team, everybody else on another. She thought her team needed more clues, then suddenly she got it.

"You think that because he's black, he might be Muslim, right?" she asked.

Henderson nodded. "He is Muslim," Chrestman said. "Ernie, that is. Is Bamia Muslim?" Tory nodded. "I didn't want to make any assumptions. A name like Bamia, you never know, and I didn't want to assume that someone had a certain religion because of his name—"

"Did Bamia and Lerner get along okay?" Tory asked Henderson.

"They got along fine," Henderson said. "Bamia never

had any problems with anybody until—'' He seemed to remember who was in the room, and stopped midsentence.

"What kind of packages did Mr. Bamia send out, when he was still sending stuff to New York?" Tory asked the UPS guy.

The man seemed to ponder her question. "Well, he always packed his stuff real careful, I can tell you that." Maybe the guy really was trying to be helpful, maybe someday he'd hit it big on a UPS Deliveryman calendar, and she'd be glad she'd been nice to him.

"Were his packages to New York the size and shape you might use for framed art?"

"Well, yes, I guess so, maybe."

"What kind of packages did he send to Bosnia?"

"Oh, none of those were packages. That would be a whole different deal, what with customs and all. No, all the stuff back and forth from Bosnia, those were letter envelopes, the kind that only hold printed matter."

"Like U.S. currency," suggested David.

"Oh, no," said the UPS man. "I don't think they're supposed to be used for that."

But David was talking to Snow now. "When we helped Cody move in here, I talked to Bamia about how his interest in art conflicted with my assumptions about Muslims. He said that many modern affluent Muslims collect European artwork just like anyone else."

"If he was selling art in New York, then sending currency back home, how was he getting the art to begin with?" asked Tory.

David shrugged. "Courier? I don't know."

"Why all the secrecy? There's nothing illegal about selling artwork for other people, is there?" she asked.

"Not unless it's stolen," David replied.

"And that's the problem, isn't it?" said Bridget, speaking up from the dining room table. "He didn't want the scrutiny that comes with selling through a gallery."

''What scrutiny?'' asked Tory, beating Snow to the punch. Cops might want to know whodunit, but engineers wanted to know everything about anything.

''Scrutiny by people looking for Nazi-seized art,'' explained Chrestman. ''There are organizations dedicated to identifying art that was seized unlawfully by the Germans during World War Two.''

''But that was over sixty years ago,'' commented Tory. ''Is it illegal now, to sell artwork that was seized by the Nazis?''

''The courts will be wrestling over that question for a long time,'' said Chrestman. ''Whether a certain piece of art is even subject to scrutiny depends on the piece, the artist, the provenance. Selling stolen art is illegal. If there's a possibility of Nazi seizure, selling might be legal but highly unethical. But if this Bamia guy was selling art, and he was sending it to Nuance, we don't even know if it was selling out the front door or the back door.''

''What do you mean, selling out the back door?'' asked David.

Chrestman didn't look enthused about giving an explanation. ''If a collector is looking for something in particular, someone who works in a gallery may know another collector—or anyone really—who's selling that item. If the transaction is arranged privately, without going through the gallery, it's selling out the back door.''

''Back door, front door, sounds like we need to get in touch with Lerner,'' said Snow. ''See what he has to say about all this.''

Chrestman cleared his throat. ''Ernie's wife became good friends with my wife while Ernie was in school here.'' Chrestman cleared his throat again. ''Ernie and his wife are staying with us for the Christmas holidays.''

''They're staying here?'' Snow was incredulous. ''At your house? This guy is at your house this very minute?'' Chrestman nodded, all the glow of viewing a Kadensky long forgotten. "Call him," Snow said. "Tell him to get over here. Now."

Chrestman said, "I'd like a little privacy—"

"You gonna tip him off or something?" asked Reeves.

Chrestman gave the cop a look of pure disgust. "His wife is six months pregnant. I don't think they're going on the run. Besides, even if Ernie was selling out the back door, it might be perfectly legal."

"Call him, tell him to come over here, now," said Snow.

"I'm not going to make that phone call, not here in front of everyone. Ernie is a friend, and I don't think he's done anything wrong."

"Okay, fine," said Snow. "But you tell him that if he's not over here in the next twenty minutes, I'm sending someone to get him."

Chrestman stood up and took the cordless phone off the kitchen wall. "I'm going into the bedroom."

"No!" and "Don't go in the bedroom!" At least three people said something simultaneously.

"My dog's in the bedroom," called out Cody. "Asleep."

"Well, I'll try not to disturb your dog then, young man."

"It's a really big dog," said Snow.

"But he's friendly," Cody added immediately.

"It's not a problem," stated Chrestman. "I like dogs." He disappeared into the bedroom, closed the door behind him, and when there was no immediate call for aid, Snow continued his questioning.

"Did Mr. Bamia tell you why he stopped making shipments to this Lerner guy in New York?" Snow asked the UPS guy, who shook his head. "This was about eight, nine months ago?" The UPS man nodded.

"That's about the same time that I started getting complaints from you," Henderson said to Kunz.

"That's when it started, back in the spring," related Kunz. "First few months, no problem. Then, problem starts. Problem gets bigger, always bigger, no matter what I tell him, no matter what I tell you.'' Kunz spread his hands so widely that he almost sideswiped his new wife, who ducked just in time. "Finally, I leave, I have no other choice."

"When Bamia started feuding with you, that's when he started the deal of hanging more and more artwork in these houses—'' Henderson broke off, and everyone looked at the walls, which had more framed art per square foot than most museums. Chrestman came out of the bedroom.

"Ernie is on his way over," the art professor reported. "He says he got friendly with Bamia when he lived here, felt sorry for the man. Bamia has a background in art, I guess his family and some of his friends had significant collections. Some of them started sending him art, pieces they'd collected, pieces they needed to turn into cash, fast. Ernie helped Bamia make a few sales here locally, then when he went to New York, the volume got big. Really big." Chrestman shook his head.

He looked shaken, and Tory wondered what names had been named in his telephone conversation. Maybe it was like being an addict working in proximity to your addiction—the constant temptation to arrange some transaction if it would give you a chance to have an idolized item to yourself, even if just for a little while.

"Did Lerner say how Bamia got the art?" asked Snow.

Chrestman shook his head. "He said he didn't know, and that he didn't ask. Ernie feels certain that the pieces came from collections of people Bamia knew back in Sarajevo, back when he was a professor."

"So it got to be too big, and your friend got scared?" Snow asked.

Chrestman shook his head again. "No. Ernie says that everything was legit, but Bamia wanted to deal with Ernie, not with a gallery. Ernie just assumed that Bamia was sending back money to help family and former friends in Eastern Europe."

"Then why did it stop?"

"Ernie says that in the beginning, Bamia took checks as long as Ernie would vouch for the buyer. Then Bamia started telling Ernie to take the checks from the buyers, turn them into cash and send the cash. Ernie offered to run the sales through his own account, then wire the money to Bamia's account. That worked for a while, but then Bamia started demanding cash, and nothing but cash, in return for the art. I guess they got into an argument, and Bamia told Ernie that he'd closed out all his accounts, he didn't trust banks any more. Ernie said he went out of his way to help the guy, because he knew there was a good reason why Bamia was doing what he was doing, but it got too weird. He said Bamia got too weird. Ernie's last sale for Bamia was sometime last spring."

"Why would anyone bury money in the backyard, unless it was dirty?" asked Reeves.

"You come from where we come from, you'd bury money, too," said Jay-Josef. "Bury gold, even better. We put money in bank, war come, money gone. We put new money in new bank, new war, money gone."

"What a waste," murmured Bridget, sounding sincerely regretful. "Burying cash in the backyard."

"If you sent money back home, would you send U.S. currency?" David asked Kunz.

The young man nodded. "U.S. money, next best thing to gold."

"When Lerner stopped selling the art for Bamia, it must have started to pile up," said Snow.

"Those cabinets in the walls were amazingly well constructed," said Tory. "What I want to know is how Bamia got the carpentry skills to build them.

"That's easy," answered Chrestman. "Lots of people who work with art—teachers, museum workers, even collectors—they develop carpentry skills because of the special wooden crates that are built for valuable pieces of art. Some museums have people on staff who do nothing but crate and uncrate art. Collectors use crates when they make sales, buy pieces.''

"Put the money and the artwork aside," David said. "Who shot Bamia?"

"Not me," stated Kunz emphatically.

"Me, either," the UPS man said. "I didn't shoot him."

"Who would stand to profit from his death?" David persisted

"Someone who took Ernie's place?" suggested Snow.

"No," said Tory slowly. "If the person who shot Bamia was in on the art sales, why leave either the art or the money? I found the art, Tango found the money."

"Maybe someone who was in on the deal, but got scared, didn't want to get caught?" suggested Reeves.

"Caught at what?" David asked.

"Smuggling art," said Reeves.

David shrugged. "If Bamia got the art covertly, it doesn't mean the art was smuggled. Covert isn't always the same as illegal, same as selling out the back door."

"What about sending currency out of the country?" asked Reeves.

"Don't look at me," said the UPS man. "Someone writes 'printed matter' down on the shipping label, that's what I put into the computer."

"How about selling Nazi-seized art?" Reeves obviously wanted to arrest someone for something.

"Ernie said—" Chrestman started to protest, but Bridget interrupted him.

"What's the point?" she said. "Even if Bamia was doing something illegal, there's no way to prove it now. He sounds like someone who needs to be helped, not punished."

"But Bridget—" protested her new husband.

She went on as if he hadn't spoken. "He was trying to help people, people in trouble." She turned to Jay-Josef. "Jay, we need to help him. He needs help. He must be a very sick man, sick with post-traumatic stress, culture shock, anxiety, paranoia—''

"Cody told us about the gun when we got here," Tory said. "Even if he didn't tell anyone beforehand." She shot her son a hard look before continuing. "The way Cody tells it, Bamia acted like he thought he had to keep the gun handy at all times. Do you think he might have been crazy enough to carry it around with him, no matter what he was doing?"

"Yes," said Henderson.

"Yes," repeated Kunz.

"Yes," echoed Cody fervently.

David said, "Define *crazy* in politically correct terms." But she ignored him.

"Let me go back next door," Tory told Snow. "I'll show you what happened—I'll show you how Bamia got shot."

"This I gotta see," interjected Reeves.

Snow stared at Tory. He was remembering, she knew it. He was remembering that other time, in another season, when he'd dismissed her statements, when he'd been wrong and she'd been right. "No," Snow said slowly to Reeves. "This I gotta see. You stay here with these people. I'll be back."

"Cody comes with me," Tory insisted. "I don't want him out of my sight."

"Done," agreed Snow.

"I'm coming," said David.

"Stay here," said Snow. "She'll be fine on her own."

"It's not her I'm looking out for," countered David, and sure enough, Snow let him tag along.

TEN

Wrapping Things Up

BY THE TIME their small group returned to Sol House, the two cops who were keeping the scene secure must have succumbed to boredom. In addition to the usual placement of crime scene tape, there was what appeared to be one continuous length of tape wrapped around the entire house, starting on one side of the front door and ending on the other side. It was the most creative use of crime scene tape that Tory had ever witnessed. If they'd only tied it off with a bow, and if the colors had been red and green instead of yellow and black, the result might even look like Christmas decorations. But then that very sort of ethnocentrism, the assumption that familiar behaviors should be recognized and adopted by everyone, was partly to blame for this whole mess.

Snow signed the four of them in on the log the two cops had started—they had obviously taken him seriously about doing things by the book. "When will processing support get here?" one cop asked Snow.

"Soon," Snow replied cryptically, and led the way inside. "Listen," he said to Tory, "I'm stretching things by bringing you back over here. What is it that you want to show me? Don't disturb anything, and make it quick."

"I'll bet I'm done before your processing support ever shows up." This earned a glare from Snow, a raised eyebrow from David and rolled eyes from her own son. "We all agree that there was no sign of forced entry, right?"

"Yeah, except for the glass door your kid broke down," replied Snow. Well, what could she expect? David had tried to tell her that it didn't pay to be sarcastic with a cop on duty.

"Except for that," she conceded. "And we all agree that it looks as though Hafiz was working on constructing another hiding place in the wall. A hiding place to be concealed by a hanging picture."

"Yeah," Snow said.

"And that he was shot in the early morning, not too long before Cody found him."

"Yeah," Snow said again.

"And that he had exhibited unbalanced behavior for a while now—paranoia, secrecy, threats. It seems he had this mission to sell valuable art for his friends and family back in Eastern Europe, but because he insisted on cash payments, he lost his means of selling, his means of turning art into money. But the art kept coming in. Maybe Hafiz had just a few hiding places to begin with, but now he needed hiding places all over the house."

"Yeah, so tell me something I don't know."

Tory continued her story. "Maybe that's when he started keeping a gun around, when this valuable art started to accumulate. At the same time, Hafiz is stuck with an enemy for a next-door neighbor, a guy who has this last name Kunz, a name Hafiz associates with some atrocity against him or his family. On top of all this, Kunz accuses Hafiz's people of being responsible for the same violence that made Hafiz leave his country. Then that neighbor is gone, and someone else moves in. Hafiz tries to be friendly, but there's another problem. The boy next door has a dog. A big dog. A dog that brings up bad memories, just like Kunz did."

"Go on." Snow didn't sound convinced, but he wasn't in such a big hurry now.

"Hafiz manages to disassociate Cody from the dog."

"Yeah, it was weird," said Cody. "When Hafiz told me all that stuff about Tango, it was like he didn't even realize that it was my dog he was talking about. And Tango hadn't even done anything."

"Hadn't done anything *yet*," David reminded them. Maybe Tory should have left Cody and David back with the others.

"So Hafiz is even more unbalanced now," said Tory. "Maybe he tries to go to sleep, but maybe he's just gotten some new art. Maybe he had something valuable sitting right under his bed, something you'll find when you search the house, something so valuable that he couldn't sleep until he built a new hiding place."

"So he gets up, gets his tools, and gets his gun," Cody said, sounding excited.

Tory shot a stern look in her son's direction. "So he gets up, gets his tools, and gets his gun," said Tory. "He puts the plywood on the kitchen counter, for later. But he puts everything else on the floor by where he's working. He measures the space that he wants to cut out of the wall, draws it in pencil. Then he decides how far above the cutout he wants to hang the picture, and he gets a nail—"

"Why put in a nail to hang the picture before he makes the cutout?" asked Alvarez. "If he was building a new hiding place, hanging the picture would be the last thing you'd do."

Now Tory shot a stern look in David's direction. Damn, she hadn't thought about the sequence of things. She was about to ask David whose side he was on, anyway, when she figured it out. "He had to put in the nail in case he got interrupted," she explained. "In case he couldn't finish building a particular hiding place all at one time. If Hafiz put in a nail before he started a cutout, he could always quickly hang a picture, cover up what he was doing. That way, he wouldn't risk having to explain why he was cutting holes in the wall.''

"Nails, *cara*,'' said David. "Hafiz would use two nails, not one, to hang a picture. Use only one, it never hangs straight.''

So he was going to be a stickler for details, so what? Besides, he had a smile on his face when he said it. "The important part is that Hafiz is going to hammer a nail into the wall,'' Tory continued. "He bends down, picks up a nail, picks up his hammer, but it isn't his hammer he's picked up, it's his gun. He's in a hurry, he's frustrated, so what? He can use the butt of his gun to hammer in one single nail.''

Snow shook his head. "I'm not buying this,'' he said.

"Wait,'' David interjected. "Let her finish. I've heard of stranger things.''

"Hafiz has the safety off, maybe he even thinks the chamber is empty, with a semi-automatic it's hard to tell. Anyhow, whether he meant to or not, he's chambered a round. He uses the gun to pound in the nail, the gun goes off.''

"He would have been blown away.'' Snow made it a flat statement.

"I didn't say he shot himself,'' said Tory. "At least, not yet. He's holding the barrel of the gun, hitting the nail with the butt. Here, give me your gun, I'll show you—''

"No way,'' objected Snow. "That would go against so many policies I couldn't even begin to count them.''

Another stickler for details. David probably wouldn't lend her his gun to prove a point, either. "Imagine it, then,'' she said, pantomiming hammering a nail in the air. "The barrel of the gun would be pointed down, toward the floor. What's on the floor?''

"Toolbox, wire snippers,'' said Snow, looking at the items in front of them.

"A pencil, a spool of wire, a yardstick," contributed Cody.

"A hammer," said Alvarez.

"Exactly," said Tory. "The hammer, something that's made of heavy, dense metal. Imagine the hammer sitting right on the floor next to Hafiz. After all, if Hafiz picked up his gun when he reached down for his hammer, they must have been next to each other. When the gun went off in his hand, the bullet hit the hammer, ricocheted up and hit him in the stomach."

"What about the wound to his head?" asked Snow.

"He could have hit his head on the floor when he fell backward," suggested David. "Or hit his head on the tool-box, depending on how things were arranged." Pretty soon David would be claiming credit for figuring out what had happened.

"Well," said Snow slowly, "I guess it might work."

"It would work even better if there's no other finger-prints on the gun," said David. "If it's been fired recently, and if Hafiz tests positive for cordite."

"If he hasn't been washed down in butadiene," Snow said thoughtfully.

"*Es verdad,* there is that," David agreed. "But maybe you'll get lucky, and they'll dig a bullet out of his gut that matches the others in that gun." Were they just going to go on talking between the two of them, as though they would have had something to discuss if she hadn't shown them how it happened?

Then Snow cocked his head, started listening to a private conversation. After a few exchanges with someone on the other end, he resumed talking to those present. "Looks good for your story so far," he told Tory. "Looks like Bamia's going to make it. He's conscious, was able to answer a few questions. He's saying that all he remembers is that he couldn't sleep, so he got up, decided to hang a picture. Says no one was with him, says he doesn't remember anyone breaking in.''

''Does that mean we can leave now?'' asked Tory. ''Can I take my son home? If we have to wait for your processing people, he might have to repeat his junior year in high school.''

Snow didn't rise to the bait. ''I still want to talk some more with Kunz and this Lerner guy,'' he said. ''But yeah, let's go next door, tell everyone what we think happened, and you can go.''

''I'd like to stick around,'' stated Cody. ''Hear what Mr. Lerner has to say. I'm doing this psychology paper about the motivations for actions based on ideologies—'' Tory stared at him. ''Or maybe I could talk to him some other time....''

''Yeah,'' said David. ''I think some other time would be a good idea.''

They returned to Con House and Snow briefed the group there. ''I'll bet we can still get him on something,'' insisted Reeves. ''Valuable paintings, bunches of cash, someone gets shot. The guy did something illegal, we just need to figure out what.''

''He needs help, not punishment,'' said Bridget. It seemed Bridget and Reeves had been carrying on a heated conversation while Tory and her group had been next door. ''What's going to happen to all his money?''

''Why?'' asked Reeves. His eyes narrowed suspiciously.

''Because I want to know,'' Bridget answered. It seemed she could be every bit as dogged as Reeves. ''If you don't arrest Mr. Bamia, if you can't prove he did something illegal, then you can't claim that the cash is evidence. If the money isn't evidence, you'll have to return it to Mr. Bamia.''

''Not if he's in intensive care in the hospital, not if they decide he's bonkers,'' said Reeves. Tory was tempted to ask Reeves to define *bonkers,* but decided that it might be going just a little too far.

"If he's in intensive care, or declared incompetent, you'd still have to return the money to someone else, to someone with power of attorney," said Bridget.

"Why are you so interested in what happens to the money?" asked Reeves.

"I'm interested in what happens to Mr. Bamia," Bridget stated, ignoring the astonished expression on her husband's face. "My father is an attorney. He's with a prestigious firm in Albuquerque and they do a lot of pro bono work."

"Why am I not surprised, your father's a big-shot attorney?" asked Reeves. "How happy is daddy going to be with you, once he finds out you ran off to Las Vegas and married a Catholic?"

"Wait a minute—" began Snow, but Bridget beat him out.

"You're just the kind of person who deserves to be a policeman," she snapped.

"Por favor, chica," David said. "Don't talk about me like that. We can learn something from all of this, *¿que si?"*

"What did you call my wife?" Kunz demanded. "What does this word *chica* mean? I don't know this word."

For her part, Bridget looked puzzled rather than chastened, but Tory wasn't sticking around to explain about David's day job.

"Let's get out of here," she told Cody.

"I need to get my stuff—"

"You can come back and get your stuff later. No, *I'll* come back and get your stuff later. Or someone will. I don't think I ever want you setting foot in this house again."

"But Mom—"

"There are things I have to say to you," Tory told her son. "Would you rather have that conversation in front of everyone?" she asked.

That effective, if admittedly underhanded ploy achieved

the desired result. Tory and Alvarez had almost reached the curb when Cody turned around triumphant. "We have to go back," he told his mom.

"Not on your life," she assured him. "No way."

"Way," he said, grinning. "We left our dog, Mom. We need to go back and liberate Tango."

David laughed. "Cody's right," he told Tory. "After all, Tango should be at home for Christmas."

EPILOGUE

THERE WAS PLENTY of illumination in the bedroom at 2:00 a.m. Shimmering light from a full moon poured in the window where Bridget Charson-Kunz lay on her back, next to her sleeping husband, scheming.

Jay was going to have to give up some of his old ideas, become more open to other ways of doing things, other kinds of people. Bridget lay planning, as countless new brides had done before her, planning what needed to be done to shape the man next to her into the man he needed to be.

It wasn't all bad, this planning, and she would never see it as trying to remake someone in her own image, not at this stage of her life. Some expectations might be realized, others not, and Bridget Charson-Kunz might feel the need to reshape her husband more than most—if this unusual pairing was to succeed. But Bridget was young, strong-willed and beautiful; she had love and sexuality on her side. That powerful combination had achieved miracles in the past, and after all, this was the season in which various people around the world acknowledged and celebrated the power of miracles—even if the miracle started out in Las Vegas.

Whatever else Bridget Charson-Kunz believed she believed in the plight of refugees, helping those who were less fortunate, and the power of compound interest. Her father was an attorney, but he and his wife had learned to heed Bridget's advice when it came to investments. Bridget sighed with contentment. That was one of the reasons why she loved her new husband so. He had absolutely no idea how wealthy he had become in Las Vegas without placing a single bet.

So Bridget planned to help Hafiz Bamia. She could get legal representation for him. She could make sure he got the medical help he needed, for both physical and mental problems. If he was raising money for family and friends in need, and if he was doing it without breaking any laws, then Bridget could help him optimize his efforts. She didn't have the required level of expertise in art, but she could find someone who did.

In the meantime, she needed to convince the man to let her help him with his short-term problem. A backyard was no place to keep money. Bridget wondered how much there was, how much more could be expected from the sale of the other items. She wondered how quickly Hafiz needed to pay out the funds. How long he held on to the money. Whether it would be better to look for income, or for growth.

She ran over a mental list of mutual fund possibilities. Since Hafiz had problems trusting people, he might be more comfortable with stocks. Bridget sighed. She hoped he wouldn't insist on bonds.

She turned on her side, snuggled up to her husband. She loved this bed, this bedroom, this apartment. Hadn't she helped Jay pick it all out when he decided to move? And hadn't she ended up here with him, just as she had planned? Turning money for refugees into more money was a pleasant prospect, a nice new challenge.

But it had been an eventful last few days, and she was

tired. Financial planning was beginning to turn into pleasant dreams. As she drifted off into sleep, a small smile held captive on her lips, one word filled her mind.

Shalom.

AFTERWORD

This is, after all, a work of fiction—don't they all say that? There was once a solar-powered research building on the campus of New Mexico State University. There is no resemblance, implied or otherwise, between this facility and the fictional Con House and Solar House. Skipper Botsford lent me his name because he has a warped sense of humor; he does not conduct research on the hantavirus. Other university-related departments, buildings, organizations and individuals are strictly products of my imagination.

However, for those who like their facts straight, news stories have reported both the accidental shooting of someone using a gun as a hammer, and the uncovering of vast amounts of cash by house sitters who happened to bring their dog along on assignment. As an engineer would say, "I have proof."

Oh, and before I forget, the dog is a fictional character, too. Any resemblance implied or otherwise... You know the drill.

STOCKING STUFFER
by Wendi Lee

ONE

I LOVE THE HOLIDAY SEASON—not just because of Thanksgiving and Christmas being a month apart, not just because it's a time for family to get together and show their love for each other—even if it *kills* them—but because the criminals are out *en force*. And with pickpockets and shoplifters comes moonlighting for private investigators who need to pick up a little extra cash.

I didn't have to look long for extra work to pick up that cash for gifts: Braden's Department Store hired me over the phone. They were looking for auxiliary security to watch the shoppers who were looking for the perfect gift, and shoplifters who were looking for the perfect opportunity to slip that little something for themselves into a pocket, a bag or under a bulky sweater. I worked after business hours until ten at night and on weekends from ten in the morning until six at night.

Braden's was upscale, complete with piano player and fountain in the middle of the store. It carried all the major designer labels for shoes, clothes and china. And jewelry—Braden's was known for their finely wrought, exquisite, expensive jewelry. Much of it was made by goldsmiths and silversmiths who worked exclusively through Braden's. To own a ring, bracelet, necklace or a pair of earrings made by a Braden's artisan meant that either you were doing really well for yourself, or you had a sugar daddy.

I was assigned to two areas: walking the floor and watching the monitors in the security office. I hated it the security office—I drank gallons of coffee, and couldn't even go pee when I wanted because someone had to be there in case there was a shoplifter to be spotted. So I had to call for someone to relieve me so *I* could find some relief.

But walking the store, pretending to be a shopper, was a lot more my style. It was especially nice to have a detail around the jewelry counter. I could look at jewelry and create a wish list in my head for some future Christmas. The jewelry was gorgeous, especially the Celtic designs done in platinum with various gems and precious jewels. I had my eye on an interesting set—bracelet, necklace and earrings, done in platinum set with lapis, rubies and emeralds.

It was late Thursday afternoon and I had just arrived at the store after a hard day's work at my own office. My Braden's security supervisor, Chuck Eddy, put me behind the monitors. Yes, *that* Chuck Eddy. He had somehow finagled the job of store security supervisor for Braden's. A few years ago, Eddy had specialized in "decoy" work, in which a client would want him to sic a beautiful woman or good-looking guy on the spouse or fiancé to find out how faithful they were. But Eddy changes specialties more often then he changes his underwear—something I really don't want to dwell on. Just last year, he'd set himself up as a security specialist for homeowners, but that didn't last long. I've heard that Eddy now has at least half a dozen lawsuits against him for installing security systems with substandard wiring that allegedly caused fires.

But now he had managed to snag the security director's position at Braden's. Man, I could just about kill him for that. And here I was, working for him.

"Monitors again? Come on, Chuck. Give me a break. Let me hang out in the store looking for pickpockets and con games."

He shrugged. "Stuckey called in sick again and we need someone on the monitors with Rick."

I groaned. "Chuck. Please. Not Rick."

Rick Branigan was an overeager twenty-year-old, know-it-all college student. He seemed to think that because he'd seen every episode of *Magnum, PI* on rerun, he was an expert on private investigation. He liked to talk down to me and everyone else who wandered into the vicinity of his vast wealth of knowledge.

Chuck paused, looked at me and sighed. "You monitor for two hours with Rick, I promise you can spend your last three hours walking the place. Okay?"

Hey, where was the Eddy I knew? The guy who always put the moves on me? "You okay, Chuck?"

He blinked. I noticed his clothing wasn't quite as neon and nonmatching as it usually was. He was actually wearing an off-white sweater over a mustard-colored polo shirt, and his pants were brown. And had he lost weight? Not a lot, but maybe twenty pounds.

"Why do you ask?" He looked at me suspiciously.

I ticked off my reasons on one hand. "You actually did me a favor without trying to make it a condition of going out on a date with you, I don't need to don shades to look at what you're wearing and I swear you've lost thirty pounds." Okay, I exaggerated that last point.

He grinned. "Got me a girlfriend."

I nodded with approval. "She's good for you, Chuckie. Am I ever gonna meet this woman?"

He shrugged, clearly pleased with the attention and praise. "She meets me here when I get off work and we go for coffee. She's a nurse at Mass General."

A *nurse?* I'd thought maybe Chuckie's girlfriend was an ex-stripper-turned-interior designer or something like that. Not someone in the healing profession.

"I'd like to meet her, Chuck."

He grinned, patted my shoulder and headed back to his office. I went back to the monitor room. Rick was there, feet up on the counter, chair tipped back and hands folded over his stomach. He was good-looking, except for his weak chin and weasely eyes and pointy nose. He was tall, with a muscular frame, wavy brown hair,. and he played basketball. There were a couple of salesgirls who drooled after him. But his all-knowing attitude tempted me to pull some incredibly elaborate joke on him to pull him down a few pegs.

"Hey, Angie. Looks like you're late." Rick reached for his cup of coffee and sipped.

"I'm on time," I said, glancing at my watch.

Rick made a big show of looking at his watch. "According to my watch, you're three minutes late."

I was tempted to continue the argument, but decided that it wasn't important enough. If he wanted to act the big man, fine. I'd take him down later. I sat in the only other empty chair and looked at the monitors.

"Any funny stuff yet tonight?"

He shook his head. "Been quiet. Lots of good-lookin' babes, though." He gestured toward the monitor outside the ladies' dressing room, then winked at me. My skin crawled.

"Maybe I should take the ladies' dressing room," I suggested.

He waved me away as if he were in charge. "Nah, I'm fine. Besides, I can't see into the dressing rooms." He said this last in a wistful tone. Christ.

I turned away from him and put my attention on the jewelry and cosmetic counter monitors. I alternated between them and occasionally the men's clothing area, especially the leather coats, which were big shoplifting items this year. Yeah, I know, the coats have those chains on 'em to keep 'em on the racks. If you think that keeps them safe from shoplifting, you wouldn't make a very good shoplifter. You have to have imagination, like the women who walk around with fake pregnant bellies that are hollowed out, or the distraction created by one person while the second person stocks up on whatever they had their eye on. Then they just walk out of the store.

Yes, it's that simple. You see, a shoplifter doesn't just walk out of the store at any old time—the most experienced shoplifters wait for a large number of buyers who are leaving, then they join the crowd walking out the door; when the security gate beeps, the shoplifter slips away quietly. Meanwhile, the honest shoppers always stop and wait for security guards to check their bags and receipts. They assume an item's tag didn't "take" with the demagnetizing machine. It does happen occasionally.

No matter how much security a store may have, the professional shoplifter can find a way to outsmart us. That was why stores were so vigilant, especially during the holidays.

I had just come back from a short break, a cup of coffee in my hand, when I sat down and checked out the jewelry counter monitor. A well-dressed frosted blonde in an Ann Taylor coat and matching hat was examining a bracelet and talking to the temporary salesclerk. I knew the sales help was temporary because she had taken out several pieces of jewelry and set them on the counter. The frosted blonde distracted the salesclerk by asking to see another piece in the case and when the clerk bent down to retrieve a necklace, the blonde whisked three or four pieces on the counter into her bag. Not exactly a professional here—she was probably a kleptomaniac.

I grabbed the walkie-talkie and alerted the floor security. "Woman wearing a long dark-brown coat and matching beret at the jewelry counter. Blond, Caucasian, late thirties or well-preserved early forties, approximately five feet seven, give or take an inch. Carrying a large red designer shoulder bag." I watched as the woman inspected the proffered necklace, seemed to think about it, then shook her head, clearly telling the salesclerk that it wasn't exactly what she was looking for. She made a show of checking her watch, looking panicky about some make-believe appointment, and headed toward an exit. "She's heading for the north exit," I said, getting up.

"Where you going?" Rick asked.

I started for the door. "There's a shoplifter on the premises and I'm going to see if I can head her off at the pass."

He stood up and blocked my way. "Why don't you stay here and keep an eye on the monitors while I go find her—I was a track star, you know."

I elbowed him out of the way, ignoring his boast. "Call Chuck. Tell him what's going on."

On my way to the floor, I got a call from Martha, one of the temp floorwalkers. "Angie, I'm at the north exit and I don't see the shoplifter."

I was near the east exit and looked around—maybe she changed direction. "Tom, where are you?" Tom was the other floorwalker.

"Angie, I'm at the south exit. Nothing here, either."

That left the west side, where Braden's meets the mall. It was the most logical place to disappear. Just then, the security gate went off, and I raced toward the west side, only to be confronted with about twenty shoppers all heading out the door, and about as many entering. Everyone stopped where they were, blocking the entrance, all of them waiting like sheep for security to come and check out their packages. I excused my way out the door and stopped just outside to encounter scads of shoppers, scads of bags, scads of frosted blondes in long dark Ann Taylor-like coats. No hats. The blonde probably took off her hat the moment she exited the store. Her red bag, if she *was* a pro, would be encased in a larger black or brown bag, or in a shopping bag from another store.

"Dammit!" I muttered, stomping a foot in frustration. I turned on my heel and marched back into the store. Martha, a plump, motherly woman who looked like the perfect shopper, and Tom, an elderly man with a basset hound face, were searching shopping bags and matching receipts with items, then thanking the shoppers for stopping.

I joined in, murmuring the phrase "Thank you for shopping at Braden's" as I pawed my way through three or four bags.

When we were finished, Chuck showed up with the store's night manager, who looked very unhappy. The temporary salesclerk was with them, teary-eyed and scared.

"Did we get her?" Gerry, the night manager, asked. He absentmindedly twisted a suit coat button.

I shook my head. "No. I'm sorry. We covered as best we could with two floorwalkers and two at the security monitors." Braden's didn't cover as well on weeknights.

Gerry was a large blustery man with a flushed face. He wore a tailored gray suit and navy tie, and his yellow—yes, yellow, not blond, not white—hair was brushed back and curled on the ends. It would have been endearing, but right now, Gerry was flustered and angry. And he was flustered and angry with me. Well, okay, not originally. He was angry at Chuck, who turned to Martha and Tom, who pointed to me.

"How did she get out of the store?" he asked me in a loud voice.

"Can we discuss this in your office?" I suggested as calmly as possible. People were staring. "Do you really want everyone in the store to know who we are, etcetera?"

Gerry blinked, looked around and nodded, leading the way to his office to the beat of some march in his own head.

Gerry shared his office with the day manager. He had his own desk, own space, but it was clear that the day manager, Herman, was the big boss. Herman occupied most of the office. Gerry's desk pretty much was it for him. I think he might have had his own hook on the coatrack.

As we entered the office, Chuck tried to slip out the door. "Chuck, I need you here," Gerry ordered. "Close the door.'' He turned to the clerk. ''Jessica, what did the shoplifter get?''

Jessica was about twenty years old and her nose was red from crying. She sniffled. ''I—I showed her a pair of diamond and emerald earrings first. Then the matching necklace caught her eye. I brought that out. While she was examining them, someone came up and asked to see an opal ring. I hesitated, knowing I shouldn't leave one customer, but the lady smiled. She said, 'I promise I won't walk off with these items if you need to see to the nice lady over there.''' Jessica put her hand to her eyes and shook her head. ''And she kept her word. I got the opal ring out and the other woman looked at it and decided it wasn't for her. So I went back to the first woman—after putting the ring away—and she was very nice. And all the jewelry was still there. So I trusted her. She asked to see a black pearl ring, a real beauty worth almost three thousand. As she was examining it, I was approached by another customer and again, the woman told me she'd stay there and watch the items.''

Gerry let out an impatient sigh. ''Ms. Burnowski, what the hell were you doing when we had the orientation for temporary help two weeks ago?''

Jessica's chin trembled. ''Wh-what are you talking about?''

Gerry's face had gotten red. ''Were you busy filing your nails when we talked about taking only one item out of the jewelry case at once? Were you thinking about your big date later that night when we discussed the shoplifting scams? Were you—''

I cut in, disgusted that this big man was pushing around a young girl who was only a seasonal temp. ''That's enough, Gerry.''

Jessica was crying, big tears streaming down her face. And she looked as if she'd lost her last teaspoonful of self-esteem.

Gerry turned on me. "And you, *Ms.* Matelli. You're no better. You let this woman get away with thousands of dollars worth of jewelry. If I didn't know better, I'd say you were in league with this shoplifter."

I slapped the edge of his desk. "That's *enough*, Gerry."

He leaned into me. "*Mr.* MacLean to you."

I came up nose to nose with him. "Gerry. I don't intimidate as easily as this young lady. I don't need this job as badly as she probably does. But I *was* at that orientation—which lasted about an hour. And frankly, I don't recall any of that mumbo jumbo you mentioned. Maybe the information was in the talk, but it was the most boring, perfunctory lecture I've ever attended and I was probably daydreaming or doodling, or thinking about ways to spend the extra money I'd earn from this job, same as everyone else. Of course, I have years more experience in this field than Jessica does. But I won't take your insulting behavior. I screwed up. You lost some inventory. I'm sorry. But I do know we have that woman on tape, and I can guarantee that she will show up again in this store before Christmas rolls around." I wish I felt as confident as I sounded.

Gerry's color had gone from red to white while I was talking—he was already getting into the Christmas spirit. "How can you guarantee something like that?" he asked. His voice had gone from intimidating and angry to soft and whispery.

Chuck finally decided to jump in. I could have used him earlier, but hey, anytime is good before I get my pink slip. "She's right, you know. A lot of these shoplifters become arrogant, especially around the holidays when they know store personnel are too busy to watch every second of a transaction. And if they got away with it once, they're tempted to try again."

"Never underestimate the ego of a successful shoplifter," I added.

Gerry's color returned to normal as he looked at Chuck

first, then me. Finally, he nodded. "All right. We still have three weeks until Christmas. Let's see what happens. Meanwhile, I'll have to contact the insurance company." There was an underlying threat there, but I wasn't sure exactly what would happen if the shoplifter didn't return and the goods weren't recovered.

As we walked out of the office, Jessica hesitated. She looked as if she were planning to go back into the office to ask Gerry something, then thought better of it. She looked at us. "Does that mean I'm fired or does that mean I should go back to my counter?"

"You should go back to your counter and keep a closer eye on potential customers," Chuck said kindly.

I stared at him. He noticed. "What?" he asked.

I shook my head slowly. "Chuck, if I didn't know any better, I'd say you're becoming a human being."

He shrugged. "Who says I wasn't before?" He walked me back to the monitor room. The hired piano player was doing a funereal version of "O Tannenbaum."

"It's just that you're dressing better, and even treating women with more respect. You haven't tried to hit on me even once since I started working here last week."

He grinned. "Yeah, I guess I haven't." He gave me a sharp look. "Want me to?"

I laughed. "No. I'm getting used to your new self." I paused, then said, "Actually, I don't think this is your new self, I think you were here all the time. It just took some time for you to emerge." I stopped outside the room. "Do I have to go back in there? I hate working with Rick."

Chuck shrugged again. "Everyone hates working with Rick. If you got here before the others, I'd put you on floor duty."

"But that's not fair, Chuck," I said, "I work at the office until five. Martha and Tom are retired and do this to pick up gift money for their grandchildren. They'll always be here earlier than me." I was starting to whine and I stopped, ashamed of myself. Chuck had always been the weird, annoying presence in my life, and now I was acting like the weird annoying presence in his life. Well, maybe he needed that for a while.

"Listen, toots, why don't you go walk the floor and Rick can sit and spin by himself." Chuck smiled at the thought. So did I.

I thanked him and spent until closing time walking around the store and checking out the clothes, cosmetics and jewelry.

Every time I went by the jewelry counter, Jessica threw a nervous look my way, as if she thought I was spying on her.

TWO

I DRAGGED MYSELF home at midnight. I'd gone with Chuck to meet his girl, Gloria, a busty thirty-something brunette with a spate of freckles across her nose and an infectious laugh. If I hadn't been so happy for Chuck, I would have been ill watching him call her his "wittle wookie"—I didn't ask—and practically rub noses with her.

Still, I was happy for him.

I went home to Fredd, my pet iguana. He was perfectly content sitting on his branch all day long, as long as I fed and watered him. He preferred grapes. I hadn't told him yet, but he was getting a new branch to perch on, and a whole gross of grapes for his Christmas dinner. Of course, he wouldn't be able to eat all the grapes at once, so he'd have plenty of leftovers.

I checked my answering machine before turning in. Ma hadn't called—that was unusual. Instead, I got calls from each of my brothers and sisters. First Ray called from New Hampshire.

"Ange? We gotta talk. It's about Ma's gift this year. I think we should all get together and get her a big present. Something she could really use and enjoy. Give me a call tomorrow."

Beeep.

"Ange? Sophie here. Ray just called. Something about all of us pooling our money on some big blowout gift. He's thinking a new refrigerator or stove. Hah! Yeah, that's a gift from the heart. Here's your new appliance, Ma, so you can spend the next ten freakin' years cookin' meals for the family. What a gift! Call me back.''

Beeep.

"Hey, it's me, Vinnie. We gotta get somethin' for Ma. Somethin' big. Ray suggested a refrigerator and stove— good stuff.''

I could hear Carla in the background. "Yeah, Vinnie, just like that new vacuum cleaner you got me for our anniversary. Real romantic. A real statement of love and devotion.''

Vinnie said something back to Carla that was muffled and she laughed. "Anyway," he said into my machine, "call me.''

Beeep.

"Ange. Albert. Ray called. You've probably heard from everyone else. Let's all get together on Friday night. Santarpio's. Ray's down here in Providence on business for Thursday and Friday and staying with us for the weekend. 6:00 p.m. Can you make it?'' "Us" was Albert and his ex-wife, Sylvia. They had divorced over a year ago, and then Albert got out of the Mob and began a legitimate toy business. Sylvia had been addicted to coke and uppers, and when Albert divorced her, it was a wake-up call. Now they had reconciled and divided their time between Albert's oceanfront condo in Providence and Sylvia's inherited Newport family home. They hadn't made it official, but we hoped they'd re-marry.

Beeep.

"Hey, Sarge. You probably got the messages from our other siblings. Knock on my door before work tomorrow. We'll talk.'' That was my little sister, Rosa, the one I was closest to—not only emotionally, but location-wise. She lived in the second floor apartment. I lived on the top floor of my three-story walk-up. The ground-floor apartment was currently unoccupied. We'd had trouble renting it out, mostly because it was small. But the tenants who had occupied it over the last four years had ranged from my older sister Sophie and her two kids—on a temporary basis, only after Ma put the screws to me about doing my duty as a blood relative, etcetera—to an elderly man who was hard-of-hearing and liked to play Enrico Caruso at midnight. He didn't last long.

It was late and I needed to get some sleep. But I had another message.

"Angie, it's Jack. I've been thinking about you. Christmas break is coming up in a few days, and I *have* no plans, no place I have to be, and if you have a little time, I'd love to come down to Boston to visit you. I don't want to put you on the spot, but I'm missing you. Call me. Night or day."

Hmmm. I hadn't heard from Jack in almost a week. He was a grad student in computer information technology at Hartmore College in Vermont. A professor in the Anthropology Department had hired me to investigate the death of a student. I'd met Jack Wade while on the case. We'd hit it off right away. I stayed on a few days after solving the case and we got to know each other even better.

Then I'd gone back to Boston, and Jack had gone back to his studies. We usually talked about three times a week, and I'd been up north to visit him for a couple of days once a month. But I could tell that we were coming to that point in our relationship where we had to either commit or jump ship.

I wasn't sure what I wanted to do. But every time I saw him, I had fun, we talked easily, and we got along well together. I wasn't sure how he felt, but I got the impression he wanted more of a commitment. The last few times we'd talked on the phone, he mentioned that his thesis would be done in April, and he'd get his doctorate in June. It never went any further than that, but it sounded like he was leading up to something.

I thought about just turning in and calling him in the

morning, but I knew Jack would still be awake, and he sometimes didn't remember what time it was, so if I didn't call him, he might very well call me at three in the morning.

I dialed and he picked up immediately. I pictured him sitting at his desk in his student apartment.

"Hey, Jack."

"Angie! What time is it?"

I laughed. "You? Worried about time?"

He joined me. "I guess I need a watch."

"Isn't that what that little clock is for on your computer?"

"So what do you think about my coming down there?"

"Sure, come on down."

There was an uncomfortable silence filled with that giddy feeling—I was sure he was feeling it, too. He cleared his throat. "Um, Angie, I don't want to make you uncomfortable. I know we've only spent a couple of days together—nothing like a couple of weeks. But I was thinking of doing some job searching down there. And a place to live. I can stay with another friend, if you'd prefer to not have me underfoot all the time."

I laughed. "Jack, as they say on the game show, come on down. I have a guest room if you need privacy, and I even have a vacant apartment on the ground floor. When do you plan to come down here?"

"How's a week from this Friday?"

"I can't wait. By the way, I hope you aren't planning to spend the holidays by yourself. You'll meet Ma and my siblings."

"I hope we'll spend some time alone," he said in that deep growl that had me twirling a lock of hair.

"I think that can be arranged. But you still have to meet the family."

He chuckled. "All at once?"

"It's the holidays. Ma does it up big and the more people, the better." I told him about all the siblings getting together to get one big gift for Ma. "We're going to pool our money and buy Ma a big gift. The boys want to buy her a stove and refrigerator."

"So she can cook meals faster?"

"I think you've got it in one. Look, Jack, I have to get some sleep. So I'll see you next week?"

"Can't wait, dollface. I've been missing you." His voice was husky and I didn't know how to respond. He was far away right now, and I wanted him. But I couldn't think about it. Not now with Christmas coming and me holding down a second job, and what to get Ma growing into a huge family preoccupation. Sheesh, this meant I'd have to spend the next two weeks obsessing about a gift for Jack as well.

THREE

FRIDAY, I NORMALLY worked at Braden's at night, but Chuck gave me the night off since I had this meeting at Santarpio's. I agreed to make it up on Saturday by working a double shift. At least Rick wouldn't be there—I was taking his place that day.

The Santarpio's meeting went about the way I had expected it to go. Ray and Vinnie wanted to buy Ma something practical so she could keep on taking care of us. The women, Sophie and Rosa specifically, thought she should have some really nice piece of jewelry or a designer dress or a fur. I drew the line at the fur. I had visions of Ma proudly walking down the street in her beautiful fox fur, and a bunch of radicals throwing red paint all over her. Then I'd have to take out my gun and shoot them like it was open season. No one messes with Ma when I'm around.

"Ma *likes* to cook," Ray pointed out. "It's her life."

"No," Sophie replied, "*we're* her life and while she likes to make those big meals, she does it because we show up for said meal."

"Well, I think a pair of diamond earrings is a stupid gift for her," Vinnie argued. "Where's she gonna wear them— to the Sunday dinners she cooks for us? I can just picture it—one of those earrings going right into a big pot of Ma's sauce. Yeah, a real practical gift."

"You don't have to be sarcastic," Rosa said in an offended tone.

And on. And on. We must have gone through four pizzas, two orders of lamb, at least a dozen glasses of red table wine, and three hours later, we weren't any closer to what to get Ma for Christmas. The only thing we had decided was that each of us would contribute an equal amount to the fund. Sophie and Rosa told me to keep an eye out for a nice bracelet or set of earrings. Ray asked Vinnie and Albert to look into refrigerators and stoves.

Albert and I were the only ones not involved much in the discussion. When everyone finally went their separate ways, we walked out together. Neither of us liked either of the gift ideas. We had to find something special for Ma, something more personal than an appliance and more practical than a piece of expensive designer jewelry that she'd never wear.

But we were out of ideas.

"Maybe one of us will get a brainstorm," Albert said before getting into his car and driving back to Providence.

I REPORTED TO WORK at Braden's early on Saturday. Chuck had the day off, and so did Rick and Gerry. There was an assistant manager named Bruce, but he made himself scarce, only showing himself when called. Chuck had effectively put me as second-in-command when he wasn't around on weekends, mostly because I had a background in security.

So I assigned the weekend help—two college students named Lindsey and Melissa—to work the monitors while Tom, Martha and I walked the floor. Martha stayed near the women's and children's clothing because she could pass as either a doting grandmother buying for her grandchildren, or a matronly saleslady in the women's clothing department.

Tom worked men's clothing and outerwear, focusing on the leather goods area.

I, of course, worked the jewelry and perfume counters.

And that was when I spotted her. I was in the middle of spraying a little puff of Opium in the air and sniffing the result as I had a few dozen times before when I spotted her from across the room. She was standing in the same place. There was a different salesclerk—Nicole—at the counter. Just like the first time, the second salesclerk had gone on her lunch break, leaving one clerk to work the entire counter by herself. My alleged shoplifter from the other day was looking at a little cocktail ring as Nicole patiently waited for the woman to make a decision. The customer let her eyes stray to something else in a far case and she said something to Nicole, pointing toward it. Nicole moved over to the case and took out a long strand of cultured pearls for the woman to examine.

I watched and waited. I could have taken her in then and there, and probably wouldn't have had any trouble prosecuting her for the previous theft, but I wanted to get more on her, to catch her in the act of shoplifting rather than using just a tape against her. I took out my walkie-talkie and spoke quietly to Tom and Martha, being careful to stay out of sight. "Thursday's shoplifter at jewelry counter. Cover north and south exits. Stand by." I pocketed the walkie-talkie and bided my time.

She was good. She bided her time as well, and when another customer distracted the salesclerk momentarily, the woman swept the diamond-and-ruby dinner ring into a large black bag left strategically on the floor by her feet. Then she waited a few more moments before picking up her bag, casually strolling over to the clerk to deliver the pearl rope into her hands. The salesclerk was clearly so distracted with the other customer that she had forgotten she'd left the ring, then the shoplifter walked away from the counter.

I had to blame Braden's for not having enough sales help over the holiday season. Like every other merchant, they were trying to keep costs down. And I suppose that hiring floorwalkers like me cut into their budget for sales help.

A moment later, I followed her as she started to walk toward the east exit. As I kept an eye on her black coat, black bag and frosted blond hair, I unclipped my walkie-talkie, which I'd hidden in my vest, and informed Martha and Tom which way we were heading. At one point, a couple of teenage girls crossed my path, lingering for a few seconds in front of me the way annoying teenagers sometimes do, and I lost sight of the frosted blonde for a few seconds. We danced back and forth for a few moments and finally got past them in time to see the woman approaching the east exit.

I broke into a trot as she passed through the east entrance. Something was wrong, but I wasn't sure exactly what. It was just a feeling. But I finally caught up to her, firmly grasped her elbow and spun her around.

"Excuse me, ma'am, but I need to see what's in your bag." I flashed my Braden's security ID, which had about as much relevance as a library card, but it looked official.

She seemed shorter when I was up close, and her look of astonishment wasn't mixed with a healthy dose of sheepish deceit. Wordlessly, she held out her bag, still in shock. I took advantage of her condition to take the bag and lead her back inside to the office. By the time we reached the office, she became vocal.

"Why me? What did I do?" she asked, her arms crossed, her foot tapping.

Bruce, the assistant manager, came into the security office, looked at me, then at the woman I'd brought back here.

"Is this her?"

I nodded in a perfunctory manner. Bruce was barely into his twenties, still had acne, and perpetually greasy hair. He had started to grow a beard and it was coming in patchy. He had thick black-framed glasses and a nervous manner. He hovered by my shoulder for a moment.

"Uh, what should I do?" He put his hands on his hips and puffed out his chest.

"Why don't you tell the salesclerk, Nicole, to come in here a moment. And find the other woman who works at that counter. She's going to have to cut her lunch short."

Bruce nodded and went back out.

I took the shopping bag, a white-and-gold Braden's bag with handles, and put it on an empty spot on the table. Funny, she was carrying a black bag in the store. Of course, shoplifters covered up the real bag a lot of the time. But there was no black bag inside the Braden's bag. My stomach did a free fall. Suddenly, I wasn't so confident. But I took a deep breath and went on. Her shopping bag held an Anne Klein tailored shirt, a couple of Tommy Hilfiger sweaters and jeans, a pair of Chinese Laundry shoes, and an eelskin wallet. All with receipts.

I searched the pockets of the jeans, checked the shoes and the box they came in and even checked the wallet. Nothing.

Martha and Tom had come in, and I told them to return to the floor. The two college students alternately kept an eye on the monitors and watched me search the woman's belongings.

I turned to her. "Ma'am, may I search your purse?"

She had crossed her arms and glared at me. "I think I need a lawyer."

"If you think so," I said, looking over at the phone, "I can bring the police into this right now. We have videotape of you dropping an expensive ring into your black bag."

She looked around, holding her arms away from her sides. "Do you see a black bag on me?"

Her purse was a rich brown leather and much too small to be mistaken for the black bag I had seen her pick up from across the counters. I went back over the time I had her in my sights. She had only been out of my sight for a total of about ten seconds—was that enough time to hide or discard the items if she suspected that I was following her?

I looked over at her. She was glaring at me. I picked up the phone and her expression changed. She blanched. I raised my eyebrows and she reluctantly handed over her purse.

A timid knock on the door, then it opened and Nicole peeked around the corner.

"Come in," I said.

The shoplifter glared at Nicole as if it were her fault that she was in the security office.

"Nicole, is this the woman who was at your counter earlier?"

Nicole, a pretty blond college student, stared curiously at the woman. She nodded. "She was looking at a diamond-and-ruby cocktail ring."

"And did you put the ring back?"

Understanding dawned on Nicole. Panic was evident in her eyes. "No, no, I—I turned to wait on another customer—" She leaned against the wall, in shock. "I—I didn't mean—"

Before I lost her, I picked up a handheld camera. "I need for you to tell me out loud," I said slowly. I had trained it on her.

Nicole glanced at me wide-eyed, the proverbial deer caught in the headlights. But she rallied. "That woman was at my counter earlier."

I did a wide sweep to the woman, who looked resentful that she was on camera. I put the camera down and dismissed Nicole. She paused at the door, looked back at the woman, then left.

I turned back to the shoplifter and her purse. Looking through her pocketbook, I found her driver's license. Her name was Ellen Bidwell, she lived in Watertown, and she was forty-two years old. Her bag held nothing else of interest. A wallet, a packet of tissues, powder compact, mascara and lipstick—Tawny Bronze—keys, and a checkbook. No dinner ring.

"Ms. Bidwell, would you please empty out your pockets?"

She gave an impatient sigh. "Oh, this is ridiculous. I haven't done anything. You obviously have the wrong person." Still, she obliged me—even turning out her coat pockets and her pants pockets as well. I frowned and had her hand her coat to me. I inspected every inch of it for hidden pockets in the lining or an opening on a seam that a person could drop small items down to the hem. Nothing.

By this time, she had crossed her arms impatiently, a hostile expression fixed on her face.

"May I go now?" she asked dryly.

I made one last attempt. I called to Melissa to play back the tape. Ellen Bidwell watched the scene I had been a part of. I watched her to note her expression.

Her lips were compressed and her eyes were narrowed at first. By the time her image came into view, her eyes widened and she didn't look so sure of herself. It was pretty incriminating, even in all its grainy imagery. When the tape was over, she was composed again.

"You have nothing. That must have been some other woman who looks like me," she said. "I wasn't *at* the jewelry counter."

I shrugged. "I was there. I watched you."

"From how far away?" Ellen Bidwell gestured to the TV screen.

I shrugged. "Twenty yards, give or take a yard."

"And how good is your eyesight?"

I smiled. "Twenty-twenty." With my contacts, I silently added.

She bit her lip, but persevered. "And did you have me in your sight the entire time, from that counter to the exit?"

I was honest. "I lost sight of you for about ten seconds."

She assessed me, cool and collected now. "All right, so what you have is a woman who looks a lot like me, someone who put something in her bag, and walked out of the store. You followed her, but lost her for a few seconds. Then I probably crossed paths with her during those seconds and you picked up my trail. Because I didn't go near the jewelry counter when I was in the store.''

I digested this information. I believed some of what she was telling me. I had to—she didn't have the stolen jewelry on her.

And I hadn't gotten an up close-and-personal look at her when I spied what she was doing and followed her.

So I had to let her go. I escorted her to the exit, and she had the injured, suffering look of a woman wrongly accused.

Except I knew something was wrong with this picture. I knew she wasn't telling me the whole truth. The way she looked when she watched herself on video, there was recognition there, something she was hiding from me.

Ellen Bidwell turned to me before she left the store and said, "You'll be hearing from my lawyers."

I smiled with more confidence than I felt. "That's your right, Ms. Bidwell. But I do have to tell you that the videotape is very convincing, and any judge in any court will hear my version." I paused, then added, "We also have a tape from last Thursday night showing you clearly shoplifting several very nice pieces of jewelry. Has it ever occurred to you that whatever you take from us just gets added to the price that other customers pay?"

Ms. Bidwell favored me with a cold smile. "For your information, I have an alibi for that night. I was at work very late. I couldn't have been here." She turned away, then thought better of it. "Has it ever occurred to you that when I went through the security gates, they didn't go off?" Her logic hit me like a bag of wet cement—hard, intense and embarrassing. I kept thinking, shouldn't I have reached that conclusion without being chastised by the injured party?

That piece of information was the thing that had been

nagging me in the back of my mind, that elusive something that had bothered me about apprehending her outside the store.

''I *told* you that I didn't steal the ring.'' With a triumphant gleam in her eye, she left me standing there, wondering if Braden's would fire me because of my sloppy detective work.

FOUR

AFTER ELLEN BIDWELL LEFT, I spent the next hour studying the videotape. The image was grainy, but it was Ellen Bidwell on that tape. Then I pulled the security video from the other day and examined it.

"Do you need any help, Angela?" Melissa asked.

I looked up. Melissa was slightly overweight. She wore baggy slacks and a shapeless sweater. Her hair was cut for ease in grooming. She had beautiful eyes and a stunning smile. I knew that Bruce had his eye on her. I also knew that Melissa was a junior G-man. She was really impressed by me and often asked me questions about my work.

"Thanks, Mel. I could use a pair of fresh eyes." I gave up my chair and the remote. "I'll take over the monitors for you while you check it over."

I spent the next half hour watching serious shoppers and overworked, underpaid sales staff coming together in a Christmas buying frenzy. Melissa came back to replace me. She was frowning.

"What did you think?" I asked. "Did you see anything that might be contrary to what you witnessed with the woman earlier today?"

She filed the tapes. "I don't know. Something seems odd, but I can't put my finger on the source."

Smart girl. Exactly my sentiments. Mel left the room and Lindsey snorted. "She thinks she's gonna be a private eye when she grows up."

I turned and stared at her. Did I mention that Lindsey is a jerk? "Maybe she will be. At least she's willing to offer an opinion."

Lindsey took a sip from her can of Mountain Dew—she always had one nearby. "I don't get paid enough to do stupid stuff like that."

I left the room before I popped her one.

THE NEXT FEW DAYS were a blur as I was called into meeting after meeting with Chuck and Gerry and Mel and Martha and Tom and Jessica and Nicole. And Old Man Braden. Stanley Braden had made a success of Braden's department store by offering quality items. But his fortune had been made on importing gems. That was why Braden's had such a good reputation for quality when it came to their jewelry—it was the Braden specialty.

On Monday, I went in at three in the afternoon to meet with Old Man Braden. He requested that I bring the tapes with me.

Braden was a handsome, white-haired man with a well-trimmed beard and piercing gold eyes. He had a golf tan and a gold Rolex. There was nothing "old man" about him. His appearance reminded me of a sleek lion.

"Ms. Matelli." Braden nodded and indicated a seat. I handed the tapes to him.

Together we watched the tapes. I occasionally made a comment to explain what was happening, or what conclusion I had drawn at a certain point.

When we finished, he popped the tape out of the VCR and returned both to me. "We have lost thousands of dollars from these two thefts, Ms. Matelli. What do you suggest?"

I looked around me, wondering why Chuck Eddy wasn't in this meeting.

"Is something wrong?"

I turned back to Braden. "Well, I was just wondering

why Chuck Eddy isn't in on this meeting. Or Gerry, the night manager.''

Braden smiled, used one manicured index finger to scratch his temple in a modest gesture. ''While I'm sure they have the best of intentions, Ms. Matelli, I've read your employee file and am impressed by the extent of your experience in investigation.''

I raised my eyebrows but stayed silent. It's amazing how much you can learn from people when you keep your mouth shut.

''For instance,'' Braden continued, ''Gerry Hasson is a very fine night manager. He has worked for our store for over ten years, and is very adept at handling the employees, keeping morale high and hiring good employees overall. Chuck is, well, very good at supervising security, but he doesn't seem to have been very successful as an all-around private investigator.''

I was confused. I wasn't sure where this was heading. ''Um, this sounds more like you're hiring me for a job rather than firing me.''

Braden straightened up, looked a little confused, then started laughing. I wasn't sure whether to join in—it sounded as if it were an inside joke among rich guys, and since I wasn't in that category, I just smiled pleasantly. ''No, I'm not firing you, Ms. Matelli. On the contrary. Both Gerry and Chuck—after a little persuasion—assured me that you did everything in your power to prevent this shoplifter from getting off scot-free. The first time, she eluded you by heading for one exit, then changing direction, misdirecting you. You couldn't have known what she was doing. And I don't know how she did it this second time.'' He shook his head. ''You have witnesses—Melissa, Lindsey and the salesclerk, Nicole—who saw you search the woman.''

Another idea struck me. ''Has Ms. Bidwell, the alleged

shoplifter, brought a suit against Braden's for being unlawfully searched?"

His brows furrowed. "Strangely enough, no. But that doesn't mean she won't contact us. And that's why I want to hire you to investigate this matter."

I nodded slowly. "I see. And I accept the case. I feel responsible for what happened, even if I couldn't prevent it. It's been gnawing at me. I need to know how and where she hid the haul from Saturday." I didn't want to bore him with the details, so he asked me to fax a contract to him, then handed me a check for my services, and told me to take off the next few days to work on the investigation.

I picked up my stuff, including signing out the two tapes, and left the store. I headed for my office, which was one T stop away from Braden's. I hardly ever worked past five, but now was not the time to think about how quiet the building was when everyone had locked up the offices.

I locked myself in since it was after business hours and only the janitor would be interested in entering to empty my wastebasket. I fired up the computer and while I waited, I checked my answering machine. The little red light was blinking furiously. I reached over and pushed the playback button.

Beeep.

"Sarge, give me a call back." Rosa, my little sister. She sounded distracted.

Beeep.

"Hey, Matelli, just checking in to see how you're doing. Call me when you're free." Lee Randolph—homicide detective, poker pal and good friend. The wheels in my little brain began to spin. I would definitely have to give him a call—ulterior motive at work here.

Beeep.

"Angela, it's your mother. Albert called me and told me your brothers and sisters are fighting over what to give me. Tell your sisters that I want that stove and refrigerator.

What would I do with some piece of jewelry?'' Ma didn't sound distressed—she sounded pleased. Her children loved her so much they fought over what to give her.

Beeep.

"Yo, Angie, Vinnie here. Ma wants the oven and fridge. Tell your sisters to stop whining and pony up the dough." Such a diplomat, my brother Vinnie is. Oh, and now they were *my* sisters, not *his?* Sheesh.

I sighed and passed my hand over my face. The phone rang.

"Angie?"

"Hey. Sophia," I replied.

"You know, I was thinking…you work at Braden's, you could find something really nice for her. They have good jewelry. Maybe a tiara or something."

"A tiara." I pictured Ma wearing her tiara in the kitchen, standing over a large pot of her famous sauce. It was all I could do not to laugh. "Um, I got a call from Ma. She knows what we're planning. I suspect Ray or Vinnie talked to her. She says she wants the stove and fridge."

Sophia sighed. "It's just so…so mundane. I mean, those items are the sort of thing you buy out of necessity. Jewelry makes a woman feel like a queen and perks her up and…" She sighed.

"So what's David getting you for Christmas?" I asked.

"A vacuum cleaner, that tornado one."

I laughed. "How romantic." I thought of Vinnie and Carla.

"Yeah, but he's so good with the kids. He's also taking us on a trip to Disney World for a week," she replied. "Now for a woman with kids, *that*'s romantic."

"That's really sweet of him." David was my aikido instructor. He was also a child psychologist. About two years ago, he set eyes on my older sister and had instantly fallen in love. The surprising thing was that Sophia had felt the same way about him. Up until that day, Sophia had been a cocktail waitress in a biker bar. Her choice of men had been lousy. The marriage that had produced her two children, Michael and Stephanie, had also produced an absentee dad, and the Matelli men had been doing their best to fill in as male role models for the children.

Within six months, David and Sophia had moved in together and now lived in Brookline with her two kids. Sophia enrolled in nursing school and was due to finish her degree in June of next year. It was one of the most astounding transformations I'd ever seen—my sister went from a complete loser who waited table in a biker bar to a professional woman with a caring relationship in a little over half a year. And Michael and Stephanie had blossomed into nice kids. I suspected David did a lot of overtime child psychology in his own home to produce such great results.

Stephanie was on the honor roll at school and Michael was going out for football next year.

"Wow, that's terrific," I said, not being able to help feeling a little envious. I reflected on my own life—I did have Jack, and things were heating up between us. If I wasn't careful, Jack would be moving in within a couple of months.

"Well," Sophia said in a defeated tone, "I guess if that's what Ma wants, that's what Ma gets."

I paused, then said, "Let me think about it for a while. There has to be a compromise—something not practical, but something that will mean something to her, something we can give her that will be from our hearts and not from our stomachs."

We both laughed before hanging up.

I stared at the phone for a while. It was after eight in the evening, and Lee would most likely be home. I dialed his number.

When he answered, I said, "Hey, you called."

"Angie. Hadn't heard from you in a while. You working hard?"

I brought him up to date on my life, my work at Braden's and the shoplifting incidents. I didn't even have to ask Lee for help. He offered to look up Ellen Bidwell's record and call me back in the morning.

"So what're you going to do for Christmas?" I asked.

"Going to spend it with my dad and sister," he said. "Noreen's making a crown roast and her husband's sisters are bringing the rest of the meal, including something called 'party potatoes.'" Noreen was his younger sister.

"Sounds festive. Are you and your dad exempt from bringing anything?"

He laughed. "I bring the beer, he brings the rolls. I imagine you're going to your ma's house," he added this last thought wistfully. "You have a date?"

"You'd think on Christmas Eve, I wouldn't have one. Everyone's usually home with their families for the holidays. But Jack's folks are out of the country, and as you know, Ma always has room for a potential husband."

We both laughed. Lee was dating a lovely woman named Megan who worked in a different precinct, but it wasn't anything serious. It never was with Lee. Some people just aren't cut out to be married, and Lee was one of them.

After wishing each other happy holidays, Lee promised to call me the next day with any information he found on Ellen Bidwell.

I sat back in my chair and stared at my computer. Then I picked up the phone one more time and called Jack.

"Hey, babe," he said. "I was just thinking about you."

"Same here. How're midterms going?"

"Same old, same old. I'm more concerned about my thesis than grading midterms. Besides, all the exams for my professor's students are on the computer. I hope you don't mind if I download the information to your home e-mail so I can work on the exams from there."

"Download away," I said. I told him what I needed.

"Ellen Bidwell," he said as he wrote the information down. "Watertown. Got it. Happy to oblige."

Jack had helped me gather background information on several suspects when I went undercover as a student at

Hartmore College. I gave him the name of the shoplifter and asked for any information he could give me regarding her—financial, where she works, any personal life information. "Can you send me what you have by tomorrow so I can get started? As you find more, just keep sending the information to me."

"No problem."

"I'll pay you. Same as you got at Hartmore."

"Consider my expertise as payment for staying at your place for a few days."

I pulled up short. "Only a few days? I—I thought you were staying with me for the entire Christmas break."

He laughed. "Don't feel slighted, Angela. I just don't think it's fair that you shoulder the burden of having me stay with you that long. There's a friend or two in Boston I can stay with after Christmas. I know that our relationship is still fresh, and I don't want to blow it with you." His last acknowledgment was said in a husky voice.

I started to play with my hair, twirling it around my index finger as I thought about it. "Look, Jack, I think I have a solution for you." I told him again about the ground-floor apartment. It was the perfect answer. It was even furnished with an extra bed that Sophia had left behind, a refrigerator and stove, a couch, an easy chair and a table with chairs that Vinnie had given me when Carla did some spring cleaning of their house earlier this year. All it needed was a few dishes and some flatware and glasses, in case Jack wanted to eat in.

Since Jack would bring his laptop, he could plug it in in the apartment if he didn't want to come up to my place. I would provide him with a key so he could come and go as he pleased, and we would work it out. Of course, I was hoping he wouldn't spend *too* much time sleeping overnight in the ground floor apartment.

FIVE

THE NEXT MORNING, I got a call from Lee while I was drying off from my shower.

"Got some info for you, Angie. Come on by the station on your way to work." I thanked him and promised to be there within the hour.

I continued to get dressed—it never took me long—a pair of jeans, a T-shirt and a light-yellow pullover sweater, and my waterproof slip-on boots. My silver turtle necklace—a gift from Jack, the flippers, head and tail moved—and an artist-signed sterling ring inlaid with coral, onyx and opal that Albert had picked up when he and Sylvia stayed a week in New Mexico. I'd started to collect sterling silver jewelry, especially Native American artisan work.

I donned my dark-green anorak and wound a soft gray muffler around my neck, with matching earmuffs and gloves, made sure I had the stuff I needed—wallet, T pass, and keys to the office.

I took the green line to Copley Square and hoofed it to the Berkley precinct where Lee worked. He was in a meeting with the chief. I had to wait about twenty minutes before Lee returned to his office. A tall, lanky blond with a mustache and glasses, I noticed there was something new about him.

I peered closely at his face. Lee blinked and grinned. "What—I got doughnut crumbs in my mustache, Matelli?"

I shook my head. "No, looks more like powdered sugar on your chin. You growing a beard, Lee?"

He shrugged. "Megan thinks I should try it. I told her it comes in patchy."

I inspected it closely. His cheeks were smooth as a baby's tush, but his chin was studded with bristles. "A goatee, maybe," I said in a dubious tone.

He grinned. "Don't take it any further than that, Matelli, or I may suddenly forget where I placed the file."

I waved a hand and laughed.

He sat behind his desk and I followed suit in the chair provided for visitors. He placed the file on the edge of his desk near me. After glancing at Lee, who nodded imperceptibly, I slid it off and glanced through it.

Ellen Bidwell was clean. Not a parking ticket, not a tail-light warning. But her kids were another story. In fact, the sheet showed that she had only seen the inside of a police station because of her children. She had been to juvie three times—twice to bail out her son, Brian, and once for her daughter, Lara. Jeez. What a family.

Of course, because the children were under eighteen, the records were sealed so there wasn't anything in there that would help me understand the family. But I was starting to feel sorry for Ellen. No wonder she was sliding little baubles into her bag and trying to screw Braden's. If my kids were this much trouble, I'd probably be a klepto or in a loony bin.

I looked up. "Nothing else?"

"What do you want, Matelli, an engraved invitation to browse through the juvie records?"

"Were the kids ever charged with anything?"

He shook his head. "Looks like all three times the charges were dropped or the witnesses were taken care of. Don't read anything into what I just said. I couldn't get near the records. They're tightly sealed."

I tapped a line on a pink form. "I noticed that the boy had been bailed out both times."

Lee shrugged. "I guess you could follow up on that if you think it's appropriate."

I got up, leaned over, punched him affectionately in the arm. "You are learning to be *such* a politician, Lee."

"You up for a game of poker next week?" he asked.

"Yeah, call me. Jack's gonna be here, but I'm sure I can get away. We haven't played for almost two months." I headed back to my office.

When I got off the elevator, the bail bonds office was open. Benny, the bondsman, was a little fireplug of a guy. Even on the sunniest summer day, his office was a smoky, dark hole. Today, one pool of light stood alone on his desk, the banker's lamp with the chipped green shade that shed light on the scarred oak desk piled high with papers and an ugly black telephone that looked as if it belonged in a 1930s noir gangster movie.

"Hey, Angie," he called. He always left his door open. It was weird to see a bail bond operation on the fourth floor of a corporate building—they usually had a storefront—but Benny had been in business for over twenty years, and didn't seem to be suffering from lack of customers. I knew that Benny had a reputation for being a stand-up guy and, if a bail jumped, for hiring the meanest, nastiest mothers in the bounty business. He paid top dollar to cover his investments. Right now, he was hunched over some paperwork. He noticed that I hadn't moved from the doorway and looked up. "What's up? You still working for Braden's for extra Christmas money?"

I stopped and leaned against his doorway. "Still am. I'm just working a different angle." I started to turn back toward my office, but a thought occurred to me. "Say, Benny, maybe you could help me with something."

He raised his eyebrows. "Is this a buddy-to-buddy assist, or is there money involved?"

I thought about it. "If you come across some information, it could involve money—Braden money."

Benny rubbed his hands together. "Sounds like it's right down my alley. How much will I make?"

I shrugged. I hadn't really thought about it. "You figure out what you think the information is worth, and submit a bill to me. Then I'll submit it with any fees I'll incur during the investigation."

Benny grinned. I held up a finger. "Just remember, Benny, the fee has to be reasonable or Old Man Braden will take notice and if he feels the bill is padded, you won't get paid."

The bail bondsman nodded, a shrewd look in his eyes, and asked, "So what is it you want me to do?"

I wrote Ellen Bidwell's name on a slip of paper I found in my pocket, and handed it to him. "Look that name up in your files. Has she been picked up for anything, charged with any offense? If you can't find her in your files, check around with your buddies, maybe some cops who owe you a favor."

He nodded. "What am I looking for?"

"Nonviolent crimes, mostly. But anything that might be connected."

He grinned. "Will do. I'll probably have something for you by tomorrow."

"Thanks." I pushed off the doorway and headed to the office.

THERE WEREN'T ANY MESSAGES, and I finished up my paperwork in under an hour.

I sat at my desk, spinning around in my new chair until I became dizzy, trying to figure out what to do next. But I kept thinking about Ellen Bidwell. My god, the woman had trouble. Divorced, raising two hellions. What more could go wrong? Oh, yes, she was a kleptomaniac.

I checked my e-mail and found an attachment from Jack containing information about Ellen Bidwell. Her maiden name was Melman, she was forty-two, and had been divorced for almost a year. Her ex-husband was a lawyer and paid child support in the sum of nine hundred dollars a month per child. That was eighteen hundred a month. I didn't have kids, but I knew that in a place like Boston, that was not enough money to raise two children on.

Her checking account had less than fifty dollars in it, and from the divorce decree, it was clear that Tim Bidwell, the ex, had gotten the better deal. He had left her with the family home that was paid for except for property taxes and insurance, and Ellen had gotten the 1994 Saab. Tim had gotten the 1999 Mercedes, the newer, more powerful of their two computers, and had moved into a brownstone in the Beacon Hill area. He also retained control of the family vacation home on the Cape—in Truro—and a ski cabin in Vermont. Ellen had gotten royally screwed on the divorce. Of course she had—never marry a lawyer without a prenup. Jack had sent a message with the attachment:

Angie,
This is what I've dug up so far. Nice ex, huh? I'm gonna do a little more digging—I'm sure he's hiding assets somewhere. Check out the divorce decree. His yearly income is ridiculously small for a partner in a prestigious law firm. Someone had friends in the court system....

                                           Jack

I printed out the attachment and put the information into the thin file I'd made up for her. I stopped and studied the divorce papers. Tim Bidwell, partner at Drumm, Best and Bidwell, had put down that he made seventy-eight thousand dollars a year. I laughed at the absurdity. Only an assistant D.A. made that kind of dough—and he or she would have to be entry level.

I wondered what judge had been stupid enough to sign off on this paper? Jack had thoughtfully provided an attachment that was a copy of the divorce papers. I studied the signature and thought it said Joanne Charles. Or maybe John Charles.

I decided to go pay a visit to Ellen Bidwell's home. She might be working right now, I thought. I wasn't sure where she worked or when. I knew that she had two teenagers, and both of them had been in trouble with the law.

I got my Bronco out of the garage nearby—my cousin managed the garage and he gave me a substantial discount on monthly parking.

Watertown was an upper-middle-class community made up of mostly professionals with kids. Most of the houses were at least one-hundred-year-old Victorians with large grassy lots and tree-lined streets. I consulted a map to find Hill Street. It was a two-block street that began on Hawthorne and ended on Fayette. I noted that it was halfway between the middle school on Bemis and the high school on Common.

I turned on Hill and drove slowly down the street, looking and finding 123 Hill with very little trouble. A beautiful pale-tan Victorian with green-and-gray trim, a detached double-car garage, an eighty-by-sixty lot with an apple tree in the backyard, it looked like the perfect house. The only difference was that all the other houses had Christmas lights and Santas and nativity scenes in their front yards. The Bidwell house didn't even have a wreath hanging on the door.

The Saab was parked in the driveway. Ellen Bidwell was there. I parked down the street from the house to get a good view of it. I couldn't walk freely around the neighborhood until Ellen left. Checking the time, I realized that the high school would be out in a half hour. The middle school got out at the same time.

I drove first to the middle school. The school was institutional yellow brick and chrome, one floor. The yard seemed deserted, but as I got out of the car, two boys came up to me. "You want someone to watch that car of yours, lady?"

I looked around. "Gee, I didn't know this was such a bad neighborhood. Did I take a wrong turn and end up in Roxbury?"

The boys were probably twelve and trying to look like Eminem. They wore baggy jeans, which just looked silly, and earrings. The taller of the boys had peroxided his hair and his roots were showing. The shorter boy had a bit more weight on him, like a wrestler might, and wore a lot of chains à la Mr. T. Both boys were smoking.

I crossed my arms. "Aren't you supposed to be in school?"

They came toward me menacingly. "And if we don't wanna go?"

Their macho posing and gangsta attitude didn't bother me at all. I could take care of myself, but I tried to maintain a readiness, and awareness in uncertain situations.

I shrugged. "Actually, I'm looking for some information."

Both boys stopped coming toward me. I'd caught them off balance. "I'll make it worth your while." I held up a ten-dollar bill. Upper-middle-class gangstas could be bought cheaply. The older one reached out for the bill. I held it away from him. "Information first."

He glanced at his partner in crime and nodded. "Okay, lady. What do you want to know so bad you're willing to pay?"

"About the Bidwell boy, Brian. He go to school here?"

"Yeah," the tall boy said. "He's my man."

"Posse?" I asked.

They both nodded, both looked uncomfortable that an older person was using their slang.

"He was picked up a couple of times. Why?"

The younger boy narrowed his eyes. "Why you want to know?"

I took out a five and held it up with the other bill. "Let's just say I'm curious, just an interested party." I held up another ten and said, "For twenty-five dollars, just the facts, kids."

The short kid licked his lips, his eyes glued to the bills.

"So what is it," I asked, "breaking and entering, shoplifting, or drugs?"

"One time was for car theft," the tall kid finally said. "It was his aunt's car, but his dad got him out on bail and talked to the aunt, who decided not to press charges.

"The second time was for drugs. He had a joint on him. We were riding around, and were stopped by the cops for a busted taillight. They rousted us without our consent. Brian's dad got us all off." Both boys laughed. "Those cops searched him without cause, man."

"What about his sister, Lara?"

The tall one snatched the money out of my hand. "That'll be extra. But it's good."

I sighed. The little racketeers were smarter than I'd originally thought. I took out a twenty. "That's highway robbery, and it's the last of the money."

The short one grinned and said, "We take checks."

I started to put the twenty away. The tall kid finally told me. Lara was in a really bad situation. Brian had confided in them that his sister was seeing another girl, but it was an obsessive relationship.

"So you're saying that Lara is a lesbian?"

The tall kid shrugged. "I don't know, man, Brian just said it was a really weird friendship and he was kinda worried about her. Funny, they never got along until their dad split."

The short kid narrowed his eyes at me. "Hey, what's your interest in all this?"

I ignored his question to ask one of my own. "Do you know if their mom has ever been picked up for anything illegal?"

"Don't know their old lady. But their old man is a piece of work—he's going to the Caribbean for Christmas."

"With his girlfriend," the tall one added. "What an asshole. Brian says his old man is hiding his assets. Brian, his sister and his mother are barely making ends meet."

The school came to life, kids spilling out of it. School buses roared to life. My homeboys looked at me, the short one took the second twenty from me.

"Anytime we can help, we're out here eighth period."

The tall kid, nodded, counting the money. "Been a pleasure doing business with you."

They sauntered away, toward the buses, tossing their smokes aside and laughing.

I went back to my car and watched the kids go by, wondering which one was Brian.

It didn't matter. I had made up my mind to help them. While I investigated the shoplifting incident, maybe I could get help for the family, get the father to cough up more money for his kids. Maybe I could be a Christmas angel.

SIX

I WENT BACK to the house to watch for the kids as they came home. I parked in the same spot and kept an eye on the house. The Saab was gone. A few minutes later, a slender boy with large eyes and a sneer sauntered down the street and up the steps to the Bidwell house. He looked around, a wary expression on his face as if he thought someone was following him, then entered the house. I studied him to make sure I recognized him the next time I encountered him.

Fifteen minutes later, two teenage girls strolled lazily up the street. They bumped shoulders, wrapped arms around each other's waists. The Saab came down the street and zipped into the driveway. Ellen Bidwell stepped out, a plastic grocery bag dangling from her hand, her shoulder bag firmly on her shoulder. She spied the girls and marched up to them. I let my window down a few inches, and took out an amplifier to hear the exchange.

"Lara, where were you? I've been driving all over God's green earth looking for you. Did you forget the appointment we had?" Her anger seemed to be directed at Lara's friend rather than at the forgotten appointment.

Lara was a younger version of her mother. Her hair was curly and dark blond, the color I imagined Ellen's hair had been before she had teenagers. Lara had large eyes and, when I used my binoculars to see up close, thick, dark lashes set in a heart-shaped face. Her clothes were straight out of the teen magazines—flared jeans, a tight top under an open down jacket. No hat, no gloves, no muffler. Typical teenager, gotta show how tough they are.

I turned my attention to the other girl. She was taller with long, straight dark hair. Her features were set close together. She looked more male than female and she had a defiant expression that probably didn't change much. Ellen must have sensed it, too, because she paused and glanced at the girl.

I was getting a definite sense of déjà vu, and I couldn't figure out what was causing it.

I listened as Ellen Bidwell turned her attention back to her daughter. "So what is so much more important that you ditched me to walk home?"

Lara had turned away from me so I couldn't see her face, but I heard the lie in her voice. "We had ninth period today."

Apparently Ellen suspected it was a lie as well because she gave Ellen's friend a hard look. "Is that true, Crystal?"

Such a delicate name for such a coarse-looking girl. Crystal crossed her arms. "Yeah. We had ninth period together." She gave Ellen a "What are you gonna do about it?" look.

Ellen pursed her lips.

"We have to go study," Lara said, pushing past her mother and into the house. Crystal followed, throwing a smirk Ellen's way.

I watched Ellen watching the house. There was sadness in her demeanor. I felt bad for her.

I started the car after a few more minutes, and drove away.

I stopped for an early dinner at a little Thai place on Comm Avenue where they served a great *pad thai,* and it seemed be a good place to think. I looked over my file on Ellen Bidwell as I slurped up rice noodles, vegetables and shrimp.

My next target was Tim Bidwell, the ex. He lived on

Beacon Hill. It was after five and time to see what he was up to. I wanted to know about the family, how they operated. The two hoods outside the Watertown middle school were quite helpful with information about the dynamics of the mother and the teens.

I drove to his brownstone on Primus Street. Actually, I parked in a garage on Cedar Street West, then walked to Primus and looked for his address. It was the third brownstone on my left. I stayed across the street and kept an eye out for the father. I didn't know what he looked like, but I knew his address, and I knew what kind of car he drove.

An hour later, a sleek, black sporty Mercedes drove up to the address and turned into the drive. I lucked out—Tim Bidwell didn't pull into his garage, which meant that he was going out for the evening. He stepped out of his car and I got my first good look at him. He was about five-ten, and had a graying beard on a face that might have been carved out of granite. He wore a gray silk suit that had been tailored to fit his physique, definitely a designer label. He carried one of those slim metal briefcases and his hair was styled, cut short on top and tousled, and shaved close on the sides and back.

He went inside. I saw lights go on in several rooms, and I waited. It was getting cold, so I took a walk to the corner and warmed up with a cup of tea. I strolled back down his street in time to see a woman in an evening coat drive up in a Lexus and park in his driveway next to his car. He came out to meet her, dressed in a tux, and they greeted each other with a kiss.

She had shoulder-length copper hair and wore large diamond earrings. Bidwell opened the passenger door to his Mercedes and she slipped inside, ready for an evening of dining and dancing while Tim Bidwell's children prowled the streets of Watertown and his ex-wife prowled the aisles of Braden's or Filene's, each in search of some relief from their sad, oppressive lives.

What a bastard, I thought.

I hoofed it to my car, hoping I could catch his car and follow it, but there was a line of cars all trying to leave the garage, and I was stuck for twenty minutes. I headed for home.

WEDNESDAY MORNING, I did some paperwork in my office at home, then got ready to go down to the law firm of Drumm, Best, and Bidwell. The offices were located on the third floor of a sober brownstone building on Tremont Street, facing the Boston Common and the gold-domed State House.

It was twenty to twelve when I walked into a deli and ordered a pastrami on rye to go. At a few minutes before noon, I walked into Drumm, Best, and Bidwell with a sandwich order for Tim Bidwell. I had decided that someone needed to tell Tim that he wasn't up for Father of the Year. Maybe I could get the jewelry back without pressing charges if I could get this dipshit to understand what he was doing to his family. He could take care of his kids' problems and get his ex-wife the help she needed. I'd thought about it all night long. Although I might be causing more problems for Ellen Bidwell in the short run—not being able to see her children if Tim took over was one of the big problems—I felt that she would ultimately thank me in the long run if I could get her the help she needed.

I thought back to two days ago when I had been gung ho about recovering the jewelry and slapping Ellen Bidwell in jail. But after seeing what a mess her life was, I wanted to make her life better. I wanted to recover the jewelry as well, but I wanted Ellen to get help, I wanted her kids to get the help they needed, and I wanted the asshole father ex-husband to become more of a human being. The closest I'd come to having a nuclear family was when I took Michael and Stephanie for a three-day weekend so Sophia and David could go away to Martha's Vineyard alone.

Christmas Muzak—a version of "The Little Drummer Boy"—was playing softly in the background. I approached the receptionist and told her I had a sandwich to deliver for Timothy Bidwell. An ice blonde with perfect sculpted hair and artistic makeup, she blinked.

"But," she said, looking mystified, "he didn't come in this morning. How could he have ordered this sandwich?"

I hadn't expected that he wouldn't be in. Of course, he might have called from court. I said as much.

"But he's a tax attorney. He rarely goes to court," she said, and smiled. "Are you sure the sandwich is for Mr. Bidwell? Maybe it's a mistake."

I pretended to study the receipt. "Yes, I'm sure. Maybe I could leave it on his desk? He might have called it in."

She frowned. "We haven't been able to reach him all morning. One of his clients called with a big problem."

I shrugged, looking confused.

"What kind of sandwich is it?" she asked.

"Pastrami and Swiss," I replied.

She reached in her purse. "I like pastrami. How much?"

"Uh, it's free for you. This must have been some prank call."

"Thank you," she said, taking the bag.

I left. I went to Bidwell's home. Two units were parked there, red lights flashing, uniforms swarming all over the place. I pulled my anorak closer around me, my hands in my pockets and looked around until I finally spotted a detective I knew from Lee's precinct.

"Detective Meyer," I called out.

Harry Meyer had been on the force with my uncle Charlie. He caught sight of me and waved me over. A large gray man, balding with yellow teeth, he smiled and hugged me.

"Angela Matelli, what are you doing here?"

I gestured to Bidwell's building. "I was going to visit Timothy Bidwell."

"You got tax problems?" he asked.

"Uh, yeah."

"Well, Tim Bidwell don't have no problems anymore."

"He's dead?"

Meyer nodded confirmation.

"Mind if I ask how?"

He frowned. "Don't know as I should tell you. Technically, you could be a suspect."

"Suspect?" I asked.

"Neighbor says she saw a girl," Meyer consulted his notebook, "about five feet five, dark shoulder-length hair, green anorak, jeans. Hanging around Bidwell's building late afternoon." He looked up. "That you?"

I sighed. "You got me. But I never met the man before now."

Meyer waved a hand. "You're off the hook, kid. We got a description of another suspect already. Someone closer to him."

"The redhead?" I asked.

He blinked in surprise. "Redhead?"

"Yeah, he went out with this woman who had red hair, expensive clothes and a dark-blue late-model Lexus."

He furrowed his brows and took notes. "Nah, that's not who we think killed him." So he knew who I was talking about. Whoever she was, she must have been somehow involved in Bidwell's death.

"When was he killed?" I asked.

"This morning. Stabbed. Weapon still there, fingerprints wiped. Can't tell you any more. We gotta clean up here, then go out to Watertown and pick up the suspect."

Ellen Bidwell. The ex-wife. I had to get to her before they did.

I started to back up, ready to say goodbye but a uniform came up to Meyer to distract him.

"Detective, they found something near the body. You oughta come see."

Meyer turned back to me briefly. "Gotta go, kid. Say hi to your uncle for me." He punched me lightly on the arm.

"Yeah, thanks, Detective."

He cocked a finger toward me. "Harry to you, kid."

I wondered as I left whether I ought to mention to "No-Legs" Charlie, my ex-cop uncle, that Harry Meyer, when hugging me, had pinched my ass. I'd forgotten what a groper he could be. But I'd gotten some information and I had to move fast.

I got in my car and drove as fast as I could to Watertown. The Saab was in the driveway. Ellen was home and the cops hadn't arrived yet.

I ran up to the door and rang the doorbell. When she didn't answer I noticed that a sign above the bell told visitors that it was out of order. Sensing that I had very little time left, I pounded the hell out of the door.

She finally answered, and she had been crying. She seemed to half recognize me, but couldn't really place me.

"I'm sorry, I'm not up for a religious tract or anything." She started to shut the door in my face.

I put my hand out to stop her and she looked at me again, this time with full recognition. "You! I don't feel like putting up with your shit right now—"

"Listen," I said with force and, I hoped, urgency, "there isn't a whole lot of time to explain. But the police are going to come here to arrest you for the murder of your ex."

"Wha—?" Her jaw went slack and I took the opportunity to push my way past her.

"Hire me," I said. I had walked into her living room and she had followed me, clearly too stunned by my knowing this information to respond properly. "I'm a private investigator by profession. Braden's is a moonlighting gig for me." I handed her one of my business cards. "We'll talk later and I'll explain everything to you. But for now, get a dollar and give it to me now so I can represent you." I wasn't sure what I was doing was kosher—after all, Braden's was already a client, and they had hired me to investigate Ellen Bidwell and recover the jewelry. On the other hand, I was being hired by Ellen Bidwell to represent her in a murder case, which appeared to be completely unrelated.

She heard the sirens and came out of her stunned state long enough to go to her purse. She paused. "I can't afford to pay you—"

I shook my head. "Doesn't matter to me right now. All I'm concerned with is getting you representation. I'll bring a contract to the jail for you to sign. Do you have an attorney?"

She shook her head. "Not a criminal attorney."

"I'll find a good one for you," I assured her. "What about the kids? Do you have anywhere for them to go?"

She shook her head.

"Your mom?"

"Dead."

"Tim's mother?"

She shook her head. "The same." Then she thought of something. "My sister, Renee. Lives in Framingham." A knock at the door, very insistent. Ellen glanced at it fearfully. "I—I don't understand what's happening, why I'm a suspect."

"I'm not sure, either. Did you visit with Tim last night or today?"

She pursed her lips and crossed her arms. "Yes. This morning. Early. I wanted to talk to him about the divorce decree." She let out an exasperated sigh. "Actually, what I wanted to talk to him about was his role as absentee father. Our children are—" She searched for the word.

"Difficult?"

She looked up and nodded. The pounding on the door was becoming more insistent. "I wanted him to know what was going on with our children—"

I cut her off because she could save it for the meeting we would have with her lawyer.

"Well, a neighbor must have witnessed you entering and-or leaving his house this morning." I thought of something else. "Speaking of the children, what's your sister's last name and phone number?"

She straightened up and started for the door. "Weston. It's in my address book in the kitchen. In the drawer by the phone."

"Answer the door," I instructed her, "and like every other good suspect in every television show you've ever seen, don't answer any questions until I get your attorney down there."

I went to the kitchen and heard her open the door. "Yes?" I heard her say.

I opened the drawer by the phone.

"Ellen Bidwell?"

"I'm Ellen Bidwell."

I pulled out the address book, bound in green leatherette, very old-fashioned. I flipped through it.

"I'm Detective Meyer, this is Sergeant Cochran."

"What can I do for you, Detective? Is this for a donation to the policeman's ball?"

Oh, she was good. Of course, I'd given her some lead time. Now she was giving me time to get out of there.

"No, ma'am. We're from homicide. We're here to arrest you for the murder of your ex-husband, Timothy Bidwell."

"Tim is dead?" she asked faintly. It didn't sound as if she was acting now. Even though I'd warned her, it was still a shock, I'm sure, to hear those words. Even if he was her *ex,* she had loved him and lived with him and had kids with him. Even if he had been a jerk, even if he'd screwed her in the divorce settlement. He was still the father of her children. And she would inherit his money through his next of kin—their children, Lara and Brian, the screwups.

I heard the detectives moving around in the front of the house.

"What are you doing?" she asked, panic in her voice.

"We have a warrant to search the premises," Meyer told her. "Sergeant, start with the living room, have the officers search the upstairs, and we'll meet in the kitchen."

I made a face and realized I was in deep shit if I didn't get my butt out of there.

SEVEN

I STUFFED THE address book in my anorak and looked around. There was a mudroom off of the kitchen that looked as if it led to the garage. The garage was usually searched last when there was a warrant—if the warrant even stipulated that the garage could be searched.

I slipped quietly out of the house and into the garage. There was a back door to the yard, and I poked my head out to make sure I couldn't be seen from the house as I exited. A shed provided shelter about ten yards away, and would shield me as I climbed over the fence and made it through another backyard to my car. It was fortunate that I had a regular habit of parking my car down the street from the place I intended to visit.

I hunched down, slipped out the back garage door, and crab-ran to the shed. Once I was behind it, I climbed the six-foot-tall wooden fence. I had a bit of trouble reaching the top—the surface was too smooth, sanded, and painted. But I turned a garbage pail over and scrambled onto it and over the fence within a minute.

I landed in someone's pile of snow-covered leaves. There was a swing set in the backyard, and three kids, a boy and two girls, were hanging out there. They were all looking at me. I stood up, brushed off the snow and leaves I'd rolled in, and walked toward them. The kids were about nine or ten.

I put on my best smile. "Hi, kids."

One of the girls, a little brown-haired, big-eyed kid, said, "We're not supposed to talk to strangers."

I nodded. "Good idea. Why don't I leave and you can get on with what you're doing."

And with that, I left them. I was certain they would talk to their mother and if she put two and two together with the police coming to get Ellen Bidwell, the neighbor in back of her, I might get a visit from the police. But I would have to leave that to chance, and hope that the police never discovered my visit.

As I drove away, I thought about Ellen's case. She had an excellent motive to kill her ex. Maybe she'd realized how screwed she'd been as she looked over the divorce decree recently and went nuts. Maybe she'd always known it had been a bad deal and she'd stewed about it for the last year. Maybe she'd discovered that he was dating this mysterious redhead I saw last night. There was any number of ways this could go with a good prosecutor.

I wished I'd had the opportunity to find out more from Ellen about her whereabouts before Meyer had shown up. I checked the time and realized that school would be out in a little under half an hour. I had to get in touch with a lawyer and Ellen's sister before picking the kids up. I couldn't be sure that Ellen's sister would be able to drive into Watertown from Framingham for the children before school let out.

I got on my cell phone as I drove back to the office, making calls to criminal lawyers that I knew. On my fourth call—it must have been a busy time for criminals—Sarah Tisdale, attorney-at-law, took the case for me. Sarah was a distant relation to me, married to one of my cousins. She specialized in criminal law and had won more cases than she'd lost. She agreed to meet with Ellen immediately, and I would meet them down at the police station in about an hour.

I called Renee Weston. She didn't answer. There was a

second number, a cell phone number, I thought. She answered on the third ring.

I introduced myself and explained the situation.

"Oh, my," Renee replied.

"Are you able to get away to pick up the kids?"

She hesitated. "Well, I have my own kids to think of—they're in grade school. At least Brian and Lara are older."

I sighed impatiently. "Is there someone who could pick up your kids while you pick up Brian and Lara? No matter what their age, this is going to be a blow to them and I don't think this is the time for them to be left alone."

She hemmed and hawed. "I suppose my husband could leave work and take care of our kids, but I hate to bother him. Would it be possible for you to pick up the kids?"

I had pulled over to the curb to talk to her. It was a very frustrating experience. "Mrs. Weston, I can't do that. I'm not a relative, or even a friend. And I have an appointment down at the precinct." Come to think of it, Renee didn't seem all too concerned about her sister's predicament. "Do you know of anyone else who would be able to take the kids?"

"Not really," she said. "Tell you what I can do. I can call both schools and have the kids go straight home. You can go there and explain things to them after you've had your meeting."

I was silent for a moment, wanting to drive directly to Renee Weston's Framingham residence and hit her in the head with a two-by-four to knock some sense into her head. "Mrs. Weston, maybe I didn't explain things very well. Your sister has been charged with killing your ex-brother-in-law."

"Yes, I understand."

"I'm sorry to say this, but you don't seem all that upset about it."

Renee sighed. "Ms.—"

"Matelli," I supplied.

"Matelli. I know I sound cold, but Ellen's life is, well, messy, and I really don't have the time to clean up after her. I've done so all of our lives, and it's time she dealt with her own problems."

"She says she didn't do it." Actually, we hadn't gotten to that, but I was pretty sure she would say she didn't kill her ex.

"Well, of course she said that," Renee replied soothingly.

I didn't know what else to say to her. I looked at the cell phone, wanting to bang it against my dashboard, but I would only be destroying a personal item, not Renee Weston's abominable behavior toward her own sister.

I finally hung up. I looked at the time and realized the kids would be out of school and on their way home. The least I could do was offer them a ride to the precinct to see their mom. Not that they knew me from a hole in the ground.

I pulled up to the house just as Brian slouched up the street. I got out of the car, intending to approach him in a sensitive manner.

"Brian Bidwell?" I asked when he got within six feet of me.

"Who wants to know?" When Brian looked at me, his eyes were like cold brown marbles. There was no emotion in them.

I gave him a card. He studied it for a moment, his lips moving as he read the words silently to himself. Then he looked up at me and said, "You the bitch was asking my homeboys questions about me?"

I narrowed my eyes at him. "I am the private investigator who was asking about you, yes."

He ripped up my card and dropped it in front of me, then got in my face. "Well, stay away from me, bitch. I don't know what kinda pervert you are, but I don't like older women." He grinned and continued to stare at me.

I held his gaze and said in a steady voice, "Your mother has been taken down to the police station on the charge of murder. I'm sorry I have to tell you this way, but your father was killed this morning. The police think your mother did it."

His face wavered for a second, then he fell away from me and headed toward the house without comment. "So the fuck what?" he said.

I called after him. "You either go with me, or Social Services takes over."

That stopped him. He spun and came back to me. I saw the vulnerable boy underneath all the bravado for another few seconds. "How do I know you're not some perverted bitch who just wants to take me from my happy home?"

Ah, some humor behind the pain. That was better than an Uzi. I grabbed one of his wrists. "You can stop calling me 'bitch' anytime now. Stick with Ms. Matelli. I called your aunt Renee and she apparently is too busy to come over here."

"Yeah, she's got her own problems," he replied, yanking his wrist away from my grip, "*Ms.* Matelli. So I'll ask you again—how am I supposed to know that you, a total stranger who has been asking questions about me and my sister, are on the up-and-up?"

"Go in the house and call the Beacon Hill precinct. Ask about your mother, then ask for Sarah Tisdale, her attorney. Ms. Tisdale can give you more information about me."

"You got the number?" he asked.

"Yeah, but if I give it to you, you might think it's all a setup because I want your skinny butt. Use Information or a Boston phone book."

He looked at me silently for a moment, then turned and let himself into the house. I stayed outside and shivered until he opened the door, phone in hand, and nodded. I entered the house.

"What time does your sister come home?"

"If she doesn't have a ninth period, she should be home any minute now."

I had an idea. "Brian, wait for your sister and explain everything to me. I need to go up to your mother's bedroom to get a few things for her stay in jail overnight."

I turned to leave and he called out after me, "What's gonna happen to us?"

I stopped and turned around. He looked scared. I walked back to him and put a reassuring hand on his shoulder. "I'm gonna try to find out the truth. In the meantime, do you know anyone you can stay with?"

"Uncle Roger and Aunt Renee."

I kept my face as blank as possible. "I've already talked to your aunt and she doesn't seem able to handle everything she has on her plate already. You may end up with Social Services after all."

"In a foster home," he said, screwing his face up as if he'd just smelled something bad.

"There are some good foster homes out there. A lot of them. But let's not think about that right now. We'll worry about that later." I climbed the stairs and found Ellen's bedroom. It was the room without the Eminem, Kid Rock and Marilyn Manson posters, lava lamps and black lights.

Ellen's room looked unfinished. The walls were white, the kind of white that sheetrock has. The bed didn't match the nightstand and neither of them matched the dresser. There were no curtains on the windows, but there were still miniblinds, a neutral beige shade. Even though it was a large, light-filled room, there was something very gloomy and dark and depressing about it.

I went over to the dresser and got out a change of clothes for when Ellen's bond would be posted. I would have to contact Benny about it. But court wouldn't convene until tomorrow, so she'd be spending the night.

I began to search the dresser for the Braden's jewelry—the necklace and matching earrings, the ruby-and-diamond dinner ring, something. Nothing. I tried the nightstand, then started on the closet.

I had just finished looking in the last shoebox and going through the last pocket of her clothes when a sniffle from behind told me that someone was in the room.

"What are you doing in my mother's closet?"

I backed out and turned around to face a teary Lara. Her friend Crystal was stuck to Lara like Super Glue and she was glaring daggers at me.

"Hi, I'm Angela, a friend of your mother's."

Lara's tears turned into a sneer. "My mom has no friends."

"Brian tell you what's going on?"

She nodded. I glanced coolly at Crystal. "This is probably not the time for friends to be here."

Crystal narrowed her eyes. "Well, Lara, I guess you're on your own. I know when I'm not wanted." She dropped Lara's hand and turned to leave.

The panic in Lara's face was evident. "No, Crystal, I'm sure Ms. Matelli didn't mean it like that...."

Crystal turned back, a sly smile on her face.

Lara turned back, her eyes pleading with me. "You didn't mean it like that, did you?" I smiled as openly and as kindly as I could, considering that I wanted to rip into Crystal with a chain saw at the moment. "I don't know what you mean. But if you mean that I think it's inappropriate for a friend to be here at a time when we need to get over to the precinct where your mother is being held, yes, I think it's time for Crystal to leave." I stepped up to Crystal and took her arm and escorted her down the stairs and out the door, whispering to her, "You can't control every situation, little girl."

I shut the door firmly behind her and turned to Lara who, if she was in a cartoon, would have steam coming out of her ears.

"You—you had no right. I don't even know you."

"As an agent for your mother, I did have a right."

"She was my only friend," Lara said, tears springing from her eyes.

"Baby," I said, "you don't know the meaning of friendship. Crystal's no friend, she's an emotional vampire and she's sucking you dry." I turned away and added, "But you're not ready to hear that now. Let's deal with your mom. Get ready to go. I'm leaving in five minutes. Tell your brother." I walked away, leaving Lara to blink back unshed tears.

I went back to the bedroom and finished my search quickly. There were other places to look, but with two teen hoodlums in the house, I figured if she had the jewelry, it was either in her bedroom or in a safety deposit box. I didn't remember seeing one listed on Ellen Bidwell's financial statement.

I went to the refrigerator, wondering if maybe she kept her jewels "on ice." I'd once found some important information for a case in the ice cube tray. Nothing in the refrigerator. I emerged, closing the door and turning to see Lara and Brian staring at me from the door that led to the dining room.

I shrugged. "I was hungry, but there's nothing to eat. Let's go." I'd left the suitcase with Ellen's things in it by the front door. Making sure one of the kids had the keys to the house, we left and headed downtown.

The police station was filled with holiday cheer. Everyone, including the criminals, seemed to be a little brighter, a little more cheery. Maybe it's the fact that we're brought up to believe that we're still on Santa's nice list, no matter how naughty we've been.

Sarah Tisdale met us in an interrogation room. She was petite with auburn curls and wore lots of pastel suits and looked totally harmless. She even affected a Southern drawl. But she was a tigress in the courtroom. The funny thing was that even though she had a reputation as a sharp lawyer, even prosecutors who had dealt with her time and time again kept falling for her act.

When she saw the children, she was all sweetness and light, reassuring the kids that their mother would be free by tomorrow noon.

"Is there any place for them to stay tonight?" she asked me.

"The kids assure me that their aunt and uncle will take care of them overnight." I didn't want to go into my conversation with Renee. I looked at the kids and back at Sarah. "Can they see their mom?"

Sarah turned to the two teens and in her best gentle voice, said, "Brace yourselves, kids, you'll be talking to her in a room like this, accompanied by a policeman."

A uniformed policeman escorted the teens out the door so Sarah and I could talk privately.

"Bring me up to date," Sarah said, clasping her hands on the scarred wooden table surface. Her briefcase placed to one side, she wore a pale-green linen skirt and jacket with an eggshell silk blouse underneath. Her reddish-brown hair was styled to curl behind her ears and was artfully rumpled. Her makeup was applied as if she wore no makeup at all and just looked that way naturally. The only thing missing was her Southern drawl, which she saved for the courtroom and for alternately intimidating and flirting with homicide detectives. When she talked to me, it was in her natural Bronx accent.

I looked around the room.

Sarah smiled. "It's clean. I checked it already. And if they *are* eavesdropping, I'll slap an invasion of privacy suit on them so fast—"

I held up my hands. "I get the picture." Nevertheless, I leaned forward and talked in a low voice. "I first saw Ellen Bidwell a week ago—last Thursday," I began, giving Sarah a concise, accurate version of the events of the past week.

When I had finished, she was silent for a moment. "Jeez, Angie, you've handed me a hot one."

I shook my head. "Just because she's a kleptomaniac doesn't mean she's a murderer."

Sarah rubbed her forehead in exasperation. "The detectives found a ruby-and-diamond dinner ring on the scene. Next to the body." She looked at me. "How would they know about Ellen's connection to it?"

I bit my lip. Of course, Chuck Eddy or Old Man Braden or Gerry the night manager—any one of them could have, and would have, reported the thefts to the police. Braden had assured me I wouldn't have to compete with the police for a week, at least. Why would he go back on his word without informing me of this new development? Maybe he didn't know. I took out my cell phone and called the store, asking for Chuck.

"Hey, Ange, you managed to get out of work this week, I see," he said in a cheery voice.

"Did Mr. Braden clue you in on my assignment?"

Chuck sighed. "Yeah. What's taking so long, Angie? You're usually on top of a case."

It was weird to talk to Chuck like he was a real human being and not some reject from a bad TV P.I. show. It was almost as if the real Chuck had been replaced by a new, improved version.

"Murder happened."

"She's dead?" he asked with alarm.

"She's being held as a suspect in the death of her ex-husband," I said. "I need to know if anyone at the store has talked to the police about the shoplifting incidents."

"Well, of course we reported that the items were missing, for insurance purposes."

"Did you mention Ellen Bidwell's name in connection to the thefts?"

"Well, of course not. We have the tapes to show she did it, but we never found the goods on her. Her name was not to be turned over to the police until you had finished your investigation.''

"Well, someone mentioned her name to the homicide detectives. Someone linked her name to an item of jewelry found at the scene of the crime.''

Chuck was silent for a moment, his wheels turning. "Rick. The arrogant bastard. I'd bet anything it was him. He was on the phone when I went up there the other day and he hung up quickly. I knew he was up to something.''

We hung up. I turned back to Sarah, explaining what had happened. She pursed her lips and frown lines appeared on her normally smooth brow. "I'll take care of it. You concentrate on investigating who else could have had it in for Tim Bidwell.''

EIGHT

MY FIRST DUTY was to take care of the devil children. Sarah got me past the uniformed officer into the room where Ellen sat with her children.

Brian sat next to his mother, her hand over his. Lara sat to the side, slumped in a chair with her arms crossed over her chest. All three had been crying. I wasn't sure if the kids were crying for the loss of their father or for the incarceration of their mother. Or both. It didn't matter.

Ellen stood up when I entered. "Ms. Matelli, Ms. Tisdale told me about—why I'm here." She locked eyes with me to let me know that she hadn't told her kids everything.

She turned to the children. "Brian, Lara, please leave the room so I can talk to Ms. Matelli."

"Mom," Brian asked, "what's going to happen to us?" He didn't look so tough now. He looked small and scared.

"Aunt Renee and Uncle Roger will take you. That's one of the reasons I want you to leave the room. I need to talk to them alone."

Well, not alone, exactly. I was in the room and she was going to use my cell phone.

As they exited the room, Lara turned back. "Mom, Crystal said I can stay at her house."

A troubled look came over Ellen's face. "Oh, Lara, I don't think—"

A black cloud passed over Lara's face. "Mom. Renee and Roger have enough to worry about. Let me stay with Crystal. It'll be easier to get to school."

Ellen looked away and hugged herself. "I'm sorry, I'm not comfortable with you staying with Crystal. Her mother isn't very attentive."

"It's only one night," Lara pleaded.

"No."

The teen's voice got strident. "Aunt Renee likes her. She took us shopping last weekend, you know."

I jumped in, annoyed at Lara's obnoxious behavior. "Your mother said no. What part of 'no' don't you understand?"

Lara narrowed her eyes at me, then whirled and left the room, slamming the door. I thought Ellen would be upset, but I heard her chuckle.

She shook her head and looked up at me. "You met Crystal?"

I nodded.

She looked down at her hands. "It's not just that I don't like the girl, there's something about her—"

"Well, she creeps *me* out," I said.

"It's not the lesbian angle of the relationship, although I do think Lara is too young to make a decision about her sexuality right now."

"I noticed that Crystal is very much in control of the relationship," I offered.

She nodded. "Ever since Lara befriended Crystal, she's lost all her other friends. It's become obsessive. Lara spends every night on the phone with Crystal, to the exclusion of all her other friends, both girls and boys. They hang out at the local mall together, and I know Lara's lying to me about this relationship. I'm afraid something more is going on there. I'm afraid I'm losing my daughter." When Ellen looked up at me, her eyes were brimming with tears. She let out a laugh. "As if I don't have enough problems, I'm dealing with this, this crazy relationship between my daughter and this girl."

"When did they start seeing each other?" I asked.

"It started about the time Tim began finding excuses for why he couldn't see his kids. He's always so busy and our children are hurting because of his lack of interest."

Abandonment by father. That was the big issue with Lara. Not that I'm an expert, but I grew up that way, too. My father abandoned me and my brothers and sisters, and we all dealt with it in our own way. Sophia became promiscuous, Rosa was a shadow, I became self-sufficient. But I remembered a time when Rosa had a friend, her only friend, and we were all concerned about her. She came out of it all right, and is now a healthy adult, but I remember Ma being worried about Rosa.

"Have you talked to Crystal's mother about your fears?"

She laughed again, sad this time, and waved a hand. "Futile. Crystal's mother thinks the sun rises and sets on her daughter. 'Crystal *always* tells me the truth,'" Ellen mimicked. "'Crystal is *very* mature for her age—when I was going through my divorce, I told her secrets about her father and she always kept them.'" Ellen shook her head. "Jesus Christ, the woman is not only a moron, but dangerous in her delusion. She thinks Crystal is normal, likes boys and never lies to her. No mother in the *world* believes that their teen tells the truth all the time."

This was turning into a counseling session. I took out my phone and handed it to Ellen. "Go ahead and call your sister."

She frowned. "Actually, I'll call my brother-in-law. Renee is a little, um, selfish and self-centered. I'd be willing to bet she hasn't even mentioned my predicament to Roger." She punched in some numbers and waited. A moment later, she asked for Roger Weston. I gathered she was calling him at his place of business. When he came on the line, she summed up what had happened, glossing over the fact that her sister had been less than helpful. She handed the phone to me.

Roger was warm, helpful, and concerned. "How is Ellen holding up?" he asked.

"As well as can be expected."

"I can pick up the kids in a few minutes, if you can wait at the station with them. It's almost five-thirty and I'm just off Copley Square."

"We can do that. I have a few things I need to go over with Ellen's lawyer anyway." I gave him Sarah's name and numbers to reach her, he thanked me and we finally hung up.

I turned back to Ellen and squeezed her hand. "It's hard to believe that the woman who searched me for some missing jewelry is helping me now."

I didn't know what to say to her. I didn't say anything.

She leaned over the table and said, "Ms. Matelli, I didn't steal that ring or anything else from the store. I was just window-shopping with my sister, Renee."

I wanted to believe her. She sounded so sincere, but she was in desperate need of money, she was going through a bad time with her kids and her ex-husband—how could I ignore the facts?

"Well, maybe you could explain how we you caught on tape, putting the jewelry into your bag."

The fire in Ellen's eyes went out and in a dull voice, she said, "I didn't do it. That's not me. You didn't find that bag on me."

I was frustrated. She was holding something back—I could tell. But busting her chops wouldn't get me anywhere. I'd just have to find a way around the wall she'd put up.

"I'll go wait with the kids and make sure Roger gets them, not Crystal."

The door opened and a policeman stuck his head inside. "Time's up."

"Is her attorney, Ms. Tisdale, still in the building?" I asked.

He consulted someone outside the room, then turned back and nodded. "She's with the kids by the candy and pop machines."

I was about to say goodbye to Ellen when I thought of something. "Ellen, you wouldn't happen to know the woman your ex was dating, would you?"

"Brian met her once. He said her name was Tia. He didn't think much of her."

"I don't suppose you know her last name."

She shook her head and stood up. "Sorry."

I found Sarah with the teens. Lara was still pouting, but Brian looked as if he were going to cry. Maybe he wasn't as tough as he tried to look. Lara, on the other hand, had some invisible wall around her.

I walked over to Lara. "What's your friend's last name?"

"What's it to you?" She spit the words at me.

"Maybe saving your mother from life in prison," I said in a mild tone.

She stuck her lip out. I sensed there were tears and a few fears behind the facade. "You plan to pin this on Crystal?"

"Not if she didn't do it."

"Abbott," Brian supplied. "Crystal Abbott. She and her mom live on Marshall Street near the cemetery. I don't know the exact—"

"*Brian!*" Lara had leaned forward, arms still crossed, eyes wide.

I reached out and touched his arm. "Thank you." I glanced at her and was about to say something when a man came toward us.

He was tall and thin, aesthetic-looking with white hair neatly brushed, wire-rim glasses perched on a thin nose above thin lips. He wore a sweater vest over an Oxford shirt and khaki slacks. "Uncle Roger!" Brian moved toward him.

Roger reached out and ruffled his nephew's hair. He glanced at Lara. "Everyone doing all right?"

I introduced myself and Sarah to him.

"Thank you for jumping on this so quickly," he said to me as he shook my hand. His grip was warm and strong without making me wince in pain.

"I happened to be in the neighborhood," I replied.

We exchanged business cards—he wrote his home address and phone number on the back of his card.

He turned to the kids. "You eaten yet?"

Lara looked down. Brian shook his head. Neither looked very hungry. Roger instructed them to wait for him by the entrance. He turned to us. "What's it look like for Ellen?"

Sarah shook her head. "Not good." She glanced at me and said, "We need to talk. I just learned new information."

Great. More bad news. Whatever she had to tell me had something to do with the ring and Ellen. I might have been able to get Ellen off by mentioning the fact that I'd searched her house and couldn't find the other jewelry. But from the sound of it, things had just gotten worse.

Roger looked from Sarah to me and nodded. "Right. I'd better take care of the children. I'll talk to you both later." He started to leave, then turned around. "When can I see Ellen?"

I found it interesting that he didn't mention his wife, Ellen's sister.

Sarah talked to him briefly alone, then came back. She handed me a key. "That's his key to Ellen's house," she explained. "In case you need to get something else out of the house."

I took it. Sarah took my arm and looked around. "The police have found a witness who saw Ellen leaving," she told me in a quiet voice. "Her name is Tia Frohm. She was dating the deceased. She claims she and Tim had been married on a recent trip to Mexico. Find out more about her."

That meant she would inherit Tim's money, along with the kids.

We parted company. It was close to seven now. I went home and heated up some lasagna that I had in the freezer from one of Ma's Sunday dinners. I poured a glass of cold red table wine and ate in front of the television. But I couldn't get the case out of my mind. I finally put aside my plate and stared at Fredd, who stared back at me.

"I know what you're thinking," I told Fredd. "I'm in way too deep." I grabbed a sheet of paper and a pencil and began writing down the facts as I knew them, trying to stay away from speculation:

1)   Ellen Bidwell came to Braden's and lifted almost twenty thousand dollars' worth of jewelry—a security camera caught her on tape.

2)   She got away the first time, but was caught the second time.

3)   I searched her, but the goods weren't on her.

4)   Tim Bidwell was murdered.

5)   A dinner ring stolen from Braden's was found near the body.

6)   A witness saw Ellen come out of her ex-husband's residence.

I reviewed my list and tried to pick it apart. What if the murder and the shoplifting incident weren't directly connected? If Ellen was innocent of one, why not the other? Who, then?

I added a couple more points to the list. The seventh point was that I lost sight of Ellen when I was following her out of the store. It was only for a few seconds, but it might be crucial. The eighth point appeared to be a minor, unrelated point, but Lara had mentioned that her Aunt Renee had been shopping with her niece and friend on Saturday, the second shoplifting incident. I wasn't sure how or if it was connected, but I had to find out.

I made a list of suspects that included Ellen, Tia, Brian, Lara, unknown enemies from work, and as an afterthought, Renee and Roger and lastly, Crystal. I don't know why I put her down, but I didn't like her. Roger seemed to be much more than a brother-in-law to Ellen, but I didn't get the feeling that they were having an affair. I got more of a feeling that there was mutual respect and understanding between them—maybe they both had married miserably?

I looked up Tia Frohm's address. She lived in an expensive condo near Fanueil Hall. The condo overlooked the waterfront. Since I wouldn't sleep until I talked to her, I got back in my car and drove through the tunnel to Boston proper. I found a place to park in a little independent parking lot and walked to Tia's place. My breath was cloudy in the frosty air.

I guess I shouldn't have been that surprised to find her at home. She certainly didn't appear shocked to see a private investigator visit her at nine-thirty in the evening.

I gave her my card.

Up close, Tia was more magnificent to look at than at a distance. Her skin was smooth porcelain tinged with blush, her eyes were framed with dark, thick lashes and her teeth were almost brilliantly white. She wore black leggings to show off her slender legs, and a loose deep-green tunic that moved to show off her toned body and red tresses.

"Ms. Matelli, what can I do for you?" Her voice was low and sweet as molasses.

"I understand you were dating Tim Bidwell."

"Yes, we were—" Her voice caught and she looked down, tears glistening on her perfect lashes. "We had just gotten married. It was sudden." She used a manicured finger to wipe away a tear.

"Why hadn't you moved in with him yet?"

She sighed. "We were still talking about where we should live—his place, my place or a new house."

"Tell me, Tia, had you met Ellen, his ex-wife, before you witnessed her leaving his residence today?"

She froze for a second. "Whose side are you on, exactly?" Her facade dropped and the real Tia came out. "Who are you working for?"

"In answer to your first question, I'm on the side of truth. As to the question of who I'm working for, I'm working for the defense."

She stood up. "This interview is over. Get out."

I stood up slowly. "Oh, so you don't want to share your information with the defense." I started to leave. "Must not be a very strong witness then."

She grabbed my arm and with surprising strength, spun me. "For your information, I recognized her from a photo in Tim's place. I saw Ellen Bidwell leaving his residence this morning. She was running, she looked frightened."

"Why were you there?" Seemed to me that a running, frightened woman who had just stabbed someone wouldn't have had the presence of mind to wipe the fingerprints off the murder weapon.

"Tim and I had a breakfast date before work." She pushed me toward the door. "Now why don't you go back to your little lawyer friend and tell her that. You can tell her I'm going to be standing up for my share of Tim's estate, too, so those two brats will have to share it with me. I'll go fifty-fifty."

"Tell me, Tia, where exactly did you get married?"

She frowned. "Mexico. Acapulco, if you must know."

"When?"

"What?"

"When did you get married?"

"November 20. Now leave, will you?"

NINE

WHEN I GOT HOME, I went straight to the computer and called up my e-mail. Jack had attached more information about Ellen Bidwell, Tim Bidwell and even information about the kids and their JD records. I didn't want to know how Jack had extracted that information. Brian's record was no surprise—his homeboys had already provided that information. But Lara's was enlightening—she had been picked up on suspicion of shoplifting. The girl she had been with at the time was Crystal Abbott.

I sat back and twirled around in my office chair. I found it soothing when I was thinking about a particularly sticky problem. Lara and Crystal—shoplifting—the teen girls who crossed my path last Saturday, lingered for a few moments, the image of the girls danced with me as I tried to follow the shoplifter…the woman who looked enough like Ellen to pass for her. I didn't know what the sister looked like, but I wondered how alike they were physically.

It was eleven o'clock. I forced myself to get ready for bed and I lay there, staring up at the ceiling for practically the entire night. Okay, maybe I dozed off sometime close to dawn. But I was up and showered by seven and out the door by seven-fifteen. Every radio station was playing some version of "Rockin' Around the Christmas Tree," so I slipped Cyndi Lauper's Christmas CD into my player and listened to some incredibly cool holiday songs, including a

Caribbean version of "Rockin' Around the Christmas Tree."

I had consulted a map last night and knew how to get to the Weston house. When I got there, only one car was in the driveway of the split-level ranch in white siding with black shutters and green roof. Santa rode the roof with his reindeer, Jesus was swathed in swaddling clothes, and his adoring parents, Magi and farm animals surrounded him. I rang the bell and heard "Greensleeves" resound in the house. A dog began barking. It sounded like a little yappy thing.

I must have looked a little disconcerted when Roger answered.

He smiled. "Come on in. Do you want coffee? I stayed home today because Lara and Brian are here. They didn't want to go to school today. I thought that would be all right."

"Yes," I replied. I looked down to find the source of the barking—a small white terrier that looked like a Scottie. I knew it was a specific breed but I couldn't put a name to it. "I'm sure a day away isn't going to make a difference. It is considered a family emergency." Roger led me through the hallway past a set of steps that led to the upper level to the bedrooms. The kitchen was straight to the back. There was a beautiful view of woods in their backyard. They had a pool as well.

The dog tried to get my attention.

"Down, Dabney," Roger ordered.

Dabney? It always amazed me how people named their pets. Of course, this opinion came from a woman who named her iguana Fredd.

Roger poured a cup of coffee into a Sylvester the cat mug and set it in front of me. "I gather you came here for a specific purpose."

I took a sip of strong dark coffee and steeled myself. "Mr. Weston, I have a dilemma and I'm not sure if you can help me."

He sat across from me and said, "Try me."

I laid out the whole story—how I got involved, picking up Ellen for shoplifting, my suspicions about Lara and Crystal's involvement. When I was done, I paused and said, "All along, I've wondered if I had the right woman." I wrapped my hands around the mug, and looked up at Roger. "Do I have the right woman, Mr. Weston?"

He didn't say anything for a long time, and he didn't look at me. The kitchen was very silent until Dabney decided it was time to eat. Then the crunching sounds of a dog eating kibble echoed through the room.

Roger finally looked up at me. "Renee is, well, we've been trying to deal with this problem for a long time. She's been seeing a psychiatrist and hypnotist about it." He closed his eyes and rubbed his forehead. "I didn't know she'd gone shopping last week."

"Mr. Weston, I'm not sure about this, but I think Lara and her friend may have been involved in the shoplifting incident this past Saturday."

"Do you want to talk to Lara about it?"

I shook my head. "Not just now. But I would like to see a picture of your wife, and if you feel comfortable, I need you to search for the items that were shoplifted."

He sighed, a big sigh. Then he nodded. "I'll do it. I know most of her hiding places."

I didn't tell him that if his wife had shoplifted the items, she might be responsible for Tim Bidwell's death. If I had mistaken one sister for another, Tia Frohm might have made the same identification mistake. I didn't know how to broach this sensitive area.

While Roger disappeared upstairs, I sipped my coffee

and played with the dog. When I looked up, a bleary-eyed Lara had entered the kitchen. She wore a T-shirt and a pair of flannel pajama bottoms. She padded over to the coffee machine and poured herself a cup, then sat at the table in the breakfast nook, trying to ignore me.

I didn't let her.

"Morning, Lara," I said, sliding into one of the chairs opposite her.

"Whatever," she replied.

"How does it feel to have knowledge that might free your mother?"

That made her stop in the middle of sipping her coffee. In fact, she spilled a little on her T-shirt and cursed. "Damn it! Look what you made me do." She glared at me and went over to the sink to dab at it.

When she returned, she avoided my eyes and muttered, "Just don't talk to me."

I smiled. "Fine. I guess we'll wait for the police to handle it."

She was silent for a few minutes, thinking it through. "What do you want to know?" Her tone was less than friendly. In fact, it was downright hostile.

I ignored her tone and began to ask questions. "When you and your friend got in between me and your Aunt Renee last Saturday, was it planned that your mother would take the fall?"

Lara was pouting now. "No, my mother wasn't supposed to be there."

"Be in the store or at that particular junction?"

"At that particular junction." She had leaned back and crossed her thin arms. Her hair hung down like a curtain, blocking my view of her face.

"So you and Crystal were in on it."

"We were helping Renee."

"So it was a planned shoplifting trip."

Lara rubbed her arms as if she was suddenly cold. She spoke into the table. "I guess so. I just went along with it."

"What about the Thursday evening before?"

"What about it?"

"Were you along to help your aunt shoplift a few items at Braden's?"

Lara sneered. "Thursday night I had play practice until eight."

The back door opened and a woman who looked almost like a twin to Ellen stepped through it with two bags of groceries. She saw both of us. "Hi, Lara, who's this, the social worker?" She put the groceries on the island and turned around.

"Renee," Roger was in the doorway with a handful of jewelry. "We have to talk. This is Angela Matelli, a private investigator who works for Braden's department store."

Renee looked stunned. I felt guilty because I was putting Renee in a tough spot. She would have to explain where she was yesterday morning when Tim Bidwell had been killed. But Ellen was in jail for something she hadn't done.

I looked over at Lara, who had a resentful expression on her face.

"What we have here, Renee, is a problem," I said, sighing.

"I'll take the stuff back," she said quietly.

Roger reached over and squeezed her hand. "We'll support you, dear. You should get off lightly since you're going to a psychiatrist. This was just a setback."

"Actually," I piped up, "it's a little more complicated than that." Everyone looked my way. I explained about the ring being found by Tim Bidwell's body. I turned to Renee. "How did that ring get there?"

Her face had gone white. "It's not what you think." She looked at Roger, whose face was crumpled, confused. "I wasn't there, Roger. I didn't meet with Tim and I certainly didn't kill him. In fact, I didn't even have the ring." She turned to Lara. "So are you so incredibly in love with Crystal that you'd rather see your mother or your aunt in prison for life than tell the truth?"

Brian came flying in, his fists striking his sister as she folded up on herself. "Tell the truth, Lara, tell them what they want you to, you big bitch. I hate you, I hate you. I want Mom back," came out of Brian in one big breath.

Great heaving sobs came from Lara. I stood up and gently removed Brian and he collapsed into my chair. Their uncle reached over to Lara and rubbed her back, saying over and over, "It's all right, Lara. Get it out of your system now."

When Lara was cried out, she raised her head and said, "It's all my fault Dad is dead and Mom is in jail. I'm responsible for everything." She took a big shuddering breath.

Her aunt had been silently weeping, tears sliding down her face, making trails in her foundation. "You're not totally responsible, Lara. Your friend had a lot to do with it. And I've played my part in this tragedy." Renee spoke in a soft voice, unlike the snippy tone she'd used with me the other day.

And then Renee began to tell me what had happened. "I was Christmas shopping in the mall last Thursday night when I had this sudden overwhelming urge to take something. I was by the jewelry counter and I couldn't help myself. I waited for my opportunity, and when it came, I just did it." She shook her head. "Crystal was there, witnessed everything. I didn't even know she was there until she helped me escape." She looked right at me. "She saw you coming toward me, apparently had picked out the two store detectives waiting by the other exits, and guided me to the open exit.''

Roger got up, brought the coffeepot and a clean mug to the table, and set the filled mug in front of his wife. Then he warmed up all of our mugs. I just hoped I'd find a man like him someday.

Renee took a sip, then continued. ''But Crystal didn't do this deed because she's a nice girl. She did it because she's a conniving, manipulative little bitch.'' She glanced up at Roger, who looked at the children. She waved a hand. ''Come on, Roger, these kids say much worse in a day.''

I reached over and touched her hand. ''Please continue.''

''Yes, please, Auntie,'' Lara said, standing up. I could feel waves of repressed anger radiating off of her. ''Tell them what a victim you were, and I was. How Crystal blackmailed you, told you she would go to the authorities about your shoplifting spree and she only wanted you to steal one ring, a ring for me.'' Lara turned to me. ''We felt married, Crystal and me. We wanted to be married. Crystal had picked that ring out for me the week before.''

I studied the girl. ''Do you have any other friends? You said to me the other day that Crystal was your only friend.''

Lara looked away. ''My other—friends—don't understand our relationship.''

Brian jumped in. ''Lara has no other friends because Crystal won't let her. Mom says that Crystal has isolated Lara from her friends.''

I turned back to Lara. I was certainly no therapist, but I had to get at the truth. I just hoped it wasn't to the detriment of these fragile teens. ''Is that true?''

Lara looked at the floor and shrugged.

''Do you think this relationship is what being a lesbian is all about?'' I asked.

Lara shrugged again. "I guess."

I sat in an empty chair and looked at her. "Well, I know a couple of lesbians, and their relationships are based on mutual trust and respect, the same as heterosexual couples. They let each other have friends and do things apart from each other sometimes. It doesn't sound like Crystal allows you to do anything without her." I touched her arm. "Lara, your mother has no alibi for the time your father was killed. But you know, and your aunt and uncle know, that she didn't do it."

Lara looked up at me. I continued, "So why is she still in jail?"

"Crystal did it." She looked away. "Mom told me that she and Dad had talked and he was concerned about Brian and me. He was sending Brian to a boot camp, and he had plans to send me to a boarding school to get me away from Crystal's influence. Crystal said if we went to talk to my dad, we might be able to get him to understand our relationship better. But he wouldn't change his mind. I kept talking anyway. I told him how much I loved Crystal and how horrible my life would be without her. Crystal must have wandered away. Suddenly—" her eyes were bright with tears and she blinked them back "—suddenly Crystal crept up behind him and he stiffened. He let out a little sound, then fell forward and I saw the knife sticking out of his back. Crystal wiped off the handle and asked me for the ring. I didn't think of it at the time. I thought she was mad at me for something. Sometimes Crystal gets mad at me for no reason at all." Lara looked around at her aunt, uncle and brother. "I didn't know what she was planning—I *swear* it!"

I called Sarah Tisdale and explained what I now knew. She told me she would get in touch with the detectives and send them to pick up Crystal. When I got off the phone, I smelled bacon and eggs cooking. Roger was making breakfast for the family and I was invited to stay.

The kids had gone up to their rooms to change into their clothes for the day. It wasn't more than fifteen minutes later that breakfast was served and Roger went to let the kids know. Renee sat at the table, hands folded.

"I'm sorry I caused all this trouble. Everything just dominoed, I guess." She shook her head. "I thought I had the stealing under control."

"What's the cause of kleptomania?" I asked. I was genuinely curious.

She shrugged. "I guess it's kind of like a bottomless pit—you feel as if nothing can fill that hole inside, but you keep trying to fill it. I guess a childhood where you didn't get enough love or security causes it. I don't know exactly, but my therapist is working it out with me. I don't know how I turned out this way but Ellen didn't. She doesn't have a lot of problems, she's always been perfect, you know." The last sentence held a trace of bitterness.

"Oh, I don't know about that," I said. "She doesn't have a husband anymore, the divorce settlement was definitely not in her favor, her kids have myriad problems to deal with. Seems to me like your life is pretty good right now."

Renee smiled. "Yeah, I guess it is. Christmas is coming and maybe we'll have everyone here for the holidays. That'll be nice."

"See? Things are looking up already."

"What'll happen with Braden's?" she asked. I saw the fear in her eyes.

"I think with a letter from your psychiatrist and the return of the jewelry, you'll probably get off with a fine if you promise to never return to Braden's."

There was a shout from the front of the house. Renee sprang up, I was a little slower. I figured it was one of the kids having a problem with something. Renee was better equipped as a parent to deal with such matters. As a stranger, I didn't feel it was my duty to interfere. But when Renee didn't return right away, I became a little wary. I heard Dabney bark once, then squeal as if he'd been stepped on or hurt in some way.

Alarmed, I walked quietly to the front hall, but didn't see anyone there. But I heard voices coming from the living room.

"Crystal, please put the knife down." That was Lara. She was crying now.

"We have to call the paramedics, my husband's bleeding." Renee pleaded, fear in her voice.

"Shut up! Get away from me, all of you. Except Lara. We're leaving, baby. I got my mom's Lexus, I got money. Check your uncle's wallet and your aunt's purse. We can use all the money we can get."

"No," Lara said.

I felt a presence behind me. Brian was there. He started to push past me but I grabbed him and whispered, "Hostage situation." I pulled him around to the kitchen. "Call the police and tell them to bring an ambulance. Your uncle's been seriously hurt."

Brian's face was pasty. His eyes fell on the eggs and bacon and he went a shade green. I pinched him, a way to get his mind off things that would make him sick. He jumped.

"I need you calm, Brian. Do what I say, then wait for the police outside and flag them down. Explain the scene in here. I'm trusting you. Everyone in there is depending on you. Do you think you're up to it?"

"Yes," he whispered.

I started to leave, then turned back. "It's cold outside. Remember to put on a coat. Your mother doesn't need a child with pneumonia when she gets out of the pokey." I smiled to ease the tension. He nodded back and picked up the phone.

I returned to the front. I heard a scream.

Lara: "Crystal, *stop!* I'll go with you. I promise."

Renee was sobbing. Roger was moaning.

"Then let's go now," Crystal said.

"I have to pack—"

"I'll buy you what you need along the way." Crystal's voice was laced with desperation.

"Where are we going? How are we going to make money along the way?" Lara asked, her voice had a hysterical edge.

I stepped into the living room after assessing the situation. A large decorated Christmas tree dominated the front window, gaily wrapped presents underneath. Crystal had her back to me. Renee was kneeling next to Roger's body. He was still breathing. The dog lay by him, a little trooper. Lara, seated primly on the pale-blue sofa, gave me away by looking right at me.

Crystal whirled, a knife in her hand.

"That the knife you stuck Lara's dad with, Crystal?"

"He was going to take her away from me. He laughed at me," Crystal said with a frown. "We love each other and he laughed. He told me Lara was his daughter. *His daughter.*" She laughed. "He didn't care enough about her to visit her when the divorce went through. He was always canceling their time together because of some meeting or some benefit dinner he had to go to. He was going to the *Caribbean* for Christmas with his girlfriend instead of spending time with them."

"But *you* spent time with Lara," I said, moving slowly toward her.

She jabbed the knife at me, keeping me at bay. "I *love* Lara. I pay attention to her."

"Yeah, you're just a couple of swell kids," I replied, "spending time 'together,' shoplifting together. A regular Bonnie and Clyde."

Crystal looked blank. "Who?"

I waved my hand casually, then clamped it on her wrist. She tried to pull away, then changed her mind and tried to stab me by lunging forward. But I was ready for her. I stepped to the side and brought my free hand to the back of her neck, pulling her in the direction in which she had lunged at me. I got her down on the carpet and kept her arm immobile, kneeling the way I was taught in aikido, and taking the knife out of her hand.

Crystal screamed. "Lara! Lara! Get the bitch. Kill her! We can still get out of here."

The sound of a police siren ended that hope.

TEN

I SPENT THE NEXT few days taking care of the details. Ellen Bidwell was released almost immediately, and I slipped her a copy of the offshore accounts that held Tim Bidwell's investments.

Roger Weston was rushed to the hospital and after emergency surgery to close the knife wound, he was expected to be home for Christmas.

Because Roger couldn't go with Renee to Braden's and the police over the shoplifting, Sarah and I offered to go with her. Armed with her psychiatrist's letter and the information that she had been pressed into the second shoplifting incident by a third party who was already in the system, we were able to get Braden's to drop the charges for the return of the merchandise.

Crystal was held as an adult offender since this wasn't her first offense. Merry Christmas to her family. I requested that Crystal be evaluated for psychiatric help. I hope her mother agreed, but from what little I knew of her, and from what I had observed, it probably wouldn't happen.

Sarah Tisdale, still representing Ellen Bidwell and her children, made short work of Tia Frohm's claim that she had married Tim Bidwell in Mexico. When Tia presented her signed document, Sarah not only had a handwriting expert verify that Tim's signature was forged, but checked with the Acapulco court system and could find no record of a marriage there between Tia Frohm and Tim Bidwell.

Faced with possible charges and prison time, Tia slithered away quietly. I'm not even sure why she thought she had a chance. Greed does that to people.

Ellen Bidwell continued with her ex-husband's plans, sending Brian to a good military academy and Lara to a respected girls' boarding school. The kids would start their new schools after the new year, so the family took the two Caribbean plane tickets Tim Bidwell had bought, and bought another ticket, and the three of them planned to go down there after Christmas. It all depended on whether Lara could leave the state, since she was party to the stolen items of Braden's. But I had faith that Sarah would get a judge to sign an order giving Lara permission to go on the holiday vacation.

As for me? Well, I found the perfect Christmas gift for Ma, and everybody agreed that it was genius! Taking inspiration from Ellen and her two kids, we bought two plane tickets for an all-expenses paid two-week trip to Italy for Ma and the person of her choice. We set up hotel reservations, transportation, everything.

Ma has already asked me to go along, but I wanted to ask my brothers and sisters if that would be okay. Personally, I thought Uncle "No-Legs" Charlie should use that second ticket, but then, who would drive the rental car? With my Braden's money, I may spring for a ticket and go along as a third person. So much for the Braden's jewelry I had my eye on.

And Jack? He showed up and things couldn't have gone better. We get along great, and he's going to rent the ground floor apartment when he gets his doctorate in May. The thing I love about him is that he seems to know when I need to be alone. But we have a lot of fun together.

Who knows? This could lead to something serious but in the meantime, I'm just happy that my Christmas is turning out so well. I have a thriving business, good friends and family, a boyfriend I'm getting serious about, and life couldn't be better.

But I keep looking over my shoulder, wondering when the other shoe will drop. It did for Chuck Eddy. He called me up the other day.

"What about your girlfriend, Gloria?" I asked.

"She dumped me." He sounded awful.

"Right before Christmas?" I asked.

"Turned out she was just going out with me so I'd buy her a diamond ring from Braden's," he replied.

"Look Chuck, don't let all the work she put into you go to waste." I'd stopped working at Braden's once I finished the case. I was exhausted from solving it, and was now spending my free time either running around like a maniac to buy gifts for my family and friends, or sleeping. "How's everything going at Braden's?"

"Rick was called on the carpet for going against store policy with the shoplifting incident. He's on notice and not as cocky as he used to be."

"It was bound to happen. When you set yourself up as being a know-it-all, prepare for a fall if you turn out to be wrong."

"Say, Angie, you wouldn't want to go out with me or anything, would you?"

"Gee, Chuck, that's awfully nice of you to ask, but I do have a boyfriend."

"Well, how about for a cup of Starbucks or something sometime? Just talk shop as friends, that sort of thing."

"Yeah, we could do that," I replied.

Gloria was missing out, I tell you. I might have to find that gal and give her a piece of my mind.

THE EMPTY MANGER
by Bill Crider

ONE

AS FAR AS Sheriff Dan Rhodes could recall, there had never been a white Christmas in Blacklin County. Not that it had never snowed there. Rhodes could remember a pretty good covering about twenty-five years earlier. Kids had made snowmen in yards all over town. But everything melted the next day.

There was certainly no chance of snow at Christmas this year, Rhodes thought. Although the temperature was dropping into the lower forties at night, it would bounce back into the upper sixties by the afternoon of the next day, and there was plenty of sunshine.

"I don't think we'll ever see snow again," Lawton said late one afternoon when they were discussing it at the jail. Lawton was the jailer. He was in his seventies, and he had opinions on everything. "Probably won't ever rain again, either. You know what that old Indian said."

"Native American," Hack said.

Hack was the dispatcher, and he was just as old as Lawton. The two of them often got into discussions that seemed to Rhodes to begin nowhere and to wind up in the same place.

"They don't call 'em Indians any more," Hack continued. "Native Americans is the right way to say it."

Lawton mulled it over.

"Well," he said after a few seconds, "I was born right here in Blacklin County. I've never even been across the state line. Been to Dallas three or four times and Houston once. I guess that makes me a Native American, too.''

''Nope,'' Hack said. ''Makes you a native Texan. There's a big difference.''

''I don't see why. A Texan's an American, too, ain't he? Look at the presidents of this country who've come from Texas. They were Americans. You can't be the president if you're not an American, can you?''

Hack opened his mouth to say something, but Rhodes, who knew from experience that these seemingly harmless discussions had a way of becoming interminable arguments, broke in.

''What did the old Native American say?'' he asked Lawton.

Lawton gave him a grateful look. For once he seemed as glad as Rhodes to get the conversation back on its original track.

''He said, 'One time, it never rained.'''

Hack looked at Lawton, then at Rhodes, then back at Lawton.

''Huh?'' he said. ''What does that mean?''

Lawton grabbed his broom from its resting place against the wall and started sweeping briskly.

''If you don't get it, I can't explain it,'' he said above the sound of the broom's whisking.

Hack turned back to Rhodes, his eyebrows raised.

''Do you get it?'' he asked.

''Sure,'' Rhodes said. ''It's perfectly clear to me.''

''Bull corn. And besides, I don't see what that has to do with snow. We were talkin' about snow, not rain. There's a big difference between snow and rain.''

He turned his attention back to Lawton, apparently ready to discourse at length on the difference between snow and rain.

''You listen to me,'' he began, but Rhodes was saved

from further argument between the two by the ringing of the telephone.

Hack picked it up and said, "Blacklin County Sheriff's Department," and then he listened for what seemed like a long time. Finally he said, "Yes, ma'am. I understand. We'll get right on that, Miz Blair."

When he hung up, Lawton had stopped sweeping and was leaning on his broom, listening. Rhodes didn't say anything. He knew Hack would tell him what the problem was in his own good time.

"That was Miz Blair," Hack said.

Rhodes wanted to say that he already knew that, but he resisted the urge. It would only slow things down.

"She's the secretary at the Babtist church," Hack continued.

"The *First* Babtist Church," Lawton said. "She's been there for about five years."

Hack, who never liked to be interrupted when he was telling something, turned to glare at him.

Rhodes wasn't sure how many Baptist churches there were in the town of Clearview, but he figured that five was about the right number. It didn't really matter. Everyone knew that when people said "the Baptist church," they were talking about First Baptist.

"What did Mrs. Blair want?" Rhodes asked, hoping to get Hack's attention and avoid another argument.

"She says there's been a kidnapping," Hack answered.

There had been a lot of crimes committed in Blacklin County, but there had never been a kidnapping before.

"Who was kidnapped?" Rhodes asked.

"The baby Jesus," Hack said.

TWO

EARLIER IN THE FALL, one of Clearview's deserted downtown buildings had fallen into the street. It was a corner building, and it had been deserted for years. The owner had done nothing about its upkeep. Advanced age, a very leaky roof and general decrepitude had all contributed to the building's demise. It fell one day with a sound that would have aroused hundreds of people if there had been hundreds of people in Clearview's downtown area, but there hadn't been that many people there in years.

Rhodes could remember Christmases of the not-too-distant past when it had been impossible to find a parking place, when the streets were crowded with shoppers carrying their wrapped and ribboned packages, when merchants put together Toylands in their stores and when there was Christmas music playing everywhere you went. Or maybe it had been longer than he thought, probably about the time of the last snow if not before then.

Things had changed a lot over the years. Now most of the buildings were empty, and some had cracked or broken windows. There were hardly ever any cars parked on the streets. All the activity was out on the highway, at Wal-Mart or one of the big new grocery stores.

Jerri Laxton, a member of the city council, had gotten the idea that it would be a good thing to "revitalize" the downtown. Her argument was that it had worked in big cities, so why not in Clearview. It was even working in smaller towns, she said, places like Thurston, just a short distance away, where many of the old buildings were being renovated and filled with antiques and bric-a-brac.

Unfortunately, you couldn't just wave a magic wand and have a bunch of antique dealers come flocking to your town. What you could do, however, was get the bricks and concrete out of the street and the lot where the building had collapsed and then paint a mural on the side of the building that was left standing next to the now vacant lot.

Jerri Laxton had approached the owner of the remaining building, and he thought the idea was a good one. After getting his permission, Jerri went to the high school art teacher, who agreed to send out some of his more talented students to paint the mural.

It was at that point that the local ministerial alliance got involved. It being the season for commercial establishments to be jolly and pretty much forget any other meaning of Christmas, the ministers thought it was time for Clearview to take a stand. They persuaded the building's owner to have the art students paint a mural depicting a manger with a brilliant star hanging over it.

After that, it was only natural for someone to come up with the idea of having a "living manger scene." Each night for a week, members of the local churches would play the parts of Joseph, Mary, Wise Men and assorted shepherds. The baby Jesus would be portrayed by a doll. Nobody wanted to risk using a real baby, but the livestock would be portrayed by actual sheep, not to mention a real donkey.

There were even goats, though Rhodes wasn't sure the goats were biblical. Every evening, Vernell Lindsey brought over Shirley, Goodness and Mercy (referred to in one of the Clearview *Herald*'s rare moments of whimsy as "the holy goats"). That is, she brought as many of them as she could round up and coax into her little trailer.

Rhodes hadn't been too sure about the whole idea from the start. In a town of any size, there would undoubtedly have been protests from members of the Jewish community, not to mention the atheists and the Wiccans. But not in Clearview. If there were any atheists or Wiccans around, they weren't admitting it, and the Jews in the area didn't seem to care, maybe because there were too few of them to mount an effective protest.

So the living manger scene went on display, and for the first two nights everything had gone well. There had been more traffic in downtown Clearview than there had in years as people drove by to have a look at what their fellow citizens had brought to pass.

The Clearview *Herald* had printed a front-page article, along with a couple of color photos. There had also been a black-and-white photo of Jerri Laxton smiling eagerly at the camera, no doubt in anticipation of her reelection to the city council for another term, thanks to her part in the revitalization of downtown Clearview. In the photo's caption, Jerri was quoted as having said that the whole thing had been her idea.

Rhodes knew that wasn't true, and so did everyone else, but most of them would probably forget by the time the elections rolled around. Not that it would make much difference, but Rhodes didn't discover that until later.

When he arrived at the corner where the store had been, the thick clouds on the western horizon were rimmed with red as the sun went down behind them. The streetlights were already on, but there was no one around except Frances Blair, who had made the call to the sheriff's department. Rhodes had no trouble finding a parking place.

Frances was standing in front of the manger, wearing a heavy cloth coat over her dress. She had a red scarf tied around her dark hair to keep it from blowing in the brisk north wind that would soon send the temperature sliding toward the lower forties. Frances had some kind of thyroid condition, or so Rhodes had heard, and it caused her eyeballs to protrude a little more than was usual, giving her a permanently startled look.

"I can't believe it," she said when Rhodes walked up. "The baby Jesus is gone."

There were bales of hay stacked all around, and Rhodes wondered briefly how the Jews of two thousand years ago had managed to get their hands on hay-baling equipment. Some of the bales appeared to have a couple of bites taken out of them, but there were no animals around now, and no signs that any had been there. Rhodes was glad that someone was doing a good job of cleaning up. He didn't like having to watch his step.

"It wasn't a real baby, was it?" he said.

Frances turned her startled eyes on him, as if she could hardly believe what she was hearing.

"Well, no, of course it wasn't real. But it's the symbolism that counts."

"Maybe some child picked it up," Rhodes said. "Somebody who didn't know you shouldn't take dolls that happened to be lying around."

"It shouldn't have been lying around," Frances admitted. "I'm the one responsible. It's my job to see that everything is cleaned up and taken home at the end of each evening. I was in a hurry last night, and the donkey was acting up. I forgot all about the baby Jesus."

Her voice cracked, and Rhodes thought she might cry. He said, "I wouldn't worry about it. You can replace a doll without much trouble."

"I told you it wasn't the doll. Can you imagine someone stealing the baby Jesus?"

Rhodes could imagine it with no trouble at all, but he didn't think it would serve any purpose to say so. Frances wasn't in the mood to listen.

"Maybe someone else noticed it last night after you'd left. They could have taken it home for safekeeping."

"No, no. I was the last one here. I had to stay until Larry

Barnes loaded that donkey on a trailer and hauled it away. My husband and I were the only ones here after he left, and I'm sure no one came by later.''

Jerri's husband, Tom, owned a service station-grocery store-video-rental store out on the highway. He'd made quite a bit of money and had recently opened a second store in another town.

"It could have been someone who came by today," Rhodes said. "No one would notice if somebody took the doll."

He looked around the lot where they stood. It was almost dark now, and the streetlights had come on. The players in the manger scene would be arriving soon, and in an hour or so, after everyone had finished eating supper, people would be driving by to see it.

But now there was no one in sight. There wasn't even a car on the street, and Rhodes knew it had been that way much of the afternoon. The building on whose wall the mural had been painted was vacant, as were most of those nearby.

"I could have a look around," he said. "It might be that someone just hid the doll for fun."

Frances looked at him with disapproval, and he knew he shouldn't have said *doll*. But it was just a doll to him.

"I've already looked," Frances said. "I looked before I called. The baby Jesus isn't here."

"Did you look in the alley?"

"No. I didn't think of that."

"I'll go," Rhodes said.

There was a narrow one-way alley that ran the length of the block. Of course there was no need for it anymore, since there was no reason to deliver freight to deserted buildings or to pick up trash from behind them. But there were still some old wooden bins in the alley, and sometimes people dumped things in them. Rhodes thought the bins should have been removed years ago.

He left Frances standing in front of the empty manger and headed for the alley. Just as he started away, Vernell Lindsey drove up with the goats. Rhodes walked faster. He didn't want to have to talk to Vernell or to help unload the goats. Vernell, Clearview's resident romance novelist, wasn't one of Rhodes's biggest fans, though he'd helped pen her goats often enough. Maybe having been suspected of murder had soured her outlook. He heard the goats clattering around in the trailer and increased his pace.

The alley was darker than the nearly vacant lot, and Rhodes didn't have a flashlight. He wasn't going back to the car for it, however. He thought he could see well enough, and he didn't really expect to find anything in the alley.

He did find something, however, though it wasn't the baby Jesus.

It was Jerri Laxton, and she was just as lifeless as any doll.

THREE

SHE WAS LYING beside and partially behind the wooden trash bin that stood in back of what had once been Frazier's Furniture store. Rhodes could remember having bought a coffee table there many years ago. The store had wooden floors and had been cooled by fans that hung from the high ceilings. It was empty now of everything except dust, like the dust that was caught in Jerri Laxton's hair. Rhodes knew instantly that she was dead. She'd been hit on the head with something, and the blood had matted in her hair along with the dust.

Her death made her Rhodes's responsibility. The town of Clearview didn't have a police department. Since the sheriff's office and the jail were right there, the citizens thought that a separate law enforcement operation was unnecessary. So the city paid a fee to the county, and the sheriff's department did double duty.

Rhodes looked around. In the back wall of the building there were two doors. One of them was the delivery door. It was wide and high, and it slid aside on a railing when it was opened. There was no visible lock, but Rhodes knew it was secured from the inside. The door probably hadn't been opened in years.

The other door was a regular door, probably the one through which the owner, Mr. Frazier, had left at the end of the day. There was a single concrete step beneath the door.

The door was open.

It appeared at first glance that Jerri Laxton had either attempted to enter or leave by the door and had fallen into the alley, hitting her head on the concrete step, but Rhodes was certain that wasn't the case. To him, it looked as if she had crawled out the door and then tried to crawl into the alley, perhaps looking for help.

She hadn't found it, however. She'd died before she could go any farther than the step, and she'd fallen off to the side, lying partially hidden behind the trash bin.

Rhodes checked for a pulse, though he knew he couldn't do a thing to help her. When he had assured himself that she was as dead as she looked, he went back to the manger scene to send everyone home.

Quite a crowd had begun to gather, some of them in costume, and it wasn't easy to convince them to leave without telling them exactly why, especially Vernell, who had already unloaded her goats.

Rhodes was afraid that if he told them about Jerri, they would all try to troop back into the alley to have a look, but when he told them that there had been a fatal accident, none of them seemed to have much desire to see for themselves, not even Vernell, who was probably afraid that Rhodes would accuse her of having had some part in it.

"There'll be a lot of people coming by," Frances Blair said, plainly agitated. "Someone needs to stay here and let them know what the trouble is."

Harvey Stoneman said, "I'll do that."

Stoneman was the pastor of the First Baptist Church. He was a short, stout man with a smooth, strong voice, but he didn't look much like a preacher at the moment. He was apparently supposed to be one of the three wise men, and he was wearing what looked like an old chenille bathrobe and leather sandals, along with a towel twisted into a turban.

Rhodes thanked Stoneman for volunteering and went to

his car to call the jail. He got Hack on the radio and told him to send Ruth Grady to the scene.

"What's goin' on?" Hack asked.

"Nothing I want to talk about on the radio," Rhodes said. "Where's Ruth patrolling?"

"Out toward Obert. She's not far. I'll tell her."

Rhodes signed off and moved his car to block one end of the alley. He got out and went back to have another look at Jerri Laxton. This time he took his flashlight.

When he returned to where Jerri's body lay, there was someone waiting for him. It wasn't his deputy, however. It was Jennifer Loam, the brand-new reporter for the Clearview *Herald*. She had graduated from college only a few months earlier, in August, and to Rhodes she seemed impossibly young. She was tall, thin, blond and intense, and Rhodes was sure she'd never had to cover a story quite like this one. She was wearing some kind of hooded robe and carrying a shepherd's crook. Rhodes didn't think there had been any female shepherds around Bethlehem, but he didn't mention it.

He also resisted the impulse to tell Jennifer that she didn't have any right to be where she was. He didn't want to listen to a lecture on freedom of the press. All he could hope for was that she hadn't touched anything.

"Is she dead?" Jennifer asked when Rhodes walked up.

"Yes, she's dead. You haven't touched anything have you?"

"I know better than that. 'A killer always brings something *to* the scene and leaves with something *from* the scene.' I had a good journalism teacher, Sheriff Rhodes, and she told us all about the importance of preserving crime scenes if we ever found ourselves at one." Jennifer paused and looked down at Jerri's body. "I never thought I'd find myself at one, though, not really."

"It's not a crime scene yet," Rhodes said, shining his light around. "It looks like an accident."

"It might look like one to you, but I don't think it was. You can see that—"

"Never mind," Rhodes said, thinking that it would be a mistake to underestimate Jennifer, even if she did look about twelve. "You could be right. One my deputies is on the way here, and we'll need to secure this area. You'd better go back to the manger area."

"I'll get out of your way, but I'm not leaving until I get a story."

"You can wait with the Reverend Stoneman," Rhodes said. "He'll be here a while. If there's a story, I'll let you know."

Jennifer said that she'd be with Stoneman, and left. Rhodes continued to look around the area, but he couldn't see anything that he thought would help. He wasn't going inside the building until Ruth Grady arrived. For all he knew there might be someone in there waiting for him.

FOUR

RUTH GRADY ARRIVED about ten minutes later. She was short and stout, like Stoneman, but her voice didn't carry as far as his, not unless she was yelling at some hapless criminal she'd caught in the act. Rhodes considered her an excellent deputy, and he liked working with her.

When Rhodes explained what the situation was, Ruth went back to her county car and parked it at the entrance to the alley at the end of the block opposite Rhodes's car, sealing the alley off from traffic, just in case someone who came to visit the manger scene decided to take a shortcut home. She left the car's headlights on.

After they had both searched all around the body and found nothing, Ruth said, "I guess we'd better go inside and have a look."

"I'll go first," Rhodes said.

Long ago, he had been told at some training session or other that the most dangerous thing a lawman could do was to enter a dark building. If there was someone inside, he could shoot at your flashlight. Or he might be standing right beside the door, waiting.

Which was why Rhodes never failed to get a laugh from the TV cops who went into a room holding their weapons out at the end of their extended arms. Anyone standing just beside the doorway could easily club their arms and get their weapons. The proper way to enter was with the pistol kept carefully close to the body. And you didn't enter at all until you'd checked to see who was there, not by shining a steady beam of light but by clicking it off and on.

Rhodes made all the right moves, or did as well as he could. It had been a while since he'd had to enter a dark building at night.

There was no one inside, however, or there didn't appear to be so he needn't have worried. The brief flashes of light revealed nothing more than dust and spiderwebs.

Rhodes went inside, followed by Ruth Grady. There was a small office partitioned off from the rest of what had been the display floor, and they started over to check it.

"There's a regular trail through here," Ruth said, shining her light at the floor.

Rhodes could see what she meant. Most of the floor was covered with dust, but there was a relatively clean path that led from the office to the back door.

"Look there," Ruth said, pointing with the light at a dark stain on the floor.

Rhodes nodded.

"Let's have a look in that office," he said.

There was no one there, but the door was open, and Rhodes's flashlight revealed that the little room wasn't empty. There was an old desk, which wasn't especially surprising, and a single bed with a mattress, which was. The bed appeared to have been used.

"Wonder what Mr. Frazier would have to say about that?" Ruth said.

Rhodes didn't venture a guess. They both looked around the office, but there was nothing that looked like a clue: no bottles or cans, no ashtrays with half-smoked cigarettes, no telltale fingerprints. There was a spot on the desk where the dust had been disturbed. Something had sat there until recently, Rhodes thought. He held the beam of his flashlight on the spot, but he couldn't tell what had been removed.

"Me, neither," Ruth said. "It was small, though."

That wasn't much help, but it was the best they could do

for the moment. Rhodes looked in the desk drawers, but they were as empty as the top of the desk. It was too bad that, while Jennifer might be right about the killer both leaving something at the scene and taking something away, it was sometimes very difficult to figure out just what had been left behind. And while it was obvious that something had been taken away, there was no way to tell what it was.

There was something else missing, too, unless whatever had been on the desk was the murder weapon. It was too bad that the killer hadn't left it behind. Rhodes wished people would be more helpful.

"We'd better have a look upstairs," he said.

The front part of the building had a very high ceiling, about two stories, but the back half was overhung by a loft where more furniture had been displayed.

Rhodes led the way up the stairs. When he got to the top there was a skittering noise and something ran across the floor in the back of the building.

Rhodes flinched, but he didn't pull the trigger of his pistol.

"Mouse," he said.

"Good thing you didn't shoot him," Ruth said.

"Nerves of steel," Rhodes told her, shining the light around the upper floor. He didn't see the mouse. He didn't see anything.

"Might as well go on back down," he said, and they did.

"Jerri Laxton met somebody in that office," Ruth said when they reached the bottom of the stairs.

Rhodes agreed that it looked that way.

"And whoever it was killed her," Ruth continued. "Probably hit her with something heavy. I wonder what it was?"

Rhodes said he didn't know. "But I think we'd better have a talk with Mr. Frazier. I'll go. You stay here and see what you can find."

"I don't think I'll find much."

"Maybe not. But give it a try. You'll need to bag those sheets. I'll call an ambulance and the justice of the peace."

"All right," Ruth said, and Rhodes went outside.

RHODES HAD HOPED there might be some clue on Jerri Laxton's body, but there was nothing he could see. He'd do a more thorough search of her clothing after she'd been taken to Ballinger's Funeral Home, but Rhodes didn't really expect to find anything helpful. In his experience, clues weren't usually easy to come by. He solved more cases by talking to people and weighing their statements than he did with clues.

He went to his car and called the ambulance and the J.P. It didn't take them long to arrive, and even less time to leave again.

After Jerri's body had been taken away, Rhodes thought about all the people he needed to talk to. There was Frazier, of course, but he could wait. The first person Rhodes wanted to see was Ron Laxton, Jerri's husband. It was a sad fact that the first suspect was always the husband, no matter how close the couple had seemed to be.

Rhodes walked back to the manger scene and told Stoneman and Jennifer to go on home. It was getting late, and he didn't think there would be anyone else driving by.

"What about my story?" Jennifer wanted to know.

"There's no story yet," Rhodes said. "We'll have to wait on the autopsy."

"She was murdered, wasn't she?"

"It looks that way," Rhodes told her. "But don't quote me."

Jennifer didn't look happy with that, but Rhodes didn't care. He had too many other things to worry about. He went to his car and got Hack on the radio.

"Call Clyde Ballinger and have him meet me at Ron Laxton's place," Rhodes said.

Clyde Ballinger owned the funeral home, but he was also Rhodes's friend. Rhodes didn't like breaking bad news to people, but Ballinger was an expert at it.

"Sure," Hack said. "I'll call him. I'll be glad to. I don't suppose you're gonna tell me why, though."

"That's right."

"I don't mind," Hack said. "Nobody ever tells me anything, but that's fine. I'm just the dispatcher, that's all. I don't really matter in the big scheme of things. I'll just keep doin' my job in the dark."

"You're just afraid that Lawton will find out something before you do," Rhodes told him.

"That's right. Treat me like a kid. I'm used to it. I don't need to know anything."

"I'll tell you all about it later," Rhodes said, and signed off.

FIVE

RON LAXTON OWNED THE local Dairy Queen, though Rhodes hardly ever saw him there. Neither did anyone else. He was an absentee manager who trusted his employees to do a good job and not cheat him out of too much money.

He had been on the school board for a while some years previously, but he had resigned when Jerri ran for the city council. He told everyone that one politician in the family was enough, though the truth was that he hadn't been very well liked as a board member, and there were three people planning to run against him if he stood for reelection. Jerri, on the other hand, had become very popular in Clearview because of her commonsense approach to some of the town's problems. She was always looking for ways to improve the town, and while some of her schemes might not have worked out, she always had the best interests of the citizens at heart. Some people thought she should run for state representative.

The Laxton house was in one of Clearview's older residential neighborhoods, but one that had been kept up well over the years. The yards were neat and the sidewalks were edged. Rhodes hated yard work, but he admired people who enjoyed it and did a good job of it. There were large old trees in most of the yards, mostly pecan trees, and their branches spread out over the street.

Some of trees were hung with Christmas lights, and on the roof of one house there was a reindeer-drawn sleigh, spotlighted from below. There was a wooden cutout of a snowman on Laxton's lawn. It wore a stovepipe hat at a jaunty angle, but it wasn't lighted. There was a Christmas tree in the front window, and Rhodes thought about the gifts that would remain ungiven.

He was glad to see Clyde Ballinger's Cadillac parked out in front of the Laxton house. Rhodes parked his car and went over to the Cadillac. The driver's window slid down smoothly and Ballinger said, "Evening, Sheriff."

Ballinger was normally a jovial man, always ready with a joke and a smile, hardly the stereotypical funeral director. But when the occasion demanded, he could be utterly serious.

"I know what this is about," Ballinger went on. "But I left before they brought the body in. I guess you want a little help in comforting the grieving husband."

"Nobody's grieving yet," Rhodes told him. "I want you to help me break the news."

"Sure," Ballinger said. "It's not going to be pleasant, though."

"It never is," Rhodes said, and told him what he knew about Jerri Laxton's death.

When he was finished, he stepped aside as Ballinger opened the door and got out of the car.

"Try to take it easy on him," Rhodes said.

Ballinger looked hurt.

"Sorry," Rhodes said. "I know you'll handle things the right way."

They went up onto the small front porch, and Rhodes rang the doorbell. After a few minutes, Ron Laxton came to the door and opened it. He had brownish-blond hair and light-blue eyes, and he was wearing jeans and a T-shirt. When he saw the sheriff and the funeral director, he took a step backward.

"What's the trouble?"

Rhodes let Ballinger handle things, which the funeral director did smoothly and compassionately. When Laxton was over the worst of his surprise but still in a state of mild shock, Rhodes asked him a few questions.

"Do you have any idea why your wife might have been in that vacant building?" he asked.

They were in the kitchen. Ballinger had helped Laxton make coffee. Laxton sat at the table, looking down at his cup, but he wasn't drinking the coffee. Neither was Rhodes, who didn't like hot drinks. He preferred cold Dr Pepper.

"She called and said she might be a little late tonight," Laxton said. "She was going to talk to someone, but she didn't tell me where or who it was. I got the idea it was city business."

"She didn't mention Fred Frazier?"

"Who?"

"He's the owner of the building where I found your wife," Rhodes said.

Laxton looked up and said, "Come to think of it, she was worried about old buildings lately. Ever since that one fell down on the corner there. She was afraid it was going to happen to some of the others. She didn't mention any names, but she said she was going to talk to some of the owners about renovating them. She was big on the idea of getting those buildings fixed up and filling them with antique dealers. Maybe she was meeting with Frazier about that."

Rhodes thought it was possible, but a vacant building seemed like an odd place to have a meeting. On the other hand, maybe it wasn't so odd, depending on what you were meeting about. Rhodes thought about that bed.

"Were you and Jerri having any problems?" he asked.

"Problems? What kind of problems?"

Rhodes didn't know if Laxton was playing dumb or whether he was still in shock. Rhodes decided to put things a little more bluntly.

"Marital problems," he said.

Laxton pushed his hands against the table as if he were going to stand up, but he slumped back in his chair.

"I resent that," he said.

"I'm sorry," Rhodes said, "but you might as well tell me about it if you were. I'll find out eventually."

"Jerri was a wonderful woman. I'd never fool around on her."

Ballinger gave Rhodes a look, so Rhodes changed the subject.

"Did she have any enemies?" he asked.

Laxton gave the ghost of a smile.

"She was on the city council," he said. "What do you think?"

Rhodes understood what he meant. Anyone holding office in a small town, and probably in a large one, was bound to make people angry every time there was a vote on an issue.

"I mean real enemies," Rhodes said. "People who might want to kill her."

"That's just silly," Laxton said. "Sure, some people didn't agree with her, and some of them thought the idea of renovating the downtown was ridiculous, but you don't kill somebody over something like that."

Rhodes thought Laxton might be surprised at some of the things people were killed for. He talked to Laxton a little longer, but he didn't get any answers that were helpful.

He did learn that Jerri Laxton drove a gray Taurus and that it wasn't in the garage. Ron didn't know where it was.

"Probably at the city hall," he said. "If it's not parked downtown."

After a bit more fruitless discussion, Rhodes said that he had some other people to see and got ready to leave. Ballinger followed him out of the house.

"I'll stay here a while," Ballinger said when they were outside. "He might want to discuss the funeral arrangements, and I can let him talk if he wants to."

"If he lets anything drop, call me tomorrow," Rhodes said.

"He doesn't know anything," Ballinger said. "But you know what they say—the husband is always the last to know."

"So that's the reason you looked at me like that."

"That's it. I don't like to repeat gossip, but you need to know this, I guess. Ron might not have thought about fooling around, but Jerri did."

"With…?"

"I'm not sure I should tell you."

Rhodes remained silent.

"All right. All right. It was Harvey Stoneman. Jerri sang in the choir, and I think they got to know each other pretty well."

"Maybe Ron did know," Rhodes said, thinking out loud.

"He didn't kill her," Ballinger said. "If that's what you mean. I've dealt with enough people to know real grief when I see it."

"All the same…"

"I'll talk to him. If I find out anything, I'll call."

Rhodes thanked him for his help and went off to have a chat with Fred Frazier. The Reverend Stoneman could wait until later.

SIX

FRAZIER LIVED IN an even older part of town than the Laxtons, where the houses and yards weren't nearly as well kept. A couple of the houses had a string of lights running along the ridges of their roofs, but those halfhearted efforts at decorating didn't do much to make things cheery.

Some of the people living in the neighborhood had money, but most of them were old and preferred not to spend any money that they didn't have to. Rhodes kept a close watch on the neighborhood because some of the residents seldom left their homes. He liked to check up on them periodically and make sure they were all right.

Fred Frazier's wife had died several years earlier, but Frazier hadn't become a hermit as some older men do. He still got out and about, though he wasn't particularly sociable with anyone, and he wasn't nearly as spry as he had been when Rhodes had bought the coffee table. For that matter, neither was Rhodes. But Rhodes had been a young man at the time he'd made the purchase, and Frazier was already nearing sixty. He had shut down the store not long after his wife's death, and it had never opened again. He'd told people that he didn't want to be there if his wife couldn't be with him.

The old wooden porch of Frazier's house was sagging a bit, and it creaked when Rhodes walked across it to knock on the front door. He waited a few seconds, and then the porch light came on. Fred Frazier looked at Rhodes through the glass top of his door, but he didn't open it.

Frazier looked really old, Rhodes thought. He was skinny, and his face was blotchy. His skin seemed to sag on him as if he'd recently lost a lot of weight. He had thin white hair combed over the top of his head, but the pink scalp showed through everywhere. His face was wrinkled, and the tips of his ears were hairy.

"What do you want, Sheriff?" he asked. "I didn't expect you to come calling on me this time of night. You bringing me a Christmas present?"

"I wish that was it," Rhodes said. "But it's not. I'm here to talk to you about your store."

Frazier stood unmoving behind the closed door.

"What about it?"

"Someone was killed there today."

"The world's a sorry damned place," Frazier said, shaking his head.

"I'd like to talk to you about it."

Frazier opened the door and stepped back to swing it inside the house. Rhodes pulled open the screen and went on in, passing by Frazier, who closed the door behind him.

"I was watching TV," Frazier said. "I like that WWF show. I know it's not real, but I like it anyway. Those wrestlers are something else. Come on back."

Rhodes walked behind him through a living room that was almost as dusty as the store had been, except for a framed photograph of Frazier's wife that sat on an end table. The frame was shiny, and the glass was clean and free of dust. The picture sat beside a pathetic little plastic Christmas tree with a couple of red ornaments hanging from its shabby branches and a strand of dust for a wreath. Rhodes supposed that the tree must have been stored in an attic without benefit of a box.

There was nothing shabby at all about the dusty furniture that filled the room, however. Rhodes could tell that Frazier had brought home only the best of the store's stock to furnish his home.

Rhodes followed Frazier down a short hall and into a back bedroom where a TV set was tuned in to the wrestling show that Frazier had been watching. Rhodes saw The Rock posing on the ropes, holding a profile as the crowd cheered. Frazier picked up a remote from his recliner and muted the sound.

"You can have a seat," he said. "I bought that recliner up in Dallas. It's the only furniture I ever had that didn't come from my own store."

There was no other chair in the room, and Rhodes didn't want to sit in the recliner.

"It's all right," Frazier said. "You can have it. I can sit on the bed."

"I'd rather stand," Rhodes said.

Frazier shrugged and said, "Suit yourself." He settled himself into the recliner and turned the remote over and over in his hands.

"Do you know Jerri Laxton?" Rhodes asked.

"That crazy woman who thinks we can bring business back to downtown Clearview?"

"That's one way to describe her."

Frazier snorted and said, "Well, then, I know her. What about her?"

"Did you see her today?"

"She the one that was killed at my store?"

"That's right," Rhodes said. "Did you meet her there?"

"Nope. Been right here at home, watching TV. Haven't seen anybody. How was she killed?"

"I don't know that yet," Rhodes said. "Do you ever visit your old store?"

"What for? There's nothing there. Let me tell you something, Sheriff. I had some happy times in that store when my wife Ernestine was alive. The two of us worked there together for nearly thirty years, side by side. Even ate our lunch in the back every day. There was never a better woman in the world than Ernestine, if you ask me. The

Lord threw away the mold when he made her. But that's all gone now. It's over, and you can't bring it back. My wife's dead, and so's the whole damned downtown. The store's closed for good, and that's that. I don't believe in living in the past, Sheriff. There's not much point in it if you ask me.''

"Did you know that there was a bed in the office there?''

"Couldn't be. I cleaned that place out completely when I closed it down. Well, just about. I got everything out except for an old desk that wasn't any good. It was cheap stuff, something I used in the office. I wouldn't want anything like it in my house. So I just left it there.''

"There's a bed there now,'' Rhodes said. "And somebody's been using it.''

Frazier thought that over for a few seconds and said, "I don't know who it could be, unless it's one of those damned homeless people you hear about. I thought we didn't have them around here. I thought they stayed in places like Dallas and Houston. You wouldn't think we'd have one here in Blacklin County.''

Rhodes could have told Frazier a few stories about homeless people in Blacklin County, but it didn't seem like the time. He said, "I don't think it was homeless people. I think somebody was using the place for a love nest.''

Frazier wheezed out a mirthless laugh.

"I haven't heard that phrase in a million years,'' he said. "Love nest. That's a good one, Sheriff. You're an old-fashioned man. But tell me the truth, who'd want to have a love nest in a dirty old place like that?''

Rhodes didn't have an answer for that. He said, "When's the last time you were there?''

Frazier looked down at the remote that he was turning in his hands and said, "Been at least a couple of years. Like I said, I don't believe in living in the past. Wasn't any bed there the last time I went, I can tell you that.''

"Did anyone have a key to the back door besides you?''

"Don't even have one myself. It's never locked. Why bother? Nothing in there to steal. Nothing but that old desk, and it's not worth a thing. And memories. There's lots of memories, Sheriff, but nobody can steal those."

"And you wouldn't like to see the building restored? Put back like it was?"

"Wouldn't mind at all. I talked to Miz Laxton about it and told her I thought it was a fine idea, except that it wouldn't work. Cost too much, for one thing, and I sure wasn't going to pay for it. For another thing, nobody'd come to Clearview to shop for antiques. There's too many other places to go. Thurston's got a big head start on us."

"It might work," Rhodes said. "You never know."

"I know," Frazier said, shaking his head. "I know. Believe me, Sheriff, downtown Clearview is dead. It was alive once, but that was a long time ago. Nothing is going to bring it back."

Rhodes didn't say anything, mainly because he was afraid Frazier was right.

SEVEN

BEFORE PAYING A VISIT TO Harvey Stoneman, Rhodes drove by the Clearview City Hall. It was only a block from the furniture store, and Rhodes wanted to see if Jerri's Taurus was there.

It was, parked in back. Someone might have seen her walk to the furniture store earlier that day, but it wouldn't have made much of an impression. And given the traffic on the downtown streets, she might not have been seen at all.

As for her killer, he, or she, could have parked anywhere: in front of the remaining downtown bank, in the alley behind the store, or in the parking lot of the only grocery store that hadn't yet relocated to the highway. Nobody would have noticed a car in any of those places.

Rhodes looked at the Taurus but found nothing that looked like a clue. He drove back to the furniture store. Ruth Grady was still there, and she'd found something.

"It was in the trash bin," she said, holding up a doll wrapped in what Rhodes guessed must be a semblance of swaddling clothes.

"That takes care of the kidnapping, at least," Rhodes said. "One major crime is solved. I guess we don't have to worry about getting a ransom note."

"Not likely. The question is, who put the doll in the bin?"

Rhodes had a guess about that.

"Jerri Laxton. She could have walked by the manger scene on her way here. If she saw the doll, she might have picked it up, intending to take it home and bring it back this evening.''

"I don't think she would have pitched it in the trash bin,'' Ruth said.

Rhodes said he didn't think so, either. He tried another guess.

"It could have been kids. They might have been passing by and looking things over. If they saw the doll, they might have thought it would be fun to toss it in the trash.''

"It could even have been the killer,'' Ruth said. "But I don't know why.''

"There seem to be quite a few things we don't know,'' Rhodes said.

"We'll find out, though,'' Ruth said.

Rhodes grinned and said, "We always do, don't we.''

"Well,'' Ruth said, "nearly always, at least.''

Rhodes nodded. "Close enough. Anyway, at least we've found the doll. Call Mrs. Blair and tell her we have the baby Jesus in our safekeeping.''

"All right.''

"And you'll have to tell her she can't have him back. He's evidence in a murder case now.''

"She's not going to like that, is she,'' Ruth said.

"Not a bit,'' Rhodes said.

THE FIRST BAPTIST CHURCH of Clearview was housed in a building older than Rhodes. He'd been driving past it all his life, and it was so much a part of the city that he hardly noticed it any more. But the church was one of the few places in the town that seemed prosperous in spite of its age. It didn't look old at all, and the congregation had just built a huge new addition that they called a "family life center.'' There was a gym, a fully equipped kitchen, game rooms and even a racquetball court. Rhodes found it hard to believe that there were people in Clearview who actually played racquetball.

The parsonage was next door to the church, and it was only about five years old, the former parsonage having been deemed by the congregation not to be good enough for their live-wire of a new pastor, Harvey Stoneman, who was leading them into a prosperous new era that had increased the size of the congregation amazingly and in a very short time, necessitating the need for expansion.

Rhodes parked in front of the parsonage. He didn't like going to a man's house, much less a preacher's house, and asking him about his love life in front of his wife.

And the Reverend Stoneman did indeed have a wife, Mona Mae Stoneman, a red-haired fireball with a temper that sometimes astonished the parishioners. Rhodes had heard one story that involved her throwing dishes out the open door and into the yard after her fleeing husband because he had forgotten to take them out of the dishwasher as she'd asked him to do.

The congregation was willing to overlook little things like that, Rhodes supposed, as long as the sermons were effective and not too long, and as long as the money kept rolling in. Preachers were only human, after all, and so were their wives. They were as given to sin as any other mortals, though Rhodes thought it would set a good example if they didn't give in to it as often as others did.

Rhodes thought about Mrs. Stoneman as he walked toward the house. If she threw the dishes at her husband when he didn't take them out of the dishwasher, what might she do if she found out he was having an affair with one of his choir members?

Rhodes didn't find out, because as it happened Stoneman wasn't at home.

"Where is he?" Rhodes asked Mrs. Stoneman, who had invited him into the living room of the parsonage. "I need to talk to him.

There were Christmas carols playing softly on a CD

player in the background. Rhodes realized he hadn't heard any all day. He recognized "O Come, All Ye Faithful."

"Harvey's where any minister would be at a time like this," Mrs. Stoneman said. "He's with a church member who's suffered a terrible loss."

Rhodes tried to read something into her expression as she told him that, but he couldn't draw any conclusions except that he wouldn't want to play poker with Mrs. Stoneman. Not that there was any danger of that happening. Preachers' wives didn't play poker, not in Clearview, and neither did the sheriff.

"How well did he know Ron?" Rhodes asked.

"As well as he knows anyone in the congregation. Very well. Harvey's a good pastor, Sheriff."

"I can see that," Rhodes said. "Did he know Jerri Laxton well, too?"

Rhodes thought that Mrs. Stoneman's mouth tightened when he mentioned Jerri's name, but he couldn't be sure. It had been tight all along.

"He's on a first-name basis with everyone in the church," Mrs. Stoneman said. "He has a wonderful memory."

Rhodes said he supposed that was an excellent thing for a pastor to have.

"It certainly is. What did you want to talk to Harvey about, anyway, Sheriff?"

Rhodes wondered what the penalty for lying to a preacher's wife was. He said, "I wanted to ask him about Jerri, whether she'd mentioned anything to him in confidence about someone who might have wanted to kill her."

"A minister doesn't break confidences."

"I should have known that," Rhodes said. "Well, I won't take any more of your time. Tell your husband I came by."

"I'll be sure to do that, Sheriff," Mrs. Stoneman said.

EIGHT

"I GOT THE BABY Jesus in the evidence locker," Hack said. "Don't seem right, somehow."

"You've been talking to Mrs. Blair," Rhodes said.

"That's right. Ruth asked me to call her. I guess she didn't want to have to be the one to tell her."

Rhodes said he didn't much blame Ruth.

"I always say it's best to tell people the truth about things," Hack said. "Let them know what's goin' on. Some people don't like bein' kept in the dark about everything all the time. Not that I'm one of 'em, you understand."

"I was going to tell you," Rhodes said.

"Well, don't let it worry you. Ruth's already filled me in."

"What about Lawton?"

Hack smiled the smile of a man who was one up on his best friend.

"He don't know a thing yet. I'll be telling him in the morning, though."

Rhodes was sure of it. But Hack would tell it at his own pace and draw it out interminably. Rhodes hoped he wouldn't be around for it.

"You say you've been talking to the preacher's wife?" Hack said.

"That's right. She's quite a woman."

"You got that right. You remember the time she tried to get Miz Coover's driver's license lifted?"

Rhodes had almost forgotten about that little incident.

Mrs. Coover was a spirited woman in her late eighties and not ready to give up her car, in spite of the fact that she often drove down the streets of Clearview on the wrong side, as if she thought she might be in England.

"I remember," Rhodes said.

"I thought Miz Stoneman was gonna bust a blood vessel tellin' you about it," Hack said. "Her face was redder than her hair, and it swole up like a balloon. That was when she and Brother Harvey first moved here, and she didn't know about Miz Coover."

Everybody who had lived in Clearview for any length of time knew about Mrs. Coover, Rhodes thought. She drove a 1978 Pontiac that had once been navy blue. Its color had faded because the car was always parked outside and had never been waxed, Mrs. Coover having long ago lost the ability to drive inside her garage without scraping the sides.

"If Miz Stoneman had been here a while," Hack said, "she'd have known to get out of the way, just like everybody else." He paused to shake his head. "Miz Stoneman didn't see it like that, though. She sure lit into you."

"She was right," Rhodes said. "I should have taken Mrs. Coover's license away."

"Yeah, but you didn't. And when you said you weren't, I thought Miz Stoneman was gonna grab you by the neck and throttle you."

"I wouldn't have blamed her. Like I said, I should have taken Mrs. Coover's license."

"Wouldn't have made any difference. She'd just have driven anyhow. She was one stubborn old woman."

Mrs. Coover had died only the previous year, but she had finally stopped driving a few months earlier after running over the curb at the grocery store and nearly going through the plate glass windows in front.

"It's a good thing Miz Coover didn't hurt anybody when she did that," Hack said. "Miz Stoneman would prob'ly have gotten a lynch mob together and strung you up. Miz Coover, too.''

"I don't think she'd go that far," Rhodes said.

"You never know what somebody might do when they get all wrought up like that. Even a preacher's wife."

"You could be right, I guess."

"I know I am. When you've had as many dealin's with women as I have, you know how far one of them will go. And that one will go to just about any length, I'd say. And that reminds me…''

"Of what?"

"Have you bought Ivy a Christmas present yet? She's a fine woman, but I'd hate to be the one that didn't buy her a present."

Ivy was Rhodes's wife, and he knew what a fine woman she was. He also knew that he always had trouble finding presents for her. Finding presents wasn't one of the things he did best. Hack knew that, too.

"I don't have anything," Rhodes said. "Any suggestions?"

"Nope. None of my business. I've already got somethin' for Miz McGee."

"What?"

"That's for me to know and for you to find out."

Rhodes started to say that he didn't want to know anyway, but he stopped himself when he realized that they'd already sunk to the level of third graders. He didn't see any need to make things worse.

"I just about forgot," Hack said. "There was a call for you. That newspaper reporter, Jennifer Loan."

"Loam," Rhodes said.

"Yeah. Loam. I knew it had to do with either dirt or money. She wanted to know about the murder."

"You didn't tell her anything, did you?"

"Who me? How could I tell her? I didn't know anything to tell her. Nobody around here ever tells me anything."

Rhodes had the feeling, not uncommon in that office, that they had been on a long trip and, at the end of it, they'd arrived right back where they'd started.

"What else did you want to know?" he asked.

"Nothing," Hack said.

NINE

YANCEY, Rhodes's Pomeranian, was bouncing up and down
around Rhodes's ankles, yipping excitedly. There was nothing unusual in that. Yancey was always excited, unless he
was sleeping. What was unusual was the little Santa hat
that Yancey was wearing. Rhodes wasn't too sure about the
hat.

"I'm not, either," Ivy said when he told her. "Someone
at work gave it to me, and I wanted to get your reaction."

"I think he looked better without it," Rhodes said. "I
don't like hats much, even on people. And they look even
worse on dogs."

Rhodes and Ivy were sitting at the kitchen table, and
Rhodes was eating a sandwich made out of some kind of
lunch meat that he suspected had a lot more tofu in it than
meat. So did the cheese he'd put on the sandwich, not that
he was complaining. He'd lost a little weight lately, and
maybe the fake food had helped.

He thought about slipping a bite of the sandwich to Yancey, thinking it might quiet him down, but Ivy got in the
way when she bent down to remove the Santa hat.

"Who gave you the hat?" Rhodes asked, and took a
drink of Dr Pepper. Real Dr Pepper. He'd eat fake food,
but he wouldn't drink Diet Dr Pepper. A man had to draw
the line somewhere.

"Carmen," Ivy said.

Carmen Boland was a partner in the insurance agency

where Ivy worked. She was also a member of the First Baptist Church.

"Has Carmen ever mentioned anything about Harvey Stoneman to you?" Rhodes asked.

Ivy tossed the little red hat onto the table. Yancey seemed to be relieved that it was gone. He lay down under Rhodes's chair.

"Why would Carmen mention Harvey Stoneman to me?" Ivy asked.

"Well, some people like to pass along interesting information. And I heard that Stoneman might be messing around with one of his choir members."

"Jerri Laxton, for example?"

Rhodes had told Ivy about Jerry's murder earlier. He always discussed things with Ivy, and sometimes she had been a big help to him.

"That's who I had in mind," he said.

Ivy said, "Carmen mentioned something about that only the other day. There's been a little talk. Some of the church members aren't too happy about it, but Carmen says none of them really believe anything was going on."

"Maybe they just don't want to believe it."

"That could be it. Or maybe someone's trying to stir up trouble."

Rhodes finished his sandwich and took the last swallow of Dr Pepper.

"Do you believe what they say about husbands being the last to know?" he asked as he pushed his plate aside.

"Not really. I think men know more than people give them credit for sometimes."

Rhodes decided not to pursue that line of thought for the moment.

"What about wives?" he asked.

"You think Ron Laxton killed his wife? Or that Mona Stoneman did?"

"I was just asking a question. Seems to me that a lot of

people know there was something going on between Jerri
Laxton and Harvey Stoneman, or think there was. Clyde
Ballinger told me about it. And Carmen mentioned it to
you. Clyde heard it from someone. So did Carmen. Half
the town must have heard something or other about it. And
everyone will be talking about the murder tomorrow. The
ones who haven't heard about that already will read about
it in the paper."

"Did the new reporter get the story?" Ivy asked.

"She was there when I found the body. She's playing a
shepherd in that manger scene."

"She's also on the ball," Ivy said. "I like her."

Rhodes nodded. "I wonder how much she knows about
Stoneman and Jerri Laxton. And how much she'll print."

"She won't print much. Even if she wants to, the editor
will never let it get in. You should know our paper better
than that."

Rhodes said, "I know. The last controversy that got any
coverage had to do with who assassinated John F. Ken-
nedy."

Ivy laughed. "I'm too young to remember that."

"Me, too," Rhodes said. "Somebody told me about it."

"I'll bet. Do you have any suspects in Jerri Laxton's
murder besides the spouses?"

"The preacher," Rhodes said. "Harvey Stoneman."

TEN

THE NEXT DAY went by so fast that Rhodes didn't really have much time to devote to the investigation of the Laxton murder.

Early in the morning, there was a traffic accident on the Obert road that involved a car, a pickup and a trailer full of cows. The cows were loose on the highway, and there was a little bit of fog that added to the unexpected thrills for the drivers coming over Obert's Hill.

After the accident was cleared up, there was a domestic dispute between a husband and wife who had somehow managed to get into a screaming match over the location of their family Christmas tree. Rhodes had a hard time convincing them that it was the season of peace and goodwill, but when he left the house, they had stopped yelling and throwing things and scaring the neighbors.

After that there were other incidents, minor annoyances and major ones, so that it was the middle of the afternoon before Rhodes got a chance to go by Ballinger's Funeral Home and pick up the autopsy report on Jerri Laxton.

Ballinger was in the little brick house where he lived at the back of the main establishment. He was reading when Rhodes came in. Rhodes glanced at the cover and saw that the book was an old paperback of the kind that Ballinger preferred, this one by someone named Gil Brewer. Ballinger put the book aside when Rhodes came in and gave him Dr. White's report.

As he looked through what the doctor had written,

Rhodes reflected that one advantage of living in a small town was that he could get his autopsy reports sooner than if he lived in a city. As long as there was a qualified doctor, which White was, and as long as White was willing to do the job, Rhodes didn't have to send the bodies of victims to Dallas or Waco. It would have taken him weeks to get a report if he'd had to do that.

Ballinger didn't seem interested in the report or its contents. He picked up his book, *Three-Way Split,* and started reading again.

When Rhodes was finished with the report, he stood up and said, "Thanks, Clyde. Did you find out anything else from Ron Laxton last night?"

Ballinger put the book down on the desk again and looked up at Rhodes.

"I was hoping you wouldn't ask me that."

"Why?"

"I like Ron. He's a nice guy, and he was really upset last night."

"I hear that Harvey Stoneman went by to comfort him."

"I know. I was still there when Harvey came. That's what I should tell you about."

"All right," Rhodes said. "Tell me."

"Ron didn't exactly appreciate Harvey's visit. He didn't take it very well."

"You want to be a little bit more specific about that?"

"Not really. But I will. Ron wouldn't even let Harvey in the front door. He called him a few names and said he didn't think Harvey was fit to be a preacher."

"I guess Ron wasn't the last one to know, after all."

"I don't know who told him," Ballinger said. "He didn't say. It sure wasn't me. But somebody must have."

"How did Harvey take it?"

"Just the way a preacher should. He was really calm and forgiving. He said he knew Ron wasn't thinking straight and that he'd come by later, when Ron was feeling more like talking.''

"And that cheered Ron up?"

"Not a lot. He was still cussing when Harvey drove off."

"Did he tell you anything about what he knew?"

"No. I told him that was no way to treat a preacher, but he just said that Stoneman wasn't fit to be a preacher. And then he told me something worse."

"What?"

"He said he was going to show the town what a big hypocrite Harvey Stoneman was."

Uh-oh, Rhodes thought.

"Did he say how he was going to do that?"

"No. I'm not even sure he meant it."

"You should have called me last night," Rhodes said.

"I know. But Ron hasn't done anything yet. He's been busy, and I don't think he feels like doing anything to Harvey. He came in this morning to make the arrangements for Mrs. Laxton's funeral, and he didn't look like a man who was going to make trouble for anybody."

"I'll tell you something about people who don't look like they're going to make trouble," Rhodes said.

"Yeah?"

"They're the worst kind."

RHODES LEFT BALLINGER'S and drove by the Laxton house, but Ron wasn't there. The afternoon was about gone, and Rhodes drove by the jail to find out if there had been any reports of trouble between Laxton and Stoneman. Hack said that there hadn't. Nothing out of the ordinary was going on.

"You know I always give you a call when somethin' happens," Hack said. "You're the sheriff. You're supposed to know what's happenin' in this town. And even if you weren't the sheriff, I wouldn't keep you in the dark about anything. I believe in sharing information. I don't hold things back from the people I work with. I—''

"I get the point," Rhodes said. "Where's Lawton?"

"He's back cleaning one of the empty cells. He figures we'll be getting plenty of customers before too long, what with it bein' Christmas and all."

Rhodes knew that Lawton was right. For some reason, the Christmas season was one of the high-crime times in Clearview, and maybe in other places, too. Maybe it was the parties, with people having too much to drink. Or maybe it was something else. Not everyone thought of Christmas as the happiest time of the year. Rhodes was sure Ron Laxton would never think of it that way again.

"Are they gonna have the manger scene tonight?" Hack asked. "I mean, the baby Jesus is still in the evidence locker, and he's the star of the show."

"I don't think that will stop them," Rhodes said. "A doll is easy to replace."

He knew as he said it that Frances Blair wouldn't feel that way, but there wasn't anything he could do about that. The doll was in the evidence locker, and it was going to stay there for a while.

"I guess you know by now what killed Jerri Laxton," Hack said.

"I got a report from Dr. White. I put it in the folder when I came in."

"I know you did. I saw the report in your hand when you walked through the door. I just wondered if you were gonna tell me anything that was in it. Not that it's any of my business. I'm just the dispatcher. It's not like I'm a big-shot crime fighter like the sheriff or anything."

Rhodes repressed a sigh and said, "Jerri Laxton was killed by a blow to the temple."

"The old blunt instrument," Hack said. "You didn't find one lyin' around, did you?"

Rhodes said that he hadn't.

"Maybe the baby Jesus was the murder weapon," Hack said. "That doll looked like it had a pretty hard head."

"It wasn't the doll," Rhodes said. "And it wasn't blunt. The murder weapon was sharp."

"Ice pick?"

"Not that sharp. More like a trowel. She was hit pretty hard. The point cracked the skull and pushed some of the fragments into the—"

"That's plenty. Sometimes I like bein' kept in the dark. Did you find a trowel lying around?"

"No. There was nothing like that anywhere in the store or in the trash bin. And no one's doing any bricklaying around there, either."

"So where does that leave you?"

"Right where I usually am," Rhodes said. "Dazed and confused."

"That was the name of one of those slacker movies," Hack said. "You see it?"

Rhodes admitted that he hadn't. If he ever had time to watch a movie, he was likely to see something with a little less class, like *Bride of the Monster* or *Francis Joins the Navy*.

"You prob'ly didn't do any Christmas shoppin' today, either," Hack said.

Rhodes said he hadn't.

"You need to get into the spirit of the season," Hack told him.

"It's hard to do when somebody's been murdered," Rhodes said.

"Yeah. But you still oughta try."

Rhodes promised that he would.

ELEVEN

WHEN RHODES LEFT the jail, it was just beginning to get dark. There was a distinct chill in the air, and he was glad he'd brought a heavy jacket from home that morning.

He drove by the Laxton house, but there was still no sign that Ron was at home. Rhodes went to the door and rang the bell. There was no answer, and there was none when Rhodes pounded on the door with the flat of his hand.

Rhodes stood on the porch wondering what to do next. He thought the best idea would be to talk to Harvey Stoneman, who would be downtown, getting ready to portray a wise man, an ironic role if there ever was one. That is, it was ironic if the rumors about Stoneman and Jerri Laxton were true. If they weren't, then Stoneman was indeed wise.

Before he started downtown, Rhodes called Hack on the radio and told him to have Ruth be on the lookout for Laxton.

"That'd be an apb," Hack said. "Right?"

"Either that or a bolo."

"Think anybody listenin' in on a scanner will figure out what all that means?"

"Probably everybody."

"Yeah, I'll bet you're right. We shoulda used the ten-codes."

"Everybody has a book with those codes," Rhodes said. "Comes with the scanner."

"Maybe somebody listenin' will find Ron for us."

"That would be fine with me," Rhodes said.

DRIVING DOWNTOWN didn't take long. It didn't take long
to drive anywhere in Clearview, or to walk for that matter.
When Rhodes had been growing up there, he had walked
everywhere. But no one walked these days. It was still as
safe as it had ever been, especially downtown. But it wasn't
safe to walk to the Wal-Mart, not if it meant crossing the
highway.

Rhodes parked the county car on the street near the manger scene. The painted backdrop was lit by floodlights hidden behind the hay bales, and there was music coming from
a boom box, also hidden behind the hay. Rhodes recognized
the voice of Tennessee Ernie Ford singing "Come, All Ye
Faithful."

Over on one side Frances Blair was getting the shepherds
lined up, and Vernell had her goats in place. Well, almost
in place. The goats were never going to be entirely cooperative.

Mary and Joseph were standing over the manger, but
Rhodes couldn't tell whether the baby Jesus had been replaced. Stoneman and the other two wise men were helping
unload the donkey from a trailer that was backed into the
alley.

Mona Stoneman was nowhere to be seen, which suited
Rhodes just fine. He much preferred to talk to Harvey when
the preacher's wife wasn't around. When the donkey was
unloaded, Rhodes strolled over to the trailer and called Harvey Stoneman aside.

"I'd like to talk to you for a few minutes," Rhodes said.
"Before things get started here."

"I think we're about ready to go, Sheriff," Stoneman
said. He looked around as if to see who might be watching
them. "Can it wait until after we're through here?"

"No," Rhodes said. "It can't."

"I can understand that," Stoneman said, though he didn't
look as if he really did. "Could we step around to the other
side of the trailer? It should be a little quieter there."

Rhodes had to admit that it was pretty noisy around the manger. People were milling around and talking, Frances Blair was giving directions, Vernell's goats were chomping on the hay, and the donkey wasn't being cooperative about his placement. Tennessee Ernie was singing "Hark! The Herald Angels Sing."

Rhodes said he thought going around to the other side of the trailer was a good idea. They moved to where the street-light shone through the trailer's board sides and made barred shadows on the side of the building that stood beside it. The building had once been an automobile dealership, but it was empty now, like most of the others.

It wasn't much quieter there, really, but it was more private, which Rhodes figured was what Stoneman had wanted all along. They were both lucky that Frances Blair was talking to the shepherds and had momentarily distracted Jennifer Loam, who would otherwise have spotted Rhodes and pounced on him immediately.

Standing beside the trailer in his robe and turban, Stoneman should have looked ridiculous, but he didn't. His forearms were thick and muscular, and his face under the turban was dark and determined.

"I think I know what you want to ask," Stoneman said. "I've heard the rumors, too, of course, and they're just not true. No matter what people think, I wasn't having an affair with Jerri Laxton."

Rhodes nodded. When someone started telling him things without his asking, his policy was simply to listen.

"I was counseling her privately," Stoneman said. "As her minister. She and Ron were having problems, but I thought I could help them work things out."

He stopped and looked around, but there was no one there except for him and Rhodes. Rhodes figured it was time for him to say something.

"What kind of problems?" he asked.

"You know," Stoneman said. "Marital problems. I really can't say much more than that. It's confidential."

"It's not like you're in a confession booth or anything," Rhodes pointed out. "Maybe you'd better tell me."

"There are some things that have to stay between a pastor and his parishioners. It's not like I'm a priest, that's for sure, but it's still a matter of confidentiality. Let's just say that Ron was having problems because Jerri was a more successful politician than he was. You may not know this, but there were even some people who were talking about her running for the state legislature."

"I heard about that," Rhodes said. "I thought it was a good idea."

"She had big plans for this town. Like what she was working on for this very block. Not many people knew what she had up her sleeve. It would have changed the whole downtown, brought in some traffic, even made it prosperous again. She could have gone a long way in politics, I think."

"I believe it," Rhodes said.

"So did Jerri. But Ron didn't. Or maybe he did, and that was what caused the trouble. He was afraid she was outgrowing him."

That wasn't the kind of thing you heard about much in Clearview, Rhodes thought, but it could have been true.

"Did Ron know you were counseling his wife?" he asked Stoneman.

"Jerri wanted to keep it a secret. She thought Ron would be ashamed if he knew she'd been discussing their personal problems with me."

By now Rhodes had a good idea what kind of personal problems Ron and Jerri had, even if Stoneman hadn't been specific.

"Isn't there a pill for that now?" Rhodes asked.

Stoneman said, "That's not the kind of thing Ron would ever discuss with his doctor, much less with his wife."

"Bob Dole advertises it on TV," Rhodes said.

Stoneman shrugged. "That's TV. This is Clearview."

"Did Jerri ever mention anything about other men?"

"Definitely not. She was a hundred percent faithful to Ron, no matter what he thinks."

Stoneman sounded utterly sincere, but then he always sounded that way. It came with his job.

"What about enemies?" Rhodes asked. "Did she mention anything about anyone who might want to kill her?"

Stoneman looked shocked.

"Who would want to do a thing like that?"

"Somebody did it," Rhodes reminded him.

"Well, yes, but—"

Stoneman didn't get to finish his sentence because that was when the shooting started.

TWELVE

THE FIRST SHOT was followed by almost total silence. The only sound was the voice of Tennessee Ernie singing "Silent Night."

The second shot blew away the boom box, cutting Tennessee Ernie off right in the middle of the phrase "all is calm." Rhodes didn't dwell on the irony of it all. He'd had enough irony for one night.

"Stay here," Rhodes told Stoneman, and ran around the trailer.

The first person he saw was Ron Laxton. That was because Laxton was the only one standing. The shepherds, the wise men, and everyone else had hit the concrete, which was apparently what Laxton wanted.

The donkey had fled the scene. Rhodes could see it running down the middle of the main street, skidding occasionally on the pavement as if it were much more accustomed to running on a dirt surface.

Unlike the donkey, the goats didn't seem bothered in the least. Two of them watched Laxton with what appeared to be mild curiosity, while the third was chewing on a corner of the boom box that had landed at its feet. Or its hooves. Rhodes wasn't sure of the correct term, not that it mattered.

"Hey, Ron," Rhodes said.

Laxton was holding a revolver in his right hand. It looked like a .38 to Rhodes, but he wasn't quite close enough to be sure.

"Hey, Sheriff," Laxton said, waving the pistol around.

It was a .38, all right, Rhodes thought.

"Where is he?" Laxton asked.

"Who?"

"You know who. The Reverend Harvey Stoneman, that's who. Reverend. What a laugh."

"I don't think he's here," Rhodes said.

"I'm not blind," Laxton said. "I can see that he's not here. I can even count up to three, and I can tell there are just two wise men. One's missing. He's the one I want."

One of the shepherds raised up. Jennifer Loam.

"I haven't seen him," she said. "I don't think he's gotten here yet."

"You hear that, Ron?" Rhodes said. "Stoneman's not here."

Rhodes took a step toward Laxton.

"Why don't you just give me that gun, and we'll go see if we can find your minister."

Laxton fired a shot into a hay bale. The bale hardly moved, but several of the shepherds twitched reflexively. The goats looked only mildly interested.

"He's not *my* minister," Laxton said. "Don't call him that again. And don't come any closer."

Rhodes didn't think that Laxton was really dangerous. He would have been shooting at something other than bales of hay if he'd really wanted to do any damage. So Rhodes went another step closer.

"I told you not to do that," Laxton said. "If you do it again, I'm going to kill one of those goats."

Vernell Lindsey, who was lying nearby, looked up at Rhodes and said, "You'd better not get one of my goats killed, Sheriff. If you do, I'll see to it that you never hold office in this county again."

Rhodes had heard similar threats for years, and he never took them very seriously. Still, he didn't want to have a goat's blood on his hands if he could avoid it. He was about to tell Vernell that, but Laxton cut him off.

"You shut up," he said to Vernell. "If anybody opens their mouth again, I'm killing all the goats."

"Now Ron," Harvey Stoneman said, stepping from behind the trailer, "you know that wouldn't be right."

Rhodes had hoped Stoneman would have enough sense to stay out of sight. He should have known better, though. Preachers always thought they were good at calming people. But usually they didn't have to deal with people who were holding .38 caliber pistols.

Laxton shot one of the top boards on the trailer. The board cracked like thunder, splinters flew up, and Stoneman ducked back behind the trailer. That made four shots, Rhodes thought. So there was probably one cartridge left in the chamber. Maybe two.

Laxton read his mind. He waved the gun at Rhodes and said, "Do you feel lucky, punk?"

Rhodes sighed. That was what was wrong with the world today: Everybody wanted to be Dirty Harry.

"Why don't you just put the pistol down on the ground, Ron," he said. "Then I'll pick it up, and we'll forget this whole thing."

"Ho-ho-ho," Ron said, but he didn't sound the least little bit like Santa Claus. "You know you'd take me off to the jail as soon as you got your hands on the gun. And I'm not going to jail. Nobody's taking me anywhere."

"He's suicidal," Jennifer Loam said in a stage whisper. "You can't let him kill himself, Sheriff!"

"I heard that," Laxton said. "Don't listen to her. That's crazy talk. I'm not going to kill anybody but that bastard Harvey Stoneman. Come out, Stoneman! Don't make me come get you."

Rhodes heard a car start somewhere down the block. Laxton heard it, too.

"The son of a bitch!" Laxton said. "He's running away!"

Stoneman had finally gotten smart, Rhodes thought, hoping that it wasn't too late.

Laxton ran past Rhodes and headed around the trailer. Jennifer Loam stuck out her shepherd's crook and grabbed him around the left ankle.

Laxton didn't fall, but he began stumbling, his arms windmilling. He lost his grip on the pistol, and it flew up over the trailer and landed on the other side, discharging a shot when it struck the concrete.

That's five, Rhodes thought.

The bullet ricocheted off the wall of the building and whined down into the street, where it twanged through the sheet metal on the side of someone's dark-blue Malibu.

Laxton came up short against the side of the trailer. He put out his hands to stop himself, but he was going so fast that his face smacked into one of the sideboards. He might have been hurt, but he hardly slowed down. Turning to his left, he ran up the alley, ducking down behind the trailer to pick up his pistol as he ran.

Rhodes was right behind him.

"Everyone stay here!" Rhodes yelled.

He hoped people would listen to him, but he didn't have much faith that they would. There was always someone who wanted to be a hero and help out the poor hapless lawman.

Rhodes peered up the alley and saw Laxton duck into Frazier's Furniture. The back door slammed behind him, and Rhodes would have to go after him.

Five shots, Rhodes thought, wondering if Laxton had brought any spare ammunition with him.

When he got to the furniture store's back entrance, Rhodes paused to look behind him. Sure enough, not everyone had stayed behind. Jennifer Loam was right there at his elbow.

"Where did he go?" she asked.

Rhodes pointed to the door.

"He's in there. I'm going in after him. You stay here, and don't let anyone else in."

"I'm going, too."

"No, you're not. You're not a law officer. Reporters don't carry badges."

"You can't stop me. Freedom of the press."

Rhodes thought that journalism teachers should clarify the amendments for their students.

"Freedom of the press has to do with what you can write," he said, "not with going into dark buildings after fugitives. You stay right here."

"Are you going to shoot him?" Jennifer asked.

"Not unless he shoots me first," Rhodes said.

Rhodes thought about calling Hack for backup, but by the time he did that, Laxton might have left the building through the front door or even through one of the windows, and there was no telling where he might go if that happened. Besides, Rhodes told himself, the odds against Laxton having another pistol on him were pretty high.

On the other hand...

"Do you have a cell phone?" he asked Jennifer.

He might as well have asked if she had a nose.

"Of course. Who doesn't?"

"Good. Call the jail and tell the dispatcher to get a deputy here as soon as possible."

Rhodes gave her the number, and she dug around in her robe for a second before coming out with a phone about the size of a matchbook.

"Are you going inside before the deputy comes?" she asked.

"Yes," Rhodes said. "When she gets here, tell her to watch the front door. You can watch this one."

"What if he comes out this way?"

"Hit him with your crook," Rhodes said, drawing his own pistol before he went inside.

THIRTEEN

THE BUILDING SEEMED much darker to Rhodes than when he had entered it perviously, and this time he didn't have a flashlight. So he stood by the wall just inside the door and waited for his eyes to adjust to the lack of light.

There was a faint bluish glow from the streetlight coming in through the front windows, though the windows were so dusty and dirty that the illumination was only slightly better than nothing. Rhodes wished he'd sent Jennifer to the car for his flashlight, but it was too late for that.

After thirty seconds or so had passed, Rhodes could see the vague outline of the office room. Since that was about the only place to hide, he thought Laxton must be inside. Rhodes started walking in that direction, trying to make as little noise as possible.

After he'd taken two steps, he heard a board creak above his head, and he thought maybe Laxton wasn't in the office, after all. Maybe he was in the loft. But then he remembered the mouse that had been up there.

"Are you a man or a mouse?" he asked of no one in particular, but of course he didn't get an answer.

He decided that he might as well try the office first. It was even darker in there than it was in the rest of the building, and Rhodes could barely see the outline of the desk and the bed, or at least he thought he saw them. He might have been imagining things. If there was anyone under the bed or cowering in the kneehole of the desk, he couldn't tell.

The good news was that no one was shooting at him.

He pushed the office door open with his knee and went inside. There was no sound, no movement. Rhodes stood on one side of the desk and shoved it with his hip. It slid a foot, seemingly meeting with no resistance. Laxton obviously wasn't there, so Rhodes tried the bed. No one there, either, which meant that Laxton was upstairs with the mouse.

Rhodes thought they deserved each other.

He went over to the bottom of the stairs and said, "Why don't you come on down, Ron? I really don't feel like climbing up there after you."

No answer. Rhodes waited for a few seconds, then started up. He stopped on the third step.

"There are mice up there, Ron. You'd better watch out."

Still no answer. Maybe Laxton wasn't afraid of mice. Rhodes climbed higher, holding his pistol close to his body and hoping that Laxton would stay put, wherever he was up there.

There was always the chance that Laxton had one bullet left, or that he'd reloaded. And if that was the case, he was just waiting for Rhodes's head to poke up over the top of the stairs, at which time he'd blow it off.

If he could see it, which he probably could. There was enough light from the street to provide a visible silhouette.

Rhodes kept as low as he could, and when he was almost to the top, he sat, keeping his head just below the level of the loft. He could smell the dust on the old stairs.

"Ron? I'm going to stand up now. Don't shoot. We can talk things over and see what we come up with."

Instead of standing up, Rhodes stuck up his hand and waved it in the air. Laxton didn't shoot at it. He threw his pistol instead.

Out of ammo, Rhodes thought, and stood, which was a tactical error. Laxton came barreling out of the darkness, his feet crashing across the floor, and hit Rhodes with a hard upper-body tackle.

Rhodes fell backward, losing his pistol in the process, and the two of them tumbled down the stairs. Rhodes hit some sensitive part of his body, including both elbows, on every single step.

The two of them landed in a heap at the bottom, with Rhodes underneath Laxton, whose mouth and nose were still bleeding from their sudden encounter with the trailer.

Laxton panted and cursed, spraying blood, as he tried to gouge out Rhodes's eyes.

Rhodes batted Laxton's hands away and made an effort to sit up. Laxton hit him hard just under the right eye. Rhodes's head snapped back, and Laxton hit him again, this time in the forehead. That was a big mistake on Laxton's part, as he was hurt much worse than Rhodes, who heard Laxton's knuckle pop just before Laxton yelled.

"Son of a bitch! Son of a bitch!"

Laxton collapsed on top of the sheriff, and after that, it was easy for Rhodes to throw him off. Laxton lay on the floor in the fetal position, whining and sucking on his knuckle. Rhodes could have told him that neither of those things would help, but his face hurt too much for him to care about anything that Laxton did.

Rhodes looked around for the pistols, but it was unlikely that he could have found them if Ruth Grady hadn't come in with her flashlight.

"I told the reporter to go around and watch the front," Ruth said. "I thought you might want a little help." She shone the light on Laxton. "But I see you didn't need it. What did you do to him?"

"I think he broke a knuckle," Rhodes said. "On my head."

Ruth turned the light on Rhodes and shook her head.

"I take it back. You could have used some help, after

all. You're going to have a real colorful eye by tomorrow, I'll bet.''

"Probably," Rhodes said.

"You're lucky he didn't break the eye socket. That can be really painful, not to mention dangerous.''

"That's me," Rhodes said. "Mr. Lucky. Help me get Laxton on his feet, and I'll take him to jail.''

"What are the charges?''

"Assaulting an officer, resisting arrest, illegal discharge of a firearm, attempted murder, and disturbing the peace, for starters. Not to mention shooting Tennessee Ernie Ford.''

"Who?'' Ruth asked.

"Never mind." Rhodes said.

FOURTEEN

RHODES SAT BEHIND his desk and thought about Ron Laxton, who was going to have the worst Christmas of his life. Not only had his wife been murdered, but it seemed likely that Laxton was going to spend Christmas in the Blacklin County Jail, which wasn't exactly festive.

"Maybe we should get a Christmas tree," Rhodes said.

"Nope," Lawton said. "They drop needles all over the place. Just be somethin' else for me to clean up."

"I think a tree's a good idea," Hack said. "We could put some lights on it, maybe the kind that flash on and off. Red and green ones. Give this place a little color. It's not like you have all that much to do, anyway, Lawton. We could get us a little tape player with some Christmas music on it, too."

"No Tennnessee Ernie," Rhodes said.

"How about Perry Como?"

"OK. Or the Kingston Trio. I always liked that Christmas album of theirs."

"I'll see what I can do," Hack said.

"Sure, go ahead," Lawton said. "Nobody cares about me havin' to clean up the mess."

"Maybe somebody'll put you a present under the tree," Hack said. "You ever think about that? Or maybe we could get us one of those plastic trees. Then you wouldn't have to worry about it droppin' needles on the floor."

"I hadn't thought of that," Lawton said. "OK, I'll go along with it if we get a plastic tree."

"What about the prisoners?" Hack asked Rhodes. "We gonna get them a tree?"

"No," Rhodes said. "They can come in and see the one in here, though."

"You're feelin' sorry for Ron Laxton, aren't you?" Hack said. "I can see why, but he doesn't have anybody to blame but himself. He could make bail if he wanted to. You know he's got the money."

"I know. But he was upset about his wife's murder or he wouldn't have acted the way he did. He just went crazy. He really doesn't belong here."

"He was downtown, shootin' off a pistol in the middle of a crowd," Hack pointed out. "If he doesn't belong here, I don't know who does."

"Whoever killed his wife," Rhodes said. "That's who."

"Yeah," Hack agreed, "but the thing is, we don't know who that is, do we."

"No," Rhodes said, thinking that he should know by now.

He wasn't the kind of lawman who relied on modern forensic science so much as he did on talking to people and evaluating what they told him. It seemed to him that somewhere in all the things he'd heard recently, he had the answer to who the killer was, but he couldn't sort it out. Maybe it was Ron Laxton. Maybe that's why he had refused to try to bond himself out of jail.

"I'll have to think about it a while longer," Rhodes said. "Maybe I'll figure it out."

"In the meantime you better be buyin' Ivy a present," Hack told him. "And you better do somethin' about that eye of yours. It's goin' to be more colors than a Christmas rainbow by mornin'."

"You're just lucky he didn't break your face bone instead of his knuckle," Lawton said.

"I have a hard head," Rhodes said.

"Speakin' of hard heads," Hack said, "Ruth fingerprinted the baby Jesus today.'' He thought about what he'd said and added, ''I don't mean she took his fingerprints. I mean she looked for fingerprints *on* him. She found some, too.''

''I'm sure she did,'' Rhodes said. ''That doll was handled by a lot of people.''

''That's what Ruth said. She said there were so many different prints that you might as well give it back to Miz Blair.''

''Not yet,'' Rhodes said, thinking there might be some prints on it that simply didn't belong. If there were, they might be important.

''You think Ruth can catch that donkey?'' Hack asked.

Rhodes said he wasn't sure. ''That donkey might be out of the county by now. The last time I saw it, it was moving pretty fast.''

''Losin' it will put a damper on the whole thing,'' Lawton said. ''You need a donkey for a good manger scene. A camel would be better, but if you can't get one, which you can't around here, a donkey will do. You need a donkey, though.''

''Maybe they'll cancel again,'' Rhodes said.

Hack didn't think so. ''Too many people countin' on seein' it. They missed havin' it last night.''

''They got a little extra show if they came early enough tonight,'' Rhodes said, standing up. ''I'm going to see Harvey Stoneman.''

''What for?''

''To finish a conversation,'' Rhodes said.

RHODES PARKED HIS CAR and looked at the new addition to the First Baptist Church. It hadn't been finished long, and there was still a stack of unused brick out back. Rhodes wondered if there might be a trowel that someone left behind, but probably the workmen hadn't been that careless.

Once again, Harvey Stoneman wasn't at home. But his

wife was there. She had been wrapping Christmas presents on a bridge table set up in her den when Rhodes came to the door, and she went back to her work while they talked. Christmas songs were playing in the background, somewhere in another room. Tennessee Ernie again. Rhodes wondered if anyone except him remembered the Kingston Trio.

"Harvey is at the manger scene," Mrs. Stoneman said. "I told him that he'd be excused if he didn't go, considering what had happened, but he told me people expected three wise men, so he was going to be sure they saw them."

"Ron Laxton tried to kill him," Rhodes said. "I don't think anyone would blame him if he wasn't there."

"That's what I said. Of course he's also worried about what people will say about him running away. He doesn't want them to think he was scared."

"He did the right thing," Rhodes said. "Other people could have been hurt if he'd stayed."

Mrs. Stoneman shook her head as she folded the corners of a sheet of red-and-white paper to fit precisely on the end of a shirt box.

"I don't think so. I don't think Ron wanted to kill anyone but Harvey."

She taped the corners of the package neatly and went to work on the other end.

"Why would he want to kill Harvey?" Rhodes asked.

Mrs. Stoneman finished taping the paper in place, then reached into a big bag of bows and brought out a big red one. She pressed it to the box, but it didn't stick. When she moved the box, the ribbon slid off. She put it back on and smashed it with a fist. The box crumpled and paper crackled. Mrs. Stoneman straightened the bow as much as she could and said, "I expect you know why, Sheriff."

There was a pause and Rhodes could hear Tennessee Ernie's deep voice singing "O Little Town of Bethlehem."

"Nice song," he said.

"You don't have to pussyfoot and change the subject around me, Sheriff. I've heard the same rumors that everyone in town has heard, but the difference is that I don't believe a word of them. Harvey Stoneman is as faithful as any man ever was. He's not one of those preachers who follows the Bible's bad examples. He's no adulterer like King David."

Mrs. Stoneman picked up the shirt box and shook it, as if daring the ribbon to fall off again. It stayed in place. Rhodes didn't blame it. He'd have been afraid to move, too. She put the box down on the floor and picked up another one, which she put on top of a piece of paper.

"I'm glad to hear you can trust him," Rhodes said.

"It's not that women don't try to tempt him," she said, taking up a pair of scissors that looked big enough to trim a hedge with.

She measured with her eyes and cut a straight line through the paper, the scissors making a quiet snicking sound. Then she folded the paper around the box and taped the seam.

"Do you think Jerri Laxton tried?" Rhodes asked.

Mrs. Stoneman folded the corners of the paper. Every line was straight and perfect.

"I don't know. But if she did, she won't be trying again, will she?"

Rhodes decided to take Mrs. Stoneman at her word and not pussyfoot around.

"Where were you yesterday afternoon?" he asked.

Mrs. Stoneman didn't look up as she turned the box and folded the paper at one end.

"Right here," she said, her eyes hard and flat. "At home, which is where a wife should be. Don't you think so?"

"Not necessarily," Rhodes said.

Mrs. Stoneman didn't answer, and Rhodes knew it was time for him to leave. He said, "Merry Christmas," but Mrs. Stoneman didn't have any reply to that, either. So Rhodes found his way out and drove downtown.

FIFTEEN

RHODES HAD TO ADMIT that the manger scene looked good. The wise men knelt by the manger with their gifts, the shepherds stood by in wonder and Mary and Joseph sat on a bale of hay and looked amazed at all the to-do.

Apparently Ruth Grady, or someone, had caught the donkey, which, while perhaps not as effective as a camel, was behaving itself very well, better than the goats, which were still nibbling on little black bits of boom box and occasionally raising their heads and looking suspiciously around them, as if they'd like to butt someone.

A steady stream of cars drove by to see the sight, more cars than Rhodes had seen downtown in a long time. It was nice that there was some traffic in Clearview for a change, but Rhodes didn't like to think of the reason people were there. He was pretty sure it wasn't just to see the manger scene. They probably also wanted to have a look to see if Harvey Stoneman had the nerve to show up.

Rhodes parked the county car and waited for about an hour, until the number of passing cars began to diminish and finally dwindled down to none. When that happened, Frances Blair walked up to the group and called out that it was time to wrap things up and go home, that everyone had done a wonderful job, especially considering everything that had gone wrong.

While people were rounding up the goats and loading the donkey, Rhodes got out of his car and walked over to have a word with Harvey Stoneman. It was colder than it had been on any other night so far, and Rhodes could feel the chill filtering in through the cotton cloth of his pants and sliding past his socks and up his legs.

Stoneman was heading for his car without speaking to anyone. In fact, it appeared that people were deliberately avoiding him.

"I need to ask you a few more questions," Rhodes said, catching up with him just past the trailer where the donkey was braying with dismay, as if it didn't want to leave. Or maybe it just didn't want to get back into the trailer.

Stoneman kept on walking, his head down.

"I have to get home," he said. "My wife will be worried about me."

"I think she'll be all right," Rhodes said. "She was wrapping Christmas presents when I left her."

Stoneman stopped and looked at Rhodes from beneath the hood of the robe he was wearing.

"You went to see my wife?" he said. "What for?"

"I really went to see you," Rhodes said. "Your wife just happened to be there. I hadn't finished talking to you before we were interrupted."

"Interrupted? Is that what you call it? I hope you have Ron Laxton locked up."

"You don't have to worry about him. He's in jail. But I don't really think he belongs there."

"I do," Stoneman said. "I believe in forgiveness, of course, and in turning the other cheek, but not in this case. The man tried to kill me."

"He thought he had a good reason."

"He was wrong. I explained that."

"You didn't explain everything, though."

"For example?"

"You didn't explain how Ron found out about you and his wife."

"I told you, rumors get started. I don't know how. And there was nothing between me and Jerri Laxton. I was counseling her as her minister, and that's it. End of story. Can I go now?"

Stoneman brushed past Rhodes, bumping the sheriff's shoulder as he went by.

"Your wife has quite a temper, doesn't she?" Rhodes asked.

Stoneman stopped and turned back. His face was in shadow under the hood, and Rhodes couldn't see his eyes.

"What do you mean by that?" he asked.

"It's just a question," Rhodes said.

"I think I know what you're implying, and I don't like it, Sheriff. I don't like it even a little bit."

"I'm sorry to hear that," Rhodes said. "But you haven't answered the question."

"I don't know what you're talking about."

"I thought bearing false witness was against your religion," Rhodes said.

"But then you're not exactly a biblical scholar, are you?" Stoneman said, turning back toward his car.

Rhodes didn't try to stop him this time, and Stoneman got in and drove away. As he did, Jennifer Loam stepped out from the shadows behind the trailer. She was still in costume, and she held her crook in one hand.

"He's pretty snippy for a preacher," she said as they watched the taillights of Stoneman's car move down the empty street.

"He's had a bad night," Rhodes told her. "You have to cut him some slack."

"Is he a suspect in Jerri Laxton's murder?" she asked. "Or do you suspect his wife? Or both of them?"

"You're pretty sneaky, aren't you?" Rhodes said. "Listening in like that."

"No," she said, giving him the look of an innocent shepherd. "I'm not sneaky at all. I just happened to be standing there, and I overheard you talking. Naturally, I listened. I couldn't help it."

"I'm sure that's exactly the way it happened. Anyway, it doesn't matter. Anything we said was off the record."

"You know better than that, but you're right about one thing. It doesn't matter. I couldn't print it anyway."

"Why not?"

"You know why not. My editor doesn't want any controversy. He doesn't want anything that might upset an advertiser. He wouldn't run the story about what happened here tonight if he didn't have to. He's afraid Ron Laxton will cancel the Dairy Queen's ads."

"That's the way it is in a small town sometimes," Rhodes said.

"That doesn't make it right. And I'm going to do what I can to change it."

"I wish you luck."

"You don't really mean that. You don't like bad publicity any better than anyone else in this town."

Rhodes thought about some of the cases he'd worked in the last few years. More than once, he'd had to deal with reporters from some of the city papers. TV reporters, too, and those were much worse.

"You're right," he said. "I don't like bad publicity. But I can handle it, so you can go ahead and do your job the best way you know how. Sooner or later, you'll get your story in the paper."

Jennifer smiled and said, "Can I quote you on that?"

"No," Rhodes said. "I don't think that would be a good idea. And I don't think it's a good idea to eavesdrop on the sheriff when he's talking to someone, either. You might hear something you shouldn't."

"That's true. I've learned a lot of things about this town that people are trying to keep secret, just by keeping my ears open. Jerri Laxton was a big one for keeping secrets, for example."

"What kind of secrets?"

"Read your local paper," Jennifer said.

She thumped the end of her shepherd's crook against the pavement and left Rhodes standing there, looking at her back as she walked away.

SIXTEEN

RHODES WENT TO Wal-Mart before going back by the jail. He wanted to have a look at the jewelry counter because someone had told him once that a man couldn't go wrong if he gave jewelry as a gift. Rhodes wasn't sure that was true, but he couldn't think of anything else to get for Ivy. She might have been dropping subtle hints for months, but if she had, he hadn't caught them. He wasn't good at subtle hints. He needed something more blatant, like a direct statement, and there hadn't been anything like that.

He knew Ivy had a similar problem when it came to buying a gift for him. Not about the hints. He didn't give hints, either. If he did, there wouldn't be any problem. Ivy could catch a hint faster than most. But Rhodes didn't drop any hints because he didn't have anything to hint about, mainly because he didn't want much of anything. Certainly not jewelry. He wore a watch, but that was it.

The Wal-Mart parking lot was as crowded as the downtown area was deserted. It was as if every car that had driven past the manger scene had wound up parked in front of Wal-Mart, where the lights threw their eerie orange glow over them and changed their colors to something that was similar to what they had been in daylight, but subtly altered now.

Rhodes had to park at the back of the lot, but he didn't mind. He thought the exercise might do him good. As he walked toward the store, he passed people with shopping carts piled high with their purchases, and he recalled the days when the downtown area had been as busy as this, or nearly so. It seemed like a long time ago.

That's because it was *a long time ago,* he thought.

He went through the doors, past the gray-haired greeter, who said she was glad to see him but didn't recognize him, and straight to the jewelry counter. There were all sorts of things under the glass: rings, necklaces, bracelets, watches. He remembered that long ago there had been jewelry stores downtown, two or three of them at the same time. If a watch broke, you could get it fixed. Now you didn't need watch repair, however. You just threw the old watch away and bought a new one. It was that way with a lot of things.

After looking for a while, Rhodes settled on a drop with a blue topaz stone set in gold and a matching bracelet. He paid for them with his credit card, glad that the gift buying was over for a while. Now all he had to do was wrap the two boxes. He wished he was as good at wrapping as Mrs. Stoneman. But he wasn't. He was barely competent. The paper never seemed quite smooth when he was done.

Before leaving, Rhodes went over to where the artificial Christmas trees were displayed. He saw a small one that wasn't too bad. He could carry the box under one arm, and he thought that he might as well buy it with his own money. The county might not want to spring for a Christmas tree in the jail, especially if the prisoners were going to be allowed to see it. But no one would object if Rhodes paid for it out of his own pocket. He got a string of lights and a box of glass globes to hang from the plastic branches and waited in line to pay for them.

While he was waiting, he saw a metal stand nearby that held Christmas CDs and tapes. There was nothing by the Kingston Trio, but there was a tape by Gene Autry. Rhodes thought he'd like to hear "Rudolph" a time or two, so he took the tape. He had a little cassette player at home he could take to the jail.

"Think it's goin' to snow this year, Sheriff?" the checker asked him when he got to the head of the line.

"I doubt it," Rhodes said. "One time, it never snowed."

The checker looked at him as if he might be a little touched.

"Never mind," Rhodes said. "It's a long story."

The checker put the globes and lights in a blue plastic bag with the tape and set the bag on top of the box that held the tree. She took Rhodes's credit card and ran it through the reader.

"Merry Christmas," she said as he signed the credit slip.

"Merry Christmas to you, too," Rhodes told her.

THE TREE DIDN'T take long to set up on a little table that Lawton found, and it looked pretty good with the balls and lights on it.

"Could've used some icicles, though," Hack said. "Icicles set a tree off better'n anything."

"Too much trouble," Lawton said. "Takes forever if you do a good job of it. You have to get 'em on there so they hang just right, or they just look tacky."

"We could get 'em on just right," Hack said. "We have time."

Lawton shook his head. "Too much trouble. I like it just the way it is. Well, mostly I like it. I'd like it better if it had a few presents with my name on 'em under it."

"I guess the high sheriff didn't think of that," Hack said. "Of course it don't matter much to me. I'm just the dispatcher. I'm just the one who has to take ever' call that comes in and be sure that it's answered and that ever'body's happy about it. Which is what I do, day in and day out. So I guess I don't need any presents. Just bein' of service to the county is enough of a present for me."

Rhodes hadn't thought about getting anything for Hack or Lawton yet, but he'd do that later, now that he didn't have to worry about Ivy's gift. He was about to say so, but Lawton cut him off.

"I'll bet Miz McGee will get you a present," he told Hack. "Prob'ly somethin' real nice, like maybe a pair of drawers with little Santa Clauses on 'em."

Hack's face got red, and Rhodes wasn't surprised. He knew Hack didn't like to be teased about Miz McGee. Lawton knew it, too, which is why he'd done it.

"At least I got somebody that cares enough about me to buy me a present," Hack said. "You'll be lucky if you get sticks and ashes under the tree."

"You could be right," Lawton said. "If Santa's been checkin' that list of his twice, I wouldn't be surprised if he put me on the 'naughty' side."

Hack nodded. "That's where you belong, all right. If you ask me—"

Rhodes interrupted them before they could really get going.

"I'm going to bring a tape player tomorrow," he said, holding up the tape he'd bought. "Anybody here object to Gene Autry?"

"Is 'Santa Claus Is Comin' to Town' on there?" Lawton asked.

Rhodes looked at the tape and said, "It's on here."

"Well, then, go ahead and bring somethin' to play it on. I like that song."

"I don't," Hack said. "That Gene Autry wasn't half the singer that Roy Rogers was."

"Baloney," Lawton said. "Gene could sing rings around Roy. Ride a horse better, too."

"You don't know what you're talkin' about," Hack said. "You ever see Gene's face when he's on a horse? He looks about as scared as if he was ridin' a bear. He didn't know any more about horses than you do."

"Yeah? Then why'd he have a horse like that Champion?

Champion was twice the horse Trigger was. Smarter and better lookin', too.''

Rhodes knew they'd go on like that all night if he let them, but for some reason he didn't feel like stopping them. He just put the tape down on his desk and left as quietly as he could, before they started comparing Gabby Hayes to Smiley Burnette, or Pat Brady to Pat Buttram.

SEVENTEEN

AS HE WAS driving home, Rhodes went through the downtown area again for one last look at the scene of the crime. He was passing the deserted manger scene when he thought he saw something moving in the darkness of the alley.

He parked the car and got out, remembering to take his flashlight with him. He passed the manger mural, his shoes crunching occasionally on tiny bits of plastic that the goats hadn't eaten.

He turned the corner of the building and switched on the flashlight, aiming the yellow beam up the alley. He didn't see anyone or anything that didn't belong there, just the wooden trash bin. Maybe he'd just imagined that something had been moving around. But he didn't think so.

He walked up the alley, shining the light into the shadows. He still didn't see anything unusual. He told himself that he was getting old. His eyes must have been playing tricks on him, though he still wasn't convinced.

He became more convinced after standing in one spot for several minutes, getting cold and then colder, waiting for someone or something to move. When nothing did, he checked inside Frazier's Furniture. There was no one there, not in the office, and not upstairs. Not a creature was stirring, not even a mouse or a rat or whatever had been skittering around upstairs before.

Rhodes left the building and started back to his car. He got almost to the corner of the building when he heard something. He turned back, shining the light along the alley wall. The wind turned over a piece of paper that scraped along for a few inches before it settled down. For some reason, the sound made Rhodes feel even colder than he already was.

But that hadn't been the noise he'd heard before. He went back into the alley until he came to the trash bin. He stood beside it, listening. There was nothing for a few seconds, but then he was sure he heard something shift around inside the bin. He shone the light through a crack on the side of the bin, but he couldn't really make out anything inside.

So he lifted the top of the bin with one hand and heaved it up and back. It thumped against the side of Frazier's Furniture, and Rhodes stuck his head over the side of the bin to see what was there.

Someone jumped up, knocking the flashlight from Rhodes's hand. The light flew behind Rhodes, and the beam lit up the sky as the light tumbled end over end. When it hit the wall on the other side of the alley, there was a tinkling sound, and the lens broke. The light went out.

Whoever was inside the bin sprang out and whacked Rhodes on the side of the head. Rhodes staggered as the figure of a man ran up the alley, sticking to the dark side. It was almost as if a shadow were running instead of a man.

Rhodes took off after the man, or the shadow. Whatever it was, it wasn't in prime condition. Rhodes caught up with it before it even got to the corner. It was a man, and Rhodes grabbed him by the shoulder.

"Slow down a minute," he said.

The man stopped and turned around. He was small, and in the bad light he looked about a hundred years old, though he was probably only in his forties. He was wearing ragged clothes that stuck out at odd angles from his body. From the way the shoulder felt, Rhodes suspected that the clothing was stuffed with newspapers as insulation against the cold.

"What's going on here?" Rhodes asked.

"Nothing," the man said. His voice was hoarse. "I just needed a place to sleep. Who the hell are you?"

"I'm the sheriff," Rhodes said.

His badge was clipped to his belt, and he showed it to the man.

"I wasn't doing anything wrong," the man said. "There's no law against sleeping, is there?"

"Not against sleeping," Rhodes said. "Loitering, trespassing, assaulting an officer, things like that, well, there are laws about those."

"Yeah, right."

"What's your name?"

"Paul Ziebarth," the man said. "Here's my ID."

He reached into a coat pocket and brought out a worn leather wallet that was spiderwebbed with cracks. He opened the wallet, pulled out a driver's license, and handed it to Rhodes.

Rhodes got his glasses out of his pocket and slipped them on. They didn't help much, but he could see well enough to tell that the photo looked a little like Ziebarth, though the license had long since expired. He handed the license back to Ziebarth, who put it away.

"Why were you in the trash bin, anyway?" Rhodes asked. "The back door to the store's not locked. It would be a lot warmer in there."

"I tried that last week. I got run out."

"Somebody ran you out? Who?"

"Some old geezer. Said he owned the place."

"And you believed that?"

"What's the difference if I did or not? What am I gonna do? Make him show me his ID?"

Rhodes ignored the jab.

"You say this was last week? How long have you been sleeping in that trash bin?"

"A week. That's it, just a week. I was thinking I might be able to get a job around here, what with Christmas coming on. Sometimes stores need an extra hand during the rush. But so far I haven't had any luck."

"You're the one who found the doll," Rhodes said.

"The doll? What doll?

"The one in the manger. It was being used in the living manger scene. You took it and put it in the trash bin."

"I didn't take any doll."

"You might as well tell the truth. It'll have your fingerprints on it."

"Maybe it will, but that doesn't mean I took it. It was in the trash bin, sure, but I didn't put it there. What would I do with a doll?"

"Sell it maybe?"

"I'm not a thief," Ziebarth said.

"I don't suppose you killed anyone, either," Rhodes said.

"Killed? What are you talking about? I never killed anybody. Are you fixing to hang a frame on me for something? If you are, I want a lawyer."

"I don't think you'll need one," Rhodes said. "What you do need is a place to spend the night."

"Yeah. I guess you're gonna pay for my motel room, what with it being Christmas and all."

"Not exactly," Rhodes told him. "But there is a little room at the inn."

HACK AND LAWTON were drinking hot chocolate when Rhodes took Ziebarth in, and Rhodes hoped they were through arguing about Gene and Roy.

He printed and booked Ziebarth, but before he locked

him in a cell, Hack had to find out his opinion of the Christmas tree.

Ziebarth gave the tree a disdainful look and said, "It'd look better if it had some icicles on it."

EIGHTEEN

RHODES PARKED in front of the parsonage and got out of the car. The lights were still on inside, though it was getting pretty late for people in Clearview to be up. Maybe Stoneman was working on Sunday's sermon. Rhodes went to the door and rang the bell.

Stoneman answered the ring. His wise man's robe was gone, and he was wearing jeans and a white shirt. He didn't look happy to see Rhodes, or maybe he was just generally depressed. Rhodes wouldn't blame him if that were the case. Having half the town believe you were carrying on an affair with one of your congregation and then getting shot at by her husband the day after she'd been murdered would depress anyone.

"Hello, Sheriff," Stoneman said. "What's the trouble now?"

"Maybe I'm just here on a social call," Rhodes said.

Stoneman rubbed his face and said, "Don't make jokes, Sheriff. It's too late, and I'm too tired."

"Sorry. I know it's late, but we need to talk. Can I come in?"

Stoneman opened the door, and Rhodes entered the house. There were no Christmas songs playing in the background this time. The house was as quiet as the deserted furniture store. Stoneman led Rhodes to what had probably been a bedroom but that now served as Stoneman's study. There was a cluttered computer desk with a closed laptop on it, and there was a bookshelf filled with books, some of them imposingly thick.

"Your wife gone to bed?" Rhodes said.

"She had a headache. You want to sit down?"

Rhodes sat in a straight-backed wooden chair, and Stoneman sat in a typing chair at the computer desk.

"I repeat," Stoneman said, "what's the trouble now?"

"It's about Jerri Laxton," Rhodes said.

Stoneman sighed. "I've told you all about that. What do you want from me now? A murder confession?"

Rhodes said that wasn't exactly what he'd come for.

"You think Mona killed her, don't you," Stoneman said.

Rhodes gave him a noncommittal look.

"What do you think?"

"I don't know what to think anymore. Mona will hardly even speak to me."

"Maybe you haven't spent enough time counseling with her, the way you counseled Jerri Laxton."

"You could be right. Sometimes I get so busy with the church members that I forget my family members. I guess I shouldn't blame Mona for being angry."

"I'd say she was storing up a lot of rage, all right."

"You said 'storing up.' Does that mean you don't think she's let it out?"

"Oh, she's let it out, all right," Rhodes said. "I saw her."

"What do you mean?" Stoneman asked.

"Let's just say I'm glad I'm not a Christmas package that she's wrapping."

Stoneman didn't get it.

"Have a look under your tree sometime," Rhodes said. "If the gifts in some of those packages are fragile, they're broken for sure."

"Oh. I see what you mean. At least I think I do. Anyway, it's true that Mona has a temper. A terrible temper. I admit that. But I explained to her that there was nothing between me and Jerri Laxton. I explained it more than once.''

''And she didn't believe you.''

''I guess not. I should have spent more time talking to her about it and let her know how much I care for her. I'm going in there and talk to her as soon as you leave and let her know that I love her.''

''Probably not a bad idea,'' Rhodes said.

''I should have done a better job of it before now. But even if I was lax in my familial duties, I'll never believe Mona killed anybody. It's just not possible, temper or not. You're looking in the wrong place.''

''I didn't say your wife killed anybody. That's not why I'm here.''

''Then what *are* you here for?''

''We never seem to finish our conversations. I still need some information from you.''

''I've told you everything I know to tell, Sheriff, and that's God's own truth.''

''I don't think so,'' Rhodes said. ''I think you know more about Jerri Laxton's plans for downtown than you managed to tell me.''

Stoneman leaned back in the typing chair and looked at Rhodes quizzically.

''You said she had big plans for that downtown block,'' Rhodes said. ''I knew about the idea of putting antique stores there, but there must be more to it than that. The new reporter from the *Herald,* Jennifer Loam, hinted at something, too, but she didn't say what it was. Apparently it's going to be in the paper sooner or later, but I can't wait for that.''

''I might know something,'' Stoneman said. ''But it was told to me in confidence.''

''It's going to be in the paper,'' Rhodes repeated. ''But I need to know about it now.''

''All right. I don't suppose it can hurt anything to tell

you. As far as I know, there's nothing firm yet, though. Nothing's been signed."

"Just tell me," Rhodes said.

"People had convinced Jerri that the antique store idea wasn't a good one," Stoneman said. "But she didn't give up. She was determined to do something about downtown. She'd been in touch with a couple of people about putting in some new buildings there, and things were beginning to come together."

"New buildings? Where, exactly?"

"Where the building fell down and where that old furniture store was. There was going to be a clinic of some kind, and maybe another business, too. Of course they'd have to bulldoze the whole block, but the new buildings would really add something to Clearview. People would come back downtown again."

"So that's what happened," Rhodes said.

"I beg your pardon?"

"Never mind," Rhodes said. "I think I have it all now. Thanks."

He didn't wait for Stoneman to say anything. He just got up and started out of the house. Stoneman caught up with him at the front door.

"What is it, Sheriff? What do you know?"

Everything had clicked into place in Rhodes's head now, like the interlocking pieces of a jigsaw puzzle assembling themselves and becoming a picture instead of a jumble of colorful fragments.

"I know who killed Jerri Laxton," Rhodes said.

THERE WERE NO Christmas lights glowing in Fred Frazier's neighborhood when Rhodes arrived in front of Frazier's house. The lights that ran along the roof ridges had all been turned off. The houses were dark and silent, except for Frazier's, where there was a light burning in the back room.

Frazier came to the door looking even older and sadder

than he had when Rhodes had talked to him only the night before. This time Frazier didn't ask why Rhodes was there. He just opened the door and let him in.

Rhodes went into the house and stopped to look at the photograph of Frazier's wife that stood beside the small, forlorn Christmas tree.

"Nice picture," Rhodes said.

"Ernestine always did take a good picture," Frazier said. "But she looked even better in person. She was the prettiest woman I ever met, and the best. Let's go on in back. I was watching David Letterman. He's not very funny, but it helps pass the time."

"I guess you've had some trouble sleeping since your wife died," Rhodes said.

"A little. You'd think a man would get used to it, his wife being gone, I mean. But I still haven't."

They entered the back room. Letterman was reading a Top Ten list, and the audience was groaning. Frazier found his remote in the recliner. He sat down and muted the sound.

"I guess that's why you've been sleeping in the store some of the time," Rhodes said. "You feel closer to your wife there where the two of you worked together all those years."

"Who told you I was sleeping there?"

"Just somebody you chased out one night. That homeless man you mentioned."

"I didn't mention any homeless man."

"Not by name," Rhodes said. "But you told me someone like that was probably sleeping there. It was you all along, though, wasn't it?"

"Okay, all right, it was me. No shame in it. I moved that bed in there when I was feeling lonesome. Ernestine and I spent a lot more time at that store than we ever spent here, and I slept there sometimes. Nothing wrong with that. I own the place."

There was no conviction behind Frazier's words. It was as if he barely had the breath to get them out.

"That picture in there by your Christmas tree," Rhodes said. "You had it on the desk at the store, didn't you."

"What if I did? I decided to bring it home. It was getting dusty."

"I noticed how clean it was. I guess you had to clean the blood off, too, along with the dust, didn't you?"

Frazier slumped back in the chair and tried to look surprised, but he didn't quite pull it off.

"What blood?"

"The blood you got on the frame when you hit Jerri Laxton with it."

"She wanted me to sell the building," Frazier said, looking at the silent TV set instead of Rhodes. "Can you believe that? She said it could be torn down and replaced with a new one. I had her meet me there so I could tell her about what the building meant to me and how much history was still there, even if the place was empty. She laughed. She said I was an old fart who was standing in the way of progress. I didn't mean to hit her. I didn't even think about it. I just grabbed up the picture and swung it at her. I hit her pretty hard. Then I left. I'm sorry she died."

"If you'd gotten help for her, maybe she wouldn't have," Rhodes said.

"I've thought about that a lot. I haven't slept since it happened."

"You told me you didn't believe in living in the past," Rhodes said.

"Yeah. Well, I don't. It's not healthy. But what choice is there for a man like me? I don't have a wife anymore, and I don't have my business. I don't have any friends. When you get to be my age, Sheriff, the past is all you do have."

Rhodes considered his own state of mind and how much

he'd been thinking about the past lately. Probably that wasn't a good sign.

"You remember that coffee table you bought from me?" Frazier said.

"I remember."

"That was a good solid-wood table. I'll bet you still have it."

Rhodes said that he did.

"That's what I'm talking about. Things that are solid, they last. You don't get rid of them."

"Things change," Rhodes said.

"Not for the better, though."

Rhodes didn't say anything. He didn't feel like arguing. Besides, he wasn't sure Frazier was entirely wrong.

"I guess you're going to take me to the jail," Frazier said.

"That's my job."

"I need to put on some shoes. You think I'll get any sleep there?"

"We'll see," Rhodes told him.

NINETEEN

THE NEXT DAY, the Gene Autry tape was playing on the little cassette machine Rhodes had brought in. Gene was singing about Santa coming along down Santa Claus Lane, and Lawton was humming along.

"I wish you'd stop that noise you're makin'," Hack said. "It's bad enough we have to listen to Gene Autry without you chimin' in."

"You need to get in the Christmas spirit," Lawton said. "That's what you need."

Rhodes thought he needed to get in the Christmas spirit himself. So far there wasn't much going on to make his spirits bright. There wasn't much satisfaction in jailing a man like Fred Frazier. It wasn't going to bring Jerri Laxton back or brighten Ron Laxton's days.

Ivy came through the door. She was carrying several packages. Her face was red, and her short hair was windblown.

"It's getting colder out there," she said. "That wind's coming straight down from the North Pole."

"You think it's gonna snow?" Lawton asked.

"Not around here," Ivy said. "How long has it been since it snowed in Clearview?"

"One time," Hack said, "it never snowed."

Ivy laughed, and Lawton, who had been humming again, nearly strangled.

"What's in those boxes?" Hack asked, changing the subject before Lawton could say anything.

"Just a little something for you," Ivy said. "And for Lawton, too. There's even one here for Miz McGee if she ever happens to drop by."

Lawton forgot about Hack's theft of his joke.

"Can we open 'em now?" he asked.

"Not until Christmas," Ivy told him.

"Is there anything there for the high sheriff?" Hack asked.

Ivy reached in a pocket and pulled out a small pad of sticky notes that she handed to Lawton.

"I couldn't resist," she said.

Printed on the top of the note page was the heading, Shoot Low, Sheriff, They're Ridin' Snakes.

Hack laughed, and Rhodes walked over to have a look.

"I don't recall that I've ever run into that situation," he said. "But it's probably good advice."

"That all you got him?" Hack asked.

"I have a little something special," Ivy said. "But it's at home."

Hack gave Rhodes a speculative look.

"Wonder what that could be?" he said.

Rhodes shrugged. He wondered the same thing.

Gene Autry started singing "Rudolph, the Red-Nosed Reindeer."

"I always liked that one," Ivy said.

"Me, too," Hack said, and he started singing along, ignoring Lawton's glare.

Rhodes laughed. He was feeling better already. Maybe it would snow after all. You never could tell.

DEAD MEN DIE

A DEMARY JONES MYSTERY

When Demary Jones stumbles over a man's naked corpse on the front steps of her temporary digs, it gives new meaning to the phrase "dead man's walk." Suspicious questions from the investigating detective rattle her almost as much as the nagging fear that she'd interrupted the dumping of the body, and that the killer would be back to clean up any loose ends—like her.

The picture darkens when ten thousand dollars in counterfeit money is wired to Demary's bank account and the treasury department is ready to foreclose on her freedom. Though jail might be the safest place for her right now, she's racing to expose the sinister truth before a killer can hide all his secrets in blood.

E. L. LARKIN

Available December 2001 at your favorite retail outlet.

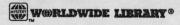

AGATHA AWARD WINNER

JEANNE M. DAMS

KILLING CASSIDY

A DOROTHY MARTIN MYSTERY

Though Dorothy Martin is quite content with her new life in
a cozy English village, she looks forward to an unexpected
trip back to her Indiana hometown. Sadly, it is the sudden
death of a longtime friend and a small inheritance that
offer Dorothy this brief holiday in the States.

Along with her inheritance, Dorothy gets a cryptic note
from her deceased friend claiming he was murdered. Now,
back among the friends and acquaintances of her past,
she must find out if one among them is a killer—and why.

"Altogether, this is a warm and worthy read…"
—Publishers Weekly

Available November 2001 at your favorite retail outlet.

🏛 **WORLDWIDE LIBRARY**®

WJD402

KILLER

A Charlie Greene Mystery

COMMUTE

California literary agent Charlie Greene starts her weeklong vacation
by shutting off the phone, putting out the cat—and finding the body
of her neighbor slumped in his SUV. With nothing but her track
record for stumbling onto bodies to incriminate her, Charlie
becomes the prime suspect.

It seems as if Charlie's dearly departed neighbor had some dangerous
secrets involving bundles of hidden cash. Soon a strategically placed
bomb, a temporary loss of hearing, a stint in jail—all topped off by
the stunning events unfolding in her own backyard—lead Charlie to
the inescapable conclusion that vacations really are murder.

"...clever and original plotting..."
—Publishers Weekly

MARLYS MILLHISER

Available December 2001 at your favorite retail outlet.

⊕ **WORLDWIDE LIBRARY** ®

WMM405